INVISIBLE
FURIES

CRITICAL ACCLAIM FOR *LOST GROUND*

Michiel Heyns has fast become one of South Africa's most respected novelists. His latest book, Lost Ground, *is among the finest to have been published in the last few years. Well-written, engaging and almost perfectly paced …*

M Blackman, *Sunday Independent*

Heyns is an ironic writer, and many of the scenes in Lost Ground *are cleverly nuanced, and often funny, although never without a powerful underlying tension.*

Margaret von Klemperer, *The Witness*

Heyns's style – his dry, funny scrutiny of his characters, his narrator's self-effacing and slightly self-mocking personal insights, his ability to convey the grainy texture of even the simplest emotion – makes Lost Ground *an unmitigated novelistic joy to stumble into.*

Karin Schimke, *Cape Times*

It's remarkable, and you should not only read it but buy a copy as you will want to look into it again. It's hard to know how Michiel Heyns does it – part magician, part juggler and fine linguist, he presents a novel that is as mysteriously alluring, yet as simple as the photo of some dorp street on the cover. It has something of the quality of a John Meyer painting: unpretentious, familiar and the light is right.

Jane Rosenthal, *Mail & Guardian*

Heyns's venture into the literary thriller is moving and humane.

Diane Awerbuck, *Sunday Times*

[Heyns] is as intent on the language and the way he writes as he is to explore and go places that will thrill and engage the reader.

Diane de Beer, *The Star*

[Lost Ground] has all the hallmarks of a great novel: murder, sexual tension, racial conflict and the existential angst of a South African grappling with returning to the country of his birth after a long time living abroad.

Charlene Rolls, *YOU* magazine

INVISIBLE FURIES

A NOVEL

MICHIEL HEYNS

JONATHAN BALL PUBLISHERS
JOHANNESBURG & CAPE TOWN

First South African Edition published in trade paperback in 2012 by
JONATHAN BALL PUBLISHERS (PTY) LTD
PO Box 33977
Jeppestown
2043

Paperbook ISBN 978-1-86842-509-9
eBook ISBN 978-1-86842-510-5

Twitter: www.twitter.com/JonathanBallPub
Facebook: www.facebook.com/pages/Jonathan-Ball-Publishers/298034457992
Blog: http://jonathanball.bookslive.co.za/

Cover design by Michiel Botha, Cape Town
Typeset by Triple M Design, Johannesburg
Printed and bound by CTP Book Printers, Cape
Typeset in 11/14 pt Palatino

For Christine, once again

Quarter of pleasures where the rich are always waiting,
Waiting expensively for miracles to happen,
Dim-lighted restaurant where lovers eat each other,
Café where exiles have established a malicious village:

You with your charm and your apparatus have abolished
The strictness of winter and the spring's compulsion;
Far from your lights the outraged punitive father,
The dullness of mere obedience here is apparent.

So with orchestras and glances, soon you betray us
To belief in our infinite powers; and the innocent
Unobservant offender falls in a moment
Victim to his heart's invisible furies.

WH Auden: From 'The Capital'

'I dare say moreover,' she pursued with an interested gravity, 'that I do, that
we all do here, run too much to mere eye. But how can it be helped? We're all
looking at each other – and in the light of Paris one sees what things resemble.
That's what the light of Paris seems always to show. It's the fault of the light of
Paris – dear old light!'
    'Dear old Paris!' Little Bilham echoed.
    'Everything, every one shows,' Miss Barrace went on.
    'But for what they really are?' Strether asked.

Henry James: *The Ambassadors*

… indeed, to be able to point to one of Gloriani's figures in a shady corner of
your library was tolerable proof that you were not a fool. Corrupt things they
certainly were; in the line of sculpture they were quite the latest fruit of time.
It was the artist's opinion that there is no essential difference between beauty
and ugliness; that they overlap and intermingle in a quite inextricable manner;
that there is no saying where one begins and the other ends; that hideousness
grimaces at you suddenly from out of the very bosom of loveliness, and beauty
blooms before your eyes in the lap of vileness …

Henry James: *Roderick Hudson*

On the whole, people that say demeaning things about our world, I think that's
usually because they feel in some ways excluded or, you know, not part of the
cool group or … so as a result they just mock it.[…] There is something about
fashion that can make people very nervous.

Anna Wintour: *The September Issue*

CHAPTER 1

To tote a suitcase in Paris is to court the contempt of the natives. Parisians never go anywhere – why should they? – and despise anyone who does. That's why they've arranged for a flight of stairs at every Metro exit, to break the spirit of anyone hobbled with a suitcase, and to ensure that the unwelcome traveller will arrive out of breath and red of face, in sweaty contrast with the Parisians, who step out of the Metro as unruffled as if fresh from a scented dressing-room.

Lugging his too-heavy case up the steps onto the rain-drenched Boulevard St Germain, Christopher indulged these musings with a vehemence proportionate to his discomfort. The ride from the Gare du Nord to Odéon had been sticky, slow and crowded, his fellow-passengers resentful of his luggage, impervious to his abject, albeit insincere, apologies. Evidently Paris had not, in the years of his absence, undergone a change of heart: she was still a whore with a heart of stone. There were no longer, it was true, evil-tempered *ponceuses* dwelling in the depths of the Metro to snarl at you while punching a hole in your ticket; but their spirit lingered on discontentedly in the windy vestibules, the impatiently slamming swing doors, in the general inimical implication of the place. It was, he reflected as he stopped to rest his suitcase arm, the same misanthropic spirit that possessed the po-faced bureaucrats in the French consulate in Cape Town, intent less on easing the way of the stranger to *la patrie* than on impressing upon him how little his presence was desired there. Ultimately, it was the gloating malevolence of the *tricoteuses* – knit-one, purl-one, slip-one as another head rolled into the basket.

In spite of the rain, he stood looking around him to get his bearings. Thirty years on, and the Boulevard had not changed, not so that he could notice, anyway: the Odéon GC cinemas showing generic American movies with French titles, the eternal cafés, their serving areas retreated now out of the rain, and cars, cars, cars. The plane trees coming into light-green leaf, the news kiosks, the round columns advertising the latest *spectacle* – it was a film set with action figures.

He stepped into the street. A strong hand grasped his arm and pulled him back from a car coming the wrong way. *'Faites attention, monsieur,'* said the Samaritan, irritated rather than concerned. Christopher's first instinct was to tell the man to mind his own business – if I want to get run over, whose life is it anyway? – but brought out a grudging *'Merci, monsieur'*, all the same. The man, without looking round, shrugged and walked away, shaking his head, probably already wondering why he'd bothered to save the life of a gormless foreigner.

'And bollocks to you too, mate,' said Christopher aloud. This was not his normal mode of expression – he'd never called anyone *mate* in his life – but he felt a need proportionate to his humiliation to adopt an assertive persona in the face of this disdainful city. More cautiously now, he crossed the road to the Cour du Commerce connecting the Boulevard with the Rue St André des Arts – that much he remembered. The cobbles of the Cour were slippery; the wheels of the suitcase were too small for the cobbles, and the bag capsized several times. If Paris hadn't been so damned picturesque, it may have been more negotiable.

The Hotel du Carrefour, too, had not changed in thirty years. Or if it had, Christopher's memory was not acute enough to register deviations. The building still seemed crazily out of kilter, not a right angle in sight, the stairs listing and veering at some perilous compromise between gravity and inertia. By rights, the whole structure should have collapsed or at least rearranged itself, but as far as he could tell, the angles were all still at odds with one another to exactly the same degree as before. The effect remained disorientating, making one doubt one's visual and spatial judgement.

The choir stalls in the foyer, ripped who-knows-when from

8

what church in a frenzy of righteous revolutionary fervour, were at this hour occupied by breakfasting guests, muttering rather than chattering, oppressed by their enforced propinquity. From what Christopher could glean in passing, the breakfast was as plain as ever: the single stub of crusty bread, the postage stamp of butter, the thimble of preserves, the dwarfish pitcher of coffee with its juglet of milk. The serving woman was too young to be the same one as had flung the bread at the guests all those years before, but the flinging action was the same, as was the air of sublime detachment: presumably one of those trade secrets that get passed on from generation to generation. An uninitiated guest was brandishing an empty coffee jug, trying to wring a refill from the *serveuse*.

The reception desk was still in uncomfortable proximity to the dining area, enabling the owner to keep an eye on the distribution of the matutinal bounty. The owner too, was the same – far older, of course, but showing, in that infuriating French manner, few effects of the passing of the years. Christopher did not think it necessary to mention having stayed here before, but the owner adjusted his eye-glasses – one concession at least to the ravages of time – and peered at Christopher's passport. 'Monsieur Turner' – he pronounced it Turr*nirrr* – 'from South Africa; ah, yes, I remember …', and from the sudden set of his features into something even less welcoming than his habitual scowl, it was clear that he did remember, remembered over a span of thirty years the blocked basin and bidet, the aftermath of an over-enthusiastic indulgence, fresh from the austerities of England, in the *vin et crudités à volonté* at the Caves Ste Geneviève.

'I never want to see a grated carrot again,' Daniel had moaned, as he voided himself of yet another largely undigested helping of crudités and sour wine. Orange and purple, at the best of times an unfortunate combination, had never composed so badly.

'Don't blame the carrots,' Christopher had replied, moralistic even in extremis. 'They're not what's making you puke.'

They had spent the night, or what remained of the night after evacuation of their meal, emptying out basin and bidet with a tooth mug into the toilet in the hallway, but without managing to clear the bowels of the plumbing. They were obliged, thus, to report the blockage to the owner – who, initially apologetic, had, after uncovering the cause of the blockage, been decidedly chilly for the rest of their stay.

'You will have room 36,' the owner said, as if pronouncing sentence, producing a heavy brass key suspended from an even heavier brass object, pear-shaped and cumbersome, presumably to prevent theft of the key – though who would steal the key to a garret room in a one-star hotel was anybody's guess.

'Ah, yes,' Christopher said, '*cinquième étage.*'

'You know it?'

'It's where I stayed last time.'

'Ah,' the owner said, gravely, as if committing himself with a heavy heart to a course he knew to be unwise. 'Ah, yes. Of course. Nevertheless. All the same.'

The little lift made its way up the first four floors as reluctantly as before, its creaks and groans, Christopher used to think, the perfect accompaniment to the grumbles of the *femme de chambre* who haunted the upper floors, the one who had complained about his pipe – like everybody, he used to smoke, then – about their unwashed clothing on the floor, about the pips from the grapes he and Daniel bought to stave off the scurvy that they were sure would be brought on by the cheap diet of steak frites.

The lift stopped on the fourth floor; one walked the last flight, dragging and bumping as best one might one's suitcase up the narrow curving staircase. Having dragged and bumped, Christopher opened the door to his room. It was the same door: he recognised the surprisingly solid feel of the door lever, its resistant spring, and the flimsy plank of the door panels. What was it a sign of, that thirty years later he had not progressed beyond the converted *chambre de bonne* that had served him as a student on a budget? Admittedly he had shared it then, and now had it all to himself, but even that suggested, to a nature not susceptible to easy consolations, a diminution rather than a gain. The room itself – well, it was tempting, for the sake of consistency, to say it had not changed much, but that would not have been strictly true. The plumbing seemed to have been done up in the last ten years or so; the tap gushed with more enthusiasm than of old, and the mattress, when he sat down on it to take off his shoes, was firmer than he remembered. But the angle of the ceiling, of course, was the same, determined, here on the top floor, by the pitch of the roof of the building; and the little window giving onto the balcony – no more than a ledge, really, from which one had a view of Notre Dame rising from the over-praised roof-tops of Paris– that, too, was the same, as was, he established, stepping out in stockinged feet, the view from it. One addition to the room was the notice on the wall: *Prière de ne pas fumer*; but the smell of the room, the strange mixture of old lavender and fresh polish and cigarette smoke and something else – something ancient and sinister and French, the blood of aristocrats, the sweat of peasants, the tears of lovers, or perhaps just rats – that had not changed.

He unpacked the all-purpose supply of clothing he had considered adequate for Paris in May, though of course nothing he owned was *really* adequate for Paris. In the wardrobe fitted under the slanting roof there was the usual rogues' gallery of hangers left behind by former occupants, some from grander establishments like the Hotel Nacional, Madrid, some from refuges less exalted even than the Hotel du Carrefour, by the sound of them – the Tallahassee Motor Inn, Sleeperz in Newcastle, the Elite Cleaners in Napier, New Zealand.

He considered having a shower; but the shower was on the third floor and cost five euros, a sign behind the door informed him. Not that he could not afford that sum, but the frugal habits of half a lifetime suggested that a shower at the end of the day would get rid of at least twice as much dirt for the same price.

He took out his address book, somewhat self-consciously compiled for this trip. At home he had no need of an address book: those people he knew well enough to qualify for an address book he could locate without its aid. He turned now to *De Villiers, Eric*, and stared a bit blankly at the number. It used to be that the first three figures were letters giving a clue as to the location of the phone; now the all-digital number conveyed no such hint. It was in any case a number, acquired at third hand, in which he had little faith.

11

Lifting the receiver, he dialled 9 for an outside number – one used to have to ask the owner at the desk for an outside line – then reconsidered, and put down the phone. He did not want to have to speak to Eric now, as his first act in Paris, to arrange a meeting, and go through the pretence of eagerness to see each other. He didn't know what would be worse, for Eric to pretend with badly-dissimulated pleasure, or, what was more likely, to make crudely apparent how little Christopher's presence pleased him. Eric was a duty, not a pleasure, and he would no doubt have an equally unflattering view of Christopher – indeed, rather more so, in that to Eric Christopher could not be other than an irksome intrusion upon what by all appearances was a singularly enjoyable sojourn in Paris. Christopher had never much liked Eric, but had tolerated him as the only and much-indulged son of his best friend, and Eric had been at best indifferent to him. Eric could wait; he had waited for three years.

Martha? He had seen her last two years ago when she'd come out to South Africa: a cordial enough meeting at dinner with common friends, on the basis of letting bygones be bygones, such ill-defined bygones as they had, Martha and he. And she'd urged him to look her up when next he was in Paris.

'I can't imagine when that will be,' he'd said. 'Paris is not really on my list.'

'Why ever not? It's still the most beautiful city on earth.'

'Oh, beauty is as beauty does. One gets irritated with the implication that one should fall flat on one's face in worship each time one turns a corner in Paris.'

'Whose implication? The Parisians couldn't care less.'

'The implication of whoever it is that designs those little blue plaques for the street names, and the red marquees outside the restaurants, and the railings around the plane trees – it's all so *deliberate*, so unspontaneous.'

'I grant you it's not spontaneous as a squatter camp is spontaneous.'

'I didn't say squalid, I said spontaneous.'

'There's no such thing as spontaneous design.'

'There is such a thing as happy accident,' he'd persisted.

'I grant you that. But you can't build a whole city by happy accident.'

Their disagreement, really only a pleasant sparring match, had been derailed by somebody at the other end of the table getting hold of the reference to squatter camps, getting hold of it as a dim dog gets hold of a stick, and not letting go until he'd got gob all over it and the table had lost interest.

And now, here he was, and there was Martha's number, on the card she'd given him: Martha Samuelson, Literary Agent, her home number scrawled on the back. He hadn't told her he was coming, not wanting to commit himself in advance to seeing her, or not wanting to commit her to a meeting she might prefer to avoid graciously on the grounds of a previous engagement. Also, his mission in Paris was one that she was unlikely to have much sympathy with.

Was ten o'clock on a Saturday morning a reasonable time to phone? Surely as reasonable as any other … he dialled the number. She picked up almost immediately.

'Martha? Christopher here, Christopher from Cape Town.'

'Christopher?' She sounded properly surprised, neither overjoyed nor dismayed. 'Where are you phoning from?'

'Here in Paris.'

'Oh. I thought Paris wasn't on your list.'

'It wasn't. But it was placed there by circumstances.'

'That sounds intriguing. Are you going to tell me?'

'Over a cup of coffee or a glass of wine, if you have time for one.'

'When?'

'Any time from now.'

'Where are you?'

'In a hotel on the Rue St André des Arts.'

'That's easy. I'm just up the street, near the Odéon. Why don't we meet for lunch?'

'Why not, indeed? Where?'

'Le Départ on the Place St Michel? At one?'

'I'll be there.'

He put down the phone. Martha sounded exactly as he had thought she would, warm enough to acknowledge a past association, cautious not to presume on it. Apart from her occasional visits to South Africa, he had last seen her almost thirty years ago, on the eve of his departure from Cambridge. He remembered taking leave of her, somewhat bleakly, in front of the University Library, where he had gone to return the last pile of books left over from his preparation for his final exam. She was to stay on, he was returning to South Africa.

'Well,' he'd said, giving her an awkward kiss, his arms filled with books. 'I hope to see you soon in South Africa.'

'Yes,' she'd said non-committally, 'but I don't know when. I'm hoping to find a job in Paris when I'm done here.'

'Shouldn't be too difficult, with a Cambridge PhD in French.'

She'd given him a wan smile. It was drizzling lightly, and droplets of rain sparkled in her red-gold hair. 'I don't have the PhD yet. Oh, and congratulations on your First.'

'Thanks. I'm surprised, really. But pleased, of course.'

'Of course. Well, I'm meeting someone for lunch at the Grad Pad. Give my love to Cape Town.'

'Will do.'

'And say hi to Daniel for me.'

That had been her only reproach, if reproach it was, for his desertion of her two years earlier. In their first year at Cambridge, in 1978, what had been a casual acquaintance at the University of Cape Town had soon developed into a friendship. Christopher was doing the English Tripos at St John's, Martha a PhD in French at Caius. He'd enjoyed her brisk, slightly astringent manner, unbeguiled by the weight of Cambridge tradition and yet insatiably curious in pursuit of its arcana: 'It really is a fully functional medieval system,' she'd said, 'with minor concessions to modern fads like women's rights.' The Cambridge colleges were just opening up to women, and they were still something of a novelty.

They met often in the University Library or on the Sidgwick Site; they walked together to Grantchester or cycled further afield, to Saffron Walden, or even, once, to Norwich, staying in cheerful, smelly youth hostels. Of an evening, they would sit reading together in his rooms – his study, overlooking the river, was more pleasant than hers – and later, walk to a nearby pub, the Baron of Beef or the Pike, for a drink before closing time. They both felt held at arm's length by the English students, who were manifestly reluctant to consort with South Africans, the country being, at the time, at the nadir of its international reputation. Too polite to be brutal, the Brits were nevertheless too embarrassed to be natural. Their friends were Australians, who were by and large apolitical, or French, who were left-wing but somehow less terrified of contamination. They spoke to the Australians about cycling, to the French about politics, and to each other about Greek tragedy and movies.

At the end of their first year, Martha accompanied him to the May Ball of his college. They got mildly drunk, and as they walked out onto the Backs, the first light of a summer's day burnishing her glorious hair, the little river making its tranquil, unassuming way beneath the solid but graceful stone bridges, a lone punt filled with tired revellers in evening dress drifting by, he thought he had never seen anything more beautiful, and he kissed her. They went back to her rooms and made love – he tentatively, his first time, she more assured, but with a certain ironic reserve which he found attractive if disconcerting.

It was assumed, without quite being spelt out, that they would spend the summer in Cambridge – they were neither of them rich enough to contemplate long journeys, in any case – making such excursions as occurred to them: they'd both expressed a desire to see Bath, he'd mentioned cycling to Lavenham in Suffolk, she'd said she wanted to see the Brontë home. The buses were slow but cheap, and, with someone to share the tedium and the scenery, might be fun. Besides, they were both lately enough arrived in Cambridge just to enjoy being there; the prospect of long summer days next to the river seemed very fair. He'd looked forward, too, to discussing with Martha some short stories he'd been writing.

And then, unannouncedly, before any of this could come to pass, Daniel de Villiers had arrived. He had, on the spur of the moment, decided to see Europe – characteristically assuming that Christopher would be available to travel with him – and by Europe seeming to mean in the first place Paris, where Christopher's French could smooth his way. As heir presumptive to a large wine estate, he had been given a generous allowance by an indulgent father, and in reply to Christopher's objection that he couldn't afford Paris, Daniel had munificently offered to pay half his expenses.

Christopher knew he was breaking an implied pledge to Martha; but it was only an implied pledge, and Daniel was very persistent. There was something flattering about his plea that he *needed* Christopher to go with him; he was not a man ever to confess to a need if he could help it, and he seemed to feel that doing so gave him the right to have it met. Although Christopher could see through the presumption of this, he was helpless against the appeal; he had never been able to deny Daniel anything he deigned to ask. So, after a rather miserable farewell to Martha where she made it clear, without spelling it out, how hurt she was, Christopher had taken off for Paris. When he returned four weeks later, she had left for the Lake District with a woman friend; he and Martha never really regained their intimacy, though they did see each other from time to time, and pretended that they wanted to do so more often. Much later, once he'd gone back to South Africa, she had contacted him once or twice while on a visit and they'd met, usually at the home of friends she was staying with. They had never again referred to their one night of passion, if indeed it had been passion.

CHAPTER 2

Christopher, with three hours to while away, walked out into the noisy Saturday morning, content to let Paris take him where she wanted. He would have resisted any suggestion that he was indulging in a sentimental revisiting of places he had formerly known; but to walk for any length of time in the Latin Quarter is to happen upon forgotten landmarks, persistent in their immutability. He walked, not sure whether he was remembering things or imagining that he recognised them. The street market on the Rue de Buci, for instance, seemed as familiar as if he'd visited it the day before; but then, most of Paris has passed into the collective memory by way of films, photo spreads in magazines, advertising posters. As, in a museum, one comes face to face with Renoir's fat pink nudes with a shock of recognition, and then realises that it's not the painting one is recollecting but its simulacrum, so in Paris one is forever rediscovering places one has never discovered in the first place.

And as he walked, Paris fell effortlessly into Paris picturesque, so often indistinguishable from Paris cliché. The basket of baguettes carried by the white-smocked young man on the bicycle: real bread, no doubt, intended for consumption in some café with a salad and a glass of wine. But in Paris bread had lost its innocence and become self-conscious. Could the young man really be unaware of *composing*, the verticals of the baguettes counterposed by the horizontals, diagonals and circulars of the bicycle frame and wheels? And the couple kissing on the Place St Michel, as couples are forever kissing in Paris: if it hadn't been for Robert Doisneau, would they have kissed right there?

He paused by a quayside bookstall specialising in 'artistic'

17

postcards of Paris, the multitudinous spawn of Henri Cartier-Bresson and his imitators. One card caught his eye: a black-and-white photograph of a little boy running down a street, carrying a baguette. He turned it over; the title was *Le Petit Parisien/The Little Parisian/Der Kleine Pariser*. He snorted. It was conceivable that the little boy, in running down the street with a baguette, was intent only on getting bread on the table, entirely unaware of being a *petit Parisien*; but once the boy had seen the picture, and he could not have escaped seeing it, he would forever after be aware of being a *Parisien*, whether little or not, would forever be posing for the candid photograph that somebody must surely be taking of him. The photograph was dated 1952; now, almost sixty years later, the boy was probably a semi-alcoholic in his sixties, playing boules or chess in the Luxembourg Gardens, corrupted for life by the seductive gaze of that camera.

So Christopher wandered and looked and recalled, or fancied he recalled. He found, not quite by accident, but not quite by design either, the Pâtisserie du Sud Tunisien, still dispensing the same sugary doughnuts; and La Petite Hostellerie, still offering a prix fixe menu with boeuf bourguignon as one of its mainstays; and there, after several more unplanned twists and turns, was Shakespeare and Company, with its wistful inscription from Whitman: *Étranger qui passe, tu ne sais pas avec quel désir ardent je te regarde.*

Christopher had, in a desultory fashion, tried to keep his little French alive, in spite of a suspicion that he would never return to France: it seemed a pity to let it languish like a neglected child. For a while, in weekly sessions with the Alliance Française in Cape Town, he had gathered with earnest housewives and with supercilious graduate students preparing for an exchange programme in France, but there had seemed no living connection between daily life in chaotic South Africa and the rigours and intricacies of the French language; so he had given up the classes, retaining a nominal connection with *la langue* through a copy of *L'Étranger* dutifully kept by his bedside – the rough little Gallimard paperback. *Aujourd'hui, maman est morte.* Not a phrase he was likely to find useful in his sojourn.

He strolled onto the Île de la Cité, thronged on this mild and sunny May morning with tourist buses and their disgorged contents. He avoided the queue snaking into Notre Dame, searched out rather the little park at the back. In the gazebo, a brass band from an American college was playing the theme from *E.T.* Nobody seemed to be listening, but the thin cheer of brass mingled pleasantly with the young green of the trees, and the amateur musicians, earnestly addressing their instruments with pursed lips and ballooned cheeks, were touchingly intent upon the trite little tune, a kind of beauty after all in their dedication if not in its result. They, too, were conscious of being in Paris rather than in Tucson, Arizona, and if they blew all the harder as a consequence, what did it matter if Paris didn't really notice?

He crossed the river to the brash commotion of the Place du Châtelet, so little adjusted to the needs of the casual stroller; it was really only a perverse instinct of curiosity that brought him back to this prosaic manifestation of pure purpose in a city temperamentally more at ease with leisure. As if intent on pursuing to some conclusion this other aspect of the city, he ventured down one of the staircases leading to the labyrinthine metro station, the subterranean nerve centre of the city. If a city could be said to have a subconscious, it must be this, he thought, as he huddled against a graffiti-covered wall, gazing at the unstaunchable flow of passengers dodging, elbowing, shouldering, striding, strutting, sauntering, each intent on a single destination, assignation, confrontation; a million uncoordinated impulses converging here to be redirected and dispatched, shunted according to the dictates of a tentacular network of electronic and mechanical components along crepuscular corridors, moving walkways and echoing tunnels, to emerge at last as purposeful human action.

He regained the open air with a sense of release: even the clangour of the Place sounded with a kind of unconfined vigour after the muffled closeness of the vast station. It was with something akin to relief that he crossed the river once more to the Place St Michel. He took a seat at one of the tables of Le Départ, on one of the little round-backed chairs arranged like seats in a theatre, facing the great stage of the street, with its troupe of strolling players, all imagining themselves at the centre of the drama – all except the poor wandering tourists in their too-clean sneakers and their floppy hats, their pink polyester tops and their pink faces, their plaid shorts and their paunches; hapless aesthetic accidents astray amidst the assured arrogance of Paris, map-flapping from guidebook highlight to highlight, or staggering footsore behind some impatiently spritely tour guide with a pennant. Victims of many delusions, believing themselves to be 'having fun', or at any rate being spiritually enriched, hoping that their blisters constituted an education, they did at least escape the delusion that they mattered personally. Whereas the Parisians – the Parisians *mattered*, because to look like that is to matter, and to matter is to look like that. *Étranger qui passe …*

Thus mused Christopher at his own little table, with the *grand crème* in front of him – mercifully, he'd remembered not to call it *café au lait* – recalling evenings here with Daniel after dinner at La Petite Hostellerie, a last glass of wine, and another, and another, those first two weeks when Paris had seemed like some infinitely ingenious conspiracy to catch him with his guard down, to startle him into some hitherto unexpected glimpse of his own susceptibility to the beauty of the past and the pleasure of companionship. They had walked the streets, they had tramped the length of the river, they had criss-crossed the parks and loitered on squares, they had bought wine and bread and cheese and idled on the prow of the Île de la Cité as the river rushed past with its businesslike barges and garish tourist boats. They had gone to cheap restaurants and noisy bars, they had talked bad French to French girls, who had giggled and replied in bad English.

But mainly they had discovered in each other a capacity for delight which nothing in South Africa, in all the years they had known each other, had ever unlocked. They had been at school together, at Rondebosch Boys' High: Christopher a day boy from Pinelands, Daniel a boarder from Franschhoek, the son of an Afrikaans father and an English-speaking mother. It was an unlikely friendship, the reticent – surly even, thought some – farm boy, and the quicker, clever city boy, the one solidly good at sports, the other articulate, witty, a writer of school plays and short stories. Christopher admired the quiet reserve of his friend, possibly interpreting a failure of human warmth as a strength; Daniel may in his turn have been attracted to the verbal facility of the smaller boy, his quick wit and ready laughter. Then, too, Christopher, temperamentally slow to assert his own claims, admired the direct, unthinking manner of the other boy: he seemed enviably free of Christopher's morbid wish to please others. And as Daniel did not mind being pleased, they were excellent friends, without ever having to account to themselves for the basis of their friendship, though Christopher was aware that others were puzzled about it. He did not share this insight with Daniel.

They both went to the University of Cape Town, where their friendship continued, though they now saw less of each other: Daniel was doing a Commerce degree, Christopher a BA in languages. They were in the same residence in their first year, and then Christopher, weary of the brash bonhomie of residence life, moved out to share a flat with friends. Daniel once let slip the observation that he didn't get on with Christopher's 'arty' friends; for his part, Christopher was quietly mystified, on those few occasions he spent with Daniel and his sporting friends, by the paucity of their conversation and the penury of their wit. It seemed strange that a group of human beings should choose to spend so much time together, with so few shared resources.

So, by the time Christopher came to Cambridge and Daniel went to the farm, the friendship was in abeyance; hence Christopher's surprise when Daniel turned up in Cambridge, and hence all the stronger the sense of rediscovering a friendship, of indeed, in the luminous medium of Paris, extending it far beyond what it had once been. Daniel didn't mind making a fool of himself; he talked freely, in a mishmash of mauled languages, to strangers, who responded with like warmth to the attractive, sun-flushed young man. And it had been a source of pride for Christopher to be the designated travelling companion of this golden youth. Paris brought out a kind of benign recklessness in Daniel that surprised

Christopher; it was an easier basis upon which to meet him than the rather wary respect they'd had for each other at home. And above all, Paris had liberated Daniel, uncrabbed by convention and uninhibited by his customary reserve, into showing affection for Christopher; and Christopher had felt confident enough to return it as freely as it was given. They had walked home in the early hours, drunk, arm in arm so as not to fall over, and had woken up in the same bed, hung over but eager for the new day.

His art history course had enabled Christopher to make the profusion of beauty on offer in the museums intelligible both to himself and his companion; no doubt his confident pronouncements and delighted discoveries would have struck a connoisseur as callow and under-informed, but they served their purpose as a clue through the labyrinthine halls of the Louvre and the packed treasure-houses of the smaller museums. There was also the novelty of being deferred to by Daniel, and the pleasure of sharing with him the ingenious insights that seemed to arise unbidden, like some heady fume, from contact with such prodigality. Christopher had seldom, if indeed ever, had such a strong sense of his intellect and his emotions working in concert, each making sense of the other, collaborating all the more productively for their difference. He had never been so conceited – or so happy.

They had followed, one day, a procession of barges on the Seine celebrating some triumph of the SNCF, a huge locomotive hunkering on the main barge, with brass bands at regular intervals along the left bank lending the occasion the air of a festival dedicated to a deity of technology, the gleaming locomotive its avatar. To Christopher and Daniel, pausing to listen to the bands, then running to catch up with the procession, there was something hilarious about the light-hearted pomposity of the whole business; and their exuberance was increased rather than dampened when they were drenched by a sudden downpour of rain. Along with such of the crowd as had not had the foresight to carry an umbrella, they squashed into the arched space under the Pont Neuf, squeezed up against each other, out of breath, wet and sweaty, but cherishing the warmth of each other's bodies. Then, miraculously, the members of a brass band also sheltering under the bridge cleared space for themselves and their instruments, and started playing, to the cheers of the crowd. 'I can't give you anything but love', they played, with a kind of earnest joyfulness; and as they played, Daniel hummed along, then hamming it up to the amusement of the onlookers, put his arm around Christopher's shoulder, made big eyes at him, and belted out with the music, in his strong tenor, 'Dream a while, scheme a while, we're sure to find happiness.' And Christopher had thought, who needs dreaming and scheming, this *is* happiness, standing under the bridge in the rain with Daniel's arm around him and a brass band proclaiming 'love's the only thing I've plenty of, baby'. At the end of the song the onlookers applauded – partly the band, but also partly Daniel's performance, and he took an ironical bow. Then the rain stopped and they ran after the barge, laughing and singing, I can't give you anything but love, baby.

'You're smiling very benignly upon the passing scene.'

He got to his feet and kissed Martha. 'I didn't see you arrive.'

'Evidently.'

They settled side by side on their little chairs and frankly in-spected each other, as if for signs of wear and tear.

'You look well,' she said. 'A bit greyer than when I last saw you, but it suits you. And I like the rimless glasses.'

'Thank you,' he said. 'You are looking better than well.' Martha had apparently caught the Parisian trick of ageing into a kind of emphasised angularity rather than the helpless South African blur of fat and wrinkles. She had always, with her cheekbones, her deli-cate nose and her grey eyes, been a beautiful woman, but now it was as if the distractions of youth had been drained from her fea-tures, leaving only a firmer kind of serenity, presided over, as it were, by an extravagant sunburst of hair – less radiantly red than in her youth, but still splendid in its gleams of old-gold and cop-per, and still unconfined.

'Thank you,' she said, easily accepting the compliment. Then she said, 'So. The circumstances.'

23

'The circumstances?'

'That bring you to Paris.'

Suddenly it seemed impossible that he should explain to Martha, of all people, what he was doing in Paris. 'Oh, yes. Shall we order first?'

'Yes, but don't think I'll forget about it.'

It was over a bottle of Chablis, then, and an omelette aux tomates, that Christopher explained. 'You remember my friend Daniel?'

'Of course I do. He spoilt, for me, what was to have been an idyllic Cambridge summer.'

Christopher sighed, half in relief. By naming it, she simplified enormously. 'Yes. I have often wanted to tell you how sorry I was.'

It was an apology that was coming thirty years late, but, handsomely, she seemed to accept it without examining the best-before date. 'I think I knew that. At least, I knew that you hadn't enjoyed it.'

'How did you know that?'

'When I saw you after your holiday, you seemed decidedly wan when I asked you how Paris had been.'

'Did I?'

'Yes. In fact, you seemed to have spent a season in hell.'

'That was rather what it felt like – the last fortnight, at any rate.'

'Hell in Paris? How did that happen?'

He had not thought he would be telling her the sorry little history, but under the spell of her candour it suddenly seemed the most natural thing to say, 'What happened was Marie-Louise.'

'Ah, did she happen here?' If there was an element of amusement in Martha's interest, that did not detract from its sustaining force. 'I knew of course that Daniel married her, but I put it down to their UCT connection.'

'In a sense, you were right. We'd both known her at UCT, Daniel rather better than I had. But yes, she appeared out of the blue one morning in the hotel here where Daniel and I were staying.'

'Just by chance?'

'So I assumed at first. But it turned out that they'd had an arrangement.'

'And Daniel hadn't told you about this when he was persuading you to accompany him to Paris?' Christopher had made much, in his shuffling excuses to Martha, of Daniel's insistence on *needing* him in Paris.

'No. No, he hadn't. When I pointed this out to him later, in a somewhat heated conversation, he claimed that his arrangement with Marie-Louise had been *provisional*. But it wasn't my impression that there was anything at all provisional about Marie-Louise's presence.'

'In fact, there was never anything at all provisional about Marie-Louise herself. She was in my residence at UCT. She made it her business to get onto every committee.'

'Well, she came to Paris intent upon, as it were, getting onto Daniel.'

'And succeeded.'

'Yes, well, her committee experience must have stood her in good stead. Oh, at first the three of us went around together, pretending to be having fun, Marie-Louise and I just about managing to conceal our resentment of each other, and Daniel opting for blithe obliviousness. I remember an utterly awful evening at Le Procope.'

'How so?' she asked, her sympathy not entirely vanquishing her amusement. 'Was the food so bad?'

'The food was the least of it, except as the occasion of Marie-Louise's petulance. It was my birthday, and Daniel, to give him his due, was feeling a bit repentant, so he offered to treat us to a special meal. Le Procope was my choice; Marie-Louise had held out for the Brasserie Lipp as *less pseudo*, but of course it was my birthday and even Marie-Louise could just about see that it made sense for me to have the choice of restaurant. But in the event she did make it her business, as you put it, to run down every aspect of Le Procope, including, and especially, the food, which was, I seem to remember, not as miraculously good as I somehow expected *real* Parisian food to be.'

'Le Procope is hardly the place to go for real Parisian food, Christopher.'

'So we discovered, to the extent that any of us were capable of recognising real Parisian food. But while Daniel and I'd have taken the disappointment in our stride and written it off to experience, Marie-Louise dwelt on every piece of gristle in her coq au vin and every grain of sand in her salad with delighted disgust, and sent back her crème brûlée because it was *lumpy*. I remember lumpy because I was instructed to convey to the waiter the lumpy state of the dessert.'

Martha laughed. 'I'm impressed that you knew what lumpy was in French.'

'That's just it, I didn't. I said *rempli de mottes*, which really seemed to set off the waiter and the kitchen staff.'

'I can see how it would. You were saying that there were clods of earth in Marie-Louise's dessert.'

'So I discovered later. Apparently the term I wanted was *grumeleux*, which I have cherished for three decades against my next visit to Le Procope.'

'It would be a pity to waste it, but I can't guarantee that Le Procope's crème brûlée is still lumpy.'

'I don't think I want to find out. It was a hideous evening, and when we got back to our hotel room said as much to Daniel, rather forcefully, in fact, after all the wine I'd knocked back in the restaurant. He was completely unrepentant, and suggested that I swop rooms with Marie-Louise the next day.'

'Which you did?'

'Which I abjectly did. Marie-Louise made it clear that she expected no less, and expressed satisfaction at having to pay only half of a double room instead of full price for a single room.'

'Which Daniel was happy to have you pay?'

'Well, if he was unhappy he didn't say so. They got to share the double room and I got to spend many hours wandering around Paris with my Green Guide.'

'Mm. Educational, but not very entertaining. Why didn't you go back to Cambridge?'

'Why not, indeed?' He considered. 'I suppose I've never been one to cut my losses and get out while I can. Perhaps I was hoping that Daniel and Marie-Louise would have a falling-out, or that she'd take off for Switzerland as she was forever intending to do, only she never did.'

'Of course not. She knew she was onto a good thing.'

'You call Daniel a good thing?'

She acknowledged his pleasantry with a quick laugh. 'Well, the farm is excellent. I've been taken to see it by my Cape Town friends.'

'Beau Regard is a beautiful farm. And the rest is history.'

'Quite a history. But the part of the history that intrigues me is how, after your holiday in hell, you kept up the friendship with Daniel.'

Christopher sighed. 'Shall we order coffee?' They had long since finished their meal, and their empty plates had been removed with brisk efficiency.

'Yes, let's,' she said, draining the last of her wine. 'But about Daniel?'

'Yes, about Daniel. Yes, we remained friends. Of sorts.'

She ignored his qualification. 'In spite of Marie-Louise?'

'Yes. She was never much more than civil to me, but never less so, either, and over the years she came to accept my occasional presence, or at least not to mind it too much.'

'As she lost interest in Daniel?'

'Possibly. Anyway, Daniel and I began to see each other occasionally. And then, when they separated last year ...'

'Oh? That's news.'

'Yes, although in South Africa it's old news. She had a well-publicised affair with a French photographer who came to photograph the farm. He also photographed the beautiful Mrs de Villiers, and photographer and subject composed well, as they say.'

'So Marie-Louise is now in France?'

'No, apparently they're living in London and New York for the time being. I think he has an inconvenient wife in France.'

'And what does this have to do with your being in Paris?'

'It's part of the back story, if you will. In the first place, as I was saying, it's meant that I've seen more of Daniel.'

'As consoler and adviser.'

'As company. I think he's quite lonely.'

'In the midst of all those hordes that descend upon Beau Regard at the drop of an invitation?'

'Yes, and many don't even insist on an invitation. The hordes come to gape, gossip and gorge; they're no real company for Daniel, though he needs their admiration, I think.'

She persisted in her sceptical view of the situation. 'How sincere can it be, the admiration of gapers, gossips and gorgers?'

'Oh, sincere enough as far as it goes. If they didn't admire the place at some level, they wouldn't turn up. And Daniel has kept his impressive looks. But, as I say, their admiration leaves him unsatisfied.'

'Like most addictions.'

'Indeed. So, every so often he phones me for a supper for two at the kitchen table, or a quiet weekend.'

'And you go?'

'I go. Why not?'

'Why would you? What has the friendship ever brought you?'

Her directness took him by surprise, but he adjusted readily to her level of confidence. 'On balance, not very much,' he said, after the slightest of hesitations. 'He didn't really encourage a rapprochement in the Marie-Louise years, and of course, that does … discourage.'

'My dear Christopher,' she asked, and now with no attempt to hide her impatience, 'how on earth does a history so lacking in reciprocity end up bringing you to Paris?'

'If you stopped side-tracking me, I could tell you,' he smiled.

'I'm sorry,' she said, only half-repentant. 'Do carry on.'

'Thank you. Well, you may know that Daniel has brought forth two children, the eldest of whom …'

'Is called Eric.'

'Oh. So you know.'

She visibly checked her first impulse of candour, and continued in a more guarded tone. 'Eric de Villiers has achieved a certain fame in some circles in Paris.'

This, in turn, checked him for a moment. 'Fame?' he asked. 'Do you mean notoriety?'

She seemed to consider this while the waiter placed two tiny cups of coffee in front of them. 'No, I mean fame, I think – though initially there was some danger of notoriety. He took a while to find his feet, morally speaking.'

'And he has now found them?'

'As far as I can tell. He is at least no longer mentioned in contexts a well-wisher would not want him to be mentioned in. He is known, to those who know that kind of thing, as *Le Bel Africain*.'

'Beauty is as beauty does. And what is it that he does?"

She sipped her coffee. 'Well, he represents Africa. The French, as you may know, think they are mad about Africa, which to them means *The Lion King* with sex.'

'And Eric gives them that?'

'Well, he does look like a young lion.'

'You're avoiding my question. I know what he looks like. Though when I last saw him, he looked more like a young buffalo. Or perhaps he just acted like one.'

'I'll leave you to decide for yourself what animal he most resembles. I take it you'll be seeing him while you're here?'

'That is *why* I'm here.'

'To see Eric?'

'To see Eric.'

'But why?'

'That is what I've been trying to tell you. Because Daniel asked me to.'

'Daniel …?'

'Yes. The thing is, Eric originally came to France for six months, ostensibly to learn more about the wine trade so as to equip him to assume his rightful place as heir to Beau Regard.'

'And he has now been here for …?'

'Three years, close enough, most of them in Paris, where I imagine very little wine is made. And he's showing no sign of any intention to return.'

'And Daniel wants him to return.'

'He does.'

'And you are here to persuade Eric?'

'More or less.'

'And why doesn't Daniel come to Paris himself to persuade Eric?' Her interrogation, for that was what it was, was unexpectedly bracing to him; her evident interest in his mission made it seem what it had not seemed before: *interesting*. It had seemed merely onerous and perhaps ridiculous, but not interesting. Well, he would repay her interest with his candour. 'Daniel doesn't think his argument will carry any weight with Eric.'

'And yours will?'

'It may. It will, of course, be the same argument, which is in itself quite a strong one. But Daniel thinks that Eric is more likely to attend to the argument if it is put to him by a third party.'

'Eric does not attend to Daniel?'

'Apparently not. Relations between them have always been strained, and things were not improved by Daniel's separation from Marie-Louise, to whom Eric was … *is* close.'

'But if Marie-Louise deserted Daniel, and by extension Eric …?'

'Quite. But Eric apparently thinks Daniel's handling of the situation lacked humanity.'

'How did he handle it?'

'Decisively.'

'You mean brutally.'

'I mean decisively. He instituted divorce proceedings and managed to get a ruling that Marie-Louise was not entitled to a cent, a drachma or a sou.'

'And you don't call that brutal? That after – how many years of marriage?

'Twenty-seven.'

'Twenty-seven years of marriage, she should be cut off without a penny?'

'I'm sure the court took into consideration everything that was relevant. Still, be that as it may, Eric is not speaking to, or in any way communicating with, his father.'

'Hm. High-minded of him.'

'Yes. Unless his way of life is so depraved as to hide its face in shame, as it were.'

'Why should it be?'

'I was hoping you might tell me that.'

'What do I know about Eric's way of life? At most, I hear about him by the way.'

'Then have you not heard by the way of his ... circumstances, for want of a better word?'

'I know that he works in fashion, if that's what you mean.'

'How can I mean that when I didn't even *know* that? What can young Eric possibly have to contribute to the fashion industry?'

'His looks?' she ventured.

'You mean he's a model?'

'I don't know. I don't think so. I was told he's associated with Gloriani.' She said this matter-of-factly, as if he should recognise the allusion.

'Gloriani? Is that good?'

'I think so, yes. In fact, it's probably excellent. Gloriani's not the latest thing, but he is a very established label, one of the last survivors of the glory days of haute couture, and nobody in the trade would willingly miss one of his shows.'

'And Gloriani himself?'

'Himself?'

'I mean, as opposed to the label?'

'I'm not sure that Gloriani exists as opposed to the label. Oh, there is a Mr Gloriani, a Signor Gloriani, a Monsieur Gloriani, but when people say Gloriani, they mean the label. But why the interest?'

'Well, there's a sense at home that Eric may have got himself embroiled with some undesirable person.'

She seemed amused at this. 'Oh? Undesirable to whom?'

'Well, to his father and his friends.'

'I see. And what is this sense based on?'

'On ... well, on the signs.'

'As interpreted by Beau Regard?'

'Yes,' he said, ignoring the sardonic reserve of her question. 'Apparently Eric is still receiving an allowance from his father, but he's no longer drawing the money. That seems to suggest that he has a … sponsor.'

'That's as it may be. I wouldn't jump to any conclusions. Besides, the sponsor might be charming.'

He looked at her over the dregs of his coffee, trying to ascertain whether she was serious; he decided she was, though also enjoying being provocative. 'Aren't sponsors normally assumed to have more or less mixed motives?'

'That's as it may be,' she said again. 'A mixed motive may be preferable to a single-minded purpose. But again, I wouldn't jump to any conclusions.'

'Well, Daniel is jumpy, and there's nowhere else to jump to.'

'And because Daniel has jumped, you do too?'

'He has asked me, at any rate, to come and find out.'

'Before you jump?'

'In a manner of speaking.'

'And may one ask, if you did jump, *how* you would jump?'

'I'd present his father's proposal to him.'

'An ultimatum?'

'No, an offer.'

'An offer dependent on his return to Beau Regard?'

'Naturally.'

'And if he does not return?'

'Then, naturally, the offer lapses.'

'Then it *is* an ultimatum.'

'I don't know. As I understand an ultimatum, it's a threat delivered from a position of weakness trying to impose itself as a position of strength.'

'And that's not Daniel's position?'

'Surely not. His … *offer* is made on the basis of, well, of all he has to offer.'

'You mean Beau Regard.'

'Yes. Between us, if Eric returns, he steps into a handsome settlement and all the privileges associated with succession.'

'To the title?'

'To the property. And it's a handsome property.'

'Oh, I know. There's none handsomer,' she said, a trifle dryly.

'But what if he doesn't?'

'Then he doesn't.'

'Step into …?'

'Step into.'

'And who does?'

'Step into?'

'Step into.'

'There's his sister, Annette.'

'She's younger than Eric?'

'Yes, by a year or so. But she's been married a good two years.'

'Would that impede her stepping?'

'Not necessarily. She's a woman of good sense, and her good sense urged her to marry Harry Krige, the heir to Le Dauphin, the neighbouring farm.'

'It would seem Harry Krige is a man of good sense too.'

'Oh, eminently so, albeit of limited imagination. It's a marriage made in heaven, if heaven can be assumed to interest itself in the preservation and extension of the ancestral acres.'

'So, if Eric doesn't return to the fold, Harry Krige will step into it?'

'That seems likely. Though Daniel is reluctant. He's never really warmed to Harry. He thinks he's an opportunist who married Annette to get his hands on Beau Regard. So naturally he's not eager to give him what he wants.'

'Naturally.' Her manner, never effusive, was at its driest in referring to Daniel. 'And all Eric will have to do is return to Beau Regard?'

'Yes. Though part of the settlement will only come into effect when he marries.'

'Why is that?'

'Daniel believes marriage is a steadying influence.'

'Marriage hardly steadied Marie-Louise.'

'But it steadied Daniel.'

'Daniel was unsteady?'

'He was, one might say, unestablished.'

She visibly refrained from taking up this point, and asked

instead, 'Does Daniel have in mind a particular steadying influence for Eric?'

'Naturally he wouldn't prescribe to him, but before Eric came to Paris there was an understanding between him and, as it happens, Harry Krige's younger sister, which pleased Daniel very much.'

'He warmed to her more than to her brother, then?'

'Oh, infinitely so. She's a very unassuming young woman.'

'And Daniel likes women to be unassuming. How vividly you make me see him.' She put down her coffee cup with as much emphasis as its size allowed. 'But how definite was the understanding between Eric and the unassuming Miss Krige?'

'As definite as circumstances allowed, I gather. An undertaking on his part to come back and claim her.'

'Would she not have been the obvious person to come to Paris to lead Eric back?'

'She is, as I've said, unassuming. And she has her pride. She won't be seen following a man to Paris to plead with him to return to her.'

There was a moment's silence, during which Martha may have been considering a variety of rejoinders. But all she said was, 'She will consent to being *returned to*, though?'

'I think so. We must assume that she's in love with Eric.'

'Poor woman,' Martha said. 'And your task is …?'

'To make contact. And then, as I've said, to present the offer.'

'Will Eric be willing to be made contact with? I mean, by you, as his father's ambassador?'

'That is what I must find out. I don't think he'd refuse outright. He was, as I've intimated, never the soul of courtesy, but he wasn't openly rude either.'

'That sounds like a slender foundation on which to build a relationship.'

'Oh, I'm not aspiring to a relationship. At most, I'd hope to reach an understanding.'

She laughed. 'Which is, after all, also a kind of relationship. But given the amenities of our century, why doesn't Daniel just email or Skype his son? And isn't everybody under thirty on Facebook?'

'Even with the amenities of our century, you still need to know the other person's email or Skype address, which Daniel does not. And no, Eric's not on Facebook.'

'You make him sound almost interesting.' She looked at her watch. 'I need to be going. I have to meet a client at two-thirty. A young American who insisted on the Deux Magots. Why are writers so self-conscious?'

'Perhaps because no one else is very conscious of them?'

'Possibly. Are you still writing, by the way?'

He shook his head. 'No. I stopped years ago. After my last visit to Paris, in fact.'

'Paris doesn't usually have that effect on people; quite the contrary, I'd say.'

'I don't know if it was Paris. I just seemed to lose the will to write.'

'Perhaps you'll recover it here, where you lost it?'

'I'm not sure that I'd know what to do with it.'

'You'd write, of course, and I'd sell your stuff. It used to be very good.' She rose to her feet. 'But I really must rush. Come and see me. I may be able to help you.'

'*Now* you tell me! But when?'

'Come to supper. Come tomorrow. Phone me for directions.'

She took the slip that the waiter had placed in a saucer on the table. He attempted to take it from her, but she held onto it. 'I'll pay this one,' she said, placing a few notes in the saucer. 'I suspect, with one thing and another, you'll be paying through your nose.'

Christopher walked back to his hotel, dodging the heedless human traffic of the Rue St André des Arts. Seeing Martha again, *really* seeing her as opposed to spending time in the same room with her and some other people, was an unexpected pleasure. But why unexpected, he wondered. He had spent days on end in her company once – but then, that was before the summer of 1979. Today, suddenly, it had been as if all the dreary history of that time had been produced, glanced at wryly, and then stowed away as redundant. Where before their meetings had been constrained by all that they were not saying, here it had been enriched by the consciousness of what it was unnecessary to say. Except, Christopher thought, if this was the Chablis talking. Wine and Paris had always been a beguiling combination.

Arriving in his room, he felt emboldened to make another attempt to establish contact with the elusive Eric de Villiers. Martha's account of him as having somehow cut a figure in Paris, or at least in a certain segment of Parisian society, was intriguing; but then, as she had also said, the French had always had a sentimental regard for the beasts of the jungle, when picturesquely presented.

He again took out his address book. With an inward groan of reluctance he dialled the number listed for De Villiers, Eric.

A voice answered in French. Christopher was halfway through laboriously asking, with all the subjunctives at his command, whether it might be possible conceivably to address oneself to Monsieur de Villiers, before he realised he was speaking to a recorded message that was now culminating in a clipped 'Merci'.

He dialled the number again and gave the message his undivided attention. It did not sound like Eric's voice, but then he had never heard Eric speak French. The message was uninformative, even by the standards of recorded messages: it said merely that one had reached the number one had dialled and that the call could not be taken, followed by an uncordial invitation to leave a message. Christopher was about to put down the phone – he had no intention of leaving a message – when a brusque voice cut in with a businesslike Oui?

Christopher explained his business as best he could: that he was from South Africa and searching for Monsieur de Villiers …

The voice switched to English: not a South African accent, though: 'Mr de Villiers is no longer living here.' The voice, cold as slate, did not encourage further enquiry, but Christopher, having come this far, pressed on regardless.

'Do you happen to know where he is living?'

'That I cannot tell you.' There was not even the pretence of regret in the voice's uninflected English.

'Do you know of anyone who might help me, perhaps?'

'No.' The monosyllable was clearly intended to terminate the conversation.

'Thank you for your assistance,' Christopher said, deliberately keeping his voice neutral.

'You are welcome.' The voice was as blank as his own.

CHAPTER 3

In spite of the rebuff to his first attempt, Christopher did not despair of tracing Eric. The young man would seem to have more of a public profile than he had imagined, which could only be an aid to discovery – unless, that is, the public profile were to prove more deceptive than no profile at all. The sphere he moved in might, for all its high visibility, be correspondingly opaque, like those stretch limousines gliding past, their tinted windows concealing what their size was intended to draw attention to. Where the aim was to be conspicuously invisible, publicity might not guarantee access.

Be that as it might, Christopher did not feel unduly hurried. With his laptop, he could quite comfortably work at the little table provided by the Hotel du Carrefour: tapping away in one of the neighbouring restaurants he considered too studiedly writer-in-Paris. One innovation the hotel had embraced was wireless internet, so he could do his online checking from his room, though the large-scale editing job he was immersed in – a matter of pruning and punctuating seven hundred pages of the ill-written biography of an undistinguished politician – did not require frequent internet access.

There was a dubious kind of advantage in being able to report at will to Daniel on his progress; he would have preferred more time to find his bearings. He did, though, email a preliminary report detailing what he had found out, or hadn't:

I phoned the number that you were given by Marie-Louise, but there was only a monosyllabic individual there, who denied all knowledge of Eric's present whereabouts. I also met up with Martha again – you may remember her from UCT and from Cambridge, before we took off for Paris.

Daniel replied the next day, in his characteristically terse style, that he was confident Christopher would in due course trace the prodigal son. Offering no advice as to how this might be achieved, he added:

> I remember her very well as somebody who had a crush on you, and didn't seem to like me. I didn't much like her either – I didn't like the fact that you didn't seem to notice that she behaved as if she had some claim on you. Is she still unmarried? If so, beware – her interest may flare up again at the sight of you. You've lost none of your faculties, as far as I can tell. And you may very well welcome a menopausal fling with an old flame. Just don't let it distract you from the business at hand.

Christopher shook his head. Whatever it was that he valued about Daniel, it did not survive the transition to the written word. The intriguing sense he could give one, when face to face, of having more to offer than he was prepared to admit, became, in writing, a simple enough deficiency in courtesy and generosity. Or was it just that he lacked the expressive means to convey tact and courtesy? And then again, were tact and courtesy not precisely a matter of successful expression?

These, however, were subtleties beyond what Daniel called the business at hand. Christopher's brief was not to figure out the father, but to find the son. He did not even know whether Eric was still in Paris. He might have gone anywhere.

He hoped, thus, for illumination from Martha when he joined her for supper the following evening in her little apartment overlooking the Odéon. They stood at her window and watched the light fade on the neo-classical pomp of the National Theatre.

'Did you know that I live opposite the site of the original Shakespeare and Company?' she asked.

'The one that published *Ulysses*?'

'Yes, Sylvia Beach's. It was right there, No 12, where that dress shop now stands.'

'I'm tempted to say,' he said, 'that only in Paris would a world-famous bookshop make way for a dress shop.'

'I hope you won't say it, because it wouldn't be fair. The bookshop moved, and then the dress shop moved in. It is true that there are many people in Paris with more use for a new frock than for a first edition of *Ulysses*, but that's true of any city anywhere in the world.'

'I grant you that. I'm just feeling a little disgruntled with Paris.'

'It's because you hate what you have to do. Why did you accept the commission?'

'I thought it might be interesting to see Paris again.'

This expressed but a small part of his reasons, and the look of amused reserve on her face suggested that she realised this; but she showed that she could go along with any reason that he proffered. 'It's always interesting to see Paris again,' she said. 'As you know, the last time I saw you, I couldn't understand why you were so resistant to the idea of coming back. Your elaborate theory on – what was it? – the self-consciousness of its beauty, didn't convince me.'

'Well, it's a theory.' He hesitated. 'It's a theory intended to dignify the fact that I was reluctant to return to Paris because I'd been so unhappy here before.'

'Ah, to be unhappy in Paris is to be unhappy indeed!' she exclaimed sympathetically. 'The place does *intensify* so!'

In her great good taste she did not press him for the reasons for his unhappiness. He guessed that she guessed that his unhappiness had been occasioned by Daniel's desertion; and it would have been inhuman on her part not to perceive a certain poetic justice here. He changed the subject, he hoped not too abruptly. 'I've drawn a blank on young Eric. He's no longer living at his last-known address, or at any rate his last-known telephone number.'

'Is there nobody there who can help you?'

'Only a singularly unhelpful person who either does not know or does not want to tell me.'

'A French person?'

'I think so, but he speaks good English, to the extent that he deigns to speak at all.'

'You mustn't read too much into his reticence. Parisians are constitutionally secretive. They reason that any information worth asking for is worth hoarding. That's why it's almost impossible to find out from a Parisian where the nearest Metro is.'

'That's as it may be, but how am I to find Eric?'

They had sat down to an excellent potage printanier. She tasted the soup, seemed satisfied, then replied, 'I think I may be able to help.'

'Ah,' he said, 'that is what you said last night – I must admit, more to my delight than my surprise.'

'Why the lack of surprise? Do I strike you as keeping a dossier on missing South African heirs?'

'No, but you strike me as universally capable where a cause engages your imagination.'

'Ah, when you put it like that! But you mustn't expect miracles. One is but human.' She paused, but he waited: he knew that she would not abandon the subject on that discouraging note. And he was right, for she continued: 'I do, though, have an idea for you. Or rather, I have a name.'

'Which is always better than an idea, not so?'

'That remains to be proved. But this is a good name. It is Zachariah V Bigler II.'

'That certainly sounds like an excellent name. For a start, it sounds American.'

'It is that.'

'And exceedingly venerable. What does the V stand for?'

'He refuses to say. And as to venerable, he is known to his friends as Zeevee, or Zeevee the Second. Does that make you see him in a less exalted light?'

'Well, yes, it does sound rather less biblical. He's a friend of Eric's?'

'An associate, shall we say.' She hesitated. 'I can't answer for their degree of intimacy. I think they shared an apartment at one stage.

He's also employed in the fashion industry, though not in the public eye, for reasons that you will appreciate when you meet him. Zeevee, apart from being a possible avenue to Eric, has the added appeal of being delightful company. He and I have spent many a pleasant evening at a café called L'Étoile Manquante, which is his preferred vantage point.'

'Vantage point on what?'

'Well, it's situated at the intersection of two of the livelier streets of the Marais.'

'You're telling me that your Mr Bigler is a frequenter of the Marais?'

She visibly quelled her amusement, before replying. 'You make the Marais sound like a den of dissolution. But if by that you mean a gay person, the answer is yes. I take it you have no objection?'

'None whatsoever. But if he shared an apartment with Eric –'

'It does rather open up the field of Eric's possibilities.' Her grey eyes rested on him with mild penetration. 'But this can hardly be a new idea for you?'

'I suppose it's not – or I suppose it shouldn't be. And yet I hadn't thought of Eric as being … aberrant in just that way.'

This time she did not bother to hide her amusement. 'My dear Christopher,' she laughed, 'the categories of aberration are myriad, and they are fluid; indeed, here they have ceased to be categorisable at all.'

'Oh, I've come prepared for anything.'

'That's good,' she declared, with every appearance of approval, 'because anything is what you must be prepared to find.'

'You know then …?'

'Oh, absolutely not. I myself am extremely interested to see what you will find.'

'And how will your Zachariah facilitate access to Eric?'

'I'm assuming that they still move in the same orbit, unless they've been estranged by the experience of sharing an apartment, which is of course a not infrequent consequence. But there's only one way of finding out. At worst, we'll have spent an hour or two very pleasantly at L'Étoile Manquante.'

'Zachariah will consent to meeting us there?'

'He will certainly consent to meeting *me* there, and will not object to you.'

'Would it not jeopardise my access to Eric, if he should get to know through this … Zeevee that I'm looking for him?'

'Zeevee is the most discreet person in Paris. That's admittedly not a very energetically contested distinction, but he really is discreet to an almost inhuman degree. It has lost him the company of gossips, but gained him the friendship of people with secrets.'

'If he's as discreet as you say, will he give us the information we want?'

'That I cannot guarantee. It depends, I think, not on the question, but on the answer. If it entails breaking a confidence, Zeevee will not oblige; but if it's a morsel of knowledge that he's gleaned by the way, he'll willingly pass it on. He may be discreet, but he's not needlessly secretive.'

'But will he know the answer?'

'If it is known in Paris, he will know it; that's the advantage of a reputation for discretion. Are you ready for the coq au vin? I can guarantee that there is no gristle in it. And a crème brûlée to follow, absolutely un-*grumeleux*.'

A meeting was set up for the following evening. It was an easy walk across the river, and Christopher set off in plenty of time. In the soft early evening the absurdly formal little park behind Notre Dame, its clipped hedges and fussy flowerbeds insistent on impeccable order in the shadow of the great pile behind them, was populated by strollers and loungers, shifting shapes arranging themselves in relation to the buttresses busily flying behind them. The visible, the visual, the vision, Christopher mused, and the confusion of the three; these secular purposes, this seasonal abundance, that sacred edifice. A young man lolling gracefully on one of the uncomfortable benches, evidently on display for commercial purposes, looked in open assessment at Christopher, got up from the bench the better to exhibit his elegant lines, lit a cigarette, and turned towards the river, where a passing Bateau Mouche was providing a convenient focal point, if need be a conversational gambit, an opening to negotiation. Christopher mended his pace; to saunter or to look back would be interpreted as interest.

So, more briskly than he really wanted to, he crossed the little bridges leading to the Marais across the Île St Louis: the Pont St Louis, the Pont Marie. So much attention to detail, he thought, each crossing a small event, a departure and an arrival.

He reached the café early – he was usually early, for fear of being late – and found a table inside; the choice tables, the ones with a view onto the Rue Vieille du Temple and the Rue Sainte Croix de la Bretonnerie, were all taken by the usual Paris mix of chatterers and voyeurs, seeing and being seen, talking and being talked at, listening and being listened to, not always in strictly equal proportions.

He hoped Martha would arrive before Mr Bigler. Of course, it was possible that the young man had already arrived, but there were only two unaccompanied men in the café, and neither of them looked as if he might be Zachariah V Bigler II, though it was, of course, not established what exactly Zachariah V. Bigler II could be expected to look like. Christopher had said to Martha, when phoning to confirm their arrangement: 'How shall I know him if he gets there before you?' and she had replied, cryptically, 'You will know him. Just look for someone who looks like Zachariah V Bigler II.'

'*No one* looks like Zachariah V Bigler II.'

'Exactly. That's how you will recognise him.'

Martha's prediction was duly vindicated when Zachariah V Bigler appeared in the crowded entrance. He was unmistakably the real thing. For a start, he was evidently American. Christopher would have been hard pressed to name the insignia declaring this identity, for there was nothing crudely stereotypical about his appearance. It was perhaps the extreme neatness of his attire that set him apart: whereas the rest of the clientele were carefully dressed, the care had gone into seeming not to care; here the care had been dedicated to seeming impeccable. The young man was wearing a light, loose woollen jacket of an indeterminate colour somewhere between ecru and fawn, and fitting his awkward frame – he was very tall and thin – as if it had been tailored for him, and revealing, under the diagonal of an elongated lapel, a brilliantly white shirt. The knife pleats of his loose-weave cotton slacks fell perfectly; unbuttoning his jacket, he exposed to view a discreet buckle in brushed chrome securing a narrow belt matching the umber of his soft leather shoes with their subdued lustre. His hands were as large as small shovels. All this Christopher took in as the young man paused at the door, scrutinising the interior with the air of having arrived not to dawdle, but to negotiate.

But it was not by his clothes alone that Christopher identified Zachariah V Bigler II. His face – well, the kindest way of putting it was that it contrasted startlingly with the regularity of his apparel. It was, in fact, the most irregular face Christopher had ever seen. Both mouth and nose were very large, but they were large on a different scale: the nose was too large for the mouth, even while the mouth was too large for the rest of the face, especially for the eyes, which were very deep set, and made to seem more so by heavy eyelids hooding the sockets in a manner half-comical, half-sinister. The ears, again, were too large for the nose, and the chin too large for the ears. The general incongruity was completed by an immense thatch of sandy hair, which seemed to have erupted by accident, so chaotically did it sprout from his scalp. Christopher wondered why he didn't have it cut shorter; but then, that might have exposed more of the ears than their owner wished to inflict on the world.

The young man was, in a word, comically tragically epically historically ugly. There was a perceptible hush in the café as his entrance was registered by the seated clientele: so, one felt, the court of King Arthur might have blanched at the entrance of the Green Knight. Then conversation resumed again, though at a different pitch, both more subdued and more intense than before, a pitch all too clearly suggesting that the newcomer himself was now the subject of conversation.

The young man looked around him. Evidently Christopher was in his own manner as conspicuous as Mr Bigler, for the latter's eyes lit confidently on the older man, and he smiled – a smile of singular charm, despite an array of teeth large even for the prodigious mouth, and by no means as even as the reputed excellence of American dentistry might have led one to expect. What the young man most resembled was a camel, thought Christopher, though he had never seen a camel smile.

'I guess you'll be Mr Turner,' he said as Christopher came to his feet. 'I'm Zachariah Bigler, but please just call me Zeevee. It's not a name I'd have chosen for myself, but it's preferable to the real thing, in which I had even less of a say.'

Christopher shook the extended hand – his own hand all but disappeared in its voluminous grasp – and said, 'And my name is Christopher, which I prefer to Mr Turner.' He gestured to a chair, saying, 'I suppose Martha will be along soon. It's only just gone seven.'

'Then she'll be here in the next minute,' said Zeevee, fitting his limbs with some difficulty into the space allocated by a parsimonious management. 'Martha's never late. It's her sole failing.'

He looked about him, and the waiter appeared with a promptness not previously displayed; there clearly were advantages to Zeevee's extreme visibility. He ordered a glass of red wine, and settled back on the little raffia-backed chair, which creaked alarmingly under his weight. 'How do you know Martha?'

'We were students together in Cape Town more years ago than I care to remember, but we didn't really get to know each other until we coincided at Cambridge some years later, and became … well, fast friends. Since then we've seen each other sporadically, when she's come to South Africa for holidays.'

'And when you've come to Paris, I take it.'

'I haven't really come to Paris all that often. In fact, the last time was when I was studying at Cambridge, thirty years ago.'

Zeevee stared. His eyes, on a closer view, were amber. 'That seems perverse.'

'Why? Is there a rule stipulating that, having seen Paris once, one must return within a certain period?'

'No, but that's because normally no rule is required. You see,' he said, leaning forward as if explaining an intricate natural phenomenon, 'Paris insinuates itself into the unconscious and brings one back without the connivance of the conscious mind.'

'Well, then,' Christopher laughed, amused at the young man's earnestness, 'in my case my conscious mind overruled my unconscious.'

Zeevee shrugged, a creditable imitation of the Gallic gesture relegating all matters to a tragi-comic cosmic state. 'And yet, after all, you have returned,' he pointed out pleasantly. 'Your unconscious has won the battle at last.'

'I'm sorry to destroy your faith in my unconscious, but I'm afraid it's very much my conscious mind that brought me here.'

The American smiled his enormous, warped smile. 'Ah, but that's just the cleverness of the unconscious mind, you see, to make you *think* you know why you're doing what it wants you to do. There is no such thing as accident. But what is it that you think brings you to Paris?'

Fortunately, Martha appeared in the doorway at that precise moment, and in the bustle of greetings, of fitting a third chair into the available space, Zeevee's question was dropped.

'Am I late?' she asked, exaggerating her own shortness of breath. 'I'm sorry, I was trapped on the telephone by a London agent. They have so little sense over there of the rhythms of life,' and she looked around her shoulder for the waiter, who, having delivered Zeevee's wine, was already hovering. 'Don't they know that the violet hour is not to be squandered discussing translation rights?' She indicated with an eloquent finger that she wanted what Zeevee was having.

There was a moment, just after she'd ordered, when all three looked at one another and, Christopher thought, stared into the abyss: what are we going to say now?

Then Martha came to the rescue, as usual by the simplest route possible. 'What a beautiful jacket, Zeevee. Is it new?'

'Relatively. Do you like it?'

'I love it. What is it?'

'A Gloriani, of course. Camel hair. I got it at a reduced price because the model showing it had neglected to shower. It was shown, for effect, without a shirt.'

47

Martha pretended to shudder. 'And dare one ask …?'

'Whether the jacket has since been cleaned? Well, yes, of course – though if you really want to know, the thought of the sweat of the most highly paid male model in Paris wasn't a complete turn-off.'

Martha wrinkled her nose just as her wine was delivered with that insolent flourish representing the Parisian waiter's concession to service. 'Is it the smell of the money he makes that you covet?'

'No, just the proof of his mere humanity.'

'You must surely have more proof of the mere humanity of models than you can deal with in a day's work.'

'Yes, if by humanity you mean ambition, greed, vanity and stupidity; but what I mean is good honest physicality, the smell of passion or of fear or even of bodily labour.'

There was something droll about the contrast between the formality of Zeevee's diction and his wildly unmatched features, and Christopher found himself smiling, he hoped not so incongruously as to seem to be deriding his new acquaintance. 'Blood, sweat and tears, you mean,' he suggested as a cover for his smile.

'Yes, though I think I may draw the line at blood.'

'That's reassuring,' said Martha, 'that you draw the line somewhere.'

There was another small silence, but more comfortable this time, masked by everyone's taking a sip of wine. Then Martha once again took the initiative. 'Has Christopher told you his mission?' she asked Zeevee.

'No, he was just about to when you arrived – or I assume he was about to, since I had asked him to tell me.'

'You'll never know now, whether he would have told you. Do you want to tell him, Christopher?'

'I think I'd rather you did, on balance.'

'Well, why not?' she shrugged. 'I have the advantage of being entirely disinterested. You can interrupt me if I get the details wrong.'

She took another sip of wine and made a face. 'I wonder what they're serving tonight. It has more edge than body. On second thoughts, perhaps we can save explanations for later and ask the questions first.'

'You want to ask *me* questions?' Zeevee asked, and arched his huge furry eyebrows. 'I thought I was asking the questions.'

'Not for the time being. Here is our first question: are you still in touch with Eric de Villiers?'

The young man blinked; he had singularly long eyelashes. 'I guess it depends on what you mean by *still in touch*.'

'Is it that ambiguous?'

'Surely. *Still* in touch, meaning in touch as we once were? To that, the answer is no. Still *in touch* meaning aware of each other's existence and seeing each other from time to time? To that, the answer is yes.'

'Ah.' said Martha. 'That's good enough for us.'

'I'm sure I'm pleased if it satisfies *you*,' Zeevee said good-humouredly. 'Is that all you wanted to know?'

'Of course not. Are you in a position to produce him?'

'As a magician produces a rabbit out of a hat?'

'Nothing as ostentatious as that. Can you quietly arrange a meeting between Eric and Christopher here?'

'I think I had better explain, after all,' Christopher interjected. 'I come as a kind of ambassador from Daniel de Villiers, to put it to his son to come back and assume the responsibilities, and of course the rewards, of the family farm.'

'You want to take him away? And you call your motives honourable?' Zeevee exclaimed – whether in mock horror or real dismay, it was difficult to tell.

'I called my motives nothing at all. But I'm sure he's needed more at home than in Paris,' Christopher ventured.

'Forgive me if I point out that you've not plumbed the depths of the needs of Paris. They are abysmal, the needs of Paris!' Zeevee's regard was as tragic as if, for the moment, the multifarious needs of the great city were incumbent upon him. Again, there was something so droll about his face that this time, Christopher laughed out loud.

'Ah, they amuse you, the needs of Paris?' Zeevee asked, without rancour. 'Watch out, you'll find that they're no laughing matter.'

'No, indeed, I assure you, I take them seriously. I only presume to argue for the greater need of Beau Regard.'

'Oh, the family farm? Eric has told me all about it. It sounds delightful, if a trifle bucolic. I believe it's tucked away in a very beautiful little valley called … French …?'

'Franschhoek. It's where the French Huguenots settled when they came to South Africa in the seventeenth century.'

'Ah, Eric is a descendant of the Huguenots?' If Zeevee was amused, his face did not betray it, except perhaps in its sudden solemnity. 'They must be so proud of him! And now he's returned to the country of his ancestors.'

'Yes, though not, one imagines, as a religious refugee.'

'No, hardly, though I did have a sense that Eric was, how shall we say, relieved to be free of the constraints of home.'

'What young man of twenty-three, twenty-four, twenty-five would not be? It's natural,' Martha said.

'Yes,' said Christopher, 'but it's natural also to want to return to one's home after a decent interval, not so?'

Zeevee examined his wine critically, as if he suspected it of harbouring a tiny insect. 'My dear sir, you use such contentious terms as casually as if you were talking of pork and beans. *Natural* – what is natural in a city like this? What, for that matter, is *decent*?' He put down his glass the more expressively to make his point. 'Oh, these things exist here, even in Paris, but they admit of a multitude of interpretations, interpretations that cannot be fixed simply by staring at them hard.'

'I was not aware of staring,' Christopher said, a trifle stiffly. He did not feel he needed lessons in semantics from such a young man.

'That is true, and I apologise,' Zeevee replied. 'I was speaking generally, and got carried away with my own theorising.'

'Zeevee has a theory for everything,' Martha contributed. 'It's in the *practicalities* that he breaks down.'

'And yet, my dear Martha, it is at your behest, I presume, that Christopher here is appealing to my practical abilities in tracing the elusive heir to Beau Regard?'

50

'Oh, I grant you, you have your gifts. You certainly know a lot of people. But whether that is or is not a practical ability does rather depend on the use you make of your acquaintances.'

'If you complain of me that I don't make use of my acquaintances, I am happy to plead guilty to that.'

Christopher had a sense that Zeevee, accommodating as he was, and good-humoured, and generally excellent company, was heading off the conversation into areas other than the whereabouts of Eric de Villiers. This, no doubt, was but part of the discretion for which he was celebrated, and as such would have been admirable had it not been so inconvenient. 'Would it,' he accordingly gently persisted, 'would it be making use of an acquaintance if you were to arrange for me to meet with Eric?'

Christopher thought he noticed a hesitation, so slight as hardly to register on his companion's expressive face; then Zeevee said, 'On the contrary, it would be rendering him a service, even making allowance for the purpose of your mission – which cannot but present itself to him as perplexing. My problem, however, *is*,' and he inclined his head in mock-deference to Martha, 'one of practicality.'

'I rest my case,' she exclaimed gaily.

'Mais que veux-tu? Quite seriously, what would you have me do? Have him packaged and sent from London by Thomas Cook and Son?'

'He is in London?'

'Yes.' Again, Zeevee seemed to hesitate a moment: the calculation of his discretion, Christopher thought. But he continued, 'I believe his mother is there at the moment.'

Christopher nodded. 'Of course, I'm aware of the separation.'

'And you will know that Eric has always been close to his mother.'

'Yes,' Christopher said. In truth, he had never thought of Eric as being particularly close to anybody, but that may well have been due to his own lack of insight. It occurred to him that the source of Eric's undeclared income might well turn out to be his mother, assuming that Marie-Louise de Villiers, in her own reduced state, had money to squander on an unprofitable son. Then again, she had presumably, in leaving her husband for a French

51

photographer, not cast all caution to the winds. All for love was not her style. But for the moment, Christopher's first interest was not in Marie-Louise.

'And Eric,' he asked, 'when he is not in London, what is it that he *does*?'

'You mean for a living?'

'Yes, or just to occupy himself.'

'Well, I don't know whether I would call it a living or even an occupation, but it is an identity. He is a *claqueur*.'

Zeevee said this as if it should explain all, but it left Christopher still nonplussed. 'What in the name of all the gods of industry is a *claqueur*?'

'The gods of industry have little to do with it. Have you not seen,' Zeevee asked, 'at a fashion show, those beautifully dressed people lining the catwalk and applauding each outfit as it struts out on the emaciated back of some model?'

'I'm not really in the habit of attending fashion shows.'

Zeevee's features assumed a tragic cast. 'No, I daresay they seem to you the height of frivolity. But nowadays fashion shows are news: you need not attend them to see them, they come to you in airport lounges and cafés. Next time you see a show in progress, steel yourself and look, not at the models, who I grant you, might not detain an intelligent man like yourself, but at the onlookers. They are the *claqueurs*. That is, the beautiful ones applauding vigorously are the *claqueurs*. They are employed to look beautiful and to applaud vigorously. The others, the plain ones who look as if they're hating the whole thing, are the fashion journalists, for whose benefit largely the *claqueurs* are planted.'

'But if the journalists know …?'

'Oh, they know. But it's a convention, a pleasant tribute to the make-believe of the fashion world, where appearance counts for all. Actually, it's a custom that's falling into disuse: seats at openings are too precious to be expended on penniless young men. But Gloriani, who is Eric's employer, is of the old school, and would no more dream of presenting his collection without the services of a *claque* than a chef would present his creation,' he looked about him for inspiration, at the food being placed on the table next to theirs, 'without a drizzle of olive oil or a coulis of raspberry. Besides, I have heard him say that Anna Wintour's presence needs to be neutralised by a few good-looking young men.'

'But this profession of *claqueur* – is it well-paid?' Christopher asked.

Zeevee seemed amused at the question. 'Well-paid, no,' he said. 'Lucrative, sometimes, yes.'

'You're being very cryptic, Zeevee,' Martha interjected. 'Do elucidate.'

'Well, don't you see, a *claqueur* is not paid at all. He is provided with an expensive outfit, which he must return before leaving the premises. But he is allowed to attend the reception after the show, which to an impecunious young person means a free meal with good wine. And, more important, networking.'

'Is that what used to be called contacts?' Christopher asked.

'It's related. In networking, the young person is exposed to the scrutiny of any number of people, with divergent needs. If the young person seems likely to meet a particular need, that could constitute a contact.'

'And Eric has met the need of one of these people?'

Zeevee's face registered the slightest tremor, then set in an expression notable only for being no expression at all. 'I couldn't tell you that,' he said, his tone as neutral as his face. He had clearly reached the point of discretion.

'Would it be possible,' asked Martha, 'for you to find out when Eric is likely to be back?'

'Yes, probably,' Zeevee said, in his normal amenable tone. 'That's to say, if Eric himself knows, and has communicated his intention to one of several people I can think of, I *may* be able to find out.'

'And then bring him and Christopher together when he does return?' she persisted.

'I can promise only to try.' He now addressed himself to Christopher. 'If, for some unfathomable reason, Eric is reluctant to meet up with you, then of course I don't have the means to force him to do so. My influence with Eric is not what it once was.'

This ranked as a confession of an intimacy that he had not hitherto admitted to. It also hinted at an underlying sadness in his friendship with the South African. All this, however, Christopher knew better than to notice. 'Oh, I wouldn't expect you to make any effort to persuade him against his will,' he said. 'But I would ask you to convey to him the benevolence of my intentions.'

'Oh, my dear sir, who can doubt the benevolence of your intentions?'

'Eric might.'

'Well, he might have his own views on the *merits* of your proposal, but your *intentions* must surely be above suspicion to anybody who has met you.'

'Even if only for half an hour?'

'Ah, some things reveal themselves in five minutes. Your good faith shines forth in your countenance.'

If there was something precipitate in Zeevee's judgement, and extravagant in its expression, he yet did not give the impression of superficiality. It was an effect, perhaps, of his youthful gravitas perched so oddly atop his high spirits, that he inspired more confidence than was strictly warranted by any solid and producible achievement. It – this combination of high spirits and seriousness – made, though, for such pleasant company that one would not wish too impertinently or, what came to the same thing, too conscientiously, to question the solidity of its foundation.

Christopher felt, however, that Zeevee's ringing declaration did rather close the book on that particular topic: may, indeed, have been intended to have precisely that effect. For a moment, again, there was a silence that lasted a breath too long for absolute ease. Martha seemed to be engrossed in watching, in one of the multitudinous mirrors, something at an adjacent table. Christopher availed himself of the oldest conversational gambit on earth: 'Where is it that you're from?'

The young man groaned. 'I don't normally divulge my origins on such brief acquaintance, but if you promise you won't despise me for it in the morning …'

'I can't imagine that I would,' said Christopher. 'After all, one's origins cannot in all fairness be counted against one.'

'So one would think. But I have known many an interesting new acquaintance to become vague and go in search of a drink when I tell them the awful truth, which, since you insist, is that I was born and raised in Houston, Texas.' He made an exaggerated gesture indicating that he'd spoken out of turn. 'There, I've gone and said it. Now you'll remember that you have to meet someone for dinner.'

'Indeed, no. I have no personal quarrel with Houston, Texas.'

'Then you have never been to Houston. To see it is to peer into the soul of Mammon.' He seized his throat and croaked: 'The horror! The horror! The horror!'

Zeevee's performance was attracting a certain amount of amused attention. Martha, by no means censoriously, but evidently intending to lower the temperature of the conversation, said, 'Ah, but where is Mammon not? This bar is not run as a soup kitchen; these streets –,' and she pointed at the Rue Vielle du Temple, now crowded with promenading pedestrians, 'are not dedicated to the disinterested pursuit of learning or beauty: they are commercial streets, every bit as avid in their pursuit of profit as … what would the Houston equivalent be?'

Zeevee shuddered exaggeratedly. 'Houston *has* no equivalent, but if you want to know where people go to spend their money and feed their faces, it would have to be The Galleria, a monstrous conglomeration of designer stores and fast-food joints with a few over-priced *boo*-tiques thrown in.'

'So what's the difference between that and this, other than the fact that here it's been done for longer?'

Zeevee regarded her intently for a moment, as if gauging her seriousness. Then he said, 'Do you see that ice-cream shop over there?', pointing at a shop diagonally across from them, open to the street, where a steady line of people had been arriving. 'Go and buy a *glace* there after supper, and you'll see. One of those charming young women in mob caps will ask you nicely which flavours you would prefer, then with a clean wooden spatula she will construct, nay *sculpt*, you an ice cream like a rosebud, each little lick of the spatula adding a petal to the whole. Then she will hand it to you with a smile and a *merci monsieur au revoir*, which will sound as if she meant it. Now picture the same thing in Houston: either you will get a pre-packaged monstrosity wrapped in yards of cardboard and tinfoil containing a glutinous mass of synthetic chocolate and artificial flavour, or you will have a dense ball of over-sweet gunge rammed into a cone like, well, like a cannon ball into a cannon. Either way, it will be flung at you by an obese person of indeterminate sex who will bid you Have a nice day or Have a good one, as if pronouncing a curse upon you and your progeny.'

'Oh, come,' objected Martha, 'there are very good ice-cream shops in America.'

'There are ice-cream shops, indeed, with folksy brand names calculated to suggest that their concoctions of corn syrup and cholesterol come out of a wooden barrel in the back yard, tended by jolly farmers and supplied by happy cows in their breaks from grazing the verdant meadows. But at point of sale, as they so lovably say, the pretence breaks down and you're served crap as if it were crap, and nobody seems to give a damn.'

'There's at least a kind of honesty in that,' Martha persisted. 'I happen to know that the shop across the way is one of a franchise erupting all over Paris. The mob caps are as fraudulent as anything in your Galleria. And I can't imagine that your little rosebud across the way contains any less corn syrup and cholesterol than the cardboard monstrosities of Houston.'

'Then the rosebud across the way will still have given me the experience of seeing the young woman sculpting it.'

'And the young woman sculpting rosebuds all night: do you think she takes such an exalted view of her calling?'

'I'll bet you my Gloriani jacket against your ... Gap? blouse ...'

'It's Banana Republic, in fact.'

'Yes, well, your Banana Republic blouse ... in any case, I'll bet she gets more job satisfaction than the person flinging the cardboard cone at me in Houston. The point is,' he intoned with mock-solemnity, 'that beauty, even when it is commercially motivated, sanctifies or at least *justifies* the endeavour of producing it, even of marketing it.'

Christopher wondered at Zeevee's passionate defence of beauty, in which he could hardly be accused of having a personal stake. Indeed, there was something touching about it: one could not escape thinking that his over-valuing of beauty was the ardour of the consciously deprived. Martha, however, had a different interpretation. 'There speaks the make-up artist,' she said.

'You're a make-up artist?' said Christopher. It had not occurred to him to wonder exactly what it was that Zeevee did in the fashion industry.

'I am,' the young man replied. 'And yes, Martha, I have a stake in beauty. I get paid to make beautiful people more beautiful.'

'So that not-so-beautiful people can buy the beautiful clothes and believe they are beautiful too,' she said.

'And where is the harm in that, pray?'

'The harm,' she said, with unaccustomed fervour, 'is in the exploitation for commercial ends of the young woman across the street making ice-cream rosebuds, or of the model strutting the catwalk till she is too worn out or too … *drugged* out or too …' She hesitated.

'You might as well say too fucked out, since that is obviously what you mean.'

'Yes, and generally just too *used* up to pander plausibly to other people's fantasies, and then she's ruthlessly shouldered aside by the next set of beautiful bones …'

'As she in her day shouldered aside the previous generation of beautiful bones. It has its law and its justice.'

'The law of the jungle, yes.'

He snorted. 'So? The jungle is full of beautiful creatures. When is the last time you heard the jungle referred to as anything other than exotic, exciting and threatened with extinction? Nature red in tooth and claw terrified the Victorians, because they thought it threatened their precious Civilisation. But you and me, we've seen what their Civilisation led to – to Houston and The Galleria as the acme of human achievement and aspiration. It's no wonder we're nostalgic for the jungle.'

'But what does your jungle produce? Labels, fodder for The Galleria?'

'Ah, The Galleria will swallow the labels indiscriminately, hogging anything of worth along with all the junk food it gorges on. I mean the clothes, not the labels, and while the ignorant are buying the labels, the artists are creating the clothes. And I mean the real artists, not the arrivistes who contrive the overpriced trumpery that washes up on *Sex and the City*.'

'But who's to tell the difference between the artists and the arrivistes?' Martha asked.

'I grant you, not the label-hunters who buy their clothes for the names emblazoned on them. But just because most of the labels have sold out to mediocre self-promoters, that doesn't mean that there are not, still, for those who *know*, some real artists behind some of the labels. So what if consumers buy the labels and don't see the artistry? Their money, or the small fraction of it that the artist receives, enables him to carry on creating beauty.'

Zeevee had been gesticulating, heedless of the reach of his long arms; as he spread his hands in the amplitude of argumentation, he grazed the head of someone who had just taken a seat at the next table. The man looked round sharply, and Zeevee promptly started to apologise: '*Mais excusez-moi …*' and then faltered into silence.

'Hey, it's you, Zeevee,' the man at the next table said. 'Excitable as always in defence of *beauty*.' He seemed amused, as if Zeevee's presence were some kind of anomaly. His emphasis was ambiguous, hinting at Zeevee's lack of that quality, or it may have been a self-conscious allusion to his own lavish endowment of it: he had the cheekbones of a thoroughbred, and the long, liquid, slanted eyes of a gazelle; his dark-brown skin glowed with the lustre of dark ale. The rest of his table, two men and a woman, gazed on, unabashed.

Zeevee flushed. 'Yes, Xolani,' he said. 'Those who possess beauty can't be trusted to cherish it as it deserves.'

Xolani shrugged, an elegant undulation of his long torso, and spread his hands in eloquent deprecation. 'Oh, please!' he said. 'You must have more faith in others.' His companions tittered obligingly.

Zeevee turned back to his own table. 'Where was I?' he asked, with a visible effort to regain his composure.

'The essential incorruptibility of beauty, if I understood you correctly,' said Martha.

'Is that what I said?' Zeevee appealed to Christopher. 'I'm sure that's not what I said.'

'Well, you did seem to imply that mercenary motives cannot degrade true beauty.'

'Ah, true beauty yes, but that is to beg the question, is it not? Because, what *is* true beauty? Beauty that cannot be corrupted; so it's really only a circular statement.'

Zeevee was holding forth again, but there was something distracted about his manner, as if he were only half attending to his own words. Martha also seemed to notice this, for she said, 'Are we going to stay here, or shall we go in search of dinner elsewhere?'

'I won't be joining you, if you'll excuse me,' Zeevee said. 'But,' he said to Christopher, 'I'll definitely be in touch quite soon. Do you have a cellphone?'

'No, I'm afraid not. That is, I do have one, but I neglected to activate the roaming facility.'

'I'll leave a message at your hotel, then, to arrange a meeting, whether I have the information you require or not.' A slight lowering of his voice and a flicker of hooded eyes in the direction of the adjacent table suggested that he did not want to broadcast this last commitment too widely. This, no doubt, was but part of his celebrated discretion.

'So, what did you make of Xolani?' Martha asked him later, at a table for two in Le Piano sur le Trottoir.

'Xolani? What do you mean, what did I *make* of Xolani?'

'What impression did he make upon you, is what it normally means.'

'Well, he's very impressive to look at.'

'That I know.'

'And since looking at him was all that I did, that is what I made of him.'

'You also listened to him.'

'The four words he spoke to Zeevee?'

'What counts are not the words, but their tone. How would you describe the tone in which he spoke to Zeevee?'

'I don't know. Mocking, perhaps?'

'Yes, or even goading. Something with an edge.'

'A goad has a point, not an edge.'

'You're avoiding the topic.'

'Why are you so interested in Xolani?'

'I'm not so much interested in him as in your impression of him. I want to know if you also thought Zeevee was rather … put out by him.'

'Yes, I did. And I suspect that that may be why he decided to leave so abruptly.'

'Then there you are. Thank you.'

'But what's it to you?'

She considered, as if to assess what indeed it was to her. 'I care about Zeevee,' she finally said. 'I don't want him to be unhappy.'

'Do you think he's in love with Xolani?' Christopher surprised himself by asking.

But she took the question in her long stride. 'No. No, it's not that kind of unhappiness. I think it's something else.'

'What then?'

'I wish I knew. It may only be something work-related.'

'They work together?'

'Yes, didn't I mention? Xolani is a model.'

'I should have guessed.'

'You should have. In Paris, anyone who looks like that sooner or later ends up on a ramp or a magazine cover, not to mention any number of unmentionable places. He is, as they say, very *happening* at the moment.'

'With a name like Xolani he's presumably South African?'

'Oh, yes, though he's been in Paris for several years. He's a bit of a trust fund kid, politically speaking.'

'Meaning?'

'Well, that he's living on his father's credit. His father was an

60

ANC stalwart in the days of the Struggle, spent time with Mandela on Robben Island, emerged a hero, grew very rich. Xolani went to Michaelhouse, studied law at UCT, but has never really worked for his money, except insofar as modelling counts as work. I've seen him at functions at the South African embassy here –'

'You attend functions at the South African embassy?'

'Not as a way of life or a favourite pastime; but I've been to two, if you want me to be precise. I represent some South African authors over here, and now and again the embassy deigns to recognise the existence and presence of one of its authors. In any case, on both occasions, I think, Xolani was present. He's much in demand as a poster boy for the New South Africa, though as far as anyone can tell, he's in no hurry to return home.' She was silent for a moment, thinking. Then, '*And* …' she said suddenly, 'I've just remembered. *That*'s where I last saw Eric de Villiers.'

'At the South African embassy?'

'Yes. And accompanied by, or more likely accompanying, Xolani.'

'How small you make Paris seem.'

'Well, the ex-pat colony is tiny,' said Martha.

'So, do you think the tension between Zeevee and Xolani may be related to Eric?'

'It's possible.'

'In your book, anything is possible.'

'Congratulations. You have mastered the first law of social living in Paris.'

CHAPTER 4

Christopher spent Monday prosaically enough, editing his mammoth manuscript. He wondered whether Zeevee would remember his undertaking: the conversation had been so full of other matters. But the young man proved as good as his word. There was a slip of paper in his mailbox after breakfast on Tuesday, informing him that 'M. Beegler' had called, and requesting him to call back at the number provided.

It was, quite obviously, a work number: there was a terrific din, as of a hundred people shouting at the tops of their voices while performing strenuous physical exercises to the beat of large hammers on anvils. Zeevee's bright American voice, however, penetrated the clamour without any apparent strain.

'Christopher! So pleased you got back to me! Look, conversation is technically impossible in this menagerie. Can you meet me for lunch tomorrow? I think I have news for you.'

'Lunch would be fine. Same place?'

'No, let's not. L'Étoile is for evenings – and, to be selfish about it, at the other end of Paris from my place of work. Do you know the Rodin museum?'

'Well, I did visit it years ago.'

'It's got a terrific garden – did it have a terrific garden then?'

'I can't remember.'

'Never mind. It does now. The restaurant is cafeteria-style, but not too dreadful.'

'That sounds good. What time would suit you?'

'One?'

'One is fine.'

'Good. Will you find your way there?'

'I think I'll manage. If I don't, I'll ask a native.'

'Good man, if you're sure of that. Sorry about the din this end. The donkeys are being fed to the lions.'

Christopher smiled as he put down the phone. For all his youth, Zeevee seemed to have appointed himself as guide, guardian, protector. He reminded Christopher of one of those huge dogs bred to herd sheep and which manage to retain, even in the unbucolic contexts to which human whim has relegated them, an instinct to round up random creatures – children, other domestic animals, even teddy bears. Zeevee, as a son of pioneers, must, for all his professions of disenfranchisement, have inherited the instinct to guide weaker members of the clan through the perils of unfamiliar territory; and he, Christopher, must have presented himself to Zeevee's racial memory as the type of enfeebled elder that a young plainsman would have been honour-bound to protect.

He did not mind the hint of condescension in such solicitude, even though he did not feel himself quite as much bewildered by the terra incognita of Paris as Zeevee seemed to assume. Still, he might yet have occasion to be grateful for the Texan's rangy frame to lean on, or even cling to.

The Rodin Museum turned out to have, indeed, a terrific garden – in the formal French style, of course, inviting aesthetic contemplation from an upstairs window rather than languorous lounging. Some concession to modern tastes and opportunities had, however, been made, by the placing of benches, comfortable by the standards of Parisian public seating, in shaded areas, and even, in a distant corner, a few reclining chairs. For the rest, it was Nature tamed and boxed and ordered and gravelled, contrasting starkly, in its rectangularity, with the writhing forms of the Rodin sculptures inhabiting the garden. Christopher, early once again, spent the time examining these monumental productions, which he was not sure he liked. Such an excess of attitude, he thought, so much expressive gesture, and such vacuity of reflection. These giant figures seemed capable of everything except thought – even, and perhaps especially, *The Thinker* on his uncomfortable perch, with his self-consciously furrowed brow. He represented, not thought, but somebody's parody of it, trying to convey through tensed muscles and involuted limbs what a subtler artist might have conveyed through the angle of an eyebrow or the curl of a lip. It was not that the sculptures were *bad*; it was that they were public acts rather than private perceptions, every nuance magnified and displayed. Where Greek statues had something naive about them, for all their physical perfection, something unaware in their simple contrapposto, here everything was striving, struggling, striding, writhing, wrestling. It exhausted one just to look at them.

'You're looking very pensively at *Le Penseur*,' Zeevee's pleasant baritone said beside him.

'Oh, on the contrary,' replied Christopher. 'I was thinking how fraudulent his pose is.'

'Then you were pensive, you were just not *pense*-ing very reverently.'

'But seriously – does one need such muscles in order to think? And such big feet?'

'Well, perhaps the better to actualise one's thoughts one does need big feet – and of course, big hands, which our guy certainly has.' With the happy air of pursuing a novel thought, Zeevee continued: 'Thought in the abstract, don't you think, is effete; constructive thought is muscular?'

Christopher was never sure, with Americans, whether the interrogative rise at the end of a sentence signalled a true question or just an unassertive way of stating a proposition. He tried in such cases to reply so as to meet both intentions. 'He does look like a construction worker,' he now said, 'if that's what you mean.'

Zeevee looked at him as if he weren't sure whether he was joking. 'It's not what I meant, but it's a thought,' he accommodatingly replied. 'That may be why he served as a symbol to the socialist cause when he was still thinking in front of the Pantheon.'

'Well, perhaps he is more than a pretty face, after all.'

'Never underestimate the power of a pretty face.'

'Or big feet.'

'I'll drink to that,' Zeevee said, glancing down at his buffed number elevens. 'And speaking of drinking …?'

'You mean, shall we eat?'

'That is, of course, what I do mean. Let's go, before the cafeteria line gets unappetisingly long.'

The two companions soon provided themselves with a slice of quiche and a tiny bottle of wine each, and settled at a little table under the spring-abundant shade of one of the aged trees.

'How have you been spending your time in Paris?' asked Zeevee.

'Oh, looking around.'

'That's never a hardship in Paris. To good effect?'

'Not really.' Christopher was aware of being stupidly unforthcoming in his replies; but he resisted being coerced, however subtly, into giving the conventional tribute to Paris.

If Zeevee noticed his recalcitrance, he was unfazed by it. 'You haven't been looking in the right places, then,' he commented with imperturbable good humour.

'Or in the right way.'

'Sure. We'll have to take you in hand.'

'You mean, make me see?'

'Well, help you to see.'

'Thank you! You don't think that the universal admiration of Paris is partly a conditioned reflex?'

'Not unless all aesthetic appreciation is a conditioned reflex. Sure, we like what we know and what we know to be beautiful. But I cannot imagine anybody from any culture finding, say, Houston more beautiful than Paris.'

'You cannot imagine – exactly. Because you're from a culture that privileges Paris and affects to disdain Houston.'

Zeevee laughed. 'I like your *affects to*!' He became more serious. 'Then how do you explain our friend Eric's evident preference for Paris?'

'Over his own native soil? I don't know – perhaps the contagion of example? I mean, so many expatriates, all implying by their very presence here that this is the most desirable place on earth to be right now …'

'Well, it sure beats being in a place everybody wants to get the hell out of as soon as possible.'

'You mean like South Africa?'

'No, I don't,' Zeevee said, looking surprised. 'Why? Does everybody want to get the hell out of South Africa?'

'Not everybody, no, not by a long shot. But a significant number of young white people do.'

'Ah, young white people! Fortune's favourites for so long, and now having to defer to the young, gifted and black,' Zeevee smiled.

'They might argue that to be young and black is not necessarily to be gifted.'

'*Évidemment*. But nor is to be young and white. And if South Africa is anything like America, they've had a very easy ride for a very long time, the young, not-necessarily-gifted and white. I know, I was one of them.'

'As was Eric,' said Christopher, hoping to bring the conversation back to its declared purpose.

'Eric. Yes, Eric.' He chewed his quiche longer than was plausible for a quiche to be chewed, then said, 'Yes. I have had news of Eric.'

'And was the news good or bad?'

'I don't know. That is, I'm not sure whether you would regard it as good or bad.'

'Perhaps if you told me, I could decide for myself.'

'Indeed and of course. Here is the news, then. It would seem that Eric is about to return to Paris.'

'That is surely, from my point of view, unambiguously good news.'

'So I have assumed. But don't you want to know *why* he is returning to Paris?'

'I assumed because this is where he's been living for the past three years, where, in a sense, his home is. Or are you suggesting that there is another reason for his return? An enticement?'

'So I believe. Or so I am told. I am not altogether sure that I do believe it, but nor am I sure that I don't believe it.'

'Why don't you stop scrupling, and tell me what it is that you know?'

'Right. Then what I've heard is that Eric is coming back to be married.'

Zeevee said this in a deliberately toneless way, like a newsreader reporting the latest global warming statistics. Christopher took a bite of his quiche to give him time to moderate his own tone before saying, 'You surprise me. Do we know to whom?'

'We do, or we can surmise. One Beatrice du Plessis.'

'That's a very South African name.'

'It's also a very French name. But she is in fact South African. Does the name mean anything to you?'

'I have heard it mentioned somewhere, in a context that couldn't have interested me very much, like netball or golf or business-woman of the year.'

'None of those. Try modelling.'

'Yes, that would rank somewhere below netball in my hierarchy of interests.'

'Then it will have escaped your notice that Beatrice du Plessis was Model of the Year some time ago, and went on to become a supermodel. Lucian Freud did a portrait of her with one of his horrible whippets, and Norman Mailer called her the secular Madonna, and Jacques Derrida wrote an essay on her called "Ironic/Iconic".'

'Mailer, Derrida … then she is not in the first flowering of her youth?'

'No, indeed. She's no longer modelling, though she is still very much a presence in the world of fashion. In fact, she has a seventeen-year-old daughter, one Jeanne du Plessis, who seems set to take her mother's place on the magazine covers of the world. She is also very beautiful, though in a less classical style than her mother. Her type is the ingénue.'

'And where is Mr du Plessis?'

'There is no Mr du Plessis. Jeanne has taken her mother's name. Her father … to be honest, I'm not sure who her father is. She was born when Beatrice was very young, barely twenty, I should think.'

'Which would make Beatrice about thirty-seven.'

'Yes.'

'And Eric is twenty-five.'

'Yes. But an older woman may in many respects be what Eric needs. She has been very good for him. And good *to* him.'

'Yes, but is he in love with her?'

Zeevee hesitated for a moment, and Christopher suspected he'd pushed him beyond the limits of even his good humour; but the resilient American said, equably enough, 'Who can vouch for anybody else's being in love? But I can tell you that before he left, he gave me every reason to believe that he was indeed attached to Beatrice du Plessis.'

There was more in this statement than Christopher felt he could follow up without over-taxing Zeevee's discretion; so he contented himself with asking, 'And you know Beatrice du Plessis well?'

'I think I know her well, but I don't know all there is to know. She is not easy to fathom.'

'I cannot imagine an unfathomable supermodel. They all seem two-dimensional to me – well, insofar as I have been aware of supermodels.'

'That is because they are dressed and made up to be photographed, which is, of course, for the time being at least, a two-dimensional medium. Beatrice certainly has depths that don't show up on even the glossiest page.'

'Do you think Eric knows …?'

'All there is to know?' Zeevee twirled his fork exaggeratedly. 'Well, you see, I don't know all there is to know about Eric either. As an informant, I'm awfully limited!'

'I wouldn't have thought there was so much to know about Eric.'

'Oh, you mustn't underestimate Eric,' Zeevee said, his pedantic manner making him seem suddenly older than his years. 'You think because you saw him grow up you know him; but that was probably not true even while he was at home, and then, of course, he's grown in the last three years.'

'So we have gathered,' Christopher said, his tone prompting a sudden guffaw from his companion. Christopher waited and then asked, 'Have you known him the whole time?'

'Pretty much. I met him not long after he arrived, and we struck up a friendship. I liked him and offered him accommodation – my apartment is larger than I need – and he accepted. I must have seemed relatively unforeign to him then; his French was rudimentary – it's perfect now, by the way, much better than mine – and he was kind of adrift in Paris. I introduced him to people who took an interest in him. When last did you see him?'

'More than three years ago. Before you met him.'

'Then, my dear sir, I'd advise you to reserve judgement until you have seen him.'

'But can't you see that *seeing* him is exactly what I hoped you'd help me to do?'

'Well, I guess in the end we all have to see for ourselves. But I may be able to place you in a relation that makes seeing possible.'

'If, by that, you mean that you can place me face to face with him, that's all I need.'

'You must not overestimate my powers. I cannot produce Eric at will. But I do at least know that he'll be back in Paris by tomorrow, and I can get a message to him to come to lunch on Sunday, if that would suit you.'

'Oh, that would suit me. But would it suit Eric?'

'If it doesn't, he'll be sure to say so. We're fortunately on a basis of complete honesty with each other.'

'That's very pleasant.'

'Well, not necessarily. But it at least saves time.'

Christopher had noticed from the beginning that there was something dry in Zeevee's tone whenever referring to his friend. He assumed that this was the unassimilated residue of a relation that had run its course, whatever its nature. However, Christopher reminded himself, this was not part of his concern, given that Zeevee's influence on Eric, whatever it may once have been, now seemed something of the past. He found himself, with a twinge of conscience, not regretting this; he would not have relished explaining Zeevee to Daniel, however much he himself liked the young man. Whether explaining Beatrice du Plessis would be any easier remained to be seen.

'But why,' he asked, pursuing aloud this train of thought, with an effect, no doubt of inconsequentiality, 'why should Eric wish to marry a woman twelve years his senior?'

Zeevee drained his glass and placed it on the table with perhaps more force than was required. 'That, my dear sir, is more than I claim to understand. Perhaps *you* will understand – when you've met him. And when you do understand – perhaps you'll tell me.'

'I sense,' Christopher risked, 'something unresolved in your attitude to Eric.'

Zeevee laughed his huge honking laugh. 'Your tact is beyond everything! Others have described my attitude to Eric in terms far less forgiving.'

'Why should it be the business of other people to describe your attitude to Eric?'

'Why indeed? – only, if you'll forgive my pointing it out, you have just done so yourself, albeit with the greatest delicacy.'

Christopher could feel himself flushing. 'I suppose so. My excuse is that I have what you might call a professional interest in Eric.'

'Oh, you don't need an excuse for your interest.' He hesitated, then plunged on. 'But given your professional interest, I guess you must be wondering about the nature of my relationship with Eric. No,' he demurred, raising a hand to quell the response that Christopher was about to make, 'no, don't say anything. I know what it must look like, our situation, and whereas *je m'en fous* in general, what things look like, I can see that as his father's representative you have a legitimate interest. So I would like to state categorically that my relation with Eric de Villiers is entirely platonic.' He smiled his off-centre smile. 'From his side, at least. I may have wanted it otherwise, but his virtue was unshakeable.'

'I suspect Eric's virtue in this instance was synonymous with Eric's convenience.'

Zeevee smiled again, more wryly. 'Who's to say where virtue ends and convenience begins?'

CHAPTER 5

The meeting with Zeevee left Christopher even more at sea than before. That Eric should be, apparently, an object of attraction for at least two people, one of whom Christopher found extremely likeable and the other of whom was apparently a woman of some consequence, was strange, given the loutish young man of Christopher's acquaintance. So either Eric had outgrown his loutishness, or loutishness was more to the taste of Paris than of poor old parochial Franschhoek. Either way, Christopher wondered what he might find to say to the son of his old friend, when at last he had the opportunity to do so. He had, in the old days, not found very much, though marginally more than the boy had found unaided: he had had a young person's indifference to older people, exacerbated, Christopher thought, by a naturally morose temperament. He made no effort to please or to be pleased: a form of integrity, perhaps, but not one that made for social ease. The opportunity would no doubt bring the inspiration; Christopher would take his cue from Eric's manner and adapt to that. But then, adapting to Eric's manner was not what he was in Paris to do, if Eric's manner was indeed by now adjusted to the Parisian measure. Christopher would be expected, at some point, exactly to counter that manner with a manner of his own – which, however, was what Paris more than ever made him feel he lacked. Manner was something that Paris so manifestly and infuriatingly dictated the terms of.

Thus Christopher reasoned and vacillated. He availed himself, the following evening, of an opportunity to lay his perplexity once again on Martha's little round table, in her pleasantly cluttered apartment, over a glass of Chablis, prior to their going off in search of what she claimed was the perfect couscous.

'What on earth do I *say* to the fellow?' he asked her, only half-simulating his despair.

'Tell him that he's breaking his father's heart and he should re-turn home immediately,' she said, matching the extravagance of her tone to his.

'Oh, his father's heart!' Christopher groaned.

'Do you mean Daniel has no heart, or the boy has no regard for it?'

'I don't think I can pronounce on Daniel's heart. But it's not an organ I'd want to base an appeal on.'

'Then you may have to use the Financial Inducement,' she said.

'Which is to say the threat that he'll be cut off with nothing if he doesn't return soon.'

'Is it as absolute as that?'

'I think it is. Daniel is very absolute.'

She got up from her chair, apparently in search of her handbag. 'Oh, Daniel!' she said, and her tone suggested that she was not in-voking their common acquaintance indulgently.

'Oh, Daniel indeed,' Christopher said, draining his glass.

'Why –?' she started, then broke off.

'Why what?'

'Well, why should you have to do Daniel's dirty work for him? It's like being an ambassador to a totalitarian regime.'

'That answers your question, then. As an ambassador is sworn to loyalty, so I am committed to … well, my mission.'

'That is abundantly clear, my dear Christopher. I'm presuming to question the basis of your commitment. An ambassador gets paid; what do you get for your pains, other than a few weeks in a seedy hotel?'

'Oh, the hotel's not seedy!' he smiled.

But she was not to be bought off as cheaply as that. 'Call it, then, quite a decent little hotel at the price; my question remains, why can't Daniel come and issue his own threats to his own son?'

'Don't you see, exactly because he doesn't want it to be a matter of threats? He's hoping that Eric will see me as a neutral negotiator rather than as a partisan.'

She snorted. 'Neutral negotiator be damned, when you're practically living at Beau Regard, and, for all that Eric knows, may owe your continued welcome there to your success in retrieving him from the fleshpots of Paris.'

Christopher was conscious of a certain bleakness in his tone in replying, 'And, to do Eric justice, that may not be too far from the truth, either.'

She had found her handbag. She paused in front of the mirror to arrange some fancied superfluity to her abundant hair. 'Do you mean to tell me *you* have also had your ultimatum?'

'No, nothing as confrontational as that. But I have had my instructions, and they naturally carry with them an implied penalty for non-performance.'

She turned away from her image in the mirror to direct her indignation at him unmediated. '*Naturally*? Are you listening to what you're saying? By what right does Daniel *instruct* you? I don't even enquire as to the penalties.'

'Well, he instructs me as he would instruct a lawyer. I think he sees it as in the nature of a business arrangement.'

'Then I hope he's paying you what he would pay the lawyer he instructs.'

'I wouldn't want to be paid.'

'Not in money, no, if you're too damn fastidious. But does he repay you in any other way?'

'I can spend as much time as I like at Beau Regard. My room is always ready for me.'

'In the attic?'

'It's been very comfortably refurbished,' he said, realising he must strike her as feeble. 'But you're not helping at all, you know,' he said, in a consciously unfair attempt to shift the burden of the conversation.

At this, she had one of those sudden changes of mood that he remembered from the past. 'Yes, I know,' she said, 'I'm a terrible friend. Take no notice of my old-maidenly strictures. I think, if you really want to know, that you're more than capable of coming up with the perfect, the complete way, of dealing with Eric de Villiers.'

'But if I don't even know what quantity I'm dealing with …?'

'My dear Christopher, I imagine that you will see, soon enough, for yourself.'

'But will I?' he persisted. 'Is it not of the nature of the situation *not* to be seen?'

To his surprise, she laughed as if he'd said something amusing. 'How many theories you have on the nature of the situation! Well, I trust in your acuteness to see *through* the situation.'

For that, then, he had to take it: her professed confidence put as effective an end to the conversation as the most acerbic snub could have done. It was possible that that had been her intention; perhaps, at last, she had grown impatient with his vacillations and velleities.

'Ah, my poor acuteness!' he exclaimed, as he got up to join her.

In spite of this disclaimer, he prepared his acuteness, such as it was, to be put to the test at the 'little luncheon' that Zeevee informed him, in a note left at his hotel on Friday evening, had been planned for the Sunday. He asked himself, indeed, how he *could* prepare such a faculty, given how little practice he had had in acuteness, moving as he generally did in circles – if such could be called his circumscribed group of intimates – only too little given to concealment, too much addicted to proclaiming their own values and priorities. There was nothing covert, for instance, in Daniel's way of meeting the world; he met it so entirely on his own terms. As for Christopher, he could at least resolve not to be taken by surprise, to be prepared, as Martha had urged him upon his arrival, for anything.

It is, however, in the nature of surprises to be unexpected. On the Saturday morning he went down to breakfast later than usual in the hope of finding the foyer of the hotel, which doubled as a breakfast room, less crowded than it generally was early in the morning.

Thinking to supplement the hotel breakfast with a croissant au beurre, Christopher stepped outside into the Rue de Buci, to the lavish boulangerie-pâtisserie on that street – as much for the early-morning bustle, with its smell of coffee and baking, as for the actual pastry.

Returning with his little paper bag, neatly twisted closed into two little rabbit's ears by the young woman in the shop, he was about to take his seat at the communal board, where there was, as he had hoped, a vacancy, when the hotel owner approached him. 'Oh, Monsieur Turner, if you please!'

This was unusual in itself, Monsieur Marcel being as a rule at this hour much occupied with departing guests; but even more uncommon was the cordiality with which he addressed Christopher.

'Ah, Monsieur Turner!' he said. 'You have an early guest this morning. This gentleman was hoping to see you, and I took the liberty of asking him to wait and offering him a cup of coffee.'

This was a liberty indeed, Christopher thought, to assume that he would want to see some stranger before breakfast, or, worse, over breakfast. But he did not have time to indulge this reflection, for Monsieur Marcel was gesturing towards a man sitting at the table, whom Christopher had assumed to be a hotel guest. The person designated had in the meantime got up and was smiling at Christopher as if expecting to be recognised.

Christopher could not have said afterwards which impression was uppermost in his mind as he faced the newcomer: one thought was that it was not surprising that Monsieur Marcel had been so cordial, since the visitor displayed more elegance than the Hotel du Carrefour was in the habit of accommodating; another was that the man's smile was beguiling. It was only as a belated impression that he realised that the smile belonged to Eric de Villiers.

In his confusion, Christopher resorted to the expedient of thanking Monsieur Marcel, thanking him perhaps more warmly and emphatically than the occasion demanded. It gave him time to prepare, as it were, a face with which to meet his young countryman.

But he might have saved himself the trouble. His guest was more than equal to the occasion. He extended his hand, expressing, with every sign of sincerity, much pleasure in seeing Christopher after – how long? – three years? – here in Paris, in this *unusual* hotel, really quite fascinating, the old choir stalls … and looking so good, too, Paris must be agreeing with him. In short, he chattered rather, but so easily that it quite carried off the slight awkwardness that might otherwise have strained the meeting. He gestured towards the table, as if inviting Christopher to partake of his breakfast with him.

'Please,' said Christopher, not intending this as a corrective to Eric's manner, though promptly realising that it might be taken as that, 'do sit down again. I'm about to have breakfast. Have you had yours yet?'

Eric made a comical face. 'No – but then I never do have breakfast.' He broke into a conspiratorial grin. 'But don't tell my father – he always made us have a full breakfast.'

Was this jocular injunction intended to signal the son's awareness of Christopher's role as an ambassador of his father, a spy, a tattle-tale? If so, there were surely graver matters to report than his foregoing the first meal of the day.

There were four other people at the table, engaging in that desultory tourist-talk that characterises communal breakfast tables in 'affordable' hotels, and inhibiting conversation about anything significant. This suited Christopher well enough, in that he could form his impressions without having to form his sentences. While negotiating the croissant with such delicacy as the nature of the pastry allowed, indeed, perhaps overdoing the meticulousness of the operation, he surreptitiously took in the details of Eric's appearance. It was at first difficult to characterise precisely the immense difference three years had made to the young man, other than to say that it was an improvement beyond what might have been hoped for or even dreamt of. Eric de Villiers at twenty-two had been good-looking in the sense that a bullock or a four-wheel-drive vehicle is good-looking: strong, stolid, well-made, not attuned to the finer rhythms of life. His limbs had had substance without shape, his face force without form. His blue eyes, which he had inherited from his mother, the colour of the sky on a winter afternoon in a dry climate, had reminded Christopher of marbles or boiled sweets; they had glistened without lustre and had looked without seeming to see.

Maturity had effected a singular change in the amorphousness of the young de Villiers. Where before his appearance had favoured his mother, his patrimony now asserted itself: he had been his mother's boy; now he was his father's son. He had gained – startlingly – definition. Where before he had been blurred at the edges, he now had outline; the chin was shaped, the cheekbones defined. His weight had been redistributed to the advantage of his whole body. Even his colouring had changed: the hair and eyelashes, which had been bleached to straw by the sun and sea of his beach-addicted youth, had darkened, adjusting the tones of the rest of his face. His eyes, in particular, with the darker lashes, now had more depth and expression, a more troubled shimmer of blues than the uniform baby-blue of old. Even his nose seemed to have more point to it, no longer the little olfactory snout of youth, but a harmonious feature of the mobile face.

But above all, his manner had changed. The adolescent indifference to others had yielded to an apparent consideration, a willingness to ask questions and wait for a reply. He was as relaxed as if he were the incumbent and Christopher the unannounced guest, and he took charge of the conversation as if it were a matter of some importance to him to make the other man feel at ease.

'So, how long is it you've been here?' he asked, with every appearance of interest. Even his voice had changed: the bray of adolescence had deepened into a light baritone.

'Oh, only about a week,' Christopher replied through his croissant. 'In fact, a week exactly.'

'You should really have let me know you were coming. I could have gone to London at any other time, you know.'

Christopher could not explain that it had been Daniel's plan for Eric to be taken more or less by surprise, that he had seemed to think it likely that his son might flee if he suspected that he was to receive an emissary from home. He said instead, 'You must know that your people at home have rather lost track of you.'

Eric laughed ruefully. 'I suppose so,' he said. 'Is Dad very pissed off with me?'

'He's not pleased, naturally.'

'The thing is, I've been moving around so much these past months, I've really not had an address to call my own or a chair to rest my butt on.'

'You hardly look like a vagrant,' Christopher permitted himself to remark, looking at the young man's cashmere sweater. 'You are looking very well.'

'Oh, I've muddled through,' Eric said, with a smile that made further enquiry seem somehow irrelevant. Besides, the rest of the table had by now given up on the relative virtues of the Louvre and the Orsay, and were unabashedly listening to the conversation of the two men. Eric de Villiers clearly excited interest wherever he went, if two Americans, one Swede and an Argentinean could be taken as a representative sample.

'I think I've done such justice to this croissant as can be expected of me,' said Christopher, carefully sweeping up crumbs from the table and depositing them in his plate. 'Do you feel like taking a stroll? It seems to be a decent day out there.'

'Oh, it's a brilliant day,' said Eric, rising from his chair with alacrity. 'Let's take a stroll, by all means.'

Under the benign gaze of Monsieur Marcel, whom Eric thanked in what sounded to Christopher like perfect French, they left the little entrance hall of the hotel, Eric passing through the awkward swing door first and holding it open for Christopher. His manners had decidedly improved.

'Did you have any particular direction in mind?' Eric asked.

'No, not really. Do you have a preference?'

'If it's all the same to you, yes, I'd like to walk towards the river. I like getting out of the noise.'

That, too, was new: Eric had usually had some form of noise-producing machine on or under or about him.

'It's down here,' Eric said as the two men turned into the Rue de Seine, 'as I suppose you know.'

'I do know that much, yes,' replied Christopher, amused at Eric's evident wish not to seem to patronise him.

The narrow pavement was at this hour so crowded with pedestrians that it was difficult for them to remain abreast, and conversation ceased until they had made their way around the domed bulk of the Institut de France and braved the traffic to cross to the river.

'Let's walk across the Pont des Arts,' said Eric, 'and then we can come back by the Pont Neuf. I like the bridges.'

'Even this one?' Christopher asked, gesturing towards the severely utilitarian lines of the bridge. It was, in fact, almost a relief to find something in Paris that was not calculated to beguile the eye.

'Oh, especially this one. It's not a particularly beautiful bridge, as bridges go in Paris, but it doesn't have any traffic, and it has a shit-hot view of the Île de la Cité.'

Christopher smiled, partly at the earnestness of the judgement and partly at the odd idiom: Rondebosch Boys' High had not altogether been supplanted by Paris. Eric, noticing the smile, said, 'I suppose you think it's crazy, me carrying on about bridges and views and things.'

'Well, it's true that it's a part of your personality that's new to me.'

Eric stopped; they were halfway up the steps leading to the bridge. In the mild light of May his hair shone, not with the bleached glamour of the surf, but with the deeper tones of old gold. His eyes, too, took the light and refracted it into splinters of turquoise. 'You might as well say I was an insensitive lout.'

Christopher could feel himself blushing at Eric's perspicacity; but as he opened his mouth to offer some feeble rebuttal, Eric raised a hand. 'And don't feel obliged to deny it. I wouldn't want you to violate your conscience for me.'

'If you insist, then,' Christopher conceded, as they resumed their walk, 'you were perhaps just the slightest bit of a lout.'

'There you are then,' Eric retorted. 'But check out that view.' With a start, Christopher realised how much the son sounded like the father – as, from a certain angle, he looked like him.

And indeed, the historic little island, floating on the shimmering river, the filigreed spire of the Sainte-Chapelle pricking up like an off-centre mast, had never seemed fairer than in the light of this spring morning. Around them, artists were setting out their wares, musicians were making their music, lovers were parading their passion, picnickers were unpacking their baskets, all in the usual promiscuous blend of commercial purpose and sensual gratification. Christopher could feel its appeal all the more strongly for his resistance to it. Ah, to be young and to be in Paris, he thought, glancing at the heedless youth next to him, is there anything more beautiful? And yet, what a trap and a delusion, too, the implication that to be surrounded by such beauty is to be happy, or that such happiness as it may offer is lasting. He had been young once, too, in Paris: he remembered standing here at dawn one morning in July, fleeing the dregs of a sleepless night in the single room handed down to him by Marie-Louise, watching the sky lighten over the island, the deep red dawn gradually blanching into the blue day, while he stood stupidly staring, dry-eyed and wondering where he would wash up if he jumped, and how Daniel would cope with the bureaucratic tangle of shipping his drowned remains home – if indeed, Daniel would bother. Well, if nothing else, it would spoil Marie-Louise's holiday, he had thought.

'You seem amused at something.' Eric said next to him.

'Do I?' Christopher replied, oddly pleased that his melancholy reflections should at some level, apparently, intrigue the young man. 'I'm not really. I was thinking of the last time I stood here, thirty years ago.'

'Must have been something pleasant, for you to be smiling like that.'

'No, it wasn't pleasant at the time. Or I certainly didn't think it was.'

'Well, I hope I can stand here in thirty years' time with that expression on my face.'

'And I hope you'll have more to show for your thirty years than I have,' Christopher said, lapsing, he realised, into self-pity under the spell of Eric's sympathy. To spare his companion the task of replying to his self-indulgence, he said, 'Still, I'm grateful to be here at all, thirty years later.'

'And this time, I hope, enjoying it more than last time.'

Again there was something so adult, almost solicitous, in Eric's tone, as if he were the grizzled veteran and Christopher the un-tried youth, that Christopher laughed – and, doing so, realised that yes, he was enjoying being just there, just like that, in the sunshine over the glittering water, with the great city that had once seemed so oppressively to crowd in upon him now decorously keeping its appointed place by the river's edge, and yet brimming with prom-ise – vague as that promise inevitably was in his case, perhaps in-distinguishable from a regret.

'Yes,' he said, 'I am enjoying it more than last time. Come, let's walk, I want to go down there,' and he pointed at the prow of the island, where already the vagrant multitude from around the world was gathering.

Eric laughed, but made no show to start walking, which Christopher took as a sign that he, too, was enjoying this moment on the bridge. 'Is that another unhappy memory?' he asked.

'Actually, this is a happy one. Your father and I used to have our lunch of bread and cheese and wine down there.'

'Dad? Were you here with him then?'

'Yes. And your mother. But she arrived later.'

'Really? He's never mentioned it, nor has she.'

'Oh, it was a long time ago, and other memories have probably got in the way.'

'They haven't for you.'

'I don't have that many other memories. Besides, I'm remember-ing now because I'm back in Paris.'

'So you've known Dad for a long time?'

'A very long time. We were at school together, and then at UCT.'

Eric nodded his head pensively, as if processing this informa-tion. 'That *is* a long time, yes. Has Dad changed much, would you say, over the years?'

'I wouldn't say so, but then, I may have changed with him. We're neither of us what we were at your age. He has a farm, a family, and all the responsibilities that go with that.'

There was a brief silence. Then, almost abruptly, 'And you?' Eric asked.

'Me?'

'I mean, what do you have?'

'Oh, I have memories.'

'If you don't mind my asking, is that enough?'

'Perhaps not, but how do you suggest I supplement them?'

'It's never too late, is it, to supplement one's store of memories?'

'Excuse me, but sometimes it is.'

'How would you know that?' Eric asked. 'Perhaps even this will be a memory one day.' The wide sweep of his arm took in the bridge with its burden of human leisure and human commerce, the river with its busy little boats, the buildings partly screened by the green of the plane trees, the two river banks with their personalities as distinct as two continents, the great bowl of the spring sky, the whole dazzling day; but Christopher saw mainly the young man at the centre of this bounty, gesturing as if it were all his to embrace or, perhaps, bestow.

'You must be right,' he said. 'Perhaps it will, one day. Shall we go?'

'Of course.' Eric dropped his arm and gave a self-deprecatory grin. 'I'm sorry, you must think I'm very pushy.'

'If you'd been pushy, you wouldn't have apologised. Besides, I give you notice that I'll be doing some pushing too. Shall we walk?'

They crossed the bridge and turned right along the river towards the Pont Neuf. The *bouquinistes* seemed, on a superficial scrutiny, to offer for sale exactly the same postcards, posters and books as three decades before, except of course for the addition of the still-ubiquitous Diana in her multifarious manifestations, coyly glancing up from beneath lowered lashes, like a glossy llama wanting its head scratched. It was only appropriate, Christopher thought, that the most photogenic woman on earth should have come to the most photogenic city on earth to die.

Eric paused by one of the stalls and selected a postcard. 'I haven't seen this one,' he said, showing it to Christopher. It was, indeed, an unfamiliar photo of Jim Morrison, though recognisably one of the Young Lion series. The cupid's-bow pout, the angled Siamese-cat jaw, the truculent stare, the famous lion's mane of hair: the whole epicene ensemble was there, but in place of the usual rebarbative sulk, a look of startled vulnerability discomposed Morrison's face, as if the camera had caught him with his guard down; and his delicate arms were extended in front of him as if warding off an invisible assailant. Yet another beautiful casualty of the beautiful city: to be young and in Paris was not, after all, to be invincible, to be proof against the heart's invisible furies, in the poet's phrase.

'I'd have thought you were too young for The Doors,' Christopher said.

'Well, I am of course, in one sense; Jim Morrison died quite a few years before I was born. But people like him become part of the collective unconscious, I suppose. Or the racial memory, or whatever.' Eric laughed, apparently downplaying his solemnity. 'And anyway, the card isn't for me, it's for a friend. An older friend, as it happens, though hardly of The Doors generation.'

'But a fan?'

'Yes. And she's South African. You'll meet her. All South Africans in Paris eventually meet one another. But I won't leave it to chance. You'll see her tomorrow at Zeevee's.'

This was the first time he had mentioned Zeevee, which was in itself rather odd, as it was presumably to this friend that he owed his knowledge of Christopher's presence in Paris. It was possible that the young American featured less prominently in Eric's life than Eric in his.

They recommenced their walk. 'Have you been to Morrison's grave in Père-Lachaise?' Eric asked.

'Yes, when I was here before. It was something of a centre of pilgrimage then. And vandalism.'

'It still is, though it's almost as well guarded as Napoleon's tomb.'

'I suppose that's one way for his disciples to show their veneration, destroying the shrine. It's their homage to the self-destructive muse.'

Christopher remembered the unseasonably rainy dawn in early July in the storied old cemetery with its crumbling mausoleums housing extinct dynasties, its pompous monuments to forgotten dignitaries, its poignant memorials to the deported. He had not gone on a conscious pilgrimage: he'd just wanted to get out of the hotel so as not to wait around for Daniel and Marie-Louise to emerge. He had wandered, not altogether aimlessly, but without any very urgent purpose, through the Luxembourg Gardens, melancholy in the wet morning, through the streets of Montparnasse, violated by the barbaric Tower, then still a relatively recent structure. Christopher was starting to detest the Parisian picturesque, but inconsistently found himself unable to embrace its brash contrary either, and it was with something like relief that he had entered, after a longer walk than he would have thought possible, the medieval gloom of Père-Lachaise.

It was early, and there was nobody else about. He was not looking for any one grave in particular, and was content to roam the endless alleys of the dead, until he came upon what a profusion of flowers and other less-appealing detritus – broken bottles, used syringes, empty Coke tins and a wilderness of inane graffiti – marked as Jim Morrison's grave. Sitting on an adjacent tombstone was a young woman, apparently in meditation, her thin white dress clinging to her spare form, her long hair plastered to her pale skin. Her face was turned up to the rain, and she was muttering something that Christopher could not hear. She was both absurd and touching in her absorption in her rite of remembrance, homage, whatever.

Christopher's foot scuffed against the stone coping of a grave. She blinked rapidly and focused on him.

'Did Jim send you?' she asked in a light, breathy American voice, tense with excitement.

'No, I'm afraid not,' Christopher said. 'I'm here of my own accord.'

Her face retained its expression of rapt transport. 'No,' she said, 'no, no, no, no. Jim said a beautiful stranger would come in the rain.'

'That's not me, then,' Christopher said, but his pleasantry was lost on her.

'When he left me he said he would send somebody to take his place,' she insisted.

Christopher suspected that she was one of the singer's multitude of conquests, duped by one of his gnomic exit lines. 'I wasn't sent,' he said again.

'Then why are you here?' she demanded.

'Because I want to be here.'

'Yes,' she said, shaking her head in evident irritation, 'but what made you want to be here?'

'I don't know, just a sense that I wanted to visit the cemetery.'

'You don't know? You see!' she exclaimed triumphantly. 'He *sent* you without you knowing it.'

'But sent me to do what?'

'To take his place.'

'Please, how could I possibly take Jim Morrison's place – a famous singer like him?'

'No,' she said impatiently, 'not his place as a singer. His place in my life.'

'And how would I take his place in your life?' Christopher asked, half amused at this instance of the fan's solipsism: I am as important to my idol as my idol is to me.

She got up slowly, her eyes fixed on him. She was very thin, and ethereally pale. Her eyes were dark, her pupils enormous. Her lips were strangely red, and when she smiled, as she now did, her teeth appeared very white and sharp. 'By making love to me,' she said. 'On his grave.'

She came towards him and started undoing the buttons of her shift-like dress. 'He knew he was going to die,' she said. 'He told me to wait by his grave every year on the anniversary of his death until he sent a beautiful stranger. I have waited for eight years, and now he has sent you.'

She extended a pale, bony hand; Christopher stepped back and stumbled over the tombstone behind him. He scrambled to his feet, but she was upon him and put her arms around him. She was surprisingly strong for such a slight person. Her hands were clawing at his clothes; he was wearing a light rainproof jacket, and he was grateful for the tough synthetic material, but her nails were sharp and he could feel them digging into his flesh. She was kissing his neck, but there was no tenderness in the kiss; it felt as if she was rending his flesh in fury.

'Jim said pain is beauty and beauty is pain,' she said.

Christopher had managed to disengage one of his arms, and he was prying her loose. 'Listen, I don't care what Jim said,' he panted. 'Just let go of me.'

He pushed her away, and in the confined space between the gravestones she stumbled, and sat down heavily. 'You are denying your true being,' she said. 'Jim said to expose yourself to your deepest fear; after that, fear has no power.'

He was backing away from her. 'Listen, I'm not interested in fear or power or beauty or pain,' he said. 'I just want to get the hell out of here.'

She was withdrawing into herself again, her fury spent, not looking at him. 'Go, then,' she said, in the tones of a sibyl, 'but you will answer to the Lizard King in the afterlife. You have failed him.'

'Shall we go down here?' Eric asked, pausing at the steps leading down from the Pont Neuf to the little park at its base. 'Where you and Dad had your bread and cheese?'

'No, I've changed my mind,' Christopher said. 'Besides, we didn't bring any bread and cheese.'

Eric laughed. 'We can always come back. Bread and cheese are not hard to come by.'

'Let's keep the possibility open,' said Christopher, indulging a luxurious sense that there might well be further excursions with this companion. He could not have said why, but he had a sense that they had discovered each other – he hoped on Eric's part with even a fraction of his own glad surprise.

After Eric had walked Christopher back to his hotel, the older man had occasion to reflect on the unexpectedness of his impression – and also on its inappropriateness. He was not in Paris to rediscover Eric de Villiers: he was here to retrieve him. One of the topics, exactly, that they had failed to broach between them, was Christopher's reason for being in Paris – which he was sure Eric must have some inkling of. Why else his failure to ask the one obvious question: what on earth are you doing in Paris? Related to this was his failure to as much as refer to his father, except jokingly. It occurred to Christopher that, for all the impression of frank and free conversation, they had discussed almost nothing pertaining to his reason for being in Paris.

This omission came home to him with particular pertinence when he sat down at his laptop to compose the letter to Daniel that he knew it behoved him to write. He sat for a long time before his little flapped-up box, with little more than Dear Daniel to show for the twenty minutes he had stared at it. What, after all, was there to say, other than that, far from having been ruined by Paris, Eric had somehow been immeasurably improved by it? This could not be what Daniel wanted to hear: he had taken his stand so absolutely on the matter of the dissolution supposedly wrought by bohemian life on the susceptible constitution of farm children. Whereas Daniel might be expected to be at least relieved that Eric was well, he would not want to know that his son was better than he had ever been while under the eye and tutelage of his father.

I have seen Eric today, Christopher started, and I am pleased to say that he is looking very well.

But what else of any substance was there to report? We crossed the Seine and he bought a postcard and I showed him where we used to have lunch? Christopher snorted. Daniel would hardly care to know that Christopher had shown Eric where they used to have lunch; Daniel probably did not remember. All Daniel really wanted to know was when Eric would be returning home, and Christopher was no nearer telling him that than he'd been on his first day in Paris.

In the end, he told himself that he would have more to report the following day, after the lunch at Zeevee's, and the promised meeting with the mysterious recipient of the Jim Morrison postcard. With a sense of relief, of a confrontation averted or at any rate postponed, he closed his computer without bothering to save the attempt at a letter, and went to visit the Cluny museum, which he had been intending to do ever since his arrival. That at least would not have changed in any perplexing way.

In the event, the Cluny let him down: it had in fact changed, if not in content, then in name, and was now known as the Musée National du Moyen Âge – rather more pompously than the homely little museum, surviving so imperturbably in the midst of the clamour of a later age, merited or desired. The interior, though, in spite of evident rearrangement and modernisation, was reassuringly the same, with the famously inscrutable Lady in her crepuscular sanctuary still presiding serenely over her little court of ladies and animals and her Unicorn.

Christopher, who had had, once, a more than passing interest in the Middle Ages, wondered afresh at the transformation of so much greed and bloodlust, so much plunder and rape and carnage, into works of such unruffled beauty. A saving impulse of mercy and pity, or the hypocritical dressing-up of a sanguinary society? Consolation or decoration? He stood for a long time pondering the stately garments, the stylised forms, the appealing animals, the whole fantasy of humans in harmony with one another and nature: had we lost the trick of it, or were we merely more honest in our exploitation of each other and our environment? Elsewhere in the museum, after all, there were quite enough reminders of the brutally bellicose nature of the Middle Ages. However beautifully worked and filigreed a sword, it remains an instrument for killing, in the right – or wrong – hands, a weapon of mass destruction. The unicorn, for all its mythical allure, was hunted – the bait, according to legend, a beautiful young woman.

He emerged with something like shock onto the crossing – confrontation, collision – of the two great Boulevards of St Michel and St Germain, teeming with the millions that a fine Saturday in Paris produces as a beehive pours forth bees on a sunny day. Pausing for a moment to adjust his eyes to the bright light, he was pushed aside, unaggressively but unapologetically, by a young couple, single-mindedly intent on their interlocked progress. An elderly woman stood with an air of serene detachment next to the railings around the museum, waiting for her dog to finish defecating in a spot where, within minutes, the results would be stepped in by some hurrying pedestrian. This, however, was not her concern: the great city invited, necessitated, the creation of private spaces in the midst of the clamorous multitude.

All was amorphous movement, purposes at cross-purposes with other purposes, pedestrians vying with one another for space on the broad pavement and with vehicles for dominance of the street: the utterly random intersection of human endeavour, imperfectly ordered into the grid of Baron Haussmann's design. For once, the Parisian Picturesque did not assert itself: the crossing was as devoid of charm, as charged with brute energy, as any in New York or London – ruled, insofar as it was ruled at all, not by any law or even accident of aesthetics, but by the phased changing of the lights. It was curiously exciting, and yet also intimidating: it did not admit of any distancing perspective, any aestheticising reduction: you had to deal with it head-on.

Christopher smiled to himself at his own theorising of a banal intersection: what was it, after all, but two streets crossing? A young woman hurrying past caught his smile and returned it, amused, uncoquettish. The smile, fleeting as it was, seemed to include Christopher in the turmoil of people; he had as much right there as anybody.

Squaring his shoulders, in a manner of speaking, with this assurance, Christopher made his way down the Boulevard St Michel to the Place St Michel, with its fountain and its shallow, littered pool, its gloomy, looming sculpture of a triumphant St Michael, and its eternal circle of people waiting for people – how many expectations had been dashed, how many relationships terminated here by the simple failure to keep a rendezvous? He continued up the narrow Rue St André des Arts, in effect a thoroughfare of holes in the wall from which and inside which food was dispensed. He could feel the pull of Paris, the facile appeal of it, which it would be so easy to succumb to, as he had succumbed all those years ago, he and Daniel.

At the hotel there was a note informing him that Monsieur Bigler had phoned, and would expect him tomorrow at noon at the address below, and please to key in the code to open the street door, and proceed to the double doors on the ground floor. The address, Christopher was intrigued to find, was on the Île St Louis; it had not occurred to him to ask the young American where he lived, and he couldn't have said where he might have imagined him to spend his private hours: Zeevee seemed to have no existence beyond his public self. He had in fact, he realised, not exercised his imagination at all on Zeevee's behalf: he seemed so perfectly a creature of the Parisian streets that one did not imagine him having a home, a setting, other than some chair in a café, or at most a banquette in a restaurant. There was, then, more to Zeevee than met the eye – which, Christopher reflected with a guilty grimace, was just as well.

CHAPTER 6

The next morning, after the usual crowded little breakfast at the Hotel du Carrefour, Christopher phoned Martha. After the slight friction of their last interchange, no more than a slight scuffing of the smooth surface of their talk, he felt the need to re-establish the cordiality of their meetings.

'Ah, Christopher!' she said. 'I trust you are making your peace with Paris.'

'I think it's making its peace with me. Young Eric came to see me yesterday.'

'Off his own bat?'

'Well, I assume he was put up to it by Zeevee, but he needn't have done it.'

'And he came to offer peace?'

'Not in so many words, but his manner was ... well, very accommodating.'

'Then that's excellent. Did you put your proposition to him?'

'No, it hardly seemed the moment to do so, on our very first meeting.'

'You didn't want to disrupt the accommodating manner?'

'Well, I didn't want to test it. Frankly, I was flabbergasted by the change in Eric de Villiers.'

'He has changed?'

'He has been transformed. But utterly. Martha, he has become *civilised*.'

'Paris has been known to have that effect – well, on those it doesn't drive mad.'

'But it would take more even than Paris to account for this change. It would take a miracle.'

She still refused to share his wonder. 'Paris has been known to effect miracles,' she said. 'But how has he changed? In appearance?'

'Well, it begins with externals and extends to intangibles. He is, for a start, immensely better-looking.'

'I told you he was admired in Paris.'

'But I thought Parisian admiration was just another species of Parisian perversity, the fascination of the abomination, that kind of thing.'

'And instead?'

'Well, you've seen him. He's improved almost beyond recognition.'

'Of course, I don't know what he's improved beyond, not having seen him in his unimproved state. But he is good-looking certainly. And the intangibles?'

'Well, he is, as I say, so *civilised*.'

'Perhaps he has just grown up.'

'Perhaps. But he's grown up into something that his young self gave one no grounds to hope for. He's amiable, he's attentive, he's humorous, he's courteous, if I may use such an old fashioned word.'

'And how do you account for this miracle?'

'I was hoping you could help me there. How would *you* account for the miracle?'

'Other than his growing up? Well, miracles are not really my province, but I would say it takes a woman.'

'What kind of a woman?'

'I would say a thoroughly superior kind of woman.'

'Which is hardly the kind of woman he has been assumed to be consorting with.'

'Doesn't that rather suggest that you may have to re-examine your assumptions?'

'My dear woman, I've been doing nothing else since arriving here. But who's going to get Daniel to re-examine his?'

'Ah, with Daniel I can't help you; there you are on your own.'

'Well, I take it you won't refuse to discuss my assumptions with me. Will you be going to Zeevee's for lunch?'

She hesitated. 'No. No, I was invited, but I shall phone my regrets.'

'But why? And how am I to face the natives without you to protect me?'

'You answer your own question. The reason *why* I won't go is *so that* you can face the natives on your own – not that there are likely to be very many natives. Zeevee's crowd is mainly composed of deracinated foreigners of one stripe or another.'

'But why should I face these deracinated striped foreigners on my own?'

'So as to form your own impressions. If I were there you would talk to me and nobody else and accept my opinions as your own.'

'Am I really so abjectly reliant on you?'

'Not in general. But there is the danger that in the face of the unfamiliar you may retreat into the relative safety of my company.'

He laughed. 'I like your *relative*!'

'Absolute, then, if you prefer. But meet me tomorrow evening for a glass of wine – and perhaps supper afterwards?'

'That sounds good. Where?'

'Le Départ at seven?'

'Le Départ at seven.'

Without the relative safety of Martha's company, then, he set out for the Île de la Cité. The spring day was as sparkling as the day before, and all of Paris seemed to be intent on taking advantage of it. Crossing, again, the Pont St Louis to the snug little island, Christopher checked the address on his slip of paper. The Rue de Bretonvilliers proved to be a tiny street at right angles to the river, somewhat dark and forbidding. Number 11 was an unassuming door between a haberdasher and an art dealer. Christopher tapped in the code he had been given, and the door clicked open. Entering, he experienced one of those surprises that Paris, so obsessively private despite flagrant public display, is so capable of springing: a small but beautifully proportioned courtyard, ablaze with the colour of a meticulously tended garden, formally arrayed in relation to a minuscule pond upon the surface of which drifted two perfect water lilies. At the far end of the courtyard a set of French doors stood open to the morning, and from it emanated the sound of conversation and music – Keith Jarrett, Christopher guessed, though it was not an album he knew.

Zeevee's message had said that his apartment was on the ground floor; the French doors, then, must be Zeevee's. They seemed grander than anything Christopher had expected; but then, he reminded himself, he hadn't really formed any notion of Zeevee's habitation. And yet he had a home, and, to judge by its exterior, a substantial one.

Christopher paused for a moment: the gravel pathway seemed so pristine that he felt self-conscious about disturbing its surface. And yet, others must have trodden there before him, apparently without leaving tracks. He ventured onto the path and was gratified to discover that he, too, left no tracks; perhaps even the gravel in Paris refused to take impressions.

The door was open, and had no knocker or bell, so Christopher had no choice but to enter the room. As he did so, he almost staggered backwards. The room before him was a temple to perversity, its contents apparently selected with a connoisseur's eye for the most hideous productions of their time. The furniture was not identifiable as belonging to any particular period or style: it was a compendium of the mistakes of all the ages, from Regency chairs with Egyptian motifs to light Swedish 1950s tables, angular and attitudinal but flimsy. The paintings ... well, the paintings seemed to have been chosen according to no principle other than that they should not on any account agree with the rest of the room – though, to be fair to the paintings, the room was not difficult to disagree with. Among the more conventionally figurative productions, Christopher recognised a Tretchikoff – one of his blue-black women festooned with carnivorous-looking lilies – and something that may have been an early Hockney, in its resolute refusal to please. The floor was covered with a rug in Day-Glo peppermint green and shocking pink, and the wallpaper seemed to have been scrawled over by a large demented child armed with a very big crayon. From the high ceiling, which was painted cerulean, was suspended a chandelier of yellow and blue crystals that tinkled in the breeze from the door. But against the wall facing the door, presiding over this phantasmagoria like a sober disc jockey at a rave, was a large oil of a young woman naked but for a pair of short white socks, leaning back upon what seemed to be a singularly uncomfortable couch. On her face was an expression of vulnerable defiance, what may, in a more moralistic age, have been called *lewdness*, an implication that the model was where she was because that was where she wanted to be, but had her doubts about the motives of the viewer. Her body was slender and small-breasted, but with a presence disproportionate to its mass, her posture a tensing for action rather than a relaxation of purpose. Her skin was stripped to the bone, arid, testifying to dry open spaces far removed from the cosy prettiness of Paris. There was repose in the face, and yet a fierce desire; something at once complacent and ravenous, austere yet licentious.

All this, however, only became coherent to Christopher later, in the tranquillity of his lodgings; what he was conscious of now was a welter of impressions, an apparently random collision of objects that yet composed uncannily around the central icon of the nude woman.

The room seemed to be empty, if a room so cluttered could be called empty. The music was coming from what used to be called a radiogram, a piece of heavy imbuia hunkering on ball-and-claw feet in clumsy imitation of some best-forgotten period of interior decoration. The silly little doors stood open, and the original workings – the radio and record player – had been ripped out and replaced with a CD player. A CD cover was lying on the cabinet – Keith Jarrett indeed, the *Carnegie Hall Concert*.

The voices Christopher had heard from the courtyard were quiet now. Then, suddenly, there was a burst of laughter, a woman's laughter, and Zeevee appeared from a room to the left, accompanied by the woman. He seemed, by contrast with his companion, very serious. 'Let me tell you, Zelda,' he was saying, 'you can't *imagine* what shit that's going to cause'; then, his eye lighting on

Christopher standing uncertainly at the door, his face brightened into his customary smile.

'Welcome,' he said. 'I'm glad you found the place. The *patron* at your hotel sounded very uncertain, as if doubting that you actually existed.'

'Oh, he sounds that way even when confronted with my person. I think he filters out South Africans.'

'Oh, you are South African?' Zeevee's companion, who had been openly staring at Christopher, now asked. 'I think that's so neat.' Her tone – truculent, resentful – contrasted oddly with the sentiment.

'I don't know,' Christopher laughed. 'Not so long ago it was the world's least-favourite nationality.'

'Like being an American until Barack Obama came to redeem us all,' Zeevee said. 'Zelda, this is Christopher.'

'Oh hi, Christopher' she said. 'It's *so* good to meet you.' She uttered her platitudes with a kind of husky earnestness, as if they were of great moment. In appearance, too, she combined the dramatic and the frivolous, the solemn and the flirtatious, to mystifying effect, seeming to frown and pout at the same time. She was all but enveloped in a large velvet cloak with gold tassels; and underneath this she wore, as far as one could tell through the interstices of the cloak, the briefest and sheerest of skirts and a pair of very high-heeled sandals secured with ribbons that wound round her thin calves to be tied at the knee with an exaggerated bow. Her face was very pale and not made up, except for two bold black slashes where her eyebrows would have been had she not plucked them. Her hair was yanked back from her face, straining at the roots and twisted into an elongated cone that exploded at the apex into a kind of feather duster. Her eyes, in spite of their coerced elongation, were large and very blue, fixing their object with a doll-like stare. The whole effect was at once infantile and sinister, like the Bride of Chucky, Christopher thought.

'Are you in the trade?' she asked; it was difficult to tell whether she was making small talk, inviting a confession, or spoiling for a fight.

'The trade …?'

'Fashion,' Zeevee explained. 'Zelda thinks everyone is in the trade.'

'I do not so,' said Zelda. 'I so absolutely do not. I met somebody last night who manufactures aluminum skillets.'

'Heavens,' said Zeevee, 'you *are* extending your range.'

'Yes,' she said. 'He was so sweet.' Her flat little voice sharpened into a squeak of approbation.

'A sweet saucepan salesman?' Zeevee asked. 'Well, why not?'

She looked at him as if she suspected that he was making fun of her, but then replied with imperturbable gravity, 'He manu*fac*tures *ski*llets. He so does not sell saucepans.'

'The difference, my dear Zelda, between a skillet and a saucepan is not worth a disagreement between our sweet selves. Let's find something to drink.'

'Yes, let's,' she said with an intensity suggesting that she was agreeing to an act of extreme daring or perhaps superior cunning. 'Are you coming?' she asked Christopher with a conspiratorial grimace that could have been a smile or a leer.

'Why, yes,' he said, 'although I would seem to have arrived.' He gestured towards the piece of furniture next to which they were standing, something he thought he'd heard referred to as a tallboy in his youth, upon which an array of bottles was displayed.

'Oh, that's what *you* think,' she growled ominously. 'You are *so* wrong.'

'Zelda will put you right on any subject you care to name,' Zeevee said. 'In this instance, what she means is that the champagne is in the other corner. Will you help yourselves? Everybody seems to be arriving at the same time now.' With that, their host moved towards the front door, where guests were indeed arriving en masse, as if by some atavistic instinct or arcane agreement.

'Zeevee thinks he has to interpret me to everybody,' the woman informed Christopher, with extreme earnestness. 'He calls me the sphinx.' She took Christopher by the sleeve. 'Come get some champagne before the rampaging citizens descend.'

Christopher allowed himself to be led to the designated corner, where indeed several open bottles of champagne were sweating in ice buckets. She seized a bottle and filled two glasses, expertly tilting them as she poured.

'There you go,' she said, handing him a glass and lifting hers as she said, 'Chin chin.'

Christopher was mainly intrigued at the extreme vapidity of this person who was clearly an intimate of Zeevee's: he found it difficult to reconcile his impression of the man with this woman, who, on a charitable assumption, was under the influence of some recondite substance, unless her manner was merely the sphinx-like quality she'd alluded to. Not really knowing how to continue their conversation – what does one say to a sphinx? – he turned to the door to survey the arriving guests.

These had apparently been selected for their picturesque qualities. The figure that stood out, quite literally, was an impossibly tall young man who had a large Dobermann in tow – if 'tow' was the proper word for a leash apparently fashioned from plaited silk scarves, appearing to great effect against the dog's glossy black coat. The Dobermann was as alert and outgoing as its owner was languid and uncommunicative. While the dog repaid with evident pleasure the attention of any one who showed an interest in it, the man seemed deliberately to repel notice, not engaging with any of the glances that he attracted. His hair was fashionably tousled to suggest, perhaps, that he had just got out of bed – and the fact that he had not shaved seemed calculated to suggest that it was not his own bed from which he had emerged. His languid manner then became referable, to the possibly over-active imagination, to the depredations of the night – an inference that was given some credence a moment later when, emerging at last from his cocoon of self-absorption, he kissed Zeevee on both cheeks, and said, 'I do hope you've provided some sustenance, I'm *famished*. These days, I fear, bed no longer comes with breakfast.'

His accent was public-school British, not quite a lisp, but with a pronounced labial slur, a function of an overdeveloped upper lip, perhaps, if not an underdeveloped power of articulation. His manner, though far too self-conscious to be childlike, had a certain sweetness, at odds with its deliberate brittleness; he seemed helplessly trapped in a world-weary public persona that he could not afford to disown, and lacked the energy to discard. Surprisingly, the effect, whether intended or not, was to make one want to get to know him. It was possible that his eyes, which were enormous and glossy-black, as naively trusting as those of his dog, contributed to this effect.

'You'll find food in the next room,' Zeevee informed his guest. 'It comes without a bed, though.'

'My dear Zeevee,' the man said, 'nothing in Paris comes without a bed.'

Christopher realised that he was staring; and if he hadn't, he would have been made sharply enough aware of the fact by Zelda's resentful little mewl at his elbow: 'Don't get too carried away now,' adding in her conspiratorial half-whisper, 'Simon's *so* not available nowadays.'

There was more in this statement than Christopher thought he could unlock with a single key, but he opted for the one that might open most doors.

'Simon?' he asked.

Zelda looked at him like a little girl whose party balloon had just unexpectedly popped. 'You mean you don't know *Simon*?'

'Well, no. I'm new here, remember.'

'I'm remembering, but gee, don't you have *movies* in Australia?'

'South Africa. Yes, we have movies, but I've probably not seen as many as I should.'

'I'll say you haven't if you haven't seen *Simon*. Simon Cleaver. Clever Simon to his friends, Simon the Cleaver to his enemies. He's been in *everything*. He was discovered by Pazoleenee.'

'Didn't Pasolini die sometime in the seventies?' Christopher asked, not without some pleasure in demonstrating that he was not quite the gauche provincial she obviously took him for.

'So he did. So?' she asked.

'So how old can Simon be, if he acted in a film nearly forty years ago?'

'Well, nobody knows how old Simon is, but he's way past his twenties, that much I know. And I also happen to know that he was discovered at the age of five.'

'I'm not sure that being discovered by Pasolini is what most five-year-olds need.'

'Simon's needs … well, I guess they weren't like the needs of most five-year-olds you've met. But the role wasn't what you're thinking – or what I'm thinking you're thinking. He was somebody's child, some woman who kills him rather than deliver him into the hands of some fascist politician. She throws him in front of a bus and then jumps herself, I saw it at the Cinémathéque last year. It's very beautiful.'

'I'm sure it was, but it doesn't sound as if Simon was the main attraction.'

She fixed him again with her doll-like gaze. 'You know what's weird? He *was* the main attraction. He just stood there with those big black eyes of his, looking … well, so a*dult*. But the *really* weird thing was that you could kind of *understand*, you know? how the fascist might fancy the little boy.'

'That does sound weird, yes,' Christopher said. 'And that established Simon as a star?'

'His career took a nose-dive after Pasolini's death, but it picked up again in the eighties when the Americans started getting into movies about child sexuality and that kind of crap, and he could play schoolboys till he was way into his twenties, so he had enough work, and he could speak Italian and French and more than help himself in half a dozen other languages, and helping himself was what he was best at? Everybody adored him and of course wanted to get into his pants. But *nowadays*,' she grimaced, 'nowadays he must take what he can get, because everybody who ever wanted to get into his pants have done so or are otherwise really pissed off because they didn't when everybody else did. So he's not exactly being in … inunud …' she stopped, without embarrassment. 'What's the word?'

'Inundated?'

'Yes, *thank* you, *inundated* with offers, but I'm thinking he's got

100

something to keep him going at the moment. I heard somebody was doing a revival of some dreadful old play about a woman who has the hots for her husband's son.'

'Phaedra?'

'If you say so, sir. Anyway, Simon's playing the son – when he's shaved and cleaned up he still looks about eighteen. Apparently he comes to a sticky end, which is what Simon will come to one of these days too, I shouldn't wonder. But he'll do it beautifully, like he does everything,' she concluded resentfully.

He glanced sideways as the subject of this ambiguous panegyric sauntered off into another room, from where high-pitched squeals of delight or alarm suggested that his arrival was not unremarked by the company there.

'It sounds as if he's popular enough here,' Christopher remarked.

'Because they screech and cackle? Oh, they screech and cackle at anything, in Paris. Besides, that was for Rambo.'

'Rambo?'

'The dog. He's very well liked. He's named after some poet you'll know about.'

'Oh. Rimbaud?'

'Sure, like I said, only you say it better. My French …' she shrugged helplessly, as if defeated by the very thought of the language. 'We models don't get paid to talk, so we don't talk.'

Around them, the company had waxed; there were now about ten people in the room, and more seemed to be arriving, for from behind the shoulders and talking heads obscuring the entrance, a strange melodious bray arose. '*Ciao bello!* What a bee-ootiful day you have arranged for us!'

The company parted as if by common consent, and the owner of the voice appeared, flinging up her arms, advancing upon her host. 'Zeevee!' she crooned, in a heavy alto. She was dressed in a metallic sheath so tight that she seemed to be extruded from it, her breasts all but spilling over the severely cut bodice. Her hair was an improbable shade of red, encouraged to stray abundantly from the rhinestone Alice band only nominally restraining it. Her nose was Roman in shape and size, and her huge nostrils flared like those of a horse, an impression reinforced by her teeth, which were large, square and protruding. She was large, almost as tall as Zeevee, and her height was enhanced by her shoes, silver wedge-shaped platforms. She loomed over the assembled company like some pagan goddess over her supplicants.

Zeevee, submitting to a triple cheek-kiss, said, '*Ciao*, Sandra. You look magnificent, as always.'

'I try my best,' she said, complacently surveying the vast expanse of flesh and cloth she offered to view. 'My secret is that I never go against nature. Nature made me beeg, so I dress beeg.'

They were both aware of being the centre of attention, and were good-humouredly performing, Zeevee taking the supporting role.

'Who is she?' Christopher asked Zelda.

She gave him another you're-so-new-in-town look, or maybe it was just her eyebrows that gave her a look of perpetual surprise. 'Oh *that*,' she burbled, 'is only about the most famous designer in the world. Alessandra *Giovanelli*? Sister of the even more famous Paolo Giovanelli? Except he's now so *dead*?'

'I've heard of Giovanelli, yes, and I've seen their stuff.' He had a general memory of glossy images of ugly, brightly coloured clothes and very large handbags.

'You see their stuff *everywhere*. I don't like wearing it, it's so *Miami*, you know what I mean?'

'I'm not sure that I do.'

'Oh, *you* know, where the Eurotrash go when they get kicked out of St Tropez. It's the last stop before rehab. Sandra's just out of rehab, she's forever just out of rehab,' Zelda added spitefully.

Zeevee was escorting the redoubtable Alessandra to the champagne table, and for a moment the room was almost quiet; but then there was a flurry around the door, not quite a commotion, more of a restless shuffling, like a herd of antelope sensing the presence of a predator. The group didn't disperse, merely lost its compactness, seemed less settled, then gradually, almost reluctantly, parted to reveal a newcomer standing in the doorway. It was a woman of indeterminate age – either a wonderfully mature twenty-five, or a miraculously preserved forty; if her skin glowed with the bloom of

102

youth, her expression had the resigned sobriety of experience. She was framed in the doorway, standing quite still, apparently alone, but as self-possessed as a queen entering an audience chamber supported by a retinue. She was dressed in a simple dress of some light-coloured stuff that seemed to have body without weight, draping her slim frame generously but without muffling its clean outlines, the shoulders covered but the arms left bare. Her neck emerged from the high collar with a classical purity of line, and her head, held high, had a kind of quattrocento asceticism about it, Christopher thought. Her rich colouring and black hair contrasted with the subdued tones of her dress. She presented, almost as if by design, an aesthetic ideal diametrically opposed to Alessandra Giovanelli's flamboyant display; and yet her presence asserted itself quite as tellingly. Her posture – calmly waiting, and yet unmistakably *waiting* – suggested that she was used to making entrances, used to being looked at, used to being met at the door; and indeed, within a few seconds of her appearance, Zeevee had materialised at her side, kissing her lightly on both cheeks, steering her into the room, engaging her in his most exuberant manner – which manner, however, she met with a grave reserve. Christopher guessed that humour was not her most natural mode, and chatter not her forte.

'You're staring very hard,' came Zelda's plaintive squeak.

'Am I?' Christopher replied. 'I beg your pardon, I was …' He faltered, not wanting to say what would have been the only true account of his feelings, that he was *overawed*.

'You were ogling, but you needn't beg my pardon for that. Or Beatrice du Plessis's pardon. She's used to being ogled.'

'That is Beatrice du Plessis?' Christopher asked.

'Oh, please, you're telling me again that you don't know?' she said, rolling her eyes. 'She's only the most famous face in the world.'

'I seem to have been out of the world, then,' Christopher said. 'I can't say I recognise the face. It's very beautiful, though,' he said as if in expiation.

'I suppose you think you're the first person to make that discovery?' she jeered.

'I was thinking she looked like a quattrocento painting,' Christopher said.

She fixed him with her hostile stare. 'I suppose you think that's clever. Well, it isn't.'

'I had no desire to appear clever,' Christopher protested, conscious of sounding priggish. 'I was just saying how Beatrice du Plessis struck me.'

'Oh, don't get worked up, I was just having you on because I don't know what quattrocento is. But seriously,' she said, rounding her eyes and hissing, 'stay away from Beatrice du Plessis!'

'Why ever?' Christopher asked. 'She seems harmless enough.'

'Oh, *seems!*' she groaned. 'Do you always trade in appearances?'

'When I have nothing else to go on, yes.'

'Well, now you do have something else to go on. I'm telling you she's dangerous. But *lethal.*'

'Dangerous in what sense?'

'I'm telling you, in the lethal sense. As in life-threatening?'

'Whose life has she threatened?'

'I don't name names. But she *eats* people. For some women it's enough just to suck the blood out of somebody and leave a pale corpse lying around behind the sofa, but *la du Plessis* – she devours them whole?'

'How intriguing,' Christopher observed, though in truth he felt somewhat alarmed. What had Eric become embroiled in?

'And I'll tell you this,' Zelda continued, 'the ones she likes are the ones who are old enough to know better. Anybody can eat boys – some guy said that under twenty, destiny is hormones? – but for the real gourmet, only well-seasoned meat will do. You'd better watch out.'

'I should think I'd be rather too well-seasoned for her.'

She snorted. 'Don't count on it. She's one weird lady.'

'Does she have a husband?'

'She had one, but she ate him.'

Zelda drifted off, leaving Christopher feeling intrigued but perplexed. Her chatter, though probably malicious, and almost certainly misleading, was interesting as a specimen of the medium in which he found himself. She seemed to be a friend of Zeevee's, and yet he could discern no common ground between them. It seemed indeed possible, then, that there was more to Zeevee than met the eye.

The woman Zelda had identified as Alessandra Giovanelli came up to Christopher, holding a glass of champagne in one hand, an unlit cigarette in the other. 'Do you have a fire?' she asked.

'No, I'm afraid I don't smoke. But I'll see if I can get you a light.'

'No, no,' she said, 'not necessary. I smoke when I have nothing better to do. Perhaps talking to you is better than smoking?'

'I can hardly say. It depends on whether you use tobacco as a stimulant or a soporific.'

She looked at him solemnly for a moment as if seriously considering her options. Then she let out a harsh laugh, like the bark of a seal. 'Ha! I think you are not a soporific.'

He inclined his head in awkward acknowledgement of what was presumably intended as a compliment.

'I am Alessandra Giovanelli,' she announced.

Some impulse of perversity prevented Christopher from acknowledging that he knew this. 'I am pleased to meet you,' he said instead. 'I am Christopher Turner.'

There was a moment during which she visibly wondered whether she should recognise the name so blandly offered as a counter to her own; then, opting for the safe refuge of generalised enquiry, she asked, 'You are English?'

'No, South African.'

'Ah, Africa, where the wild animals are. I would love to go and see for myself the wild animals.'

'They no longer walk the streets,' Christopher said. 'You have to go to a game park to see them.'

But she had lost interest in the wild animals. 'Don't you love this room?' she said abruptly.

'It is certainly unusual.'

'It is be-oootiful! It is by Kelly Wearstler,' she said. 'You know Kelly Wearstler?' she added, responding to his blank expression.

'No – should I?'

'She is very big right now, very big. She has turned Hollywood kitsch into a style statement. Every piece is a collector's item; that chandelier is from the most exclusive bordello in Memphis, in America. They tore it down to build a Holiday Inn, very sad. But this room, it reminds me so much of the sitting room of my *nonna* in Chiusdino! But my grandmother was not a collector, these pieces, they were just what she had in her house.'

'Chiusdino?' Christopher repeated, wondering whether this was another allusion he should recognise.

'Aah, you have not heard of it. Of course. Nobody has heard of Chiusdino. Is in Tuscany, a teeny-teeny little village where nothing happened from the time San Galgano's horse knelt there before the Jesus Christ in the twelfth century. The stone, it is still there, with the prints of the horse's knees.'

'The horse's knees left an imprint in stone?'

'Yes, yes, miracle, you know. My grandmother, she said always the horse made the miracle; they should have made the horse a saint. My grandmother was the most modern woman in Chiusdino. She was the dressmaker, she taught me everything I know about fabric.' She fingered the cloth of her dress, which was indeed of a stuff so fine and yet so strong that it draped effortlessly where it found room to do so, and supported without evident tension where it was called upon to do so. 'I am a designer,' she said, having evidently decided that a South African could be forgiven for not having heard of her.

'And your mother,' Christopher asked, 'was she also in the fashion business?'

'My mother?' Her voice hit a high note. 'No, no, she *hated* dressmaking, and she hated Chiusdino. She used to say everybody is related to everybody else's goat. She went to Siena as soon as she could, she became a prostitute. She told me I must become an actress. She loved Gina Lollobrigida. Do you know Gina Lollobrigida in Africa?'

'Yes … yes, we do. *Buona Sera Mrs Campbell.*'

'Yes, yes, Mrs Campbell, exactly, you have heard of her.' She lifted her glass as if to toast Mrs Campbell. 'I think my mother

106

she thought she was Mrs Campbell. But the problem – no GIs in Siena! But me, I am not an actress type. I am more the natural type, don't you think?' she crooned, embracing herself, her razor-blade fingernails glinting turquoise against the hard gleam of her dress.

Christopher was trying to come up with a tactful response to this self-evidently outrageous claim. Fortunately Zeevee, squeezing past on his way to the drinks, overheard and said, 'Sandra, if you're the natural type, I'm Tarzan.'

'Well?' she said. 'You can be Tarzan, why not? I think you will look good in a leopard skin. I will design you one.'

'Thank you, dear, but I'm not sure that that's my style. You know I prize skilled artifice above brute nature.'

'Ah, you make-up artists, you are all the same,' she sighed, then turned back to Christopher. 'If I could, I would live in the jungle.'

'Then how did you come to be a fashion designer?' he enquired.

'Ah, that was my good fortune. My mother was in Siena most of the times – she worked every day except Mondays – so I lived with my grandmother, you see, and so I could sew before I could talk, and I would have become the village dressmaker after her if it had not been for Paolo.'

'Paolo?'

'Paolo, my brother. You have not heard of Paolo Giovanelli?' She seemed to feel that there were limits to the levels of ignorance she could countenance, even from an African. 'He is very, very famous.'

'I've heard of him, of course,' Christopher said, with a silent thank you to Zelda.

'Yes, of course you have. Very famous. He was younger than me, two years younger. When he was twelve years old the village priest, how you say … molested him.'

'That is very terrible.'

'Yes, terrible, *terrible*. But Paolo, he discovered that for him it wasn't so *very* terrible to be molested. So he decided he wanted to be a dress designer, and he made my grandmother teach him everything she knew, and when he was eighteen, he went to Rome and took me to be his assistant. I was always his assistant and when, you know, his boyfriend killed him, I took over the business.'

'Your brother's boyfriend killed him?'

'Yes, yes, very sad, it was in all the papers, about four years ago. Rinaldo was a very jealous man, and Paolo … well, Paolo was very beautiful.' She said this as if it explained all, as if it was the natural fate of beauty to be killed. 'And somebody *very* high up in the Vatican, he fall in love with Paolo. And Paolo, after the priest, you know, he always had something about the church. And Rinaldo did not like that.

'And that is why, you see,' she continued, 'the Giovanelli label is now Alessandra Giovanelli. *Time* magazine has called me the "New Face of Giovanelli".' She turned her face to him as if to demonstrate what the New Face of Giovanelli looked like. 'Is not as beautiful as the old face of Giovanelli, but will do.'

'I'm sure it will do very well,' Christopher said uncomfortably, not quite sure what the face would do *for* – but yes, as the public face of a corporation, it would do admirably. It was arresting without being assertive, vivid without being garish, unusual without being freakish. It would look good on a postage stamp or a commemorative medal. But no, it was not beautiful.

'Ah,' exclaimed Sandra, 'there is the divine Beatrice!' She pronounced the name in the Italian fashion. Beatrice du Plessis had indeed re-entered the room, now accompanied by a man, olive-skinned, lean as a lizard, his neck-length hair a discreet shade of silver, perfectly coordinated with the pearl-grey linen suit he was wearing.

'And who is the man with her?' Christopher asked, intrigued by the man's air of quiet authority; he made no show of greeting anyone, but seemed as much at ease as if he had been in his own home. Though not overtly friendly, his manner somehow signalled good intentions and a placable temperament.

'Ah!' exclaimed Sandra, 'you don't know? That is the diabolical Gloriani!'

'The designer?' Christopher was pleased for once to recognise an allusion.

Sandra seemed less than impressed. 'Of course the designer,' she said dismissively. 'But I think he has not designed anything in years. All his designs are made by his assistants. People tell a story that Gloriani woke up one morning and told everyone that he had during the night lost the gift, he could no longer design. Now he is waiting for the gift to come back. Perhaps Beatrice will help him, she can inspire anybody, even a charlatan like Gloriani. I have made Beatrice the most beautiful clothes. She can wear even a sack and she can make it look beautiful, but when she wears *my* clothes they look like they were designed for the Holy Mother of God herself.'

'I thought she looked like a quattrocento painting,' Christopher said, tentatively; hoping his sole observation would find more favour here than with Zelda.

'Quattrocento?' Sandra said critically. 'Yes, maybe, the lack of expression. But the colouring, it is much *richer*, it is more like Caravaggio.'

This, coming after Zelda's warning, seemed ominous. 'You mean Salome with the head of John the Baptist?'

She barked again. 'I was thinking of the – how do you say – Conversion of Maria Maddalena.'

But the subject of their conversation was now on her way over to them, guided at her elbow by Zeevee, clearly intent on introducing her to Christopher.

'You must meet one of your compatriots, Beatrice,' he said as they approached. 'This is Christopher Turner.'

Beatrice extended a slim hand. 'Hello,' she said in a low, colourless voice. 'I'm Beatrice du Plessis.' She pronounced it in the Afrikaans way, *doo*-plissy.

There was a short uncomfortable silence, broken by Zeevee. 'You know Sandra, of course?'

'Of course,' said Beatrice unhelpfully, her tone leaving little room for elaboration or even improvisation.

Sandra came to the rescue. 'Ah, you were with Signor Gloriani. Where has he disappeared to?'

'You know one never has more than five minutes of Gloriani's time. He's moved on to a more deserving cause.' The lack of animation in her voice dulled any satiric edge her statement might have contained.

'Ah, you are too modest!' Zeevee exclaimed. 'He is talking to Marcel about the catering for his next show.'

'And is that not a more deserving cause?'

'Perhaps a more practical concern right now for him. Gloriani is more nervous than I've ever seen him before a show.'

'Maybe it is because he is afraid,' said Sandra. 'Maybe the people will see that the Emperor has no clothes?'

Zeevee gave a gentle laugh. 'Oh, Gloriani has plenty of clothes!'

'But are they *good*?' Sandra persisted.

'Gloriani's clothes are always good,' Beatrice said gravely but unemphatically.

'Ah, my dear, you say so because *you* are so good,' Sandra said. 'Me, I am not good, I say what I think.'

'I also say what I think.'

'I know, and that is what makes you good, that you think such good thoughts. Me, I think bad thoughts. I think Gloriani is *finito*.'

'That is a bad thought indeed. And professional jealousy has nothing to do with your opinion?' Zeevee ventured.

'I don't know, maybe, maybe yes. As I say, I am bad. But to me, his designs look secondhand, it looks like he has a clever apprentice who make them.'

'Did you have in mind any particular clever apprentice?' Beatrice asked mildly. Christopher found himself staring at her, so startling was her beauty at close quarters.

Sandra raised her eyebrows – they were heavily pencilled, and with the movement, a minuscule bit of glitter seemed to drift to her chest. She said, '*Cara*, you must ask Zeevee if you want to know about Gloriani's apprentices. He works for the man.'

'All the more reason not to ask me, I'd have thought,' said Zeevee. 'You know I never talk out of the bedroom – or out of the shop.'

'Yes I know, you are very *boring*.' She looked around her, then abruptly turned to Christopher. 'Everyone seems very boring today, don't you think so, Mr Turner?'

Christopher, taken aback at this sudden challenge, said, 'Why no, I find everybody fascinating. You must remember, I come from Cape Town.'

'And in Cape Town you have not people more interesting than this?'

'I can't say that I know anybody here well enough to judge.'

'You know them as well as you will ever know them,' Beatrice contributed in her neutral voice. 'In Paris, what you see is what you get. Appearance is all.'

'It is fortunate, then, that everybody here appears to such good effect,' Christopher risked.

'And I say no, what you see is what they want you to see,' Sandra chipped in. 'What you get is something else *completamente*. My dear Mr Turner, you must beware!'

'Oh, I'm in no danger,' Christopher said. 'I'm only a visitor.'

'That is no safeguard,' Zeevee said. 'Visitors are, if anything, even more prone to being taken in by appearances. Even the American tourist stopping over just for a day may buy what looks to him like a genuine work of art in Montmartre.'

'But who says it is not?' Beatrice asked.

'You know, and I know, my dear Beatrice, that your piece of Montmartre art is merely mass-produced kitsch.'

'But if your tourist gets pleasure from something he believes to be a work of art, has he in fact been deceived?' she asked, suddenly animated, as if she had a vested interest in the topic. 'What measure of worth is there, other than the pleasure he takes in his purchase?'

'Surely,' said Christopher, 'there is a more objective measure of worth?'

'But who is to determine it?' Beatrice asked.

'It *has* been determined,' announced Sandra, 'by the rules of beauty.'

'As decreed by whom?' Zeevee asked.

'Oh, please, Zeevee *caro*, you know, of course, when I design a dress I am not indulging a ... *capriccio*. I use everything I know, everything about the rules of design, everything about the cloth, everything my grandmother taught me, and everything I have learnt myself, and only then ...' she raised a finger, 'only then can I say that my personal inspiration, my *creativity*, comes into the picture, otherwise,' she smiled, 'otherwise, you see, my designs they look like Gloriani's, copies of copies.'

'And yet Gloriani is the most celebrated couturier of his day,' Zeevee objected mildly.

Sandra snorted like a horse. 'Celebrated by whom? All the, how you say, arse-lickers, *claqueurs*, people who are paid to applaud, people who understand nothing about tradition or originality – they are agents and models and photographers, they are all vultures, they are hyenas at a kill.'

'But who is killed?' Christopher asked.

'Oh, there are many victims, *molto* – the models, when nobody wants them any more, the agents, many become alcoholics, and of course the photographers, too much cocaine.'

'So today's vultures are tomorrow's victims?' Christopher asked. 'There seems to be a kind of justice to that.'

'Do you think the victims find that a consolation?' Beatrice asked. 'Wouldn't they rather believe that they were being unjustly punished?'

'I shouldn't think their wishes are consulted in the matter,' Zeevee said. 'You see, my dear Christopher, what an infernal business fashion is. And I am condemned to the lowest circle of hell.'

'The one reserved for traitors?' Christopher asked.

'No, no, no,' Sandra interposed. 'Zeevee, he is not a *traditore*. You must find him another circle.'

Beatrice smiled for the first time. Her teeth, though perfect, were small and pointed, and Christopher caught himself thinking of Zelda's allegation that she'd eaten her husband. But what she now said lacked bite. 'But why a circle of hell at all?' she asked. 'We all know Zeevee is an angel.'

'Ah, now you are mocking me,' the subject of her encomium said. 'Rather find me a comfortable circle of hell, with some congenial fellow-sinners, than an eternity of angelic duty. Being good is such a strain, don't you find?'

Sandra shrugged. 'Ha, I don't know, I have never tried. You must ask Beatrice. She is good.'

To Christopher's surprise, Beatrice blushed, the first sign she had given of any social discomfort. 'Good for what?' she asked. 'It's no good being good unless one is good for something.'

'Whereas being bad is an end in itself?' Christopher asked, partly to divert attention from her. Beatrice darted him, he thought, a small grateful look.

'Being bad, surely,' said Zeevee, 'is not an *end*. It's an unintended consequence of some entirely unrelated end.'

'You say being bad is an accident?' Sandra gave a huge baying laugh. 'I like your theory very much. I shall say to the priest tomorrow when I go to confession, father I have sinned by accident.'

'I said *unintended*, not unforeseen,' Zeevee objected. 'If you think you can foresee the consequence of a deed, but it turns out in a way that you did not intend, then it is no accident.'

'Ah, you are too fine for me!' exclaimed Sandra. 'These things make me hungry. Where is your food, Zeevee?'

'In the next room. Come, let's all go, before Simon feeds it all to Rimbaud.'

The next room was a surprise. For a start, to call it a room at all was an understatement. It was, Christopher thought, what the Italians would call a *sala*: an official chamber. It was a long oblong space running, as soon became evident, along the left bank of the island and overlooking the swift river, silvery in the early afternoon sunshine. The windows were uncurtained, to let in the view and the light, though there were internal shutters should privacy be required. In the near distance, through the green of its surrounding trees, rose the sublime prow of Notre Dame. As if not to compete with the scene outside, the room's interior was as understated as the other had been extravagant. The floors were bare, palest oak, and the walls were the lightest of greys, with a dull shimmer of what Christopher took to be silk. There was almost no furniture: a few low wooden benches of simple design stood in the centre of the room, as in an art gallery; and along the wall furthest from the windows was a long table where the promised food was arrayed. Behind the table was the most ornate feature in the room, a massive neo-classical fireplace of carved marble. People were crowding around the table; Christopher hung back, but Alessandra joined the fray with the determination of a healthy appetite, with Zeevee behind her.

'You're not going to eat?' Beatrice asked.

'Not just yet,' Christopher replied. 'I don't like elbowing people out of the way to get to my food.'

She looked at him solemnly. 'I suspect you don't like elbowing people out of the way, period.'

'Why? Do I seem so unassertive?'

'Well, not the elbowing kind. You wouldn't prosper in the fashion world.'

He laughed ruefully. 'I haven't exactly prospered in any other!'

She declined to respond to his levity, and asked with sweet earnestness, 'Why? What is it you do?'

'I'm a freelance editor, if that means anything to you.'

'I know we models are reputed to be barely literate, but yes, it does mean something to me.' She said this with such absence of rancour that he felt no embarrassment at her misunderstanding of his intended meaning, and she continued: 'Have you always been an editor?' she asked.

'No, I used to teach – at Rondebosch Boys' High, which is where I went to school.'

'And you studied at UCT?'

'You mean have I spent all my life in Cape Town? Yes, I did, or most of it. I did spend three years in England, in Cambridge, studying.'

'Never to return?'

'Not to Paris, anyhow. I did return to Europe, but not to Paris.

'Why not to Paris?'

'I suppose I didn't really want to come back, otherwise I'd have done so. And yet, it was always there, a feeling that at the right time I hadn't made all I could have of … of the immense *opportunity* of Paris.'

She smiled again, her quiet smile, and asked, 'What do you imagine the opportunity to have been?'

He laughed. 'I don't know! I missed it, you see. But you … *you* didn't miss it.'

'If you mean I came to Paris and didn't leave again – yes, I didn't miss it.'

'You have been, I am told – for I must confess yours is a world I don't know much about – extremely successful, have really in a sense conquered Paris and Europe.'

Her expression, when he said this, was so wan that he regretted his comment. But she replied with her customary composure: 'I have been successful, yes, in a manner of speaking.' She seemed disinclined to elaborate on her statement, so Christopher refrained from probing further. He asked instead, taking recourse to the debased currency of expatriates everywhere, 'Where are you from in South Africa?'

'From Potchefstroom.' She offered this factually, for what it was.

'Ah,' he said, not knowing what else to say. Potchefstroom did not open up many avenues of conversation. But he found one. 'I spent three months there when I was in the army.'

'Yes, many people did. Not many remember it with affection.'

'No, I don't think I do either. But we were out in the veld, mostly. I remember it as very barren.'

'The town was no less barren, in its own way. It's known mainly for having the biggest army camp in South Africa and for being the national headquarters of Calvinism. I couldn't wait to get away, but my parents decided that I should go to the University of Pretoria, which was really, in those days, just an extension of the Potchefstroom mindset.'

'You were unhappy there?'

'I don't know. I wasn't really brought up to think I had a right to happiness. I attended my classes regularly – I did a degree in English and French – and I acquired a boyfriend, which was more or less one's duty in those days. I wasn't very ambitious.'

'But how did you end up in Paris?'

'At the end of my final year a modelling scout came to Johannesburg looking for a "new face". They're always looking for a new face, they use up the old ones so quickly. My best friend, who was terrified that I'd marry my boyfriend – he was a theology student – persuaded me to go for an audition, and, well, my face

115

was what they happened to be looking for that year.'

'You've been in Paris ever since?'

'Yes, though of course with modelling you travel a tremendous amount – if it can be called travelling; every city gets reduced to a backdrop.'

She was facing the door behind Christopher as she spoke, and from a sudden tightening of her facial muscles, the merest contraction around her mouth, he guessed that somebody had just come in who mattered to her in one way or another. He didn't want to look round, but she greeted the newcomer with a slight nod of her head, which he felt gave him licence to turn round.

Coming towards them was a man of indeterminate age, possibly in his mid-forties, dressed in a carefully contrived casual style – a black long-sleeved cotton shirt with a four-button placket, and on the pocket a red logo, arcane to Christopher but no doubt quadrupling the price of the garment. With this, the man wore white jeans, cut very low in the waist and very narrow around the legs. The shoes were shiny black leather sneakers with the same red logo on the heel.

The whole outfit displayed to good effect the trim body of the wearer. If the clothes were, to Christopher's mind, rather too young to suit the wearer, they did at least fit admirably. The man's face, which must once have been striking in a street-urchin kind of way, seemed puffy around the eyes.

'Ah, Beatrice!' the man said, also sounding the name in the Italian way, though less convincingly than Alessandra; indeed, when he spoke next it was clear that his origins were decidedly English proletarian, though Christopher's ear was not well enough attuned to locate it more precisely than that.

'Where's Jeanne, then?' he asked, ignoring Christopher's presence.

'She's with friends. You know I don't like bringing her out into' – she gestured vaguely – 'into this.'

'This what, then?' the man demanded.

'This rough and tumble. This … scramble.'

'For food, you mean to say?' He gestured towards the table,

where indeed the company was congregating with more urgency than decorum.

'No, you know what I mean to say.'

'You can't keep Jeanne out of the rough and tumble for ever, you know. One of these days she's going to start scrambling off her own bat.' Rolling his r slightly, he pronounced it *scrumbling.*

'All the more reason not to expose her to it prematurely, then.' As if to make up for the man's rudeness, she turned to Christopher. 'Jeanne is my daughter. She's only just turned seventeen.'

Christopher nodded. 'I have heard her mentioned.'

The newcomer laughed. 'Oh, you'll *hear her mentioned* quite often, I should think. She's a beauty in the making.'

'I'm not sure that a beauty is what I want her to be,' said Beatrice. Her manner with the man was very dry: she evidently didn't like him, though his familiarity suggested that they were old acquaintances. Beatrice seemed, for some reason, reluctant to introduce him to Christopher, and the man made no attempt to introduce himself; he had the air of not needing an introduction to be at home anywhere he found himself. His hair, cut very short, was a grizzled black, and his eyes were the yellow-green of a ripe avocado: not in all respects a reassuring colour in eyes, but certainly striking. He must have been a formidable denizen of this world, one of the panthers of the jungle, when he was younger, Christopher thought, and even now was probably a force to be reckoned with. He seemed energetic, coiled, perhaps even dangerous.

Clearly ill at ease in the man's company, Beatrice du Plessis said at last, evidently to steer the conversation away from the subject of her daughter, 'Christopher, this is Charlie Winthrop. Charlie, Christopher Turner.'

The man favoured Christopher with a half-smile, but without offering to shake his hand. 'How do you do,' he said, satirising Beatrice's formal manner. Christopher nodded with conscious stiffness.

'You're South African,' Winthrop said, a flat statement unrelieved by a hint of interrogation.

'I am,' said Christopher. 'And you are British.'

117

'Yes.'

On this, the little group stood in rather blank silence, with Winthrop looking about him as if in search of more interesting company.

'Don't let us detain you,' Beatrice said to him. 'I'm sure you have other obligations.'

'And you know how seriously I take my obligations, don't you?' Winthrop said, and moved off without any leave-taking other than a terse, 'Time for nosh.'

'I'm sorry,' Beatrice said. 'Charlie has no social graces. He thinks they're middle-class. He himself is working class, which is to say the new upper class.'

'Is he also in the fashion industry?'

'Yes, although he pretends to detest it. He's a photographer; he claims that he wanted to be a wild-life photographer but found it lacking in blood and guts, compared with fashion photography. I think he means he wasn't able to terrify the animals as he terrifies his models.'

'Does he terrify you?'

'Ah, I'm no longer a model,' she said, and if she was evading his question Christopher didn't feel he could say so. He had already perhaps exceeded the limits of intimacy warranted by their acquaintance; but it was part of her effect on him that he felt more freedom in talking to her than he generally allowed himself with acquaintances of much longer standing. It would not do to exceed the limit too far; and yet, it was an open question of what, then, they would talk about if they were to avoid the personal note altogether.

She seemed also, from her silence, to be considering this question; but their quandary, if such it might be called, their standing there in companionable silence, was interrupted by the arrival, unheralded and unremarked, of Eric de Villiers.

'I'm pleased to see you two have made acquaintance.' He kissed Beatrice on the cheek, and shook Christopher's hand. 'I'm sorry I'm late. I was, as they say, unavoidably detained.'

If there was something incomplete in this explanation, his

manner, unaffectedly warm without being presumptuously intimate, disposed of it, as, Christopher felt, it would always dispose
of inconvenient questions: his youthful candour seemed to make
all questions fall away as irrelevant, even impertinent.

'Where is Jeanne?' he asked Beatrice.

'She's visiting friends in Montmartre. I told her to be home by
six.'

Eric frowned. 'How will she get home from Montmartre?'

'By metro, I suppose. How else?'

'I don't like her to use Pigalle or Blanche on a Sunday.' He said
this as a statement of mild fact, but it was clear that he took for
granted that his likes would be taken account of.

'Oh, she knows her way around,' Beatrice said, also quite
unargumentatively.

'Yes, but that's not really the point,' Eric said. 'Young women
have been known to disappear from those stations. And you know
what they look like on a Sunday evening.'

'I'll phone her and tell her to take a taxi,' said Beatrice.

'Yes,' he said, 'yes, I really think that would be better. Or I could
fetch her.'

'Thank you,' Beatrice said, then turned to Christopher. 'Isn't he
solicitous? Was he always so?'

'No, I don't think I would have called him solicitous,' Christopher
said.

Eric laughed, a rich young laugh that made several people
around them look up and smile. 'You might as well say right out
that I was a selfish little prick,' he said.

'That's not how I would have put it.'

'Of course not. But that's what it would have amounted to.' Then
he turned back to Beatrice. 'I'm starving. Shall we go and pile in?'

'Yes, let's,' she said, with a smile at Christopher that may or may
not have been an invitation to join them.

'I'll keep my distance a while longer,' he said, surveying the
crowd around the table.

'You're too fastidious,' she said, taking Eric's arm. 'You'll lose
out on the oysters.'

119

'There won't be oysters,' Eric said. 'Not in May.'

'I'm happy to lose out on the oysters, whether they're there or not,' Christopher said.

'I told you you weren't the elbowing kind,' she said, moving off on Eric's arm. Like Titania and Oberon, Christopher thought, or perhaps Cleopatra and Antony.

CHAPTER 7

The afternoon unwound in a leisurely round of food, further introductions and more-or-less aimless exchanges about as many aspects of the apartment's interior as lent themselves to sociable small talk. Christopher was not bored, but he felt the strain of constant renegotiations: every introduction seemed to entail an obligatory resumé of his life, which could not but, he felt, strike a new acquaintance as inordinately meagre. At his age to have so little to show for his life – at home, where one's achievements are in general either taken for granted or assumed to be not discussible, it had not been so inescapably evident exactly how little that was.

Gazing out over the glittering Seine in the waning afternoon, he reflected that since he was last in Paris, nothing had happened to him. He had returned home from Cambridge with a first-class degree; though St John's had offered him a research fellowship on the strength of his results, a misguided impulse had suggested to him that his native land was the proper ground for the cultivation of his gifts. He had soon discovered, however, that there, his first class degree, instead of opening all doors to him, admitted him to a paucity of possibilities, the most pleasant of which seemed at the time to be a teaching post at his old school. It was, as schools went, a good school, and teaching there was undemanding, at times even inspiring – ultimately, taxing only in the toll it took of his youth, his enthusiasm, his love of his subject, his belief in the value of literature. More and more, latterly, as so-called outcomes-based education was inflicted upon him as on the rest of the system, he was made to feel that his subject mattered only insofar as it could be shown to contribute to some vaguely defined result, the holy grail of the *outcome*, which would in theory bring about social justice and prosperity. And more and more his pupils – or 'learners' as they were now called – questioned the value – they called it 'relevance' – of literature; and as they questioned, so he questioned the value of his own exertions. The outcome in this instance was that he left, to pursue a freelance career in editing, which he hoped would leave him freedom to take up again his own long-abandoned novel. He found, though, that to edit for a living was a full-time occupation, and he settled down resignedly to mulling over the outpourings of others, a task which, though hardly creative, did enable him to exercise to the hilt his rage for order.

What price order, he wondered as he gazed over the drifting company, listening to the polyglot chatterings, observing the flamboyance of gesture, the extravagance of expression, and the shifting kaleidoscope of colour, the hard glint of steel and silver, the soft sheen of velvet and silk, the brushing and swishing of texture against texture, the clatter or shuffle on the wooden floor of punitive heels or of soft leather soles. The clothes covered the whole gamut, from supremely elegant to stupendously outré, calculated to take one's categories – call them moral, call them aesthetic – by surprise, designed to conceal while they revealed and to reveal while they concealed. There was clothing that courted the grotesque and clothing that aspired to the sublime; Christopher had not realised that merely covering the human body could be such a multifarious business. Had Adam and Eve known, in covering their shame, what they were starting, they may have left their shames uncovered as the lesser of two evils. He felt oddly at peace in his own unassuming cotton suit that did not take issue at any point with the extravagant declarations of style surrounding him. He was invisible, which was what he wished to be: invisible, but far from insentient.

He smelled the drift of perfume from heated bodies in motion, the mingled odours of the food, the sharp clean tang of lemon, the decadent stench of raw fish wilting, the mellow warmth of melted butter – the first of the season's white asparagus, he'd heard somebody comment. Was it this, this extravaganza of colour, of sound, of smell, this convergence and divergence of purposes, this conglomeration of flesh and cloth in a beautiful space, that he had foregone in all those quiet years? But no, this would never have been his natural medium, even had he opted to stay in the world, even if the world had condescended to admit him: he could never have submitted to the crass externality of it all, the credo and ethos of a society dedicated to and defined by appearances. He looked about him, bemused anew at the contrast between the restrained, chaste elegance of this room and the vulgar display of the other.

'Mr Turner, you are very, how do you say – *pensieroso*?' Alessandra Giovanelli's alto sounded next to him.

'I am puzzled. This room is so different from the other.'

'But why does that puzzle you? They are two different rooms, no?'

'Yes, but looking at that room, I would have judged Zeevee's taste very differently from what this room suggests.'

'Ah, but *taste*!' She flared her huge nostrils. 'That is such an old-fashioned idea. That is what your grandmother had, it was something she got from her grandmother – and never changed. She has good taste, we say, or she has bad taste, like we say she has a big nose or a small bosom, just a fact. It is not interesting, taste.'

'But if not taste, what? This room is decorated according to *some-body's* taste, not so?'

She shook her head, sending sparkles into the air. 'No, no, not so. This room is decorated in a certain *style*. That is very different from taste. So it is decorated in a different style from the other, *si*, you are right. That room was Kelly Wearstler, this is Michael Smith, they are, how do you say, cheese and chalk? But taste – no, taste has nothing to do with it. *Le goût, c'est rien. Le style, c'est tout!*'

She looked around her as if afraid she would be overheard, then leant towards him. 'I will tell you a little secret. If people all had taste, as our grandmothers used to say, meaning *good* taste, they would not need me. Me, the designer, I create a new style that makes people feel that if they wear it they will look stylish. Not beautiful, not tasteful: *stylish*. They pay me to think up a style for them. They no longer have good taste or bad taste. In the world of fashion, there is no good or bad – except,' she added sotto voce, 'where you have bad design, as in the case of the gentleman now approaching us. You will excuse me, I have used up all my funds of insincerity for this afternoon,' and she shimmered and clattered off, leaving him exposed to the approach of Gloriani, who to Christopher's surprise did seem intent on addressing him.

'I am Giancarlo Gloriani,' he said, extending a blue-veined hand.

'I am pleased to meet you. I am Christopher Turner.'

'So I have been informed,' Gloriani said. 'And you are from South Africa, Zeevee tells me?' He spoke a carefully modulated, only very slightly accented English.

'Yes, I am. I am only visiting for … well, for a while.'

'We must hope it will be for a long while.'

'I will stay for as long as I can.'

'Ah, no doubt you have responsibilities at home too. What is it that you do?'

'I work for myself. I'm an editor.'

'What is it that you edit?' Gloriani's questions were not the less irksome to Christopher for seeming perfectly sincere, though it was in fact unthinkable that the man could really be interested in what on earth Christopher edited.

He shrugged. 'Really anything that anybody's written: novels, articles, reports – lots of reports.'

Gloriani nodded sympathetically. 'Ah, I can imagine. And not always very fascinating, no?'

'No, not always very fascinating.'

'And you are a friend of Eric de Villiers, no?'

'Yes, I am. I'm a friend of his father's really.'

'Ah, you must tell me about Eric's father.'

'What is that you would like to know about him?'

'Anything. What kind of man is he?'

'He is a good friend of mine, so I find it difficult to describe him with any objectivity. He is taller than Eric, lean …'

'No. No, I mean morally, intellectually, spiritually, what is he like?'

For a moment Christopher thought of saying, well, he's intellectually quite sound but I wouldn't answer for his morality or his spirituality, but, given the extreme earnestness with which Gloriani was regarding him, he tried to come up with something worthy of his attention. 'He is very different from Eric,' was the best he could manage.

'How, different?' he insisted.

'As different as you'd expect from a fairly large age difference,' Christopher said, perhaps a bit impatiently, not convinced that Gloriani was entitled to interrogate him. Then he relented. 'Daniel is rather a quiet man. He doesn't say very much.'

'Ah. That is different indeed. Eric talks, talks, talks, always delightfully.'

This was a new light on Eric de Villiers for Christopher. It was difficult to tell whether Gloriani's gravity was natural or whether it masked a subtly ironic take on Eric, and possibly on Christopher himself. 'In fact,' he said, 'you may know Eric better than I do. I haven't seen him for three years, and I get the impression that he's changed very much in that time.'

'He has changed since I have known him. Eric was at first a little,' Gloriani paused, 'irresponsible, perhaps.'

'Yes, irresponsible is what I would have called him,' Christopher said.

'And not very interesting, at first. Irresponsibility,' Gloriani shrugged expressively, 'is interesting only to the person irresponsible. Now *responsibility* –'

'Is interesting to the person responsible?'

Gloriani laughed, a contained yet exuberant chant of pleasure. It would not have shamed Monteverdi. 'Ah, my dear sir, what is it that you know about our young man?'

Christopher thought that he knew less than ever about our young man. 'I don't really know,' he confessed, with a consciousness of appearing rather lame under the sharp scrutiny of his interlocutor.

But Gloriani seized upon his reply as if it were a choice bon mot. He laughed again his attractive laugh – impossible that he could not have known it was attractive – and said, 'You don't know what you know? That would have been the most abysmal ignorance if it hadn't been the subtlest of strategies. How can anybody find out what you know if you don't know yourself?'

And with a last effusion of his laugh he twirled around, his restless energy seemingly seeking a new focus.

Christopher was once again on his own, leaning against one of the silk-covered walls, then bethinking himself: silk-covered walls are probably not designed to be leant against. He was still nursing a drink somebody had long since poured him. This was not a company in which to get drunk, though every other excess, he seemed to gather, would be countenanced.

He looked around for Eric and Beatrice. He had not forgotten that it was on this young man's account that he was just where he was; and it occurred to him that if it was a matter of making up his mind about Eric and his associates, he was no closer than he'd been when he arrived, though not for a lack of impressions. Indeed, it was precisely because of a kind of overload of impressions that he felt his bafflement increased rather than alleviated by his afternoon's experience. That Eric was moving in brilliant company was evident; it was less clear what the company was brilliant *at*, and, more pertinently, how much light their brilliance shed on Eric himself. That he was an accepted member, or at least a licensed visitor to the company, was clear; and yet Christopher could not rid himself of the impression that there was in their attitude to the young South African a guardedness, an ambivalence – not quite a distrust, but an uncertainty in the face of what they seemed to regard as an unknown quantity. This, in a company that in general struck Christopher as recognising few limits to their own insights and judgements, was odd indeed; but then again, what business was it of Christopher Turner's, that Zeevee's guests were less than sure of Eric de Villiers's qualities? Christopher Turner's business was to get Eric de Villiers back to South Africa, where he belonged.

As if divining these reflections, the subject thereof appeared in the generous doorway leading to further rooms at the back of the house; he was in conversation with Beatrice du Plessis, but something about the angle of his head, the tilt of his shoulders,

126

suggested that his attention was not undivided. A moment later, this impression was reinforced when his face registered – not relief, not joy, but the clear recognition of an anticipated presence. Christopher, out of his line of vision, was free to turn to see who it was that thus affected him; and in the doorway, recently arrived, it seemed, was Xolani. He stood there in all the arrogance of his splendour, his long lean frame draped in an overcoat that would have been unseasonable in the mild May afternoon had it not been made of the lightest fabric, a pale taupe that complemented to perfection the rich brown skin and the lustrous black eyes.

Xolani was looking about him with the bored air of somebody who couldn't see anybody who particularly interested him. Catching Christopher's eyes on him he inclined his head slowly, mock-ceremoniously.

Then, unobtrusively, Zeevee appeared from behind Xolani. He took him by the arm – that is, Christopher could see his huge hand circling the other man's upper arm in a grip that seemed more prehensile than affectionate. He said something in Xolani's ears that caused the latter's eyebrows to rise sharply; but the next moment Xolani had again relaxed into a languor, his reply apparently prompting Zeevee to release his grip and walk away.

In the meantime Eric had left Beatrice's side and was making his way, through the groups of people, to Xolani; and Beatrice herself was coming towards Christopher. He would have been interested to watch the interaction between Eric and Xolani, but Beatrice was now before him, addressing him with the expectancy of her regard. Then she said, 'I shall have to leave shortly; but I don't want to do so before I've secured your promise that you'll come to see me soon.'

'I'd like that very much,' Christopher said.

'I shall phone you, or ask Eric to get hold of you. Do you have a number?'

'The Hotel du Carrefour, on the Rue St André des Arts.'

'Ah, that's easy. I'll ring you there. I want you to meet my daughter Jeanne.'

'I'm sure that would be a privilege.'

'It will be, for her. She has met too few South Africans of the right sort.'

'And what is the right sort?' He asked this jocularly, but she gave the question her earnest attention, making him wonder again if she were deficient in humour.

'I think,' she said at length, 'the right sort loves Paris without wanting to stay here.'

He laughed. 'Then you are the wrong sort?'

'Oh, definitely.'

'And I may be too. I am not at all sure that I love Paris.'

'That is because you are not so superficial as to make that decision after a week. But you will love Paris before you leave.'

'And yet then leave?'

'Yes, I think you will leave,' she said, still with her mild earnestness. 'Eventually. But here comes Eric to tell me we must leave. He is concerned about Jeanne. I tell him she is perfectly capable of looking after herself. But' – and she lowered her voice – 'to tell you the truth, I'm very happy that Jeanne has such a watchful guardian.'

The unlikely guardian had by now come across to them. If his encounter with Xolani had ruffled his composure, it did not show on his smooth young face or from the collected way in which took his leave. 'We must get together very soon,' he said to Christopher. He took out a slim leather wallet and extracted a card. 'Give me a ring tomorrow, if that suits you, and we'll arrange something.'

'I'm also going to arrange something with Christopher,' Beatrice said. 'I want him to meet Jeanne.'

'Oh, he must definitely meet Jeanne. But we'll have a male bonding session before then.'

The two went off, the glittering reflection from the river so lighting up the young man's fairness and so vividly etching the woman's exquisite lines that they seemed transfigured, of another essence from the guests lingering in the beautiful room. Christopher glanced at the oblong card he still held in his hand, like some talisman. Off-white, it bore on its matt surface the embossed inscription, Eric de Villiers, and a telephone number, but no address.

Was this because Eric was in fact of no fixed address? And yet, the phone number was a landline. Somewhat mystified, Christopher put the card in his pocket and looked around for Zeevee. Although there were still quite a few guests remaining, he felt that he had done enough and seen enough for one day.

But apparently that was not for him to decide. As he turned around, he found himself entangled in a coil of brightly coloured scarves. The exuberant Rimbaud had changed direction abruptly on his way out of the room, managing to wind his leash round Christopher legs; the Dobermann was now gazing rather foolishly at his owner, who was standing nearby.

'Oh, I do beg your pardon,' Simon Cleaver said. 'I've not been able to train him not to do that. It's most inconvenient.'

'Think nothing of it,' said Christopher. 'I feel quite festive, wrapped in these scarves. Like a maypole.'

'Or something wrapped by Christo,' the dog's owner grimaced. 'Except Rimbaud lacks the artistic touch.' He had a humorously lugubrious air, emphasised by a slight lisp. 'We shall have to dis-entangle you. Now, if you don't mind my passing the leash around you – just so – and again – voilà! You have been freed from your silken trammels.'

Some bystanders were commenting animatedly on the pro-ceedings, and Christopher felt thoroughly exposed; and yet, he felt, there were worse social situations to be caught in than being wrapped in silk by a black Dobermann.

'There!' said Rimbaud's owner. For the first time, he looked into Christopher's eyes and smiled. He was almost shockingly good-looking: his eyes were dark to blackness, set deeply and framed by exquisitely arched eyebrows. The nose was not small, but formed as if by a sculptor, the nostrils so delicate that they seemed more decorative than functional. The complexion, though roughened by a day's growth of stubble, was like unblemished velvet. The mouth with its full lips was frankly sensual, but with an austere set to it, softened now by a smile, which revealed, without overt display, a formidable set of teeth. Looking at such perfection, it was difficult to credit the extravagant aspersions cast by Zelda; and yet, weren't those aspersions premised exactly on the value of such beauty as a negotiable commodity? Poor Zeevee, Christopher thought: not possessing beauty of his own, he has opted to surround himself with it, perhaps even to pay for the privilege of being surrounded by it.

Christopher may have gazed a moment too long; the object of his ruminations was regarding him with a quizzical smile. He recovered himself and said, 'Thank you,' for want of anything else to say: what, after all, is the proper response to being disentwined from a Dobermann?

'Oh, we must thank *you*,' the man replied. 'For being so patient. Rimbaud, thank the man.'

Rimbaud, who by now was sitting, wagged his stump of a tail so vigorously that it produced a little drum roll on the wooden floorboards. He looked up at Christopher with a kind of bright intelligence not unlike that of his owner; indeed, in general, his allure was so consonant with that of Simon Cleaver, his glossy black coat and dark almond eyes complementing so well the colouring of his owner, that it seemed likely the dog had been selected as a fashion accessory.

'There you go,' said Cleaver, 'that means thank you.'

'You're welcome,' said Christopher to Rimbaud, aware that this was probably not the correct form of address to a dog.

'Come, Rimbaud,' said his owner, 'we've held up this gentleman for long enough.' And with another glimmer of his unexpectedly warm smile, he led Rimbaud through the thinning crowd.

Sandra Giovanelli rustled up again. 'Ah! You were talking to the sublime Simone! Is Simone not as beautiful as the angel Gabriel?'

'He is very good-looking, certainly,' Christopher replied.

'Good-looking?' she asked. 'Do you mean he looks like a good person?'

'No, I mean he is … handsome.'

'Ah, you English! What is *handsome*? It is what a horse or a sofa is, no? It has no spirituality, no music, no,' – she agitated her taloned hands searching for the missing quality – 'no *pain*! But Simone – his beauty has pain, it is dark and deep as death. My brother Paolo, he worshipped him; it was he who gave him Rimbaud, as a, how do you say, *cucciolo*?'

'Puppy?' Christopher suggested.

'Yes, puppy, and he gave him the scarves too. They were the last things Paolo designed before he died.' Her extravagant features set for a moment in an expression of epic grief; then she shrugged her huge shoulders and insisted, 'But we – we are alive, we must live, not so?' She waved at Christopher and undulated purposefully across the floor towards the table, where there were still a few stragglers finishing the remains of the spread.

Christopher could not see Zeevee, and assumed that he was in the front room, bidding farewell to his departing guests. But the front room was almost empty, except for some people engaged in desultory farewells by the front door. From another room, however, the one from which Zeevee and Zelda had originally appeared, there was the sound of voices, and thinking that there might be a third public room which he had overlooked, Christopher moved over to an interleading door that stood ajar.

It led into another small drawing-room, decorated in yet another style as eclectic as it was difficult to identify. There were only two people in the room, Zeevee and Xolani. They were standing with their backs to the door, and Xolani was saying, 'I cannot see how you can dictate the terms.'

Zeevee replied, 'I'm not dictating the terms, I'm asking you to let him go.'

'So that *you* can have him?'

'No, so that he can be free to decide for himself.'

Christopher considered it best not to draw attention to himself and to retreat as quietly as possible. He could always phone the following day, and make his excuses. Whatever Zeevee was negotiating or trying to negotiate with Xolani, it was probably not something he would want interrupted. And he, Christopher, had accumulated enough impressions to deal with in one day.

CHAPTER 8

Returning to his hotel room, Christopher would have preferred to take to his bed with a book, something straightforward and un-Parisian, but his inconvenient conscience could no longer convince itself that it was in Daniel's interest not to be informed of his impressions thus far. The problem was that his impressions were as unformed and contradictory as ever – indeed, rather more so after his bewildering exposure to the array of Zeevee's guests. And then, was he obliged to give Daniel a full account of his own impressions, if those didn't concern Eric directly? Except that, since Zeevee had been introduced to him as Eric's friend, all Zeevee's associates were presumably also Eric's, and therefore part of Christopher's brief? He told himself, or tried to tell himself, that he had been given no brief, that Daniel's instructions were as taciturn as most of Daniel's communications – 'Go and find out what the boy is about and bring him back,' was about as explicit as he got.

Well, what the boy was *about* was turning out to be more difficult to determine than Daniel could have foreseen. Or Christopher, for that matter. Somehow, finding out what Eric was about seemed also to entail what he himself was about. But that, precisely, was what Daniel would not be interested in hearing.

Perhaps, after all, writing to Daniel might force him to order his welter of impressions into a coherent account; even if it left Daniel little the wiser, it might help him, Christopher, achieve some much-needed clarity, an overview of a situation that he felt he was too close to for any coherent perspective. So he duly sat down at his laptop and addressed himself to the blank screen.

My dear Daniel, he wrote, conscious of the fact that Daniel would probably find the appellation overly intimate:

I realise that you must be impatient for news of Eric. I've waited this long because I've judged that you'd rather have a substantial report than dribs and drabs amounting to very little. You must decide whether this constitutes a substantial report or just a conglomeration (puddle?) of dribs and drabs, after all. It is, at any rate, what I have been able to ascertain.

Eric is back in Paris. He came to see me on his first day – I gather that he's been to London, I would assume to see Marie-Louise, though he did not in fact tell me that. He struck me as vastly improved, both in appearance and in manner. I realise that this may not be what you want to hear, in that it has been your (our) belief that the boy has somehow been led astray by the wiles of Paris. On the other hand, I should think it would be a relief to you to hear that he seems to be thriving. To which you will reply yes, but on what? to which I must as yet confess ignorance. He has no visible means of support, but then, Paris is not Franschhoek, where one comes with a label, as it were, and a certificate of authenticity. He may well have a perfectly respectable source of income; I must confess that I have not yet felt free to ask him to his face. He moves, at any rate, in very comfortable circles, from what I've seen – mainly in the fashion industry, where he seems to have many contacts. He has a young American friend, a man who seems to me the soul of responsibility and even respectability. He is also on a very friendly footing with one Beatrice du Plessis, a South African as it happens, who was, I am told, a 'supermodel' a few years back. You may know the name; you are more in touch with the great world than I am. I have met her and she is very lovely; also, as far as I could tell, a gentle soul. She has a young daughter on whom she dotes and over whom Eric seems to extend a paternal hand. So, really, there is little evidence of the riotous living that we imagined your son to be indulging in. Of course, as yet there is little evidence of any kind, but I am giving you what there is.

And no, I've not had a chance to put your proposition to Eric. Apart from our first, relatively brief, meeting, I've seen him only once, at a fairly large gathering today where there was no occasion for confidential talk. I do, though, now have a phone number for him, and a promise that we'll meet soon. He seems quite prepared, even eager, to see me again. So I hope soon to be able to send you a fuller account.

Christopher hesitated a moment before hitting 'send'. He realised that there was much in his letter that might irritate Daniel – the implication, for instance, that Paris had done for Eric in three years what Daniel had not managed in twenty, that is, to civilise him. And then, he could see that a father might be less cavalier about the sources of his son's income than Christopher pretended to be. It was perfectly true that he had found Eric immensely improved, but he was starting to see, or see again, that producing impressions was what Paris was best at. The trick was to see past the impression – assuming, always, that there *was* something beyond the impression. If Christopher's letter left Daniel unenlightened – well, after all, he could not shed light where he himself was in the dark.

On Monday morning at ten o' clock, which he judged to be a civilised hour, Christopher phoned the number Eric had given him. The phone rang for a while, and he was on the point of deciding that Eric was out, when the phone was picked up.

'*Oui?*' said a sleepy-sounding voice.

'Eric? Did I wake you up?'

'No, no … who is this?'

'Christopher. Look, I'm sorry …'

'No, that's fine, I'm still a bit groggy, late night last night, but I was getting up anyway. What's the time?'

'Ten o' clock.'

'Oh god, where did the night go? What's up, then?'

'I was hoping we could arrange to meet somewhere – you know, we spoke yesterday about getting together.'

'Yes, of course, of course, I remember.' Eric was gradually regaining his genial social manner. 'Let's do that. When did you have in mind?'

'Some time today? My day is wide open.'

'Mm. I think my day may not be that open. Just a minute.' There was a rummaging and a paging at the other end. 'No, afraid the day is chockablock, starting in just over an hour, so I'll have to move my arse. But tomorrow seems more promising.'

'Fine, any time will suit me.'

'Good man. Listen, I must go for my morning run tomorrow, I missed yesterday and I'm going to miss today, so why don't we meet after my run?'

'That's fine. Where and when?'

'I run in the Luxembourg Gardens – you know where they are?'

'Of course.'

'Then why don't we meet at that fountain – the Medici fountain – at eleven? If you don't mind me being a bit sweaty.'

'No, I think I can handle that,' said Christopher, amused at such a qualm from someone he remembered as pretty much permanently sweaty.

Christopher spent the day catching up arrears of editing – he hadn't factored in whole days spent lunching when he'd drawn up his schedule. The biography of the politician seemed more tedious than ever, the shabby aspirations and shallow successes of its subject less worthy of commemoration, the recollections of his associates less worth recollecting, his fall from grace less tragic and more ignominious. But the comfort of editing, which is of a piece with its tedium, is that one does not take responsibility for anything other than the correct arrangement and punctuation of the material. It imposes some sort of order without requiring or even allowing a moral judgement. Just at present, that came as a relief to Christopher. So he worked away steadily, eradicating dangling participles, inserting semi-colons where sentences had been joined with commas, rearranging paragraphs and even chapters in an attempt to lend some shape and consequence to the baggy account of an inglorious life. Having failed in all else, the politician would at least have had a good editor.

That evening, meeting as arranged at Le Départ, Christopher and Martha decided that the weather had turned too chilly for the terrace outside, even with the aid of the gas heaters flaring away in the evening air, and they sought the noisy warmth of the interior – no longer the smoke-filled cavern that Christopher remembered from a less puritanical time, but still, with its fug of coffee, liquor, human breath and body odour, hardly the modern ideal of air-conditioned spaciousness. And, as always, the din, not of amplified muzak, but of two hundred people articulating exquisitely at the same time.

The café was full, and to get to two vacant chairs they had to squeeze past several clusters of intent *discutants*. Christopher wondered impatiently as he dodged the energetic gesticulation of one such declaimer why everything should be a matter of passionate *emphasis* in Paris.

'There we are,' Martha said, as they sidled to their chairs. 'The fight for love and glory is as nothing to the tussle of finding a seat in a crowded café.'

'You wonder, don't you – don't these people have homes to go to?'

'Oh yes, they have, but that's for much later. The Parisians sleep at home – generally – and get dressed at home – invariably – and if they have children they store them at home, but for the rest, they far prefer the streets. Apart from anything else, their dogs have more room in the streets to perform their various functions. '

She lifted a finger in that expert manner that Parisian waiters respond to promptly – Christopher had tried it and failed – and ordered two glasses of wine.

'But you have something to tell me?' she asked.

He demurred. 'I'm not sure that I do. I may simply have increased my befuddlement.'

She laughed, but with a slight strain of impatience. 'Oh come, Christopher, in the end it was just a group of people, not a mystical experience. You did at least discover the identities of the *people*? In short, you are in a position to tell me who was there?'

'Oh yes – that is, most of them, or some of them, or enough of them. What I can't tell you is how they all relate to one another.'

'That's no great cause for despair; it's a condition of social living here, to be aware of more relations than you have the key to,'

Martha declared. Besides, you do have the key: they were all there because they all know Zeevee.'

'So Zeevee is the key?' This was a new light on Zeevee.

'Well, obviously, in one sense: he was the one who invited them all there. But it is quite possible that his guests may have designs of which he in his innocence has no inkling.'

'Zeevee is innocent?'

She hesitated as the waiter placed their wine in front of them. 'As innocent as it is possible to be in this place and in his situation.'

'And this qualified innocence is taken advantage of by his associates?'

'I'm not saying it is. If you tell me who was there I could hazard a guess as to their relation to Zeevee.'

He lifted his glass at her and took a sip of wine. 'Where do I start? I seem to remember mainly somebody called Zelda and someone called Sandra Giovanelli.'

'Yes, friends of Zeevee, both. Zelda is not as vacuous as she pretends to be and Sandra is not as worldly-wise as she pretends to be. They would both do anything for Zeevee, and he would do anything for them.'

'Then they, at least, would not take advantage of Zeevee?' He felt himself suddenly oddly protective of the ugly young man.

'That does not follow. Loyalty may still avail itself of advantages, and Zeevee … well, he has advantages.'

'Such as?'

'Such as that he is just immensely, fabulously rich. Or did you think ground-floor apartments on the Île St Louis were rent-controlled?'

'No, I noticed, of course, that there was money; I just didn't realise it was quite as plentiful as you seem to imply.'

'Oh, think of a number and multiply by millions.'

'I assume he didn't make these millions doing make-up?'

'No, indeed. You remember that he mentioned his origins in Houston, Texas.'

'I do indeed.'

'You must know that people don't live in Houston for its

natural beauty; they live there because that is where they make their money. And Zeevee's father, Zachariah V Bigler I, made piles and piles of it.'

'Oil?'

'Indirectly. He's a plastic surgeon who made a fortune out of rendering the wives of the oil barons fit for their illustrious place in society. And he invested shrewdly in property in downtown Houston.'

'So the dreaded Galleria is, in a manner of speaking, paying for Zeevee's apartment on the Île St Louis?'

'You could say that. And for everything, or should I say everybody, who comes with the apartment.'

'And what does Zeevee get out of it? I mean out of the apartment and everybody who comes with it?'

'Who knows? Perhaps the illusion that he is liked and admired.'

'Need it be an illusion?'

She considered. 'No, I grant you, it needn't be. Zeevee has enough about him to like and admire without his apartment; but it's an open question how many people would have discovered that if he'd been just ... well, just an ugly American.'

'And yet, you say, Zelda and Sandra are loyal to him.'

'Oh yes, if one didn't have loyalty one would be lost.'

'Lost? How?'

'Well, that world they move in, call it the world of vain appearances, can be ruthless: human beings are commodities and are traded as such; everybody who can be used is used, and anybody who can't be used is discarded. Without some loyal allies, one could be very vulnerable.' She paused. 'And even one's loyal allies, as I've said, have their price.'

He thought this over; loyalty, by her account, was not the uncomplicated social contract he'd imagined it. Then, inconsequently, he said, 'And then there was Beatrice du Plessis.'

Martha looked at him quizzically. 'I've been waiting for you to mention her and wondering why you didn't.'

'Well, now that I have mentioned her you can tell me why you've been waiting for me to mention her.'

'Simply because she's clearly an agent in the fate of your young man.'

'Zeevee?'

She laughed. 'No, I didn't realise that you'd appropriated Zeevee as well. I mean of course Eric de Villiers.'

'Of course. But how do you know she is an agent in his fate?'

'I don't *know* anything. But they are constantly seen together. And to look like that – I mean to be really as beautiful as Beatrice, is to constitute a fate.'

'Her own?'

'Certainly. But also that of susceptible young men in whom she takes an interest.'

'How do we know she takes an interest in Eric?'

She fixed him with her gaze, almost a glare in its intensity. 'Christopher Turner, are you playing games with me?'

He tried to assume an air of outraged innocence. 'Would I play games with you? *Could* I play games with you?'

'A few days ago I wouldn't have said you would or you could, but now I'm not so sure. I think you know more about Beatrice du Plessis than you're letting on.'

'Well,' he relented, 'it's true that I was hoping to get information from you before tendering the little I have.'

'You have, in short, learnt the Parisian trick of bartering. Nothing is given for nothing, and everyone hopes to profit by the exchange.'

'I'm pleased to hear that I'm acting in accordance with some general principle. I thought I was just blundering along, trying to make my way in this hall of mirrors.'

'Even a hall of mirrors has its general principles. It distorts, but it can only distort what is there. But now that I've rumbled your little subterfuge, you can tell me what it is that you know about Beatrice du Plessis.'

'I'm not sure that I *know* anything. But it has been suggested to me as a possibility that Eric de Villiers is planning to or is about to marry her.'

She raised her eyebrows. 'Oh? And how reliable is your source?'

'You will be a better judge of that than I. My source is your friend

Zeevee, though I gather that his information is not first hand, so it is only as good as his source, I suppose.'

'Zeevee's information is as good as Zeevee's discretion, which is excellent. He wouldn't pass on information that he suspected to be unsound.'

'Assuming then that the information is good, what do you make of its drift?'

'I make of it what *you* make of it,' she said obliquely.

'And I make of it what Daniel makes of it.'

'Have you told him, then?'

'Heavens, no. I mean I make of it what I *think* he will make of it.'

'And what is that?'

'Well, I think he will make the best of it. I can't imagine that a thirty-something mother of a young daughter is what he had in mind for his son, but Beatrice is after all not your average thirty-something. I think Daniel will appreciate her qualities.'

'As you clearly do. What qualities do you have in mind?'

Her question seemed innocent, but proved difficult to answer. 'Now you ask me that, I'm rather at a loss for a reply.'

'Is it possible that she *has* no qualities – apart of course from her beauty, which may have dazzled you into imagining all sorts of other qualities?'

'I suppose it's possible, and until I've come up with a list of qualities unconnected with her beauty, you may have to take it for that.'

'So that her qualities may have been generated by the activity of your prodigious imagination?'

'I don't know if my imagination has done anything except go round and round like a guinea-pig on a treadmill. But where, would you say, does Beatrice du Plessis fit in, in the rather frightening world that you have described?'

'Oh, I think she's frightened. But she, too, has Zeevee as a protector; she really in a sense made him, when it was in her power to make people. For even with money, lots of money, you need some entrée in Paris; and Beatrice, as the face of the century, could provide that. She still has some power of her own, in that she has influence over the older designers like Gloriani, and she is respected as a kind of éminence grise. But she made some mistakes in her youth, and there are those who will not allow her to forget them.'

'What kind of mistakes?'

'Youthful mistakes, the kind we all make, only in her case the consequences were more severe.'

'My dear Martha, you are being very elusive.'

'Am I? Well, yes, I suppose I don't want to prejudge too many things for you. I want you to make up your own mind first. Only, I seem to guess that you *have* made up your mind to like Beatrice du Plessis.'

'Like?' He paused a second. 'Yes – yes, decidedly.'

'Why do you say that so undecidedly?'

'I'm not quite sure why I liked her as much as I did, for there wasn't, you know, all that much of her to like.'

'There is never very much of her. But what there *is* …'

'Exactly. What there is, is breathtaking.'

'Oh, she is one of the beauties of the century – that is, of the last century. But you needn't meet her to know that. And in any case, do you always *like* what is beautiful?'

'No, but such beauty with such an unassuming manner is rare. And then, I must admit, I was touched that she seemed to like me. Why should she, after all, bother even to talk to a middle-aged South African man of no importance?'

'There *is* always the possibility that she liked you for yourself. On a more cynical hypothesis, you might after all be important to her through your connection with Eric de Villiers.'

'It is so little of a connection.'

'Do you call it a little connection? You are his father's best friend, and you are here to persuade him to leave Paris, which inevitably means leaving Beatrice du Plessis.'

'But she doesn't know that.'

'Don't count on that. Information doesn't come in a shrink-wrapped package, hermetically sealed until opened by the ad-dressee. It disperses like a vapour and lodges in the most unlikely places.'

'But how? I haven't told anybody but you. And of course Zeevee.'

'And I haven't told anybody. And Zeevee, as I have said, is discreet to a fault. But it's not impossible that word has made its way from South Africa to France along, well, along any number of channels. I'm not saying that it has, mind; I'm just saying that Beatrice, and for that matter and by that token, Eric, may not be as unaware of the reasons for your presence here as you assume.'

'So that I must reckon with that possibility in my dealings with them?'

'It may be as well to bear it in mind.'

'But what *about* Eric?'

'What about him?'

'What about him and Beatrice? What is, well, the basis of their relationship?'

She lifted an ironical eyebrow. 'Haven't we assumed that it is of benefit to him?'

Well, he could match her irony, he always could. 'Oh, whatever else it is, it is bound to be that.'

'I mean of moral benefit to him. It has done him good.'

'Do you mean it has *made* him good?'

'That I can't answer for. I haven't even spoken to him. But you have. Did he seem *good* to you?'

'Now you're mocking me. The question of goodness hardly arose. But he was, as I've said, extremely civil, even solicitous.'

'Solicitous of what?'

'Well, of my comfort and well-being, and of Beatrice's comfort and well-being, and of Jeanne's safety.'

'A kind of all-purpose major-domo, in short.'

'You are rather dry.'

'You must remember that I haven't experienced at first hand the powerful charms of Eric de Villiers. But I trust your rendering of them. It accords with what I've heard elsewhere.' She hesitated for a moment over her wine, which gave, for Christopher, more point to what she proceeded to say. 'Still,' she said, 'don't make up your mind just yet about Eric de Villiers. Wait.'

'Wait? For what?'

'Till you've seen all round him. You've seen only the facets that have been held to the light for your inspection.'

'You think he has hidden facets?'

'I'm not saying he has. But he would be singularly uninteresting if he didn't.'

'Uninteresting is exactly what he used to be.'

'But isn't it exactly your contention that he has changed beyond recognition?'

He groaned. 'Goodness knows what my contention is!'

CHAPTER 9

The next morning dawned cold and wet, and Christopher considered phoning Eric to change their venue to somewhere less exposed, but by nine o' clock the rain had stopped, and it seemed likely that with no more than ordinary luck they might have a relatively dry, if not a particularly warm, meeting. Leaving the hotel at ten-thirty, he took along an umbrella and, mindful of wet chairs, a small towel – one of his own, which he had brought along in case the hotel towels should, as in his youth, prove inadequate.

The Luxembourg Gardens, which in Christopher's memory always had a rather dusty and gravelly aspect, its pleasures very public and physical, now, under the sheen of wetness, seemed less like an exercise area and more like a private retreat. This impression was at its most compelling under the trees next to the Medici fountain, from which the rain had driven the normal complement of entwined lovers and engrossed readers. Only Ottin's two swooning lovers lingered on, reclining in smooth unconscious marble next to the water, with Polyphemus and his fatal rock louring over them.

The last time he had examined this little triangular group, all those years ago, he had been aided, as in his exploration of the rest of Paris, by the tersely informative Michelin Green Guide, and he had duly noted the features pointed out by that august publication. He'd had an appetite, then, for the dryly informative; he'd indulged in an orgy of instructive visiting. It was one way of pretending to himself that he was gaining something from the Parisian holiday that he had imagined spending with Daniel in more congenial if less educational pursuits. But Daniel was spending the same holiday, which somehow no longer was their holiday, with Marie-Louise, emerging unbreakfasted at ten o' clock and making only the feeblest of pretences at wishing to join forces for an assault upon the sights of the city.

So Christopher had ventured forth on his own; and now, waiting for the offspring of that invidious union, he remembered sitting here, early on a July morning in 1979, engrossed in the voluptuous surrender of Galatea, and the delicate, almost inquisitive tilt of Acis's head over his compliant mistress, and then noticing, almost with a shock, the uncouth bronze Polyphemus, lifting his great left hand in horror at his discovery of the lovers. Contemplating the blissfully oblivious lovers and their lurking Nemesis, Christopher had reflected that the ugly one-eyed giant's urge to crush his effete rival with a rock seemed, if not excusable, then at least understandable. Only, he would have aimed the rock at Galatea rather than Acis.

Christopher's reflections were interrupted by the breathless arrival of Eric de Villiers, glowing, indeed apparently steaming, with the exertion of his run. He was wearing running shorts and a sleeveless singlet, with a fleece-lined top tied round his waist. He stopped in front of Christopher without saying a word, catching his breath, then did a few quick stretches. He had lost weight since leaving home, and gained definition; the long limbs were limber, and the sculpted shoulders tapered down to narrow hips. He had lost, too, the deep bronze that at home seemed to last through summer and winter; his skin, lambent with its light layer of sweat, now had the smooth pallor of marble.

Christopher, aware of staring, busied himself drying two chairs.

'Can I borrow that when you've done?' Eric asked. 'I'm sopping.'

'I'm sorry,' Christopher said, 'I should have thought of that. It's all wet now.'

'No sweat. I'm sure it'll get me dry. Thanks.'

He took the towel, dried his face and arms, then put on his fleecy top. 'There,' he said, 'snug as a bug.' He did another stretch, then sat down on one of the chairs. 'Good spot, eh?' he said. 'I always come here to cool down after my run.'

Christopher sat down next to him. 'Yes, it is a good place to cool down, I should think.' But in fact he felt even here the pressure of the aesthetic, the evasion of the moral: lust and envy elevated to the condition of art. And, next to him, the feckless son of his best friend, by an accident of bone and sinew aspiring to the realm of the aesthetic, claiming a place next to the achievements of an earlier age.

'So?' Eric asked. He was leaning forward, his elbows on his knees, and glancing back at Christopher, his face a study in alert expectation. 'You had something to say to me?'

'Yes. Yes, very much so. You might even say that that's why I'm here.'

'Here ...? In the garden?'

'Yes, but also here in Paris. I've been charged with a message.'

The young man was now looking ahead of him, ostensibly at a water lily floating on the surface of the pond. 'I think I can guess that the message is from my father.'

'It is, indeed.'

'And the gist of it, roughly, is that I should come home or else.'

'Roughly, yes.'

'Then Dad could have spared you the trouble of coming here, and issued his orders to me direct, by email or whatever.'

'You forget that you weren't replying to emails or whatever.'

'Yes. I suppose that was quite shabby of me.'

'It was inconsiderate, certainly. Your father was very concerned about your whereabouts.' Christopher heard himself, and cringed at his droning moralism.

Eric did not look round, though a slight shrug of the shoulders seemed to dispose of his father's concern. Nevertheless, his tone had nothing dismissive about it when he said, 'I *couldn't* write to Dad to tell him my whereabouts. I didn't *know* my own whereabouts.'

'You didn't know ...?'

'In a manner of speaking. I didn't know where I was and what I was about. How could I write *that* to Dad?'

'Your father may have preferred a frank declaration of befuddlement to a complete silence.'

'Yes, but don't you see, I was in no state to consider Dad's preferences.'

'You must have been in quite a state,' Christopher permitted himself to remark.

But his companion did not take up the invitation to elaborate. He said instead, 'But you're not here to talk about my omissions and commissions. You were telling me why you are here.'

'*My* commissions, you mean?' Christopher smiled. 'Well, the reason for my presence is that your father thought that I, as a relative outsider, could more dispassionately, as it were, put to you his proposition.'

Eric remained looking in front of him, the merest tightening in his neck signalling a quickened interest. But his voice betrayed no particular perturbation. 'A proposition? Not an order or a threat?'

'A proposition. Even a peace offering, if you will.'

'Hell, is Dad mellowing with old age, or what?'

'I think he realises that orders and threats are not likely to have much of an effect.'

'Then he really is mellowing. But what's his proposition?'

'In the first place, of course, that you return home.'

'That bit I guessed. But it still sounds like an order.'

'Yes. But he is offering, in return, greater independence than you had in the past.'

'That wouldn't be difficult.'

'No, but he intends the terms to be generous.'

'Is that a general intention, or is it itemised?'

'Oh, there are items. Your father has given it much thought.'

'Have you memorised the items, or do they come in a separate document?' The young man's tone, though light, was not flippant, and Christopher guessed that he was at least interested.

'I can tell you the main items. But there is in fact a document of sorts.'

Eric nodded, still staring ahead of him at the water lily. 'Okay, tell me, then, what the main items are.'

'In the first place, your father thought you might find living in the house with him a constraint.'

'You might as well say that he might find living with me a constraint.'

'I don't think that's what he does mean, but either way, then, he or you or both of you might find relief from too close proximity if you moved, he suggests, to the slave quarters.'

Eric's laugh rang out so loudly that a bird that had settled on a nearby rose bush flapped away in alarm. 'The slave quarters? Does Dad have no sense of irony?'

'It did occur to him, yes, that the designation is unfortunate. But then, the designation can be changed.'

'It would take more than a change of designation to make the slave quarters habitable.'

'Your father proposes renovating the quarters to your specifications – within reason, of course.'

'My specifications as specified by him?'

Christopher smiled. 'Well, your specifications as moderated by him. But there is room for negotiation on all his proposals.'

'I can certainly see that there's room on that one.'

'Yes. Then he proposes paying you a salary, rather than the allowance he's given you up to now.'

'Is that also just a change of designation?'

'No, I think you'll find that it's a handsome salary.'

'Handsome is as handsome does. What does he call handsome?'

'That's also open to negotiation, but he's proposing forty thousand rand a month as a starting salary. Plus a bonus when a vintage is declared.'

'And what will I have to do to earn this salary?'

'You'd have to learn everything your father and his foreman know about wine farming; and you'd have to learn it by practical experience.'

'Working on the farm, in other words.'

'Yes. If you prefer, he'll send you to an agricultural college for a course in viticulture, but that too is –'

'Negotiable.'

'Negotiable. He doesn't want you to see the farm merely as a centre of sport and recreation.'

'As I've always done,' Eric proposed, without rancour.

'Well, yes, rather. But nor does he want it to be a kind of Siberian penal colony. You will of course be free to come and go as you please.'

'Subject to his moderation.'

'He intends to be very tolerant on that score.'

Eric laughed again. 'I'll note the intention. And is that it?'

'No, there's one more item. Your father proposes to settle a considerable sum of money on you if you get married.'

Eric looked back at Christopher as if to gauge whether he was serious. 'I won't ask what the considerable sum is, but I will ask: why?'

'Your father thinks marriage is a stabilising institution.'

Again the young laughter rang out. 'I hope that's Dad's term and not yours – a stabilising institution! It sounds like a rehab clinic.'

'I think the way he put it was that it would help to settle you.'

'Does he have in mind any particular aid to settlement?'

Christopher hesitated. 'He has his preferences, but they are not absolute.'

'Preferences? You mean he has in mind more than one?'

'No, I think one will do.'

'And that *one* is …?'

'I think he's hoping that it will turn out to be Elmarie Krige.'

At this, Eric, who by now was leaning forward, apparently engrossed in the behaviour of two birds on the railing in front of him, turned his head to face Christopher.

'Tell me,' he said, with unexpected seriousness, 'you who have seen something of how I live here and the people I live with, can you really picture me spending the rest of my life with Elmarie Krige?'

Christopher hesitated. This was the first time the young man had challenged him to a judgement on his Paris life, but more than this, he was asking him to assess it against his potential life in South Africa. Christopher was fond of Elmarie Krige – she was as vigorous and candid as any of the horses she rode with the ease of habit – but her qualities, admirable as they were, seemed unlikely to attach for long a restless spirit such as Eric's. At length, Christopher answered him, 'Frankly, no, I can't really picture that. But then, your father hasn't seen how you live here, and it's his ideas that we're discussing.'

'But aren't you a sort of spokesman for his ideas? Isn't that why you're here?'

Christopher winced. He didn't need reminding why he was here. 'Yes,' he conceded, 'which is why I'm putting to you what his ideas are. But can't you see that, by your logic, what I think of your circumstances here is irrelevant to my function?'

'Okay then, I'm not speaking to you in terms of your function. I'm speaking to you as a friend, and asking you whether *you* can see me living happily ever after with Elmarie Krige?'

'Ever after is more than anybody can answer for,' said Christopher, conscious of being evasive. 'But you mustn't assume that Elmarie Krige today is the same as she was three years ago, any more than you are.'

'I'm sure she has developed. But she's hardly likely to have developed in the same direction as me.'

'True. But I return to my original contention that your father has no more than a *preference*. It's certainly not a condition that you should marry Elmarie.'

'The difference between Dad's preferences and his conditions wasn't always clear.'

'He's aware of that, and has really, I think I can honestly say, made up his mind to meet you more than halfway. Elmarie Krige is certainly not a precondition,' he repeated.

Inconsistently, the young man said, 'Poor Elmarie. She was a good sort.'

'Oh, I don't really think she's languishing at home,' Christopher said, as a corrective to what struck him as a touch of condescension on Eric's part.

'Of course not,' Eric said promptly. 'I just mean that it seems a bit callous to discuss her as if she were a mere term in a contract.'

'Yes, well, but my point is exactly that she's not.'

'But even without Elmarie, what Dad wants is pretty radical,

150

don't you think?'

'It is radical, yes, in that of course it requires your leaving your present way of life. In another sense, it's not radical at all, in that it requires no more than that you return to what is after all a pretty comfortable destiny.'

'But you, you've seen what you call my present way of life. I'm sure you recognise that it has its own claims on me.'

This was the closest either of them had come to mentioning Beatrice du Plessis, though Christopher guessed that she had been as much on Eric's mind as on his – how could she not be, if Zeevee's information contained even a grain of truth? He was disappointed that Eric had not of his own accord introduced her name, but that, too, may have been an instance of delicacy on his part: after all, it was not for him to publicise what might be a private understanding.

'I think I do recognise that, yes; but are those claims necessarily incompatible with your father's proposals?'

Eric was silent for a while; then he sighed lightly and said, 'I wish I knew. To be honest, I'm not all that clear myself on what those claims are compatible with. I'm not even quite sure what they *are*.'

Christopher had an old-fashioned sense that obligations made themselves known to you if you stared at them hard enough, but forbore to say so, saying instead, 'Well, it's not a decision you need make here and now.'

Eric got up from his chair. 'I think I'm seizing up,' he said, flexing his shoulders and bending to do some leg stretches. 'We must talk again soon.'

Christopher got up. 'How soon?' he asked.

Eric looked at him. 'As soon as I've made out more clearly where I am.' His smile, direct, frank, made up for what could have been seen as evasiveness in his reply. 'I promise you I'll be giving it some thought. And I'll tell you more about my Paris life.'

The rain had stopped some time before and the sun was breaking through the dense foliage above them, fitfully illuminating the placid fountain and its little tableau of passion and jealousy. The recumbent lovers were in shade; but Polyphemus, crouching over them, was in full sun.

'Beatrice said something about having you over soon,' Eric said, mopping his face and passing the towel to Christopher. 'We'll be in touch.'

'I look forward to that,' Christopher said, as the two men walked towards the ornate exit gate of the garden and the roar of the Parisian morning.

CHAPTER 10

That evening, tired of the interminable biography, and of mulling over his conversation with Eric in the Gardens, Christopher crossed the river to the Marais. The sky had cleared, and the evening was luminous, the river glistening, the buildings just starting to light up for the night.

He walked slowly, not quite aimlessly, but with only a general sense of destination. He wanted to be among people yet not with people – a common enough condition in Paris, as in most cities. What Christopher wanted, though, was not just the presence of other people, but the curious kind of proximity, even intimacy, that some quarters of Paris could still give one, a sense of people conducting their lives in public and not caring who saw them at it.

He felt his way, as it were, along the narrow streets of the Marais, testing them for just the right combination of conviviality and privacy, a place where he could observe without being conspicuous. When at length he found the right place, he was not surprised that it turned out to be L'Étoile Manquante, where he and Martha had first met Zeevee. A table cleared in the sought-after front row, and he quickly claimed one of the two chairs nominally allotted to the little table, feeling an ignoble satisfaction as two young women, fractionally too late, expressed their disappointment in loud Afrikaans.

'*Ag kak!*' said the one, Oh crap, secure in her illusion of unintelligibility. '*Nou't daai poephol ons tafel gegryp!*', now that arsehole's grabbed our table.

'*Ag kom,*' said the other, older one, Oh, come on, '*Ons sou dit ook maar gegryp het as ons eerste was,*' we'd also have grabbed it if we were there first.

'*Ja, maar daar's net een van hom en daar's twee van ons,*' yes, but there's only one of him and there's two of us, said the younger, more bellicose one.

Christopher was amused, torn between blowing his cover and waiting to hear what else they would say. But as they seemed about to proceed down the street in search of a table, he thought it opportune to suggest that next time they'd have to be quicker, '*Jammer, juffrouens, maar volgende keer moet julle vinniger spring.*'

Taken aback, the women took a moment to register his words; then they exploded in embarrassed giggles.

'*Haai, ekskuus, oom,*' one apologised. '*Ek het nie geweet oom is Afrikaans nie',* I didn't know you were Afrikaans.

'*Ek is nie,*' he replied, I'm not, '*maar ek weet wat 'n poephol is,*' but I do know what an arsehole is.

'*Haai, oom , ek het dit nie so bedoel nie,*' said the one, hey, uncle, I really didn't mean it like that, and the two, still giggling, made their way down the bustling street. They looked like any other young tourists: healthy as puppies, gormless and guileless in their hideously coloured Crocs, the one dumpy, the other thin as a breadstick, both dressed in jeans that hung too low and tops that rode too high, exposing midriffs that nature had not intended for public exhibition, toting gaudy canvas bags and clutching water bottles. Christopher was put in mind of Eric's question that morning, whether he could see him living happily ever after with Elmarie Krige. Looking at his two young compatriots, Christopher had to grant Eric's point: after the knowing sophistication of Paris, the naive spontaneity of the home-grown product would be like custard after caviar. And then, again, both Eric and Beatrice were home-grown products; sophistication, after all, was not a matter of genetics or fate. Being altogether a question of social behaviour, it could be acquired relatively quickly – unlike, he wryly thought, morality, which somehow had a more obscure provenance and a slower maturation.

The table next to him had been vacated and was immediately claimed by new occupants. Christopher was aware of more than the usual scuffle attendant upon the business of manoeuvring oneself bodily into a space designed essentially for conversation and the consumption of beverages. Two men were wedging themselves into place, with some bumping against his table, and he grabbed his glass of wine to save it.

'*Ah, excusez-moi, monsieur,*' said the bumper. '*C'est mon chien, vous voyez.*'

The next moment the dog implicated in the apology appeared next to Christopher's table, waggling its stumpy tail as if expecting to be commended for some deed of derring-do. It was trailing a banderol of brilliantly coloured scarves – the rambunctious Rimbaud, then, Christopher guessed before glancing up at the dog's owner to confirm his assumption. It was indeed Simon Cleaver, his smile of polite apology setting into something akin to perplexity as he seemed to scan his memory for Christopher's identity. Then he visibly got it – 'Ah yes,' he said, 'the gentleman from South Africa. Mr ...'

'Christopher Turner.'

'Yes, of course. The friend of our beautiful Eric.'

This last sentence was directed at the person with him rather than at Christopher. The two men had taken their seats, the other man on the far side of Simon, and Christopher could see little of him other than a bare forearm sporting a thin silver bracelet. But Simon's words must have awoken his interest, for he now leant forward and peered at Christopher, nodding his head in acknowledgement of what could be taken as an introduction.

'This is Fabrice,' Simon said, 'and I am Simon Cleaver.'

Christopher nodded too, not thinking handshakes were required or, under the circumstances, practicable. Nor did he think it necessary to acknowledge that he knew Cleaver's name.

'It is right?' Fabrice asked. 'You are a friend of Eric de Villiers?' His accent was light, his enunciation careful but fluent. He pronounced the surname in the South African manner. His head was shaven, gleaming in the evening light, the skin stretched tightly over the well-formed skull. His eyes were almost unnaturally blue, as if chemically tinted. The mouth and chin were emphatic, not allowing for compromise or concession. He was wearing a dark-blue shirt that accentuated the colour of his eyes; the sleeves were very short, revealing a pair of strong arms. He was compact, powerful, direct. Next to the languid elegance of his companion, he seemed like a bull terrier warily flanking a Borzoi – alert, suspicious. His head, too, had something of the brutal bluntness of a bull terrier, the lashless eyes fractionally too small for the face.

'Yes, I am a friend of his father's,' Christopher said. 'Do you know him well?'

'Eric?' His smile was a superficial grimace. 'Yes, I think I know him well enough.'

'Well enough for what?' Christopher permitted himself to ask.

Fabrice laughed, a mirthless staccato exhalation. 'Well enough for my purposes,' he said, his tone not inviting further enquiry.

'You must excuse Fabrice,' his companion said. 'He is constitutionally secretive. If you asked him the time he'd fob you off with an equivocation.'

'Fob you off? Please, what does that mean?' Fabrice demanded.

'It means … what *does* it mean?' Simon turned to Christopher with a disarming air of helplessness. 'You must never ask me what the words mean that I use. I use them because they sound right.'

'Ah, you English,' Fabrice growled. 'Your language is so insipid, you have to invent words you do not know the meaning of.' Then he addressed himself to Christopher with exaggerated politeness. 'I am very pleased to have made your acquaintance,' he said, his words clearly intended as a termination. He said something to Simon in rapid French and the two men launched into an animated discussion that Christopher could not have followed, even if he had made the effort to eavesdrop. He sat back in his chair with his wine, gently pulling at the ear that Rimbaud seemed to be offering for attention, and reflecting that not all Eric's acquaintances were equally prepossessing.

There was something about Fabrice that nagged at Christopher's consciousness, a sense that he had met him before somewhere, although, glancing surreptitiously at the profile, he could not recollect any of the features. Then the Frenchman's pronunciation of De Villiers came to mind, an anomaly that triggered a memory of the brusque voice on the phone when he had tried to contact Eric. Straining his ears now to catch the sound of the man's voice – precise, flinty – Christopher persuaded himself that the voice at the other end of the line, and thus in some sense cohabiting with Eric, had been Fabrice. In that case, his knowing Eric 'well enough' would seem to mean knowing him well enough to share, or to have shared, a house or apartment with him. This was a thought to bring a worried frown to Christopher's brow as he sat idly crumpling Rimbaud's ear. It made him feel how shallowly he had yet plumbed his young friend's life in Paris.

He got up, braving Rimbaud's reproachful gaze, and nodded at the two men, who, deep in conversation, returned the most perfunctory of greetings.

At the Carrefour, a message lay next to his key: 'M. Turner, Pls phone Mme du Plessis at this number, if possible this evening.'

He took the slip upstairs and dialled the number. The phone was answered with such promptness that he was almost caught unawares.

'*Allô?*' The second syllable was extended into an unassertive, languid interrogative.

'Hello, is that Beatrice?' Christopher asked.

'No, this is Jeanne.' The voice modulated into a colourless statement of fact; the universal teenaged indifference to the adult world and its affairs.

'This is Christopher Turner. I was asked to phone your mother. Is she available?'

'One moment, please.' The voice, Christopher decided, was not sullen, simply disengaged.

He could hear unhurried footsteps retreating – Beatrice's apartment obviously had wooden floors – and a voice calling, without much urgency, like some functionary announcing the arrival of the three-fifty-five from Peterborough: '*Maman! Téléphone! Monsieur Tourneur!*'

'*J'arrive!*' sounded from a distance, suggesting that the apartment was sizeable, an impression reinforced by the length of time it took Beatrice du Plessis to reach the phone.

'Hello,' she said, her voice making up in warmth for her daughter's signal lack of that quality. 'Thanks for calling back.'

'No problem. I've just come in …'

'Yes, I phoned only about twenty minutes ago. I wanted to ask – can you come to supper tomorrow?'

'Tomorrow – that's Wednesday. Yes, I can't imagine that I've got anything on. Thank you, I'd like that.'

'Good. Come at about six, so we can sit on the balcony. The evenings are so lovely at the moment.'

'I'll do that. But how do I get to get your place?'

'Oh, of course, you don't know it. I'm close to you, actually. Rue de Bellechasse no 43. I'm apartment twelve, on the second floor.'

'I'm sure I'll find it.'

'I'm sure you will. Oh, and the code for the gate is 6D23.'

'Thanks, I've made a note of that.'

'Good.'

There was a momentary lull, neither of them knowing whether to terminate the conversation, and how. Christopher had just resolved on the simple 'Well, see you tomorrow, then', when Beatrice said, 'Eric will be here too.'

'Will he? Good – though I'd assumed that, in fact.'

'Yes, yes of course.' She evidently wanted to say something more, but was hesitating to do so. 'I want to tell you that I am pleased, for Eric's sake, that you are here.'

This admitted of a variety of interpretations: did she mean, for instance, that she was less pleased for her own sake? But all Christopher said was, 'I wonder if Eric is also pleased.'

'Oh, Eric,' she said, not quite minimising his importance, but somehow implying, perhaps, that he didn't know his own mind. 'I wish you could …'

Christopher waited; but she checked herself, and he could hear a quick exchange, and then she said in her normal, unemphatic way, 'I'm sorry, I'm going to have to hang up. We have a teenager waiting for the phone. Her mobile was stolen on the metro today, so her life is on hold.'

She said this with such gravity, as if not attempting an

extravagance or a pleasantry, that, under the spell of her earnestness, Christopher felt almost rebuked. 'Well, we must not chatter then. I'll see you tomorrow.'

'That would be delightful,' she said, almost, he thought, as if he'd been the one to suggest the meeting.

CHAPTER 11

Christopher left early for his dinner engagement on Rue de Bellechasse: apart from his chronic fear of being late, he enjoyed the crowded, narrow streets of what he was starting to regard as his *quartier* at this hour, when the pace of life seemed to slow down, the cafés starting to fill up with people intent on nothing more taxing than a *coupe* or a glass of wine, the pedestrians serenely impervious to the frustration of motorists who had unwisely ventured into the medieval labyrinth, the tourists starting to abate, making their footsore way to tour buses parked in a less frequented corner of Paris, relieved that the day's sightseeing was over, looking forward to the bland dinner in their budget hotel at the other end of Paris. So, at any rate, Christopher interpreted the look of exhaustion leavened by hope on the faces of the shuffling hordes, briskly shouldered aside by purposeful Parisians on their way to assignations or perhaps only untidy studio apartments. A young woman pushing a stroller was eating a gargantuan sandwich, her swaddled infant blinking up at her with the dim incomprehension of a young animal in the face of sensory overload. Thus, perhaps, were Parisians conditioned: by early exposure to a complex reality. The mother, meanwhile, seemed oblivious to the bits of tomato she shed as she alternated bites of the sandwich with grimaces at her solemnly gazing baby. A smartly-dressed middle-aged man walking behind her, his attention on the display of charcuterie in the shop window next to him, slipped on a slice of tomato, momentarily lost his balance, then regained his footing. He lifted an elegant shoe and examined the smooth leather sole, disfigured by the splotch of squashed vegetable matter. His face registered fastidious disgust, and he looked around for a place to scrape his sole;

but then he shrugged lightly and tittuped on his way, none the less briskly for his tomato-plastered shoe. Christopher smiled to himself, trying to fashion the little incident into a metaphor or parable of city life, but gave up the attempt: all it really exemplified was the need to watch one's step in Paris.

At two minutes past six he stood in front of the entrance to 43 Rue de Bellechasse. The building was grand in a rather austere manner, the windows onto the street shuttered and uncommunicative. But the little door in the gateway clicked open to reveal a courtyard of some magnificence, cobbled in the centre, but bordered with an extravagant display of flowers, all with that recently manicured look that Parisian parks so miraculously sustain. The effect of contained exuberance was reinforced by the building itself, which here, secluded from the public eye, relaxed into something like whimsy: the wrought-iron balconies were supported by stone satyrs in various poses of abandonment, apparently uninhibited by their load-bearing function.

There were various doorways, flanked by discreet wooden plaques listing the apartments on each staircase. Number 12 was on the central staircase, which it shared with only one other apartment. Christopher climbed the imposing stone stairway to the second floor – there was a lift, but he preferred the solid elegance of the stairs to the makeshift flimsiness of the relatively modern contraption – and there pressed the bell next to the door on the landing.

It was opened by a woman *d'un certain âge*, conservatively dressed in a black skirt and white blouse. She could have been a secretary or a housekeeper; it was difficult to tell.

'You must be Monsieur Turner,' she said, in lightly accented English. 'Please come this way. Madame du Plessis will be with you in a moment.' There was something in her manner that suggested controlled agitation; but who was to say what pressures a secretary-housekeeper in an all-female household had to contend with? She led the way down a passage, her low heels clacking on the herringbone parquet. Opening a double door, she stood back. 'Please,' she gestured. 'If you take a chair, I shall inform Madame that you have arrived.'

Christopher stepped into a large, light room with several French doors opening onto a balcony at the far end. Beyond the balcony there appeared to be a garden: from where he was standing, Christopher could see the tops of trees. He proceeded into the room, and more of the garden came into view; it was almost park-like in extent, a wooded enclave in the centre of the bustling city. The room itself was restful, a quiet composition of ecru and brown, the only darker accent being a woven rug in burgundy and dark blue. The room, like the park beyond it, had an air of cultivated tranquillity about it.

Quick footsteps sounded on the parquet flooring. Beatrice du Plessis appeared; the placidity that had marked her on their previous meeting was less in evidence than the effort to appear calm and collected. She was evidently in a state of high tension: the ivory pallor of her cheeks was overlaid with a flush, and the hand she extended to Christopher felt cold and almost clammy.

'Oh, Mr Turner – Christopher – I'm so pleased to see you. Please have a seat.' She gestured vaguely towards a sofa, but as she made no attempt to sit down herself, he remained standing too.

'Eric will be here in a second. He's just making a phone call.' Her distraction was so severe that Christopher felt no qualm in asking, 'Is anything the matter?'

She looked at him for a moment, her mind elsewhere. Then she collected herself, and said 'The matter? No … that is … well, yes, why shouldn't I tell you? Yes, there is something the matter. Jeanne – my daughter Jeanne – has … well, she has been doing some modelling, and now she's gone off on a shoot to Florence.'

Christopher looked at her in incomprehension. Why was her going off to Florence any more of an event than any other modelling assignment? But she was looking at him as if he should understand the catastrophic nature of this event.

'Why … why is that a cause for concern?' he asked. 'Isn't that normal, in the modelling world?'

'You don't understand,' she said, with a hint of impatience. 'It's one thing for a seventeen-year-old girl to take part in a shoot here in Paris and come home at night and go to school the next day. It's quite another to go away for days to a foreign city with a whole crew of … well, irresponsible and unscrupulous adults. I know, I've been there myself. It's not … Besides, she's supposed to be at school, not travelling all over Europe. And she left without telling me, just left a message. I found it not half an hour ago when I went into her room. I think she deliberately left it there so that I'd only find it much later.' Her account was distracted, disjointed; she was literally wringing her hands. Christopher felt powerless to say anything; he felt he didn't understand the enormity of the situation. 'Oh, where *is* Eric?' she asked fretfully.

There were rapid footsteps outside, and Eric appeared in the doorway. 'Bloody hell,' he was saying, 'there are no flights tonight …' then stopped as he saw Christopher. 'Oh, hello, Christopher,' he said; he transferred a sheet of paper he was carrying to his left hand and shook Christopher's hand. 'Sorry, things are pretty hectic here at the moment.'

'I understand that. I think I should really rather leave you to sort out the complication.'

'Oh, I'm so sorry,' Beatrice said. 'I did so want to introduce you to Jeanne ... but now …'

'Of course, said Christopher. 'I'd better be on my way.'

'No, stick around, please,' said Eric. 'There's not a hell of a lot we can do now anyway, and we may need a level-headed adviser.'

'Yes, please, do stay a while,' said Beatrice, recovering something of her poise. 'If you don't mind us fretting and carrying on.'

Christopher felt strongly that he would rather not stay: there was, in spite of Eric's assurance, really no capacity in which he could be anything but, at best, an observer, at worst a distraction. But to insist on leaving would be another distraction, so he decided to stay, as inconspicuously as possible. He sat down on the chair closest to him, a strange design that looked like an open hand. It was surprisingly comfortable, but he couldn't help feeling the slightest bit ridiculous, perched on a hand that seemed to cherish him in a bizarre simulacrum of intimacy. The others, though, were too much occupied with their crisis to notice.

'There are no flights tonight to Florence,' Eric repeated.

'There aren't many flights to Florence at the best of times,' Beatrice said. 'How about Pisa?'

'Nope. Last plane is about to leave from Orly.'

'Trains?'

'Yes, there's an overnight at eight-thirty-three, getting there at eight tomorrow morning.'

'Would you …?' She was almost pleading.

'Of course. It's … what?' He glanced at his watch. 'Quarter past six now, I could easily make it.' He turned to Christopher. 'But that means I'd be abandoning you here.'

'Please,' said Beatrice, with a conscious effort to recall herself to her duties as hostess, 'you're not abandoning him, you're entrusting him to my care – though heaven knows what's happened to our supper in the meantime.'

'Unless ...' said Eric.

'Unless what?' Beatrice asked.

'Unless Christopher came along with me to Florence.'

'But does Christopher want to go to Florence?' she asked. Christopher had an odd sense of being the subject of a conversation he wasn't part of. Eric must have sensed this, for with a light laugh he turned and said, 'We'd better ask the man himself. How about it? When last were you in Florence? Though I can't promise a visit to the Uffizi; you'd really just be going along to keep me company.'

'I think it's been at least ten years. But … what about you?' Christopher said to Beatrice. 'Isn't it …?'

'You mean isn't it my duty to go and collect my own daughter? Yes, I'm sure it is, but my influence with my daughter …' she shrugged ruefully. 'Let's just say that my presence wouldn't necessarily persuade her to come back.'

'Whereas Eric's would?' Christopher took the liberty of asking.

She looked at the young man as if she expected him to answer, but he did not respond. 'Well,' she said, 'it might. Jeanne … respects Eric.'

'It's worth a try, I think,' Eric said, then turned to Christopher. 'How about it?'

Christopher was not in the habit of doing things on impulse; his instinct was always to want time to think things over. But suddenly, in the bright light of Eric's invitation, even in the midst of the general perplexity, it seemed natural to say, 'Well, why not?'

'Good man,' said Eric. 'But we'll have to lace up our boots and pack our sandwiches.' 'Don't you want to eat something before you leave?' Beatrice asked. 'Even if it's just some bread and cheese?'

'Thanks, but no,' said Eric. His fingers brushed Beatrice's cheek as he said, 'We can grab something at the station.'

'You're leaving from the Gare de Lyon?'

'I think so.'

'Oh, you must have a drink at the Train Bleu. It's so beautiful.'

'If we have time.' He turned to Christopher. 'We'll go by your hotel for you to pick up a toothbrush and a pair of socks.'

'And a passport.'

'Of course. Excuse me for a moment and I'll grab my own.'

'But do you know where to find Jeanne?' Beatrice asked.

'I know where they're staying. I phoned the agency.'

'Did you speak to Nathalie?'

'Yes; she was a bit reluctant to tell me, but I said I was phoning on your behalf.'

'Did she say what on earth she was thinking, booking Jeanne on this shoot? She *knows* …'

'No,' Eric said, 'I didn't really have time to go into all that. And after all, she's a booker, her job is to book her models. Anyway, I was only too grateful that she'd given me the information.'

'Yes, but she *knows* …'

'I know, it's a bummer. But I have to get going.'

He bustled off – though *bustled*, Christopher found leisure to reflect, imperfectly represented the young man's air of being in control of a fraught situation, like an exemplary sea captain overseeing the loading of the lifeboats.

'I'm sorry,' Beatrice said again. 'You must think I'm making a fuss about nothing.'

'No, indeed. I should think any parent would be concerned.'

'The thing is,' she seemed to feel the need to explain, 'it's not that

165

unusual for young girls of seventeen to go off on photo shoots, and Jeanne has done it before. But this particular one ...' she sighed. 'Well, let's just say I have a bad feeling about it. And the fact that Jeanne didn't tell me about it doesn't help. Of course, that may just be because she knew I'd object to her missing school. I want her to finish her Baccalauréat before she starts modelling full-time. But young people ... I remember, my parents were horrified when I left for Paris. To them it was Sodom and Gomorrah and Babylon rolled into one. And yet I've survived,' she gestured vaguely at the room, as if to adduce that as evidence, 'after a fashion.'

'You've survived beautifully,' Christopher said.

'Oh ... *beautifully,*' she said, as if that were a negligible achievement. 'In Paris beauty is a commodity like any other. I paid somebody to come in and arrange some sofas and chairs in a way that pleased me.'

Christopher was about to protest that he wasn't referring to the decor, when Eric appeared in the doorway. He had put on a jacket, something light and expensive-looking, and was carrying a small overnight case.

'Shall we go?' he said. 'It may take us a couple of minutes to find a taxi.'

'Yes, go,' said Beatrice. 'But wait – I have something I want you to take.' She went across to an antique bureau. There were writing materials on it, and a sealed grey envelope, which she took up and handed to Eric.

'There,' she said. 'Give that to Jeanne, but only as a last resort.'

'A last resort?' Eric asked.

'If she should refuse to come back.'

'You think a letter will achieve what your presence couldn't?'

'It may. It contains a fairly persuasive argument. Now go. Did you buy tickets online?'

'No, we'll get them at the station. There's enough time.'

He kissed Beatrice on both cheeks, lightly, no more expressively than if she were any established acquaintance. She seemed to want to say something, but checked herself, just trailing her hand along the sleeve of his jacket as he turned from her. She put out her hand to Christopher. 'I'm so sorry our supper has turned out like this. But we'll make it up to you when you get back.'

'I'll look forward to that,' he said, hardly knowing what he was saying. He was torn between genuine pity for her distraught state and, suddenly, a rush of excitement at the quickness of it all, at the fact that it was possible without forethought to get onto a train to Italy in pursuit of a runaway girl – it was so exactly the kind of thing he could imagine Eric de Villiers doing, and by the same token so exactly the kind of thing he could never have imagined Christopher Turner doing.

'Come,' said Eric, as they reached the street, and the door clicked shut behind them. 'We may have to walk to the Boulevard St Germain for a taxi. In fact,' he said, 'we may as well go past your hotel before we find a taxi. It would take a taxi an hour to negotiate the Rue St André.'

The two men walked back to the hotel, as briskly as the sidewalk traffic allowed. Christopher admired anew the skill with which his companion made his way through the intransigent human mass that clogged the sidewalks of the Latin Quarter at that hour: without physically touching anybody, he seemed to possess to an extraordinary degree the knack of imposing his presence, so that the hurrying multitude parted before him. It was all Christopher could do to keep up, his presence in Eric's wake apparently not possessing an equivalent power. When they reached the Hotel du Carrefour, Christopher ran upstairs (the lift, he reasoned, would take twice as long) and grabbed toiletries, a change of clothing and his passport. His laptop's carrying case was big enough to double as overnight bag, and in what he thought a commendably short while, he was downstairs again, where Eric was talking to Monsieur Marcel, who, once again unusually cordial, wished upon Christopher a bon voyage and various other unintelligible blessings. Christopher reciprocated as best he could, and the two men set off to find a taxi, barely twenty minutes after leaving Beatrice's apartment.

Luck was on their side. As they emerged from the Cours du Commerce onto the Boulevard, a taxi pulled up next to them to disgorge a passenger, an elderly lady who carefully examined each note she handed the driver as if to make sure it wasn't a thousand euros.

'Oh come *on*,' Christopher muttered under his breath. 'Are you going to take forever?'

Eric laughed as he said, 'Hey, it's only been twenty seconds or so.' He held open the door for the offending passenger; charmed, she said, *'Mais merci, monsieur,'* and tripped off.

'Are you always so charming to leisurely old ladies, or is it only to show up my churlishness?' asked Christopher as they settled back into the taxi.

'Oh, always, of course,' Eric laughed, and for the moment it was possible to believe him.

CHAPTER 12

As the taxi drew up at the station, the great clock in the tower was just showing seven-thirty.

'Good,' said Eric. 'We've got an hour.'

'*Dix-sept euros, s'il vous plaît,*' the driver said.

Eric reached for his wallet, opened it, then said, 'Oh, could I ask you to pay for the taxi? I'll have to draw money at the station.'

'Of course,' said Christopher, and reached into his pocket. He opened his wallet; he didn't have anything smaller than a hundred euro note. As he reached across to pay the man, he became aware of a presence next to his window: standing right next to it, very close to the car, was a young girl of thirteen or so, dusky, with a headscarf. She was staring at his wallet.

The taxi driver, too, noticed her, and opened his window. '*Allez!*' he shouted, waving his hand. '*Allez-vous-en!*'

She ignored him, just stood staring.

Christopher was uncomfortably aware of the roll of notes he had produced to pay the fare; uncomfortably aware, also, of the change the driver was giving him.

'*Donnez-moi la monnaie,*' the girl said, so close to the window that he could hear her through the glass, staring at the wallet Christopher was fumbling back into his pocket.

'Careful,' said Eric, 'she's taking note where you're putting it.'

The driver, opening his door, made a threatening gesture towards the girl, but she remained standing, unmoved and unafraid.

'I'll get out on your side,' Christopher said to Eric, wanting him to get out, impatient with himself for not daring to open the door in that impassive girlish face.

'Just hang onto your wallet,' Eric said, and got out. Christopher followed, and the next moment the girl was at his elbow.

'*La monnaie,*' she kept chanting, '*la monnaie.*' Then she added a new note. '*J'ai faim.*' Her eyes did not meet his, were fixed on the pocket where the wallet was. Christopher knew that she was calculating the chance of pouncing, of knocking him to the ground, grabbing the wallet and running. She was utterly unafraid of the threats of the taxi driver, who had by now walked to the passenger side of the vehicle. There was something feral about her, like a desperation-driven creature, in survival mode – a lynx, a cougar – trapped out of its element.

The girl was crowding him now, crooning her mantra '*La monnaie*' in a shrill whine. The technique was partly one of intimidation, partly a question of making her presence so unbearable that she would be paid to go away.

'*Va-t'en,*' Christopher said in her face, '*fous-moi la paix!*'

He had been told that this was the strongest discouragement one could offer a French person, but she hardly glanced at him. '*La monnaie, la monnaie,*' she keened.

'Come, let's go,' said Eric. 'Ignore her.' Then she was next to Christopher as he shouldered his case; he had an uncomfortable sense that she was not alone, that her reinforcements were closing in now that the taxi driver had got back into his vehicle. With his right hand holding his case – she might snatch it, thinking there was a laptop inside – he was helpless to ward her off should she physically tackle him, and he knew that she had the power and the courage to do it. Her face was delicate, her expression neutral; she did not seem to hate him: he was just a job she had to do. He noticed with a start how beautiful she was.

His helplessness translated into a blind fury and he yelled, straight into her face, 'Fuck off, you miserable little cunt!' But he was more shocked at the violence of his words than she was. She merely kept looking at him, unblinkingly, with a kind of stoical indifference. She must have been called every name under the sun in her wretched career as a juvenile mugger.

Then there was another, uniformed, presence, brandishing a kind of truncheon, shoving the girl out of the way, shouting something at her too rapidly for Christopher to follow. It was an official of some kind, perhaps a security guard posted precisely to deal with the teeming vultures of the Gare de Lyon, to protect passengers from the depredations of the scavenging natives.

The girl retreated, shouting abuse at the man, at Christopher, at Eric, at the whole cursed, privileged edifice of the Gare de Lyon and all it represented.

They entered the great forecourt of the station, Christopher too disconcerted to talk, Eric intent on finding the ticket office. 'We have an hour,' he said. 'Why don't you wait for me upstairs in the bar of the restaurant while I draw money and get the tickets?'

Christopher would have preferred to go along to buy the tickets, but he could sense that Eric thought he could do it more quickly on his own. 'Fine,' he said, 'but please take this for my ticket. Is it enough?' He held out a two hundred euro note.

'Oh, please,' Eric said. 'You're coming to keep me company. I'm paying.'

Christopher tried to protest, but Eric held up his hand. 'Please,' he said, 'no arguments. I'll meet you in the bar of the Train Bleu.' He pointed towards a staircase, 'Up there. It's called the Big Ben Bar. I think you need a drink.'

Christopher ascended the stairs. He had heard about Le Train Bleu, one of those self-perpetuating legends that Paris produces so prodigally; and entering the vast space, he could see that in this instance there was, if not substance, then at any rate plenty of gilt and glitter to the legend. The place looked more like some royal reception chamber than a station restaurant, even in spite of the expanse of white tablecloths boxed in by leather chairs and banquettes. The curlicued alcoves, the scenic murals like altarpieces, the gilded arches, the coffered vaults, the wood panelling, the great clear windows, the whole extravaganza conspired to overawe the traveller with its sheer excess. It was a secular temple, but it was difficult to say who or what the presiding deity was, in the absence of both God and king. Food, of course, as always in Paris, was part of the mix – the French would celebrate the Second Coming with a three-course dinner (à la carte, to discourage the Americans in

171

search of a prix fixe) – but here even food was subordinated to some larger Idea – the idea, perhaps, of travel, for the murals all depicted destinations of the now decommissioned Blue Train. But travel, for the Parisians, had always been something other people did; so this vast caravanserai, too, was perhaps intended to speed the foreign hordes on their way with a last flourish of brass and mirrors – at the price of such *monnaie* as remained to them after other onslaughts of the city upon their solvency.

Christopher was directed, after a swift professional scrutiny by a supercilious functionary in morning coat, to the Big Ben Bar to the left of the main restaurant. He found an empty seat – a capacious leather armchair in an alcove – grateful for this refuge from the unforeseen perils of travelling. He felt drained – not physically, although there had in fact been something breathless about the sequence of events since his arrival at the Rue de Bellechasse, but emotionally, by the ugly confrontation on the station forecourt. He felt violated, not by the young girl's assault – if it could even be called that – as much as by the vehemence of his own reaction. He had for a moment experienced a hatred as absolute as anything he had ever felt, which seemed to show him some truth about himself that he could neither fathom nor disregard. It was, for want of a better word, the sheer unexpectedness of it, this access of loathing for … what? In the long run, a defenceless young girl. But there was something in her assurance, in her contemptuous disregard of him and his puny proprieties, her strange imperviousness to shame, that made the whole of the Gare de Lyon, all the brazen frippery and gilded trumpery of the restaurant, seem tawdry and meretricious, calling into question all his certainties – such as they were. For in the end, that was what the Train Bleu was a temple to: the security of being included in an order that excluded others. It was designed so that people could come here and admire – and admire most of all the fact that they were there to admire it. He glanced at the *carte* on the little table in front of him and winced: for the price of a beer, he could have made the young girl's day.

The bar was full, and service was not of the promptness that, Christopher guessed, such a bar would normally pride itself on

172

maintaining. But it suited him to wait for Eric; there was something about the place that intimidated him, and made him feel the need of the young man's unwavering confidence.

He did not have to wait long. Eric came into the bar, his long strides only marginally checked by the crush of drinkers. Christopher raised a hand to attract his attention, but Eric had already spotted him. He came up to him, but didn't sit down.

'I had a bit of uphill,' he said. 'Damn nuisance. Have you ordered?'

'Not yet.'

'Good.'

'We haven't missed the train?'

'No. Not yet. But it's not leaving from this station.'

Christopher looked at his watch. It was a quarter to eight. He got up from his chair. 'Then we will miss it?'

'No, not necessarily. It leaves from the Gare de Bercy, which is really just across the street – well, down the street. And they did sell me the tickets. But let's get going.'

They hastened out of the bar, past the doorman, who now greeted them as graciously as if they had consumed a five-course meal and a bottle of vintage champagne.

'I don't know why I assumed the train leaves from here,' Eric said, as they crossed the forecourt to a side entrance, 'except that most of the trains to Italy do leave from here. It's just this one that's different. It's a special train, apparently. The Artesia, whatever that means.'

Special trains, Christopher knew, cost special prices. It occurred to him to wonder again at Eric's apparently untroubled relations with money, which in turn suggested untroubled relations with human beings possessed of money. Part of his, Christopher Turner's, brief was presumably to disrupt that harmonious and lucrative relation – instead of which, here he was, profiting by it, taking special trains to Italy at its expense. He was in it up to his ears, Eric's relation to his world, and he had no idea how he would explain it to Daniel and what Daniel would think of such poor explanation as he might offer. Then, as Eric shouted at him,

173

'Come, jump for it!' and they sprinted across the street in the face of an oncoming Citroën, its headlights flashing indignantly, and as he reached the other side of the street breathlessly laughing, it was as if he had arrived also on the other side of his dilemma: he needn't mind what Daniel thought, he realised with a heady sense of liberation. He was where he was because he wanted to be there, and rushing for the special night train to Florence with Eric was thrilling precisely because it was not part of Daniel de Villiers's brief for him.

It was just before eight when they entered the Gare de Bercy, a quieter affair altogether than the Gare de Lyon: a soulless modern structure, after the garish hullabaloo of its older neighbour. But to Christopher it was transfigured by his discovery, so late in the day, of his independence and of the use that might be made of it, if only one knew to grasp at it; the starkly pillared platforms seemed like so many corridors to destinations all the more fabulous for being unknown.

'There's a lounge somewhere,' Eric said, 'but we may as well find our compartment first. I got us a sleeper for two, if that's okay by you.'

'I'd have preferred a couchette for six, but I think I can make do with a compartment for two,' he said, and Eric grinned at him.

Even the train, sleekly waiting next to the platform like some powerful but docile sea creature, contributed to the sense of taking off, of disregarding consequences; throbbing quietly, it was an image of latent force, to be released at the proper moment in a smooth rush of controlled energy. They were shown to their designated compartment by an official whose sole function seemed to be to smooth their passage.

'Phew,' Eric said, as they sank into the leatherette seats. 'That was a rush. Are you feeling knackered?'

'Not really,' Christopher replied. 'Just a bit winded. And still, I think, a bit disconcerted.'

'Disconcerted? Oh, by the girl at the Gare de Lyon. You shouldn't let that upset you. They're at all the mainline stations. They're planted there by their parents.'

174

'Yes, but I think what really disconcerted me was my own response.'

'It was certainly expressive. I didn't realise you could use language like that.'

'Yes, but don't you see? – I never do use language like that. There was something completely disproportionate in my reaction.'

'Don't let it bother you. The city gets to you that way – puts you in touch with your inner wild animal.' He was sympathetic, he was supportive, but he didn't understand; so Christopher let the subject drop. But to his surprise, Eric took it up again.

'Isn't it maybe because it reminded you of South Africa? Being brought face to face with other people's poverty when you're doing something extravagant?'

'I don't know. It may be that. But I felt it as something more basic, a kind of revulsion at the girl's deliberate debasement of herself.'

'*Was* it debasement? I thought she managed to hold on to some … I don't want to call it dignity, but some kind of self-possession. She wasn't begging, she was *demanding*. Maybe that's what got to you?' Eric seemed oddly intent on getting to the source of Christopher's perturbation.

'I don't know,' Christopher said. 'Perhaps. I did feel threatened, challenged at some level. It was as if my notion of humanity was being confronted, exactly because she was so beautiful. It was as if such beauty had no right to demean itself like that.'

'Maybe it wasn't demeaning itself. Maybe it was just exercising its power.'

'You mean *I* was being demeaned?'

Eric seemed to be considering this, but before he could answer, there was a rattle at the door and a uniformed attendant appeared, to ask whether they'd be having dinner in the dining car.

'Yes, definitely,' Eric said. 'I'm starving, aren't you? Poor man, you were invited to supper at six!'

'Yes, I am hungry, I must admit.'

'*Deux couverts à vingt-et-une heure,*' the man said, and gave them a ticket. '*C'est juste à côté.*'

'You see,' said Eric after the man had left, 'that's one thing you

175

didn't mention, when we discussed my going home. I mean, what kind of country would I be returning to?'

'You should know. It hasn't changed that much while you've been away. The gradual degeneration of an august liberation movement into an undignified jostling at the trough – well, that was well on its way by the time you left. The government may be a bit more corrupt than before, the rich a little richer than when you left, the poor a little poorer.'

'Exactly. And I'm not sure that I want to return to a country that's so unequal that one part of the population is driven to prey on the other.'

'Of course, it's not reassuring to be preyed upon. But as for the inequality, that's hardly alleviated by your staying here.'

'No. But as you've just experienced for yourself, it's not pleasant to be forcibly confronted by it.'

Without any clanging of bells or shrilling of whistles, the train started moving, smoothly, almost soundlessly, rapidly picking up speed, transfiguring the drab purlieus of the station into a concatenation of glamorous light.

Christopher nodded. 'Yes. We prefer to get into our train and leave it behind.'

In truth, he felt he was leaving everything behind.

CHAPTER 13

Seated at their table for two in the restaurant car, the darkening French countryside blurring past, Christopher felt again a sense of release – from what exactly, he couldn't have said, but it was as if he was without antecedents or responsibilities, enclosed in this capsule hurtling through an alien landscape at hundreds of kilometres per hour. He seemed to have left all connection behind him; his only link with his past, and indeed his present life, was the young man seated opposite him holding up his wine glass to the light.

As he himself took a sip of the wine, which seemed to him excellent, he felt that one effect of their shared isolation, this sudden rupture with context and history, was that he could ask Eric anything, as if there were no impediment to a free exchange of confidences.

'You know,' Christopher said, 'I've never really understood how you came to be in Paris in the first place. I mean, weren't you supposed to be tilling the soil in Burgundy?'

Eric did not seem discomfited by the question; he smiled amiably and said, 'I was indeed, and let me tell you, I tilled like hell for a while.'

'How long a while?'

'Oh, six, seven months. Yes,' he said, glancing with comical self-deprecation at Christopher, 'I know, I know, not a very long time in the scheme of things, but when you're tilling the soil from, oh, six in the morning till six at night, it can seem like a bloody eternity. And it's not as if I was really learning anything. I was doing what at home we paid someone five hundred rand a week to do.'

'I suppose you could see it as healthy outdoor exercise.'

'Oh, it was that all right. I lost a lot of fat and put on a lot of muscle.'

'I noticed,' Christopher permitted himself to comment.

Eric grinned. 'Yes, it's an odd thing, but my spell in the country really did prepare me for my stay in the city. I mean, I would have had to spend several hours in the gym every day for the same result.'

The conversation was interrupted for a few moments while they made their selections from the menu; then, still with his luxurious sense that the speeding train constituted some privileged space, Christopher asked, 'So why did you leave?'

'Just plain boredom, I think. I mean, I *liked* Burgundy, I liked the people I was working with, the place was very beautiful – have you been to Burgundy?'

'No, I haven't.'

'Well, as I say, it's very beautiful, but it's beautiful as Franschhoek is beautiful, vineyards and old buildings, cows and oak trees, sort of *countrified* beautiful – in fact, it doesn't even have the Franschhoek mountains, so as far as that's concerned I was better off at home. And it was all so *tame*; even the cattle were somnolent, and the people were so slow, as if they had forever to cook their stews and ferment their grapes. And of course, they did have forever. The château where I worked has belonged to the same family for five hundred years, which is a great thing, I suppose, but I don't think they've had an original thought in all that time. I mean, they thought *tractors* were new-fangled, and Wellington boots were sissy.'

'So you came to Paris looking for something less … tame?'

'I didn't know what I was looking for. I just knew I had to get away from the château before I started gibbering or mooing.'

'Couldn't you tell your father this?'

'Have you ever tried telling Dad something he doesn't want to hear?'

'I suppose I have, yes.'

'Then you'll know that he goes into a mode of disengagement, if you know what I mean.'

'Yes, I think I do.'

'Yes. He simply disregards what you've said – or, in my case, written – and carries on as before. I mean, I wrote him something to the effect that I wanted to come home immediately. In his reply, which wasn't a reply at all, he didn't mention this, just said, when you come home at the end of the year, *as we agreed*.'

Christopher knew that his official duty was to defend his friend's position against his son's strictures, but he also knew it would be mere cant, and recognised as such by the young man. So he confined himself to a neutral question. 'So what did you do?'

'I literally ran off in the night like some rebellious apprentice. I'd been earning a modest wage, and Dad had been sending me a bit, and I'd spent very little of it, so I thought I could survive for a while in Paris.'

'Why Paris?'

'Why not? If you're in France, why go to some provincial dump when you can go to Paris? Anyway, I knew some people in Paris, friends from varsity who were working in the city and squatting in an apartment on the outskirts – Malakoff – and they said I could stay in their back room, which was really more of a broom cupboard, without windows or ventilation. It smelled of old shoes. Actually, that was good, because it forced me to get out and explore Paris. I walked everywhere and lived on bread and fruit. I think I know the city better than most Parisians now, not just the glamorous bits, but the parts where no one who doesn't actually have to *live* there ever goes. I mean, I know what it's like to be poor in Paris, and to look at all it has to offer from the other side of the divide. And you know, it was, I don't know, strangely *exciting*.'

'Poverty – exciting? Like that poor girl at the station?'

'Oh, not the poverty itself, that's just a very hard grind. But I mean, the feeling, the knowledge, that that world of privilege is vulnerable, is penetrable, that the divide isn't as absolute as they think, the people on the other side. And I kept thinking something was going to happen to me, I don't know what, but just something more … more *important* somehow, than inheriting a farm and settling down to being a local bigwig.'

179

'Some people might think inheriting Beau Regard is quite important enough.'

'Yes, I've seen those people, the people who come to the farm and drool all over Dad. Sorry, I don't mean you …'

'Be careful how you put the idea into my head.'

'No, truly, you know the people I mean. Look, I suppose it is a beautiful farm, I always loved it in my way, but … well, I mean, it was like that château in Burgundy, everybody carrying on about how old it was, but I was looking for … well, as I say, just something more *exceptional* somehow. And I thought I might find it in Paris. The place itself … well, it's beautiful obviously, but what appealed to me was the sense of a hidden life behind all those beautiful exteriors, behind those little doors in the gateways that you need a code to get into, those doors that click open to the people who know the code and then click shut behind them.' He was getting agitated, the effort, apparently, of expressing thoughts he'd never expressed to anyone before; then, glancing up and finding himself the object of Christopher's attentive gaze, he said, 'I'm sorry, I know this sounds fucked-up, but I wanted the code, the Open Sesame to that secret world behind the door. Sometimes I'd stand in front of one of those buildings, and see the people coming in and out, or I'd listen to the chatter, when the parties spilled out onto those wrought-iron balconies, and I'd say to myself *that's* what I want, to know the code and to go in and be one of those people, people who belong here as I belong on the farm in Franschhoek. And I noticed how they wore their clothes, how they moved about the streets and how they parked their cars illegally, all of Paris belonging to them. And I wanted to look like that and move like that and live like that. I didn't want to be rich so as to have fancy cars or phones, that's just bling and flash, but I fell in love with the clothes, the styles but also the fabrics, the silk and the linen and the leather, the colours and the textures …'

He stopped, embarrassed at his own effusion. Their first course had arrived, and he availed himself of this plausible interruption to his train of thought. But Christopher was reluctant to abandon Eric's outpouring. 'I wouldn't have thought that you'd be interested in clothes,' he said, to encourage Eric to continue. 'You used to wear old jeans and ragged T-shirts.'

'Hey, we've agreed that I used to be a dolt. Mind you, the jeans and T-shirt weren't the worst of the doltishness. But in Paris I became aware of clothes as ... I don't know, as a way of asserting yourself in public – no, asserting's not the right word, a way of *presenting* yourself, if you know what I mean. I suppose you think it's a very superficial way of presenting yourself, but then, I'm not saying you have a meaningful relationship with people you pass in the street.'

'But does one have *any* kind of relationship with people one passes in the street?' Christopher asked, and then was afraid that his question might just seem facetious.

But Eric took it for what it was, a serious question, and answered, 'Yes, I think you do. It's usually very fleeting, of course, but it all adds up to, well, an identity, a persona.'

'To an image, in short.'

Eric pondered this. 'I suppose so. Except it's reciprocal, which an image isn't. It's an awareness of oneself in relation to others.'

'An awareness of their awareness of you?'

'Yes. And almost anywhere else in the world, probably, there would be something sexual or even aggressive about it – I can't imagine it on the London tube, for instance – but in Paris it's just part of some social contract, that you look and are looked at.'

'And to be part of this social contract you have to dress the part?'

'Well, you have to *look* the part, and dressing is one way of looking. There are others, of course ...' He hesitated.

'Such as?'

Eric made a face. He was uncomfortable under Christopher's probing, but had now committed himself to his own account of himself. 'I guess it helps if you're good-looking,' he said, 'and I couldn't help noticing that some people seemed to find me worth looking at, in spite of my down-at-the-heel shoes and my frayed cuffs.'

'Some people?'

'Yes.' Again he visibly forced himself to continue. 'Women, you

181

know, older women. Some men. So in certain places I could feel that I had some legitimacy, that I was contributing my part to the social contract, because I was, well, worth looking at.'

'Certain places?'

'Hell, you *are* getting me to *préciser*, aren't you?' But if he was discomfited, he was not irritated, and he pressed on. 'Well, then, yes, certain places – the Marais, of course, where people go who like looking at people.' He paused for a moment, then plunged on. 'Look, I wasn't cruising or anything, I was just enjoying the sense of for once being admired simply for being young, in this city where my youth seemed to count for so little. Paris, in case you haven't noticed, worships age and experience the way Cape Town adores youth and energy. That's why the lady in the taxi could take her time counting her money this evening, knowing she was entitled to do so. Anyway, so I did from time to time, well, *gravitate* to the Marais, and when I had the money, I'd have a drink in one of the bars.'

Christopher said nothing, and Eric, after another pause, continued, 'And then, one evening, I was spoken to. Oh, I was spoken to quite often, but usually by people who backed off when they discovered I wasn't interested in being spoken to. But this guy didn't back off, he just kept asking me questions, in English, completely unfazed by my monosyllabic answers. After a whole lot of one-sided exchanges he said, You are new in Paris? I was pretty narked and said, Is it as obvious as that? Then he said, Not to everybody, maybe, but me – I have an *eye*. And you know what he did? He pointed at his eyes, which did have, you know, a kind of glitter to them, as if he could see beneath the surface of things. Then he said to me, You are too natural for a Parisian, you have not the air of being fatigued with the effort of being beautiful. I remember he said *fatigued*, because for the rest his English was very good, just now and again a direct translation from French.

'I didn't know whether he was having me on, but I didn't really mind. I thought I was in control of the situation, and he seemed quite an interesting guy, and I didn't think he was hitting on me in the usual sense; I mean, he was quite good-looking himself, and

182

couldn't have been hard-up for sexual partners, if that was what he wanted. So I said, What do you mean *natural*? Do you mean I look like a peasant? And he said, No, you are not heavy like a peasant, you do not have mud on your boots or straw in your hair. No, not a peasant. But not from Paris, no, from somewhere with much fresh air and healthy food and much sunshine.'

Eric had immersed himself in his impersonation of this new acquaintance, with such attention to the detail of the man's utterance that it was clear to Christopher that he relished recalling the encounter. As if to confirm this impression, he carried on: 'I was quite impressed with the guy's savvy, and also flattered, I suppose, at the attention. It was the first time I'd thought *not* being from Paris could be enviable, or at least *interesting*. I mean, up to then I'd just felt that I didn't belong, but now, suddenly, I could see myself as contributing somehow to the Parisian mix-and-match. So when the man offered me another drink, I accepted, and another, until I realised that I'd missed the last metro to Malakoff, and was facing a long and wet walk home. The liquor made it easier for me to accept the guy's offer to spend the night in his apartment,' Eric looked at his father's friend as if to gauge his reaction, 'and he made it clear that he had a spare room.'

'Not everybody would have believed him.'

'Are you implying that I was naive? Okay, maybe I was, but he did seem, I don't know, sexually indifferent to me, only interested in me as a kind of phenomenon. And, in case you were wondering, the night passed without incident. His flat was right there in the Marais, though a bit further up, on the rue Notre Dame de Nazareth – do you know it?'

'No, I don't think I do.'

'It's a nondescript little street, lots of dreary little shoe shops selling fake designer stuff, but behind the facades there are some very well-appointed interiors. So, anyway, at last the little door clicked open for me and clicked shut behind me, and I was admitted to the … what shall I call it?'

'The belly of the beast?'

Eric laughed. 'No, that's too harsh. But not the heart of it either

– let's say into the enclosure where the beast roams and rampages. As enclosures go, though, this one was very comfortable; Fabrice's apartment was big and airy --'

'Fabrice?'

'Yes, didn't I mention his name?'

'No, as a matter of fact.' Christopher's surprise at the name cropping up was, he realised, less intense than his relief: by introducing the name so openly, of his own accord, Eric was somehow defusing it, rendering it relatively harmless. As an acknowledged acquaintance, Fabrice might leave some questions open, but as an unacknowledged connection he had seemed to make all questions impossible, hinting at depths of concealment that Christopher might yet, indeed, shy away from plumbing. His face must have registered something of his relief, for Eric was looking at him enquiringly.

'Why, do you know him?' the young man asked.

'No, I don't think I do,' Christopher replied, then realised that now the burden of dissimulation had passed to him – or else he had assumed it, without quite knowing why. If Eric could mention Fabrice, why couldn't he? But in the meantime the young man was continuing his account.

'Well, Fabrice – his apartment in fact had *three* bedrooms, one of which faced the street and the synagogue across the way, two others facing inward, into a courtyard. It was the first real Parisian apartment I'd been into – my friends' expat squat in the *banlieue* didn't count – and I took to it, well, like a duck to water. I liked how small it was and yet how well proportioned, how there was a place for everything and nothing seemed cluttered. I liked the wooden floors and high ceilings, the big sash windows, the shutters, the light and air and calm. I mean, at home everything is so *heavy*, all that yellowwood and stinkwood and brass, you know?' He glanced at Christopher as if for confirmation before continuing.

'At Fabrice's, though, everything was light. The furniture was very plain, all angular and monochrome, and the only wall decorations were two big black-and-white photographs framed in stainless steel, one of a horse shying from something or someone, its eyes rolling in its head, the mouth foaming, really terrifying and beautiful, the other of a young black man taken from behind, naked except for an anklet of beads, his back disfigured by a single weal, his shoulder hunched against the next lash of the whip.'

Christopher marvelled anew at Eric's power of recall, his evident fascination with every aspect of Paris life. But all he said was, 'Pardon me if I say that as decorations go, these sound rather grisly.'

'Well, they were and they weren't. They were grisly if you thought about them, about what was *happening* there, but just as objects they were very beautiful.'

'I don't know if a picture is ever only an object – but sorry, I didn't mean to interrupt your account.'

'No sweat. So anyway, there I was the next morning, eating fresh croissants with Fabrice and dreading going back to my broom cupboard in Malakoff. Of course, I'd told Fabrice all about my situation the night before, what with all the wine and all his questions, so he knew all about it, and as I was getting ready to leave, he said, Why don't you stay here until you find something of your own? I said, Do you mean that? and he said, Would I offer what I don't mean? I have an extra room, as you see, and I don't think we will get in each other's way. I told him I couldn't afford to pay very much, and he said, I won't expect any money, but I may ask you now and again to help me in my business.'

'Did you know what his business was?'

'Only vaguely. He'd mentioned that he was an events organiser, without specifying what kind of event.'

'And you were prepared to take it on?'

Eric shrugged. 'It's not as if I had many options. But you know, the prospect of my own airy room in that apartment, as against the broom cupboard in the noisy, smelly place in Malakoff, well, it was too attractive to resist, and so I moved in the same day. My friends made a decent show of regret, but I could tell that they were relieved, too, to have one fewer person battling for the bathroom in the morning.

'Anyway, my new lodgings turned out to be pretty comfortable.

185

Fabrice was out a lot of the time, and I could continue my aimless but, you know, satisfying exploration of Paris, and at least I now had some kind of foothold in the great city. The jobs I was given weren't exactly strenuous – checking whether venues were available for particular events, that kind of thing,' he grimaced. 'It turned out that Fabrice specialised in fashion shows and the after-parties – and of course whether certain celebrities were available – an event tends to be structured around a few high-profile guests, who have to be induced to attend.'

'And your French? Was it up to the level of negotiation required?'

'Yes, pretty much. I picked up the trade jargon very quickly – after the first evening, Fabrice made a point of speaking French to me all the time – and – well, I was meeting a lot of people and I seem to be quite quick at picking up languages.'

He said this unself-consciously, as he might have confessed to an aptitude for juggling. But it was of the essence of Eric's social manner, Christopher reflected, to have as little self-consciousness as a pure-bred horse: he simply was what he was, and accepted other people's attention not so much as his due as part of the medium in which he naturally moved.

But Eric continued, 'The thing is, when you're in survival mode like that, you develop skills you didn't know you had.'

'And suppress inhibitions you might otherwise have had?'

He seemed to give this his earnest attention before replying. 'I wasn't aware of suppressing any qualms of conscience, if that's what you mean.' His face, as he said this, was lit by a candour that it was difficult to imagine ever having to contend with qualms of conscience: whether from having a clear conscience or from not being prone to qualms, it wasn't clear. Or perhaps, Christopher reflected, it was just an effect of the soft lighting on a young skin. It did at least make for ease of congress, all awkward questions being so smoothly disposed of even before they were permitted to arise. 'But the point is,' Eric continued, 'even if I had qualms, I couldn't really afford to be too picky about my source of income.'

'And yet you were too *picky*, far too fastidious, to accept your father's allowance.'

186

'Yes, it did seem wrong, you know, to carry on drawing his money when I wasn't doing what he in a sense was paying me to do.'

'He might have preferred you to do what in a sense he was paying you to do,' Christopher said, then realised that he must be sounding drearily moralistic. Eric had paid him the compliment of full disclosure; the least he could do was to give him an equally candid hearing.

But if Eric was put out, he didn't show it. 'I guess he might have,' he agreed with his easy affability. 'But I wasn't really into consulting Dad's preferences, if you know what I mean. I didn't want to take his money under false pretences, but I didn't think I owed it to him to live my life according to his ideas either. In a way, by not taking his money, I felt freer to run my life in my own way, if that makes sense.'

Christopher nodded. 'That does make some sort of sense, yes.' He picked up his glass, examined its dwindling contents, and swirled it. Then he glanced up at Eric and said, 'And you stayed with Fabrice for how long, were you saying?'

'About three months. Then, one morning, he asked me to stay home that evening, which was unusual. As a rule he made it clear that I wasn't included in his social circle. Anyway, what he said was, I'm having friends to supper that I would like you to meet. He didn't explain why, just said, I think you will find them interesting.'

'And were they?'

'Interesting? Yes, they were. You've met them, I think – Gloriani and Xolani?'

'Yes. That is, Gloriani I've met. Xolani I've seen at a distance. I wouldn't have connected them with each other.'

'Oh, in Paris everyone is connected with everyone else. The trick is to know the nature of the connection.'

'And what is the nature of the connection between Gloriani and Xolani?'

'Ah, I don't claim that I've got to the bottom of *that*. But there is a relatively superficial connection in the fact that Xolani was once one of Gloriani's *claqueurs*.' He paused. 'You know what a *claqueur* is?'

'I do now. Indeed, I was told that you were one.'

'Yes I was, and occasionally I still am – as a matter of fact, as a result of that meeting at Fabrice's. Xolani had just graduated from *claqueur* to model, and Gloriani was looking for a new *claqueur* – somebody who'd clean up well, as they say, and look good in a well-cut suit. It turned out that Fabrice had arranged for me to be there so that Gloriani could look me over without my knowing I was being looked over. In any case, he seemed to like what he saw, because he asked me that very evening.'

'The job must have appealed to you, with your new-found appreciation of fancy clothes.'

'Okay, you can mock me, but yes, in fact, I loved it. And I'll have you know I was a damn good *claqueur*,' he grinned.

'It takes skill …?'

Eric laughed. 'You mean anyone can put their hands together and clap? Maybe – but to clap with conviction, that's rare. And the thing about me was that I was sincere: I really admired Gloriani's designs, you know, and I really loved the suit I was given to wear, always the same one: an unstructured woollen suit, a pale grey-blue, it was designed to be worn with a waistcoat, but without a shirt. I didn't mind that this showed a bit of skin. I was in pretty good shape, remember, after all that time in the vineyards. I knew I was being admired, and I enjoyed admiring what was *made* to be admired, and envying what was made to be envied. In a way, you could say I'd found my vocation as a *claqueur*.' He relaxed back into his seat and folded his hands behind his head. 'You know, I could happily spend my life applauding the excellence of others without being asked to produce anything other than my approval.'

'Forgive me for pointing out that while this may be an admirable vocation, as a profession it lacks a certain … well, something.'

'You're welcome to point it out, though I know it well enough for myself. What the job lacks, of course, though you're too polite to point it out, is some kind of financial return.'

'Exactly.'

'Exactly. So you're wondering what I'm living on.'

'I'm not sure that it's any of my business.'

At this, Eric shot him a sharper glance than he'd yet ventured. 'Isn't it your business to find out what I'm up to in Paris?'

'Only insofar as that's relevant to persuading you to quit Paris and return home.'

'You mean you may need to know what exactly I'd be *quitting* in quitting Paris?'

'It might conceivably be relevant, yes.'

'Then, I don't mind telling you that at the moment there's no great financial inducement. Fabrice does pay me, and pays me quite well, but I'd never be more than a kind of personal assistant, and I do have larger ambitions than that.'

'Such as?'

'Well, such as striking out on my own in some way that's connected with the fashion world. I might even start my own agency – Eric de Villiers has a certain ring to it, don't you think?'

'It would certainly translate well into several languages. But I'd guess that one needs more than a name to start an agency?'

'Oh, yes. Much more. But you know, I have moved on since my days with Fabrice.'

'And where exactly is it that you've moved on to?'

'Hm. I like your *exactly*!' He paused while the unobtrusive waiter served the main course. 'But fair enough,' he said then, 'I did say I'd fill you in on the details of my life, so I guess I owe you the full account, without omissions, suppressions or evasions.'

'I don't know about *owing*. But it would certainly help me to fix more or less where *I* am if I knew exactly where *you* were.'

'Fair enough,' he said again. 'Well, Gloriani's shows, okay, they didn't really pay me anything, but they have been really useful – apart from coming with lots of free meals, if you can call a selection of snacks on sticks a meal. But I did meet a lot of people – it was all a kind of training in social skills,' he observed wryly. 'My French was rapidly improving, and I found that I could move fairly easily in circles that I couldn't possibly have, if I'd had to buy my way in. I wasn't exactly fêted, but I was accepted without question, or with only the most superficial of questions as to my origins – which aren't too bad, I suppose.' He said this with mild chagrin.

'I'd say they were excellent.'

'Well, let's say good enough, then, to pass muster. In Paris, in any case, if you look good you're generally regarded as being good enough. So I was content in my little corner of this world that I'd so badly wanted to penetrate. Gloriani was really kind to me, and seemed to take a personal interest in my welfare. And then I met the people who worked for him, the models and stylists and bookers.' He paused. 'And, of course, Zeevee. That was, I suppose, decisive.'

'What did it decide?'

'It decided, to be melodramatic about it, my future. No, that's *too* melodramatic. It determined my movements for the next few months.'

'It? You mean Zeevee?'

'Well, yes. But *it* in the sense of the situation. You see, apart from being the kindest and sweetest guy this side of a Disney movie about a dog, Zeevee is also quite susceptible.'

'Susceptible to you, you mean?'

'I meant susceptible in general, but yes, as it turned out, to me in particular.'

'He fell in love with you?'

'Nobody confesses to falling in love any more. But he certainly showed signs of being strongly attracted.'

'And you reciprocated?'

'Oh, I liked him, of course. Everybody likes Zeevee. But no, if you mean did I like him as he liked me, no, I didn't.'

'And he knew this?'

'Oh, yes.'

'How?'

'I told him, of course. Come on, what do you take me for?'

'I don't know. You may not have felt called upon to disillusion him.'

'I wasn't so much called upon as compelled. Zeevee is one of the most direct people I have ever met – by Parisian standards almost touchingly so – and lost no time in declaring his feelings. So of course I had to declare my, well, regretful inability to *reciprocate*, as you put it.'

'And how did he take it?'

'As he takes everything, calm as an angel. He even invited me to stay in his apartment, without obligation, as he put it, for as long as I wanted.'

'And you accepted?'

'I did. Do you think that was wrong?'

'I don't think there's any wrong or right about it. I'd have thought, though, that you might have felt a little uncomfortable, accepting Zeevee's hospitality ...'

'Without offering anything in return, you mean? Yes, I did feel that, but Zeevee has a way of simplifying, of making you feel as if you're doing him a favour by partaking of his bounty.'

'And Fabrice?'

'What about him?'

'He didn't mind your leaving?'

'No, I suspect he was only too pleased to have his apartment to himself again, though he did in fact deny that.'

'And you and Zeevee ... '

'Oh, we cohabited very well. To be honest, I liked his apartment as much as he seemed to like me. What I really loved was its air of outrageous opulence, of never taking itself terribly seriously ... but of course you can only afford that attitude when there's absolutely no doubt that you could have had just about any alternative if you'd wanted it.'

'That's also a good description of Zeevee himself.'

'D'you think so? I'd have said his attitude was more a question of adapting himself with good grace to, well, the necessities of his situation.' His voice trailed off and there was a brief silence.

'The necessities of his situation are hardly of the most rigorous.'

'Financially speaking, no. But aesthetically ...'

'You mean he's not beautiful as his world measures beauty. Does that matter?'

'I think it matters to him. Zeevee worships beauty.'

'And in taking you into his house he was paying tribute to it?'

For the first time, Eric flushed. 'That's not what I was implying. I'd hope that Zeevee was attracted to something more than my blond hair and blue eyes – why are you smiling?'

'I'm remembering a poem by Yeats: *I heard an old religious man But yesternight declare That he had found a text to prove That only God, my dear, Could love you for yourself alone And not your yellow hair.'*

Eric laughed, his equanimity restored. 'And Zeevee isn't God just yet. True enough, but as I've said, he's pretty close to an angel. In any case, for whatever reason, he was a generous and undemanding host.'

'Then why did you move out?'

'Yes. Yes, that was a slight awkwardness, but not one that caused any permanent rift, I think. Zeevee's too big for that.'

'But why ...?'

'Yes. Well, because of Beatrice, really. I met her soon after I moved in – in fact, Zeevee introduced us, they're old friends. And we – well, we took to each other, and then I moved in with her.'

'You're nothing if not mobile.'

Eric looked at him as if to gauge his tone, which was in truth a shade dry, but let it pass. 'Yes,' he said, 'I know, it must seem very fickle.'

'But you've kept good relations with all your past landlords.'

'Yes, though Fabrice I don't see too much of.'

'That's probably just as well.'

'He's not a bad guy, really.

'I'll take your word for it.'

'You'll have to, since you haven't met him.'

They had long since eaten their main course, finished even the dessert they had ordered merely as a reason to linger in the muted dining car speeding through the darkness. They were now lingering over the excellent Italian coffee the attendant had produced, unprompted.

Eric stifled a yawn. 'Sorry, it's been a long day. Shall we go to bed? We've got to change trains in Milan at some unearthly hour, five-thirty or something.'

As they prepared for bed, a little awkwardly in the cramped space, the train's gentle rocking motion complicating the business of brushing one's teeth at the minuscule hand basin, Christopher tried to order the mass of impressions the evening had left him with. There was no denying that Eric had sailed very close to the wind; had, morally speaking, been close to landing on the rocks. He might, indeed, be said to have trimmed his sails to the wind, perhaps as an act of cold-hearted expediency. But by his own account he'd been in survival mode; and a healthy young animal in survival mode might perhaps be exempted from the sterner strictures applicable to mere middle-aged mortals.

Looking at this particular young animal, now slipping into the crisp white sheets that had been prepared while they were at dinner – 'Can I grab the upper bunk?' Eric had said, 'or do you want it?' making this concession to Christopher's age seem like a boyish preference – and looking at the smooth flesh exposed to the glow of the bulkhead light, Christopher wryly recognised his special pleading for what it was: a judgement beguiled by beauty and befuddled by half a bottle of wine. He lay awake for a while, soothed by the smooth undulation of the train, amusing himself – and it was, somehow, an amusement – by wondering what Daniel would say if he could see his emissary now, speeding to Italy with the object of his mission. Daniel would certainly see it as an act of flagrant disloyalty, even betrayal; but what was there in their friendship, his and Daniel's, to be loyal *to* or, conversely, to betray? Their loyalties were things of the past, as were their betrayals. Did this sense of his, of having superseded Daniel, mean that he had incurred new loyalties? Had Eric's candour, in recounting the history of his sojourn in Paris, established a bond to replace Christopher's bond with his father? He drifted off, leaving that quandary unresolved.

CHAPTER 14

The morning, which seemed to come with almost brutal dispatch, was a matter of changing trains in Milan, and settling into the local train to Florence, a considerably less streamlined experience than the Artesia. The train was full, and the two men, sitting opposite each other but flanked by businessmen engrossed in their documents, did not talk. Eric seemed pensive, possibly because of the imminent interview with the fugitive Jeanne. Only once did he say, 'We'll be in Florence at about eight, fortunately.'

'Why fortunately?'

'They won't have gone out on their shoot, so I should be able to find Jeanne at her hotel.'

'You know where the hotel is?'

'Yes, more or less. It's not far from the station. We can walk there.'

'Shall I wait for you somewhere?'

'No, why do you think I brought you? I need moral support.'

'I certainly can't give you any other kind.'

'I don't need any other,' said the younger man.

Florence station was oddly dark and functional-looking, bustling at that hour with people on their way to work, the waves of tourists not yet having arrived in full force. Indeed, on the barren Piazza della Stazione outside, with its tacky souvenir stalls, there was already a half-hearted massing of tourists, as of cattle sensing a trip to the abattoir, interspersed with *stranieri* of indeterminate origin and dubious intention – all impatiently negotiated by the heedless Florentines going about their business. Christopher had somehow recollected Florence as resplendent and radiant; but today it presented a rather stony and dusty aspect. Having produced so much beauty over the ages, it seemed to have relaxed or relapsed into sullen indifference. Even so early in the morning, it was hot, the atmosphere already exhausted.

'The hotel is on the Via dei Cerretani,' said Eric, 'I think it's over there.' He produced from somewhere a map of the city, consulted it, and said, 'Right, follow me.'

The Via dei Cerretani was a noisy, narrow thoroughfare, lethally congested: the ancient layout of the city was not hospitable to modern means of transport. Christopher found the entire place oppressive: Florence had not managed the transition from former magnificence to modern amenity as graciously as Paris had done.

'Not a very welcoming place, is it?' he said to Eric, as they narrowly missed being run over on a pedestrian crossing.

'No, but which city is, around its main station? Careful, there's a Vespa coming round that car – run for it!' He grabbed Christopher's arm and pulled him onto the pavement, which was itself so crowded that he had to shove to clear them a space.

'Right,' he said, apparently unconcerned by what had seemed to Christopher a narrow escape from death or disability, 'the hotel should he here somewhere. Ah, there we are, the Hotel David. Looks splendid, doesn't it?'

'I don't know,' said Christopher. 'Looks rather over-decorated to me.'

'Sure, splendid, as I said. The Italians don't hold back on the gilt.'

They pushed open the heavy glass doors and entered the sumptuous lobby, in all its magnificence of crystal and marble.

'If you'd like to wait on that uncomfortable-looking sofa, I'll see if I can locate Jeanne,' Eric said. Christopher did not really relish a spell on the piece of furniture indicated, with its curlicued frame and brocaded surfaces, but it was clear that Eric needed to see Jeanne on his own. So he sat down on the gorgeous sofa – it was even more uncomfortable than it looked – and looked around him at the foyer, which at this hour was teeming with departing guests. The place resembled, in its overblown trumpery, the foyer of a provincial opera house, though its field of reference was in the visual rather than the performing arts. In keeping with its name, the hotel was dedicated to the effigy of David, in all his avatars. Christopher amused himself by trying to identify the various versions of the boy hero. Next to his seat, half-hidden behind a coffee machine with a sign saying *Fuori Servizio/Broke*, there was a copy of the Donatello David, effetely dangling his big sword. He looked incongruous behind the machine, but not flustered. Having faced worse perils than incongruity, the triumphant youth stood nonchalant in his languid grace, his left foot poised delicately over the severed head of Goliath, as if too fastidious really to grind it into the dust. He was an unlikely sort of giant-killer, with his slim, smoothly androgynous torso, undeveloped biceps, rounded tummy and reticent penis. There was, in the armoured calf and heavy sword, a concession to the more robust virtues represented by the little figure, but these, in ensemble with the helmet that looked like a spring bonnet, seemed like fancy dress, a boy dressing up for a charade, rather than a warrior's panoply. One could imagine him lurking with his little slingshot, sly, stealthy, and felling the giant with his pebble; what one could not imagine was this fastidious youth hacking the giant head off the trunk. He was too decadent for that.

The lobby was, unsurprisingly, dominated by a more than life-sized copy of Michelangelo's version of the young hero, posed in front of an ornate mirror. Now *him*, Christopher reflected, one could imagine dangling the trunkless head of Goliath in vulgar triumph, the brutal, vain, cold-eyed, full-veined, taut-muscled, flat-bellied, prominently-cocked adolescent, the beautiful brat. Michelangelo had had no need to include the decollated head of Goliath: he knew he could leave it to the viewer to imagine it. Donatello's David had to prove he could do it; Michelangelo's did not.

Intrigued now, in spite of himself, by the hotel's display of the gory exploits of its eponym, Christopher got up from his gilt perch and wandered up to a large painting mounted on the wall opposite the reception desk. It was a reproduction, in a Technicolor surely more virulent than the original, of perhaps the least pleasant of all the Davids, Caravaggio's fierce little boy, looking with disdain at the perplexed head of his victim. If one were to commit some atrocity, *that*, Christopher thought, was the spirit in which to do it: unrepentant, clear-eyed, unappalled, certain of the rightness of one's deed. Only Caravaggio could have imagined so precisely the contrast in texture between the rough adult head of Goliath and the unformed features of the young David, the slender arm of the boy grasping the great head with its bleeding wound where it had been struck by the fatal pebble. Christopher remembered reading somewhere that David has the face of Caravaggio's lover, Goliath the face of the mature Caravaggio; if so, Caravaggio had clearly had no illusions about either his lover or himself: the painting could serve as an allegory of Youth scorning Age. It was enough to make one nostalgic for a good pink Madonna with chubby Child.

He turned from the complex horrors of the painting to find Eric coming towards him.

'Oh, there you are … I thought I told you to stay on your sofa,' he joked.

'Sorry, it was more than the human frame could bear.'

'I'm afraid I'm going to ask you to bear with me for a while yet. Reception has managed to wake Jeanne, and she's coming down to see me. But I imagine you wouldn't want to be part of what is likely to be a delicate negotiation?'

'No, really not. I can go off and find a cup of coffee and a roll, if you like, and meet you here … when?'

'Good man. Half an hour should do it. We'll probably be in the residents' lounge over there.'

Christopher left the garish hotel behind him with something like relief, but wondering at Eric's notion of moral support, which seemed not to require his presence at the actual event they had come to Florence to arrange. Well, he thought, it suited him well enough to leave the matter to his companion. And a visit to Florence, no matter how brief, must be reckoned as an experience in itself.

The street outside the hotel was if possible more congested than earlier, but it did provide, in its straightforward squalor, some respite from the aesthetic overload of the lobby. He followed signs to the Duomo, which turned out to be surprisingly close to the hotel. The area had been pedestrianised, and the last of the delivery trucks were leaving before the traffic barricades went up and the pedestrians took over. A qualified hush was descending on the area, like an unlooked-for benediction. Christopher walked round the pink and green and white cathedral, almost frivolous in the midst of the dour Florentine granite, and yet so serene in the harmonious disposition of its coloured lozenges. He wondered if he had time for a visit; but finding that the church did not open till ten, he contented himself with a slow wander around, marvelling again at the inhuman lengths to which mankind had gone in pursuit of ... what? Immortality? He couldn't imagine that the architects and engineers, the builders and masons and workers in bronze who had designed and constructed that sublime heap had had in mind the greater glory of God. The whole thing was a statement, an assertion, not of divine grandeur but of human ingenuity: looking at it, he had the thought that it wasn't so much that God was great, but that man was capable of almost anything. Perhaps, then, it was a monument to the desire for beauty? But was the inspiration behind it at one with the instinct that produced Caravaggio's smirking David, or Michelangelo's brute beauty? And what did it all amount to in the end?

Watching the first of the day's troops of tourists turning up and taking up their stations in the queue already forming outside the Baptistry, Christopher mused: could the impulse to beauty withstand this crude assault, the commodification of the past? The tourist stalls just opening up all featured, clearly as a hot seller, aprons emblazoned with David's naked torso. Whatever the religious or, more likely, nationalistic impulse behind the biblical account of David's victory over the Philistine giant, how much of it had survived the transition to tourist trinket?

He glanced at his watch. Allowing seven minutes for the walk back to the hotel, he should be leaving about now. He was strangely reluctant to meet the young Jeanne du Plessis. He imagined, from his not very extensive experience of seventeen-year-old girls, a petulant young woman, peeved at being dragged away from what must at present be the centre of her world. He could not assign, in his own mind, any substance to the ambition to pose in rarefied attitudes wearing outrageously overpriced garments: as professions or even just pastimes went, it seemed singularly lacking in intellectual or emotional stimulation. To be reduced to a face was surely a very diminishing experience; but in a world that elected its celebrities on the most tenuous of grounds, to be reckoned a Face must, he supposed, constitute some kind of an achievement. And young Jeanne was, apparently, a Face in training, though he was hard pressed to imagine what kind of training being a Face could require. He thought again of the Michelangelo David: did the sturdy young labourer who got his kit off for the famous sculptor achieve a kind of fame in his native town on account of the job? Did he become sought-after as a model? As a lover?

Christopher shrugged. These were imponderables, and pondering them was going to get him nowhere. Better return to the practical question of how to get a recalcitrant young woman back to where she belonged – though the problem, he recognised, was Eric's rather than his. All he could lend to the occasion was such authority as his grey hair bestowed – not, he feared, very much, in the scale of values of a seventeen-year-old girl.

The lobby of the Hotel David was, if anything, more crowded than earlier, with departures and even some early arrivals. Christopher threaded through mazes of luggage and lines of people to the residents' lounge, which was at this hour a haven of tranquillity amidst the hurly-burly of the lobby. He paused at the entrance and took in the space: its only concession to the national addiction to all things beautiful, however hideous, was a large chandelier, Murano-made to judge by its gaudiness, suspended over the room like some ill omen. The room had no windows, and the only illumination was provided by a standard lamp in the far corner, next to the chairs where Eric was sitting, engrossed in a conversation with a young woman whom Christopher took to be Jeanne du Plessis. Christopher hesitated, reluctant to impose his presence on what might be an awkward conversation; from where he was standing he could not hear anything, but it was clear from Eric's posture – leaning forward in his chair, gesticulating with his right hand – that he was putting his case with some urgency. For her part, Jeanne was sitting well back in the low chair, almost as if retreating from Eric's adjuration. For a moment the scene, the two young people in profile in the lamplight, seemed to freeze into a tableau, some allegorical genre painting – The Plea or The Ardent Lover – he all earnest entreaty, she all reticence, seeming somehow to carry more significance than the merely figurative – a moment captured as if on film, for the significance to emerge later, like a photograph being developed.

Christopher, thinking it best to leave the young people to their colloquy, made to turn back; but the movement must have caught Jeanne's eye, because she turned her head to look at him, and the next moment Eric was on his feet, motioning to Christopher.

'Ah, there you are!' he said, and if there was any awkwardness in the situation, nothing in his manner betrayed that fact, except possibly the unwonted formality in the way in which he said, 'Allow me to introduce Jeanne … Jeanne this is my old friend Christopher Turner, of whom you've heard me speak.'

The young woman did not get up, merely turned her face towards Christopher. It was a slight movement, but with something of the force of an event: for such a face to be turned to one was to take one's categories by surprise. To say that the face was beautiful was somehow inadequate, for the term failed to convey the dynamic quality of the beauty, the play of feature so subtle as almost to escape detection, the delicate range of hue from pale ivory to rose, the velvety texture of the skin, the depth of the great dark eyes in the gloom of the secluded corner. At this hour of the morning she wore no make-up; but her youthful complexion needed no help to make it glow with health and vigour. There was enough, in her beauty, to remind one that she was the daughter of Beatrice du Plessis; but there was also something else, a quality of suppressed energy, that Beatrice in her serenity did not aspire to, or had relinquished with good grace. The energy may have been repressed

200

agitation: there was something in the formality with which she acknowledged Christopher's presence – a slight nod of the head, a constrained little smile – that suggested that the interview had not been an easy one for her. And yet there was also a kind of excitement: how irresistible to the young imagination, after all, to matter so much that a handsome young man is sent to retrieve you! Christopher had likened her mother to a quattrocento painting. He searched his categories for one that would accommodate this young woman, but she was not to be classified under the periods and styles of achieved art: she was altogether a force of nature, a thing of changeability, of whim and instinct – a young animal delighting in its free movement – a colt, perhaps, or a tiger cub. Then, perhaps uncomfortable under a gaze that she may have experienced as too searching, she smiled again, with, as it were, more intention. Her smile was not the languid glow that irradiated her mother's features so beautifully; it was a sudden apparition, a flash of teeth, a deepening of dimples, an enlivening of the dark eyes. It engaged the onlooker rather than expressing a state of mind or spirit; what it communicated was not some truth about her – unless the desire to please the onlooker might be seen as a truth. In a photograph, he imagined, she would seem to invite the viewer into the frame, although he wondered whether a medium as static as photography could render the lambent quality of her presence: it would take a painter of rare genius to do that.

Christopher went forward, and took – with a slightly absurd formality, he suspected – the hand that she extended to him. This was when he noticed, in her left hand, a grey envelope – Eric, then, had had to produce the letter that Beatrice had entrusted to him 'as a last resort'.

'I am pleased to meet you,' he said.

She nodded again, gravely, and still with the smile that evidently cost her an effort. There was something admirable, he thought, in such restraint in a person so young. 'And I you, of course,' she said, 'though this is perhaps not the best occasion for us to meet. It seems I have really upset Maman.' Once again, the restraint, not only in her utterance, its content, but also its tone. Her manner spoke of an

Upbringing, Christopher thought, a correctness enhanced rather than detracted from by her slight French accent.

'She did seem concerned, yes,' Christopher said.

'I am sorry about that. The call from the agency came through only about half an hour before we had to leave, so I only had time for a note. And I did think,' she said, turning now to Eric as if to exculpate herself to him, too, 'that Maman would know we are always well chaperoned on shoots.'

'Not to worry about that, now. No harm done – but I think you'd better come back with us now.'

'But they're relying on me,' she said, not plaintively or argumentatively, stating it merely as a fact that might be taken into consideration.

'Come, we've been over that,' Eric said. 'They'll have to use a substitute.'

Christopher was struck by his note of authority: young as he was, Eric had assumed some kind of parental role in relation to the girl, one that she seemed to accept with demure contrition. Nothing could have been further from the sullen resentment he had anticipated; if she found this interference with her professional life irksome, there was nothing in her manner to draw attention to the fact. Christopher wondered what role the letter from her mother had played in her persuasion – or coercion, perhaps, if her resistance had been more spirited than her present manner suggested.

'Go and pack your stuff now,' Eric said to her. 'We'll probably have to get a flight from Pisa at midday.'

She made a little *moue*, and said, 'Dreary old Pisa.' But it was a half-humorous protest, with nothing petulant about it, and she got to her feet. She was informally dressed, in jeans and T-shirt, but it was evident that she had already caught the trick or acquired the skill of wearing clothes to maximum effect. Her tall frame effortlessly carried the cotton fabric, which lightly covered rather than clung to her.

'I won't be a minute,' she said, and left the room unhurriedly but with every appearance of purpose.

'Well!' Eric said. 'Mission accomplished, I suppose.'

'You suppose? Don't you know?'

'Oh, for the moment I do know, yes. She'll come back with us. But under protest. She's given notice that in future she'll want more of a hand in her own destiny.'

'She seemed remarkably amenable to reason.'

'*Seemed* being the operative word. Jeanne may be young, but she's been around long enough to have learnt that there are more effective ways of getting what one wants than loudly insisting on having it.'

'And what is it that she wants?'

'What all seventeen-year-old girls want, or think they want. Independence. Freedom of movement, freedom to make up their own minds, to make their own mistakes.'

'You sound sympathetic to the endeavour.'

'So I am, up to a point. I was seventeen myself not so long ago. But I also know that one's own mistakes – well, they're not necessarily any more pleasant to deal with than other people's.'

Christopher had not sat down on the ornate chair vacated by Jeanne, and Eric now got to his feet. The two men stood there, somewhat incongruously in the large airless space, like two guests at a grand reception who had got the time wrong. But their awkwardness lasted only a moment, for it was interrupted by the entrance, rapid, purposeful, of a clearly agitated man. He had, to judge by his unkempt hair and generally dishevelled air, his rumpled T-shirt and tracksuit pants, just got out of bed – and, judging by his demeanour, on the wrong side of it. Christopher was sure he'd seen the man before somewhere; and now, as if from nowhere, the name Charlie Winthrop presented itself: the photographer he had met, in a manner of speaking, at Zeevee's lunch. But where, then, he had been sleek, suave and dangerous, like a cougar or some near-mythical creature, he now seemed merely ruffled and cross, like somebody's neglected pet mongrel barking at the gate.

'So what's this, then?' he said, as he advanced upon them. 'Just what is it you think you're doing?'

'I've come to take Jeanne home, where she belongs.'

'And who may you be, to decide where Jeanne belongs?'

'I'm Eric de Villiers, I'm a friend of the family.'

'Yes, I know who you bloody well are and *what* you bloody well are! I want to know what you're thinking, barging in on a frigging shoot and fucking up my schedule.'

'I'm sorry, but your schedule isn't my prime concern.'

'Yes, I can see how sorry you are, you're bleedin' broken up, aren't you? Well, I can tell you, you're going to be even sorrier before you're done. I'll bloody well have your balls on toast for breakfast.'

Eric, though paler than usual, revealed no other sign of perturbation at this exotic threat. 'I'm afraid you'll have to make do with what the hotel provides,' he said. 'If you'll excuse us, we have a plane to catch.'

'You've got more'n a plane to catch, and you're going to catch it sooner'n you think, you bloody Saffer git.'

'If that's a threat, I stand warned and prepared,' Eric said, turning his back on the irate photographer. 'Come, Christopher, Jeanne is meeting us in the lobby.'

'So the toyboy's turned cradle-snatcher?' the man shouted after them. 'How about finding yourself a proper job and letting the rest of us get on with ours?'

These questions did not seem to require answers, and, ignoring them, Eric led the way into the foyer, where Jeanne was just making her appearance. Her training as a model had stood her in good stead, for in a remarkably short time she had effected a complete change of clothing, and was now dressed in a two-piece suit, looking more like a secretary than a model. The smile she gave the two men, too, though not perfunctory, was almost professional. Young Jeanne du Plessis was clearly not the kind of girl who made scenes. In that respect, Christopher thought, she could teach Charlie Winthrop a thing or two.

The return to Paris lacked, in all respects, the glamour of the night train. They took a local train, hot and crowded, to Pisa, from where they were to take a flight to Paris. Pisa airport coped as it could with the crush of bargain airlines, but there was no way that the wait to check in, the rush to the desks as they opened, the long delay in a crowded departure lounge, the frenzy to find an unreserved seat on the plane, could figure as a pleasant travel experience, as anything indeed but what it was: a quick and cheap way of getting from one point to the next. It was to Europe what the minibus taxi was to South Africa: affordable mass transit.

Christopher found a seat a few rows behind Eric and Jeanne – though Eric had offered him the seat next to the young woman, he had declined. The two young people, he assumed, had plenty to discuss, whereas he had no idea what he would find to say to Jeanne du Plessis, pleasantly amenable as she was.

The adventure, then, was over almost before it had started. If he had imagined a fraught confrontation, a desperate flight from Florence in the face of violent resistance, then reality had proved anticlimactic: Jeanne had been told to come home, and she had come home. He hadn't even seen the inside of the Duomo. But that was not what remained with Christopher as he buckled himself into the confines of his airline seat; what remained was his memory of the night train, of Eric's earnest account of his own life, of Christopher's sense that he was being let into that life and allowed to share its perplexities. It had not been an exemplary life; but it had been a life, which was more than Christopher would have claimed for his own existence since leaving Paris three decades years before. And in being admitted to that life, he felt, he was regaining something of his own sense, now long in abeyance, of the potential of all life, including even his own.

He lay back in his narrow seat, closed his eyes, and slept.

CHAPTER 15

He slept late on Friday morning, in spite of going to bed absurdly early the night before. He had taken his leave of Eric and Jeanne at the Orly bus terminal at Denfert-Rochereau, both of them expressing gratitude at his participation in what Eric called 'the rescue'. Christopher could not see why Jeanne professed gratitude at what she might with some justice have seen as meddling in her affairs; but she in fact seemed quite sincerely grateful, even pleased to have been brought back to Paris, which Christopher ascribed to Eric's sage advice on the journey back. Returning to the Hotel du Carrefour less than twenty-four hours after quitting it in haste, it was difficult not to submit to a sense of anticlimax, and he had, after a light meal of salad and a glass of wine, taken to his bed and slept the sleep of the just.

He was woken by the telephone at eight-thirty.

'Christopher? I hope I'm not waking you, but I wanted to catch you before you went out.'

For a moment he thought it was Martha, and realised that he'd not spoken to her since Monday evening; realised also, with a guilty start, that he did not relish submitting his account of his impulsive train journey to her ironic gaze. But then he recognised the flatter vowels and more hesitant manner of Beatrice du Plessis.

'Not at all,' he lied. 'I'm generally up at first light.' That, at least, was true.

'Good. Firstly, of course, I wanted to thank you for your part in,' there was a pause, 'retrieving Jeanne.'

'Oh, my part was a purely passive one. It was Eric who did all the work.'

'Still, I know it meant a lot to him, having you along. And Jeanne was very much taken with you.'

'Was she?' He wondered whether this was a pleasant exaggeration: the young woman, though pleasant and attentive, had not seemed to pay him any particular regard, and he would not have expected her to. 'I liked her very much too,' he added.

'That's kind of you, considering how much trouble she caused you.'

'It wasn't trouble, really – well, it was a change of routine, certainly, but a very pleasant one for me.'

'I'm glad. Still, I haven't forgotten that you never had the meal you came for. Can I make it up to you?'

'Not that it's necessary, but it would be pleasant to see you.'

'And I do want to see you. So when would suit you?'

'Any time, my time's my own.' Saying that, he realised how true this was. And if there was something exhilarating about this freedom, there was also something forlorn. He was now in Paris with no function to perform, no reason, really, to be there. He was not of the school of sentimentalists who maintain that one does not need a reason to be in Paris; but he had now perforce joined their ranks.

'Well, shall we say tonight, then? At the same time?'

'That's perfect.'

'I don't think Eric will be able to join us. Friday nights are difficult for him. But perhaps that's as well. I can really get to know you.'

'Oh, that shouldn't take you a whole dinner. A cup of tea would suffice.'

But if he expected his pleasantry to be met with like lightness, he was disconcerted, for she retorted, with a certain grave emphasis, 'I don't believe that. And I don't believe you believe it either.'

Her gravity was oddly disarming. He couldn't quite meet it in kind, but he couldn't really sustain his levity either: the best he could manage by way of a reply was, 'Well, I'm more than prepared to submit to a dinner, if that is what is required.'

He once again found his way to the Rue de Bellechasse, and was admitted as before by the secretary-housekeeper to the large cool room overlooking its secret garden. The room was as yet unlit and there was, in its clear spaces and empty prospect, an air of melancholy tranquillity, as if the place had been intended for more festive uses, and was now graciously adjusting to its diminished share of life.

Christopher went and stood by on the balcony; the garden below, in the fading light, offered a prosaic rebuttal to his romantic reflections: two deckchairs were sprawled on the lawn, one with a towel draped over it; next to one a copy of *Paris-Match* lay facedown on the ground. A sprinkler had come on and was reducing the magazine to pulp.

A door closed in the distance, and footsteps approached on the parquet. He stepped back into the room to greet Beatrice du Plessis, who had paused at the door, as if taking in the scene.

'It's rather gloomy in here,' she said. 'Shall we have some light?'

'Not for my sake,' he said. 'I love the half-light.'

'So do I,' she said eagerly, as if gratified at their concurrence. 'Let's have a drink on the balcony.'

She came closer. She seemed older, tonight, not in any identifiable feature, but in her general bearing, in something indefinable that had changed in her. And then, looking again, Christopher realised that what had changed was not something in her but something in him: he had, since last seeing Beatrice, seen her daughter – and having seen, as it were, the younger incarnation, Christopher could not but be struck by the contrast. It was not that Beatrice was any less beautiful than before – it was just that one saw her now through the filter of her daughter's fresh beauty.

This, though, was the impression of a moment, while he accepted her offer of a drink – turning down more exotic possibilities for a glass of red wine – and settling down, at first somewhat awkwardly, to what he realised was their first meeting on their own.

'Jeanne will be joining us for supper,' Beatrice said, 'but she has asked to be excused till then. She has a lot of school work just at present, with examinations coming up quite soon.' She made a face over her drink – she was having, he noticed, only a Perrier with a slice of lemon – and said, 'Which is one reason I was so upset at her taking off for Florence so suddenly. You must have thought I was making a fuss about nothing.'

'No, on the contrary,' Christopher said. 'It must be disconcerting to find that one's child has taken off for a foreign city.'

'Yes,' she said. 'But it was more than that …' She trailed off, evidently divided between the need to explain herself, and some constraint of discretion or delicacy. 'Still,' she quickly said, 'that's not important. What's important is that she came back, for which I partly have you to thank.'

'Oh, my part in it was minimal. In fact, I did nothing at all.'

'You made it much more bearable for poor Eric, having to travel to Italy at such short notice. He was very grateful for your company.'

'Oh … my company!'

'Don't disparage your company,' she said, disregarding as usual his jocular tone. 'We are all, as you see, cultivating it for all we're worth.'

'I have certainly been received very hospitably. I just meant … well, that for a young man like Eric there might be more exciting travelling companions than a fifty-year-old friend of his father's.'

'That's certainly not Eric's take on the matter. It is true that in general he spends time with younger people. But that may be exactly why he enjoys something calmer, someone, as he says, one can discuss things with rather than chatter.'

'As he says?' Christopher could not help echoing. He felt the glow of the compliment even as he felt the absurdity of his pleasure from such a source.

'Oh, yes. Did you think I was inventing it?'

'No, I'm not sure what I thought.'

'You thought that Eric was incapable of appreciating adult company?' she asked, he was not quite sure with what degree of seriousness.

'I wouldn't have put it like that. I would just have thought that he could probably have his pick of company.'

At this, she laughed – for the first time he'd known her, he realised. Her face in repose was beautiful as a painting or statue is beautiful; irradiated by laughter it had the beauty of a vital creature at play. 'And you assume he only picked you because better company wasn't available?'

'Not at such short notice, no.'

She became serious again. 'Please – that's not fair to either Eric or yourself.' She paused. 'I think you're inclined to make yourself smaller than you are.' Then, as he said nothing, pondering this sudden intimacy that had seemed to establish itself between them, she continued, 'I hope you don't think I'm being very forward, talking to you like this.'

'Not at all. I'm flattered by your interest.'

'There you are again, making yourself small,' she said. 'You should accept other people's interest as your due, not as some kind of favour. Certainly I know that Eric values your company and your presence in Paris. He says ...'

This was interesting to him. He had never thought of his company as a gift or a favour meriting gratitude; at most, if he had thought about it at all, he had considered it something he imposed on more or less appreciative recipients. So he found himself hoping that Beatrice would elaborate; but at that moment the enigmatic woman in black appeared in the doorway to announced dinner, and he was never to know what it was that Eric had said.

The dining room, also overlooking the garden, was a smaller, more cosy affair altogether than the sitting room, adjusted to family living rather than social occasions. It seemed likely to Christopher that there was a grander room elsewhere for the dinner parties he could not imagine not happening in an apartment that seemed in every other respect so dedicated to public ceremony. But for the time being, this small, companionable room served admirably its more modest function; and here they were presently joined by Jeanne, looking suddenly, in jeans, T-shirt and sneakers, like the schoolgirl she was rather than the model she aspired to be. She greeted Christopher rather formally with a handshake and gave her mother a kiss on the cheek.

'You could have honoured us with something a bit more formal,' her mother commented, though in good-humoured indulgence rather than reprimand.

'Oh, Maman,' Jeanne said, 'what's the point of getting dressed for supper only to get undressed again afterwards?'

'What's the point of ever getting dressed, then?' her mother asked. 'If you just have to get undressed again?'

Jeanne made her little *moue*. 'I think there's something wrong with your logic, Maman,' she said. She turned to Christopher. 'Don't you think so, Mr Turner?'

'I wouldn't dare to arbitrate between mother and daughter,' Christopher demurred.

'Ah, that's as good as saying you agree with me but are afraid to disagree with Maman,' Jeanne replied. 'You needn't be afraid, you know. She's really very mild.'

'Far too mild, I'm afraid,' Beatrice said with an exaggerated sigh. 'I'm afraid I've indulged you hideously.'

'Oh, there's nothing to be afraid of, Maman. You've brought me up beautifully.'

There was between the two of them a pleasant warmth of shared irony, sharp without being astringent. They clearly enjoyed each other's company, though to an old-fashioned eye there might, Christopher conjectured, have been too little consciousness of difference between parent and child. He chose, though, not to identify with this more critical view; there was something very fine in the easy exchange of pleasantries between the two women. The slightly stilted nature of their exchange suggested that they might more customarily converse in French. Their English was not at all awkward, but they were obviously unhabituated; it was as if they were dressing up in costume for each other's amusement and perhaps even partly for his entertainment. Christopher could not help wondering, given their easy commerce, why Beatrice had preferred to send an emissary to retrieve Jeanne – unless indeed it was precisely because their relationship was not based on authority and submission that she had felt the lack of some enforceable code in dealing with her daughter's delinquency. What this said about Eric's relation to

Jeanne was not clear; but Eric's relation to Jeanne could look after itself: for the moment, Christopher had enough to consider without concerning himself with that.

The food was brought in soundlessly, almost invisibly, by the woman in black, as Christopher had now taken to thinking of this functionary. Beatrice made no attempt to introduce him to her, and she did not acknowledge his presence in any way other than in refilling his wine glass or removing his plate when he'd finished eating. The food was what Christopher thought of, without having given it much thought, as typically French: a clear vegetable broth, followed by roast chicken aromatic with tarragon, a simple green salad, an excellent crème caramel.

The conversation was muted, a matter of recollection on Beatrice's part of her youth in South Africa, supplemented with such information about his own origins as she solicited – and never had his history sounded as uneventful as recounted here in this mellow chamber overlooking the darkling Paris garden. Beatrice du Plessis had somehow made the transition from Potchefstroom to Paris, bringing with her only her beauty, and had gained … what? Clearly, a life she could call her own, and a daughter who was a precious possession. Was she happy? It was impossible to tell, looking at the finely chiselled face, to say what it expressed: serene contentment or stoical acceptance – or, indeed, anything at all. Perhaps the habit of years or the necessities of her profession had imparted to her lovely features a kind of negative capability, the capacity to adapt and adjust themselves to any situation, allowing the spectator to project onto them whatever meaning suggested itself to him.

Jeanne listened attentively, passed the odd comment, posed the occasional question, and for the rest chattered about the work she was preparing for her examination. It was on English literature, and she expressed delight at discovering Christopher's expertise in the subject. She asked him if he didn't agree that Catherine Earnshaw was 'the most superb heroine in all the world', and when he teasingly disagreed – 'Wasn't she just a spoilt child who didn't get her way?' – Jeanne accused him of being 'just like Mr Lockwood'.

It was instructive comparing the composed countenance of the mother with the expressive, labile beauty of the daughter, whose pleasure and displeasure seemed to lie just under the surface of her smooth young skin, erupting at the slightest provocation. One felt that Jeanne's features contained surprises, sudden twists of plot; Beatrice's face was like a sonnet, complete, contained.

After the dessert, Jeanne asked to be excused; her mother waved her away and proposed coffee and cognac in the sitting room. They retreated to the restful room, still open to the balcony and garden. Beatrice sat down on a low sofa and gestured towards an easy chair close by. Someone – presumably the woman in black – had placed coffee and cognac on a low table, and Beatrice poured, without asking, two small cups of coffee, and some cognac into the single glass that stood there.

'You're not having any?' Christopher asked, sniffing at the amber liquid.

She shook her head. 'No. One glass of wine an evening is my limit.' She reached for an enamelled box on the table in front of her. 'But I do allow myself two cigarettes after dinner … if you don't mind?'

'No, please, go ahead.'

'Thank you.' She lit a cigarette and sat back. They sipped at their coffee and Christopher savoured his cognac in a silence broken only by desultory observations. It was as if they both knew that between them they had not yet arrived at a frankness that both of them wanted, yet were wary of. It was a question of who would take the initiative, and along what lines.

Since the topic they were avoiding was obviously Eric, Christopher thought that a neutral enquiry might clear the way. He put down his coffee cup. 'What is it that Eric does on Friday evenings?'

But if he had hoped that this would open a vein of conversation, he was disappointed. She seemed, if anything, taken aback by his question.

'Who told you that he does anything in particular on Friday evenings?' she asked.

'Why, you did. That is, you said that Friday evenings are difficult for him.'

'Oh,' she said, 'that. Yes, I did say that, but I only meant that he often chooses to see his young friends on a Friday evening, no particular friend, just an evening on the town, as he used to have before he moved in here.'

There was nothing in her manner to suggest that she resented this harking back to his single state: her tone was neutral, factual; and yet Christopher fancied he saw a shadow pass over her features, an intimation of unease. It was difficult to know how to respond to this, and while he was still wondering, she continued, 'It's understandable, really, isn't it? I mean, cooped up here in this house of women, any young man would want some male company from time to time, don't you think?'

'Yes, I should think so,' Christopher said, 'though I think I've lost touch with what young men want and don't want.'

She hesitated again and Christopher sensed that she didn't quite want to let go of the topic, so he waited. 'Do you …' she began.

'Do I …?'

'Do you find Eric much changed?'

His first impulse was to tell her all, tell her how near-miraculous he thought the change – because she had that effect on him, of wanting to tell her the truth, wanting to pay her the tribute that he was sure was her due. But a certain instinct of caution intervened to block the impulse: to give her her full due, after all, would be to reveal how little the untransfigured Eric had had to recommend himself. So he said only, lamely, 'Oh, without a doubt, he is much improved.'

Meagre as this was, she accepted it with touching eagerness. 'I'm so pleased to hear you say that,' she said. 'Then you don't think that between us we – all of us here in Paris – have spoiled him?'

'On the contrary,' he said, 'I think you – and I don't know if it's you personally or all of you here in Paris – whichever it may be, you have done him a world of good.'

'Oh, I'm so pleased,' she said again. 'Then you … you won't necessarily want to take him home?'

This question, artless as it was, started more hares than Christopher knew how to track down in a single reply. 'It's not a question,' he said, grabbing at the first aspect of her question that he could get hold of, 'it's not a question, really, of me *wanting* to take him home. The fact is that his father wants him to return, and my only function is to put his father's wishes before him.'

'But you *can* influence his decision, can't you?' she asked.

'My dear Beatrice,' he said, with a sudden rush of affection for this beautiful woman in obvious distress, 'how could I do that? I'm merely a kind of messenger; I *have* no influence.'

'I think you do,' she persisted. 'I know Eric respects you, he has told me how much he likes you.'

Again there was too much in this simple statement for Christopher to deal with in a single reply. Again he reached for its most salient aspect. 'I'm pleased to hear that, of course, but I doubt that in a matter as important as this he's going to be swayed by me – even if I should want to sway him,' he conscientiously added.

But artless as she was, she was not to be bought off with this. 'To sway him?'

'Yes. To persuade him to stay.'

'But he does not need persuasion. Eric *wants* to stay. He has said so to me. All I'm asking is that you don't try to persuade him to leave. All you need do is … nothing.'

She hadn't switched on any lights, and with the waning dusk outside, the large room seemed to grow more cavernous, more amenable to the hushed urgency of her appeal. It was for a moment as if the two of them were alone in the great city.

'But in a case like this, to do nothing is also to do – I mean, given that I was sent here to do *something*.'

'You were *sent* …?'

'Yes, in a manner of speaking. Eric's father asked me to come. I thought you knew that.'

'Yes, I did know, but when you say you were *sent* that makes you sound so … passive.' For the first time a note of impatience stole into her low voice.

215

'I guess that's what I am … passive,' he said ruefully. 'Or active only in the service of another.'

'I don't believe that,' she said, now with a sudden injection of passion. 'You have eyes to see, you have a brain to think, you have feelings, you can draw your own conclusions and act accordingly, you're not some *commissar* with authority only to implement the policy of some higher authority.'

She paused, while he reflected on how best to meet this unforeseen onslaught. But as he reflected, she continued. 'You say you can see how Eric has benefited from Paris and all it contains, you say it has done him a world of good, and yet you can't find it in your heart to *tell* him that, to make him see that to go back home is to return to a life of privileged boredom – I know, he's told me, how he is the son and heir, on the one hand given everything he wants, on the other hand watched every moment to make sure that he'll be worthy of his destiny as lord and master of Beau Regard, how he's always felt pampered and yet never free.'

'But if he knows that, I needn't tell him that.'

'I think he may be forgetting it, may be thinking that once he's the owner of the farm he'll have his own way.'

'Which is true, surely?'

'Is it?' Her question, though tinged with scepticism, was not merely rhetorical. 'I've been away a long time, but can South Africa have changed that much? Even as the owner of the leading wine estate in the Cape, *especially* as the owner, wouldn't he be under constant surveillance and scrutiny, with his father's judgement projected onto the community, and probably magnified? Wouldn't he be a prisoner of his own status? Is that not so?'

'I don't know. I quite honestly don't know. Eric is an independent man, he has a mind of his own, there's no need for him to become a helpless conformist.'

'Eric … I'll tell you something about Eric. He has a strong personality, socially he is supremely self-assured. But character, well, that's another thing altogether …'

She stopped; he could see that she saw that she'd betrayed an uncertainty, a fear. 'Oh, I'm talking nonsense,' she said. 'Eric is what you see, the most agreeable, the most helpful ...' She left him wondering what noun she would choose to cap those workaday adjectives.

But she didn't finish her sentence. She drew on her cigarette and looked around vaguely, as if searching for something in the dim reaches of the room, then returned her gaze to his face.

'Please,' she said, 'forget what I've said. I have moments when things seem uncertain, and I feel frightened.'

'Frightened of what?'

'Of people, of things, of myself. I'm afraid of what awaits me in this foreign country, but more afraid even of returning to a country that's no longer mine. But most of all, I'm afraid for Jeanne.'

'Why? She seems like a very confident young woman.'

'That is what I'm afraid of. Confidence in a city like this ... it betrays one into situations a less confident person might avoid. You think you're all-powerful, and then you discover your power has been lent to you – most often by people who have their own uses for it.'

She took a sip of her coffee, then put down the cup and stubbed out her cigarette. 'I'll tell you something,' she said, 'something that very few people know. I don't know why I want to tell you this, other than my feeling that I can trust you. And perhaps also that I want you to understand me better.'

He nodded. 'Of course you can trust me to keep what you tell me to myself.'

'Yes. I know. I can see that.' She took a deep breath. 'Do you know why I was so upset when Jeanne went off to Italy the other day?'

'Yes, I think so – you told me that you didn't want her to miss school. And I can imagine that the world of fashion is one that a mother would have very mixed feelings about committing her daughter to.'

'That's true, but in a way I've had to come to terms with that aspect of Jeanne's career. I've had to rely on the upbringing she's had, which will, I hope, protect her from the worst excesses of that world. But this ... no, this was different. You see, the photographer on this

217

shoot was Charlie Winthrop.' She said it as if that explained all, but it merely left him mystified. He remembered Charlie Winthrop as an unpleasant person, and he remembered also Beatrice's evident dislike of the man, but that did not tell him what it was that made Winthrop a more sinister prospect than any other photographer would have been.

'And that is bad?' he asked.

She glanced at the night outside. 'That is bad. Charlie Winthrop is the most … notorious of them all.'

'Are there degrees of notoriety?'

She gave a tight little smile. 'I know, you may think that a girl can be ruined only once. But there are ways of being ruined, and with Charlie it's always, well, humiliating. He's not content simply to take a woman to bed, he also has to demean her somehow. He says that he wants from his models the look of a violated slave.'

'And that's a look that sells fashion?'

'Who can tell what sells fashion? But it pleases the editors of the fashion magazines, and they are the gods who run the show. In any case, Charlie Winthrop is now the top dog.'

'So you were naturally reluctant to have Jeanne go to Florence as part of his pack, so to speak?'

'Yes, naturally.' She hesitated. 'But that isn't the whole reason.'

He waited while she lit another cigarette. 'You see,' she said, 'when I first came to Paris … well, I needn't tell you I was inexperienced, and I was scared and, with my schoolgirl French, totally out of my depth. Charlie was just starting out, he was about my age, but about six times more experienced, and already making a name for himself. He took me under his wing, and because he spoke English and was young like me, I found him a comfortable sort of companion. Only, his idea of companionship – well, it included a good deal more than I'd imagined. And so, in an almost ludicrously short time after arriving in Paris, I was pregnant.'

'By Charlie?'

'By Charlie. Only, I told him that it wasn't by him, that I'd slept with another man. He was so promiscuous himself that he believed me, and, of course, it suited him to believe me, not to take responsibility for my pregnancy.'

'But why? I mean, why did you tell him –'

'That it wasn't his child? Because I decided I wanted to have the child, and I didn't want him to have any part in it. You see, I'd started to see through Charlie by this time, and I didn't want him in any relation to the child.'

'So you were all on your own?'

'Yes – or rather, not quite. My stylist was a woman of experience, but also great compassion, and she arranged a low-profile birth. She also went to Gloriani and explained my predicament – he's one of the few people who know my history – and he took me back as soon as I could start working again. He's a kind man, whatever people say about him.'

'And so Jeanne, she's …?'

'Yes, Jeanne is Charlie Winthrop's daughter. Only, she doesn't know it. And he doesn't know it.'

Christopher raised his glass to his lips but put it down again without drinking. 'And Charlie, he's –'

'He's a sexual predator who prides himself on *initiating* the young models, as he calls it.'

'And now …'

'Now I can't tell him that Jeanne is his daughter, because he'll lay claim to her – not as father to daughter but as photographer to model, as a valuable asset. Besides, telling him that Jeanne is his daughter – well, I really don't think that that would deter him if he really wanted her. It might even add to the thrill.'

'Then why not tell Jeanne?'

'I wanted to spare her the knowledge, but of course, when this happened, this trip to Florence, I realised that I wasn't doing her any favours. So I asked Eric to tell Jeanne the truth, as a last resort.' She smiled wanly. 'Yes, I know we've come to a pretty pass when the truth becomes a last resort. But that's the pass I've come to.'

'And he told her?'

'Yes, in Florence. He gave her the letter that I wrote to her as some kind of ultimate argument. He says she was remarkably calm about it – conceded that it was probably a good idea to keep

Charlie Winthrop at a distance, and agreed to come home. We've since discussed it, and she seems strangely unperturbed by it.' She smiled, without joy. 'I hope she's not burying it in some dark recess of her unconscious. But I think she can discuss it with Eric, he's closer to her in age, and he's a good listener, so maybe it won't come to that.'

She looked at Christopher. 'I suppose that's also why I'm telling you this – so that you'll realise what it means to me to have Eric here to help me, how helpless I'd be without him.'

'I understand that, of course. And I appreciate your confidence. But as I've said, I have no real power to sway Eric one way or the other.'

But she would not allow him that excuse. 'But will you use whatever power you do have? *Will* you help me?'

So here it was, the challenge to put into practice the change he had revelled in, on the way to Italy, the shift in allegiance from Daniel to his son and to this woman softly pleading in the dusk. And yet he hesitated, counting the cost, the repudiation of half a lifetime's fealty to Daniel de Villiers. He was sacrificing little enough, he realised, in terms of any reward for his loyalty; but his loyalty had become a habit, had become its own reward, had in a way become what he *was*.

Well, if he was determined by his choice of loyalties, he could still, to that extent, choose what he was. So it was with a sense of turning his back on a former self and facing a still unknown future self that he said: 'I will help you as best I can.'

CHAPTER 16

'So you just upped and flew to Florence?' Martha asked the next afternoon, as they settled down to a glass of wine at the Closerie des Lilas, which she had insisted he should see.

'We didn't *up*, really, since we went by train, but if you mean that it was unexpected – yes, it was.' Christopher looked about him at the mellow interior. 'This *is* a pleasant place.'

'Thank you. I'm worried about you, you know,' she said. 'I think you're losing your gravitas.'

'Did I have any to lose?'

'Oh, decidedly. You clearly regarded all of Paris as insufferably frivolous.'

'I never regarded *you* as frivolous.'

'You didn't? But then, I'm not Paris. I'm not even *of* Paris, the Paris that the Parisians claim to love.'

'I thought only ex-pats like Cole Porter admitted to loving Paris. And of course Hemingway and Fitzgerald and everyone else commemorated here.' He gestured at the brass name plates affixed to the tables around them.

'You may be right. The Americans, those who don't hate Paris, think they invented it and love it accordingly. The Parisians pretend to take it for granted. But tell me, did Jeanne du Plessis meekly abandon her shoot and trot off home with you?'

'Yes, if by *you* you mean Eric and me, and indeed much more specifically Eric than me.'

'He must have remarkable powers of persuasion. The sixteen-year-old girls I've known have generally had the tractability of a Chinese tank commander.'

'She's seventeen, not sixteen, but I take your point. As far as Jeanne is concerned, I wasn't present at the interview, so I don't know what arguments Eric used.' He said this with a twinge of guilt: already his promise to Beatrice was demanding the sacrifice of older loyalties. 'Young people lead such complicated lives,' he ventured, as a safe enough generalisation. As he said this, he had an unexpected, luxurious sense that what he was involved in – or exactly *not* involved in, was only a spectator to – was of a high order of interest, with ramifications and implications beyond his knowing.

'I get the impression,' Martha said, 'from the relish with which you say that, that you don't really mind being embroiled in this little imbroglio.'

'Embroiled in an imbroglio? Do I strike you as so tautologically immersed?

'You're in over your ears. And for someone who used not to risk getting his toes wet …!'

'Oh, my toes aren't wet yet. I'm only an onlooker.'

'Be careful. Imbroglios don't distinguish between participants and onlookers. You may find yourself in the thick of it yet.'

'Well, even that …!'

'Even that what?'

'Well, even that may be a change – I mean to be in the thick of something.'

'You have changed, certainly,' she said, a trifle dryly. 'But as onlooker, then, what were your impressions of young Jeanne?'

'Favourable, on the whole. We had to come back by plane from Pisa, which is an experience to fray the best of tempers, but she remained perfectly polite and even considerate throughout, rather more so than many of our adult fellow-passengers. She is very finished, if you know what I mean.'

'Oh, I know exactly what you mean. The French specialise in finishing their children. It makes them easy to get on with but difficult to know. But how does all this affect your mission? After all, you also have a problem child to retrieve.'

'I do indeed. Only I no longer know that that is what I want to do.'

She looked at him strangely. 'Has it ever been a matter of what you *want* to do?'

'Yes, in that what I wanted to do was what I felt I *should* do.'

'And you no longer want to do what you should?'

222

'I no longer know what I should do. Oh, I know what I'm supposed to do, that is, expected to do by Daniel; but whether that corresponds to some kind of moral duty is another matter.'

'It would depend, wouldn't it, on your impression of what Eric's continued sojourn in Paris *means* …?'

'Means to him, you mean?'

'No – or rather, not only to him. What it means in the larger scheme of things, in the moral order of things, to adopt your scale of values.'

'Oh, the moral order of things!' he groaned.

'Have you given up on the moral order of things?' she asked.

'Oh no, I cling ever more desperately to the moral order of things. It's just that it's become so difficult to tell it from all sorts of other orders of things.'

'Such as?'

'Well, obviously, the aesthetic order of things,' he said, gesturing at the interior of the Closerie, with its carefully preserved air of urbane living, 'but also the pragmatic order of things, the politic order of things, the expedient order – and even just the merciful order of things.'

'To whom do you feel you owe mercy? Not Eric de Villiers?'

'No, I don't really think mercy is what is called for in his case. But Beatrice du Plessis, perhaps, may be a candidate for mercy.'

'Not from you, surely?'

'Probably not. And yet she seems to think I could be of help to her.'

'Help to do what?'

Well, he could tell Martha this much without betraying the other woman's confidence: 'To persuade Eric to stay here.'

'Have you pointed out to her that that's the exact opposite of what you're here to do?'

'Not in so many words. But she knows that.'

'And yet hopes to persuade you?'

'The truth is, she has persuaded me. That is, for better or for worse, I now believe that the morally responsible thing for Eric is to stay in Paris.'

A look of incredulity flitted across her face. 'That's more than a change, it's a volte-face.'

'I suppose so.'

'And have you told Daniel of your change of heart?'

Christopher glanced at her, over a sip of wine. 'I've told him. That is, I sent him an email last night, I've brought him up to date on my movements.'

'He can't be pleased with your haring off to Italy with the errant son.'

'He could, if he chose to, see it as my attempt to win Eric's confidence and trust.'

'Is that how you presented it to him?'

'No, I remained silent on my motives, and left it to him to fill them in for himself.'

'Is he likely to give you the benefit of the doubt?'

'No. But I think I don't care too much any more what benefit Daniel gives me or does not give me.'

She looked at him as if gauging the sincerity of this declaration. Then she asked, 'Did it take your coming to Paris to decide that?'

'I don't know. It may have taken Paris to make me see what I'd in fact decided a long time ago.'

'Then coming to Paris will have achieved at least that.'

'I think it has. I think coming to Paris has made me see things for what they are.'

'And has it made you see people for what they are?'

'You mean Daniel?'

'That, too. But I meant Eric.'

He considered. 'I suppose it's more than one could ever say about anybody who is not a totally rudimentary human being, that one can see him for what he is. But I do feel I have a clearer view of Eric, yes, than I had.' She had a look on her face something like disbelief, but he ignored it and took a deep breath. 'On a clearer view he strikes me as admirable.'

'Admirable?' she echoed the word not sceptically, but as if turning it over for inspection. 'What is it that you admire about him?'

'His general facility, his bright young courage in dealing with complex situations.'

'His practical abilities, you mean?'

'It is partly a matter of practical abilities, yes, but only insofar as tact and consideration are practical abilities.'

'As I suppose they are – I mean, tact and consideration are surely nothing if not manifested practically.'

'Yes. And Eric does manifest them practically.'

'How, exactly?'

'Oh, your exactlys! But exactly, then, in managing, with a skill beyond his years, what seem to me to be Beatrice du Plessis' somewhat tangled affairs. And then, he has arranged his own life, here in Paris, quite beautifully.'

'Beautifully?'

'Yes, I think beautifully, in negotiating the treacherous shoals of such a life, and emerging, by and large, without too much of a dunking.'

'On what do you base your assessment?'

'On what I see. But also on what he told me, the other evening, on the train, about his history here in Paris.'

'Eric told you his history?'

'Yes, or as much of it as seemed relevant, I daresay.'

Martha shifted in her chair, and stared at him. 'When you say relevant, do you mean to his needs or yours?'

'His, I suppose. After all, he is only human. But I should hope that his needs in this respect are compatible with mine.'

'One should hope so, yes,' she said, but did not venture any further comment on his hopes, and did not press him to reveal what Eric had told him about his history. Then she said, 'You say you are struck by, I think you said, Eric's tact and consideration?'

'That's what I said, yes.'

'His treatment of his father – would you say that that was characterised by tact and consideration?'

'No. No. It wasn't, of course. But then … I'm not sure that Daniel … well, that he deserves tact and consideration.'

'That is quite a statement. You used to accord him quite a bit of consideration.'

'I suppose I did.'

'Then how has he changed?'

'He hasn't changed. He's the same. He's more than ever the same. But I do what I didn't before – I *see* him.'

'Oh. And what is it that you see?'

'Do you mind awfully if I don't spell it out? It's not something I've lived with for long enough to discuss.'

She took it as she took everything, with easy cordiality. 'Of course. Forgive me for being a meddling old biddy.'

He smiled. 'You couldn't be an old biddy if you tried.'

'But meddle I can?' She was following a train of thought of her own. 'By the way,' she said, but he interrupted her.

'I dread your by-the-ways,' he said. 'I know they're by no means as incidental as you pretend.'

'Oh dear, am I that transparent? Well, then, tell me *not* by the way, why you left Cambridge to go and teach school, why you didn't take up the research fellowship?'

'I don't know. It seemed like the right thing to do at the time.'

'The right thing? To go back to South Africa in 1981? Were you intending to become some sort of political activist?'

'No, you know I was never an activist of any kind. But I did think I could, well, in some way, *do* something ...'

She hesitated. It was not often that Martha evinced any diffidence about the pertinence of what she had to offer, which made what was to come all the more interesting to Christopher, and he waited. 'Was it perhaps,' she said at last, 'to do with Daniel de Villiers?'

Well, her candour deserved to be repaid in kind. 'I suspect it was,' he said.

'You *suspect?*'

'Yes. I suspect. Do you always see your steps that clearly as you take them?'

'I think I do, when they're as momentous as that.'

'Then all I can say is you are remarkably lucky and remarkably clearsighted. I don't think I was at all clear as to why I went back to South Africa.'

'But you are now?' she pressed.

'Does it matter?' he asked. 'Now, after all these years?'

'Yes, it matters. It matters that you should see, before it is too late, what Daniel did to you.'

'What was it he did to me?' Christopher asked, surprised alike at her frankness and at his own mildness in the face of it.

This time she did not hesitate; she said, with a promptness that in anyone less urbane may have come across as brutality, 'He robbed you of your self-respect and then he robbed you of your youth.'

It was strange, the extent to which he still felt the need to defend Daniel de Villiers, who had never needed his defence. 'I needn't have gone home,' he said. 'He didn't ask me to. He never gave me any reason to believe that I was anything but a convenience to him – except when I was an inconvenience,' he added with a consciously wan smile.

But she did not share the smile. 'That's unworthy of you, to be so abject,' she said. 'You know that he gave you just enough encouragement to keep you hanging around. And he gave you nothing in return.'

'What was it that he could have given me?'

'A less provisional friendship, a friendship that wasn't always subordinated to some other claim on his time and attention.'

'Isn't that what friendship is? A supporting role?'

'In general, yes. But wasn't the support rather one-sided in this instance?'

For the first time, in her insistence, she struck him as lacking in – well, in tact and consideration, he thought wryly. Her emphasis on Daniel's failures as a friend reflected also on Christopher's abject willingness to put up with those failures; and, however accurate that reflection might be, it was not a light in which at this hour of the day or night he cared to view himself. He could tell her, probably should tell her, that her strictures were now out of date, that he had the night before acted under precisely the persuasion she was now urging upon him. But some perverse instinct of ... of what? of belated loyalty to Daniel? of misplaced pride? prevented him from telling her. He would tell her in due course; at present it was too raw to handle, his defection from his abysmal servitude. To glory in it would be also to admit to the loss of half a lifetime. She couldn't know, and he couldn't tell her, how once, long ago, for a fortnight, he had been happier, here in Paris, with Daniel, than he had ever been before or since; and that his servitude had been determined by the vain hope of someday recovering something of that happiness.

So he said, to terminate the conversation, 'You may be right. But that is now water under the bridge. Shall we go?'

She regarded her empty glass as if wondering how it had reached that state. Then she said, 'We may as well. I'm never going to get you to see the light on this.'

'Oh, I've seen the light,' he said, as they got up from their seats. 'But what to do with all that light?'

He walked her home, through the bright Paris afternoon, in a silence companionable enough not to reflect invidiously on their recent conversation, and, turning down her offer of a cup of coffee, he returned to his hotel. He had thought that he was relatively indifferent to Daniel's response to his letter, but, as he walked down the Rue de l'Odéon and crossed the Boulevard St Germain, he realised with some apprehension that there might well be a reply waiting to be downloaded on his laptop – and into his lap, he thought ruefully.

It was true, as he had told Martha, that he had written to Daniel. What he had not told her, perhaps as a last forlorn act of loyalty to his absent and erstwhile friend, was the exact tenor of his letter; indeed, he could even be said to have misled her on the nature of his letter, since he had not even mentioned his excursion to Italy. He had had other matter to impart:

Dear Daniel,
You must be wondering what's become of me, or rather, what's become of my undertaking – or your brief – to bring Eric back with me. I realise that you must be anxious and I apologise for prolonging that anxiety. Believe me when I say that had I been able to, I would

have kept you informed much more assiduously than I have. The truth is that I haven't known what to write to you.

I came here on the assumption, shared with you, that Eric was leading a dissolute life from which it was one's moral duty to try and extricate him with such arguments as one had at one's disposal – of which you supplied me with several good ones. Those arguments remain excellent, of course – it's just that I'm not sure about the assumption any more. Eric's life here, as far as I can judge, has certainly been different from what it would have been in Franschhoek, but I don't know if it follows that it's been dissolute. Of course, I can't claim to know all the details of that life – though Eric has been very candid with me – but I can see the results, and I must say that I find him much improved. He has grown up, as, quite obviously, he would in the natural course of things have done had he remained in Franschhoek, but he has here been exposed to influences that, contrary to our assumption, have apparently formed him into a mature and civilised young man.

So, to get to the point that you must have seen coming, I can't in all sincerity urge Eric to go back to Franschhoek. Yes, I can point out to him the material advantages of going back – in fact, I've already done so – and put before him your generous offer as persuasively as I know how; but what I can't do is to pretend to him that this will in some way make a better human being of him. Of course, that was never part of your plan, that I should use that as an argument, but it's been implicit in our assumptions. And though I will continue to put before Eric the advantages of going back, I need to say that it will be without the conviction with which I came to Paris in the first place.

I also need to say that Eric himself seems not totally averse to the idea of going back; but his life here is complex, and he has incurred responsibilities that it would be difficult for him simply to turn his back on. Forgive me if I sound evasive; I just don't want to be in the position of a spy reporting back on Eric's movements. Suffice it to say that it's my impression that his present life is constructive, if somewhat unconventional, and that his associates wish him well and, if you'll forgive the phrase, are good for him.

This is not what you had in mind when you sent me to Paris, I'm well aware of that, and so, of course, I'll not expect you to pay for my stay here – which has, in any case, become rather more extended than you can have had in mind.

Christopher had known, as, after a long breath, he clicked Send, that he was not only abdicating from his appointed task as ambassador, but surely severing, in Daniel's eyes, their ties of friendship. So it was now with an apprehension bordering on dread that he called up his inbox from its electronic lair. But there was no reply; either Daniel had not yet read his email, or, the more likely explanation, he was biding his time and leaving Christopher to stew in anxious apprehension.

Well, Christopher wasn't going to stew, he resolved. He had, under the pressure of Martha's vehemence, had two glasses of wine in quicker succession than he normally allowed himself, and he felt mainly a certain languor, not unpleasant, a sense that events should take their own course; that he, Christopher Turner, had now interfered enough.

CHAPTER 17

If Christopher had imagined that he had played his hand and could now sit back and regard the game with the serenity of an onlooker, he was promptly proved wrong. He had hardly closed his laptop with a sense of closing a chapter or even a book, when the phone rang.

'Christopher? This is Eric. Where have you been all afternoon?'

'I was out with Martha.'

'I hope you didn't have a huge lunch.'

'No, in fact it was a liquid lunch.'

'Good. Are you free for dinner? I know it's late to ask, on a Saturday –'

Christopher laughed. 'You mean, given the pressure of my social calendar? No, by the merest chance I am free tonight.'

'Good man. I'll come by your hotel at about eight.'

'I'll be ready. Where are we going?'

'I'll keep that for a surprise. See you tonight.'

'How do I dress?'

'Well, but not formally.'

'I think I can manage that.'

'So where are we going?' Christopher said, getting into the taxi that Eric had seemed to make materialise at his bidding.

'Ah. To La Coupole. You've heard of it?'

'Of course.' Christopher did not want to spoil the young man's evident pleasure by confessing that he'd been to La Coupole on a memorable evening many years ago: that could wait for later. 'Sartre and De Beauvoir are reputed to have danced the tango there, though the thought of those two sourpusses doing the tango does rather strain credulity.'

'I don't know,' Eric said. 'In Paris, even Marxist existentialists do the tango.'

'But do they do it well?'

'That's maybe more than we can hope for. But isn't the important thing that they do it?'

'For them, perhaps. But the poor onlookers couldn't have been charmed.'

'Since when are you so aware of what things look like?'

Christopher sighed. 'Since arriving in Paris, I suppose.'

The maitre d' greeted Eric by name, whether through some sixth sense matching reservations to faces, or because Eric was a regular there. Either way, there was in his welcome that mixture of cordiality and deference that only the fortunate few manage to inspire in the professional hosts of Paris.

As they were shown to their table, Christopher noticed the slight check in conversation as they passed, glances flicking over them, resting momentarily on Eric, sometimes lingering longer than necessary before returning to the circle of sociability: the near-automatic visual frisking that animates the great people-watching centres of Paris. He experienced again the vicarious pleasure of entering such a centre under the aegis, as it were, of the cynosure of the place; a pleasure he remembered experiencing just here, thirty years ago, when entering the same place with Daniel and Marie-Louise – though then, the pleasure had been mixed with the bitterness of recognising that part at least of the tribute was being paid to Marie-Louise, luminous in the flush of her newly won conquest of Daniel. It had been her idea, after the disaster of Le Procope, that they should come here; and her every little cry of admiration at the brilliant interior, the flamboyant decor, the self-conscious art deco, the glitter and clatter and hum of the place, was by implication a comparison with the dismal experience of a few evenings before.

But now he was here, he noted wryly, with the fruit of that union; and whatever pleasure he took in Eric's company was in a sense referable to Marie-Louise's invidious triumph. Was he being belatedly recompensed for the discomfiture of that last visit?

'You're smiling very enigmatically,' Eric said, as they took their seats in the vast pillared and coffered hall.

'Am I? I'm recalling my last visit here ...'

'So now you tell me you've been here? You should have said so.'

'So what? I've been to Notre Dame as well. That's not a reason not to go again.'

'Not that La Coupole is quite Notre Dame, but I take your point. Anyway, you were saying?'

'I was saying? Oh, yes, the last time I came here. It was with your mother and father, in fact.'

'Ah, another idyllic meal in Paris. You and Dad seem to have lived it up here.'

'You could say so, I suppose.'

'That sounds less than whole-hearted.'

'Well, your father and I had quite a complex relationship.'

Eric cocked his head, 'Oh? To me, you always seemed to get on just fine.'

'By the time you were old enough to notice, we did. But it took us a while to get there.'

'And Mom?'

'What about her?'

'Did you get along with her?'

'Do girlfriends and best friends ever get on very well?'

Eric laughed. 'I haven't had the experience, I wouldn't know. But are you saying there was rivalry between the two of you?'

'No, I never counted enough to be a rival. But there was tension, in the early days.'

'Mm, I can understand that. Once Mom has set her sights on something, she can be pretty damned pig-headed.'

They had been handed menus and Christopher's attention was divided between Eric's indulgent characterisation of his mother, and the restaurant's offerings, some of them rather bewildering to him. On the latter, though, Eric relieved him of the burden of a decision.

'The Irish smoked salmon and the lamb curry are excellent here.'

233

'Then that's what I'll have.'

'Right. That's quite straightforward, then.'

And with what Christopher had come to recognise as his easy command, Eric placed their order and decided on the wine. He settled back in his chair. 'So you and Beatrice had a real heart-to-heart last night?'

'Is that what she said?'

'That's not how she put it, no, but that's what I gathered.'

'And what did you manage to *gather*?'

'That she told you her history, and her anxieties about Jeanne.'

'Yes, she did. I appreciated that.'

'And she appreciated your sympathetic ear.' Eric was silent for a while, helping himself to a bread roll. Then he said, 'But how sympathetic was your ear exactly?'

'How does one measure levels of sympathy?'

'Call them degrees, then, ranging from …' he mock-seriously counted off on his fingers, 'a complete lack of sympathy, through some understanding, then moderate partiality, imaginative identification, ending in total empathy.'

Christopher pointed at his fourth finger. 'I think that would come closest, a kind of imaginative identification.'

'So you're on our side?'

'Are there sides?'

'Of course. My father wants me to go back to South Africa, Beatrice wants me to stay here. I'd have thought the sides were clearly defined.'

'I suppose I was surprised for a moment to hear you refer to *our side.*'

Eric flushed. 'You mean you doubted which side *I'm* on? How could you, when Dad's had to send you here to drag me back?'

'I was sent to point out to you the advantages of returning. I don't think that's dragging.'

'And I don't think you're answering my question. Whose side are you on?'

'Does it matter?' Christopher was aware of being evasive, but he did not want, for the moment, to tell the son of the letter he had written the father, which had been about as definite a taking of sides as the situation permitted. Once Daniel had replied, he would have more to tell Eric – who, in the meantime, was politely persistent.

'It matters tremendously to Beatrice, and yes, to me too,' said Eric.

'Do you mean that you might be swayed one way or the other by my opinion?'

'It would certainly be a factor in my decision.'

'Your decision?'

'Yes, as to whether to stay or to return.'

'So you're not as established as all that in your own mind?'

'Are you trying to catch me out here?' Eric asked; he was taking more of the initiative in the conversation than he'd done up to now, but without losing his good humour. 'Let's say, then, that I'm tremendously taken with Beatrice and with Paris and with everything it has to offer. But, as you yourself have pointed out to me, I'm at a crucial stage of my life, and the decisions I take now may have repercussions on the rest of my life. So, naturally, I want to keep an open mind.'

'Naturally. And your options open, too.'

'That sounds quite cynical. But yes, it's natural, I think, at this stage of my life, to consider my options very carefully. And what you've done is to place a viable option in front of me.'

'Then you *are* tempted?'

'Dammit, you really do take things literally! Okay, yes, I am tempted – in the sense of wondering what it would mean to take one course of action rather than another. But my dedication to Beatrice and to Jeanne – about that I have no doubt.'

'Doesn't that dedication become a somewhat theoretical affair if you are weighing it up against alternatives?'

'Look, what do you want me to say? That no matter what else turns up, I'll stay here in Paris as a *claqueur* and be Beatrice's kept man for the rest of my life?'

'Is that how you see yourself?'

Their first course had arrived, their wine poured, and Eric had every excuse to delay replying. But he did not avail himself of the convenience of smoked salmon. 'Yes,' he said, 'it is. I know you don't want to hear it put like this, you've probably got your own version of my relationship with Beatrice, and it's a very beautiful version, but it leaves out of account a whole lot of practical questions.'

'I know what the practical questions are. I'm supposed to be their spokesman. But your version of your relationship with Beatrice also leaves out of account almost everything of value.'

'Such as?'

'Such as the immense debt you owe her.'

'Oh, make no mistake, I'm as aware of the debt I owe her as it's possible to be.'

'I'm not speaking of monetary debt. I'm speaking of what she's done for you in other ways.'

'In other ways?' He seemed genuinely bemused.

'Yes, in every way that matters. You were, you won't mind my saying, rather rough and unformed ...'

'Oh, I know, a total lump of clay.'

'And Beatrice has formed you and shaped you into ... well, into one of the nicest young men I've met.'

Eric smiled. 'It's difficult to decide whether that's the worst insult anybody has ever paid me, or the greatest compliment. So, I'm the proverbial sow's ear?'

'Well, let's say you were.'

Eric paused while their plates were removed and the *agneau au cari* was served. 'But then,' he continued, over his curry, 'by your logic, if I am now the silken purse ...?'

'Yes?'

'Shouldn't I hold out for the highest price I can fetch?'

Christopher looked up from his plate to ascertain whether Eric was joking; and there was indeed a glimmer of saving irony in the young man's quizzical regard. As ironical, then, he took the question, and replied, 'Oh, who's to say what your value on the open market would be? Silk purses are such an unstable commodity in today's market.'

'So I'd better stick to what I have, then?' Eric asked, manoeuvring some sauce onto a morsel of bread.

But Christopher had reached the end of his irony. 'Make no mistake,' he said, 'if you desert Beatrice you'll be ... well, simply a brute.'

'A brute?' Eric repeated, not without amusement. 'Is that what I strike you as capable of being?'

'No, no. Not at all. Which is why it would be such a pity if you were to revert –'

'To the brute I used to be, you mean?' Eric insisted.

'Well, when I knew you, you were too young to be a thorough brute. But I wouldn't have ruled it out as one of your possibilities.'

This seemed to satisfy Eric. 'You may have been right. But as far as Beatrice is concerned, you needn't break your head. I'm not the least little bit tired of her.'

'No,' Christopher said, 'that would be unthinkable.' And unthinkable indeed was the idea of this young man, splendid and beautiful as he was, growing tired of as superior a creature as Beatrice du Plessis.

'You're really taken with her, aren't you?' Eric said.

'Yes, I am. She strikes me as ... well, of course, as beautiful, but also very fine. She has such composure, and yet such depth of feeling.'

'Oh, she's everything you say and more.' For the moment, that tribute, cursory as it appeared to Christopher's sense of its subject, seemed to bring the discussion to an end; an end that, Christopher guessed, had brought Eric as little certainty as to him. But Eric's uncertainties were now his affair; Christopher had laid his cards on the table and could only wait for the other to respond in his own time.

But that time, it seemed, would not be tonight. They finished their meal, which was indeed excellent, at leisure, and lingered over their wine. The restaurant was now, at nine-thirty on a Saturday evening, packed to capacity, and the warm brew of the rich interior combined pleasantly with the effect of the wine to induce in Christopher a feeling of immense well-being: sitting here, in this opulent space, opposite this glamorous countryman of his, seemed at the furthest remove from his daily life in Cape Town, which, yes, had its pleasures and its satisfactions, but lacked *this*, the effortless – not to say artless – merging of urbanity and congeniality and amenity and civility and courtesy with beauty and energy. And for the moment Eric de Villiers seemed to embody, in his person and his manner, all this.

They had ordered coffee, which was now brought to them in dainty porcelain cups, individually decorated in the restaurant's eclectic style.

'Pretty cup,' Eric said; and at this, the memory Christopher had been suppressing all evening broke to the surface, and must have registered on his face, for Eric asked, 'What's the matter? Don't you like the cup?'

'Oh, no, it's a beautiful cup. It's just that it did bring back a bad moment. From the last time I was here.'

'With Mom and Dad?'

'Yes, though it's still difficult for me to think of them as your mom and dad. You see, in my mind, these last few days, they've been roughly the same age as you. Certainly when we were here – yes, we were only slightly younger than you are now. And, of course, Paris preserves memories as in aspic or amber. Changing so little herself, she takes you back to what you were.'

'And what *were* you?' Eric asked. 'I mean, as regards coffee cups.'

'Ah, yes, the coffee cup. You see, on that evening, too, the coffee was brought in these pretty little cups. And your mother said, Gee, I'd really like one of these cups. Do you think I could take one home? And your father said, Don't even think about it. And we none of us thought about it again until the waiter came to clear the table after dinner, and announced, in loud French, so loudly that the surrounding tables looked up with interest, There is one cup missing.'

'Oh shit,' Eric said. 'That must have been bloody embarrassing.'

'Yes,' Christopher said. 'Yes, it was embarrassing …'

But stronger than his embarrassment had been the murderous hatred that Christopher had felt as Marie-Louise looked about her blandly and asked, 'What's he saying?'

'He is saying that there's a cup missing.'

'What a moron. Is he accusing us of stealing one of his cups?'

'Yes, he is. Have you got it?'

She'd shrugged. 'You find that out. You can always search me, if you don't trust me.'

In the meantime the waiter had stood stolidly looking on, then had said, this time in perfect English, 'I must ask one of you to accompany me to the manager's office.'

Marie-Louise had said. 'I can't speak French. You'll have to go, Christopher.'

'And what shall I tell them?' he'd asked, in cold and helpless fury.

'Tell them to put their little cup up their arse.'

'Thanks, that's very helpful.'

'Explain to them, Chris,' Daniel had said.

'Explain what, exactly?'

'That we're tourists, and just wanted a souvenir.'

For a moment, Christopher had given his anger free rein. 'You think they've never heard that excuse from some stupid spoilt bitch from Kansas City or Tallahassee?'

'Are you saying –' Marie-Louise had demanded, but Christopher had turned his back and followed the waiter to the manager's office.

The manager was severe but not outraged. He had seen such larcenies and worse in his career. 'Monsieur, please tell your little *copine* that here at La Coupole we like to provide beautiful tableware as a compliment to our clients because we believe they will appreciate it; but we also believe that stealing is not a form of appreciation.'

'I'll tell her,' Christopher had wretchedly said, knowing that he could never deliver such a message to Marie-Louise, who would somehow turn her contempt for it upon him as the bearer.

'We will say no more about it,' the manager had said. 'The price of the cup will be added to your bill.'

Returning to the table, now red-faced under the amused contemplation of onlookers, he had said, 'Okay, let's go. They'll add

239

the price of the cup to the bill.'

'And how do we know that they don't over-charge us for the cup?' Marie-Louise had demanded. 'Did you ask him what the cup cost?'

'No, I did not. I was only too pleased to get out of there without them calling the cops.'

'That's ridiculous, it's only a little cup. I think you should query the amount.'

By this time, even Daniel had had enough. 'Oh, come, Marie-Louise, I don't think it's for us to make a fuss. We're hardly in a position to be bolshy.'

'So who's making the fuss? *They're* making the fuss, *Christopher's* making the fuss, *you're* making the fuss, it's all just a storm in a teacup. Or a coffee cup,' she'd added, pleased with her bon mot.

They'd paid the bill, Christopher paying his third of it. The others had not commented on the fact that he was now subsidising Marie-Louise's theft, and he'd not pointed it out.

'Let's get out of here,' Marie-Louise had said loudly, with all the aggrieved aplomb of the injured party. 'This place really sucks.' There were sniggers from an adjoining table, and Daniel had had the grace to look embarrassed. 'Oh, for fuck's sake, Marie-Louise,' he'd muttered, leading the way out of the restaurant, leaving Christopher to take charge of the sashaying Marie-Louise in a humiliating travesty of their triumphal entry.

On their way home, walking in silence down the Boulevard St Michel and past the Jardin du Luxembourg, Marie-Louise had paused on the pavement, opened her bag and taken out the cup. 'Oh, all right,' she'd said, 'I'm bored with the two of you moping. It's only a fucking *cup*, for God's sake,' and she'd thrown the delicate little cup and saucer into a rubbish bin.

'So it was Mom who had pinched the cup, I take it?'

With Eric's question, Christopher lurched back into the present. 'It was indeed.'

Without blinking, he asked, 'What did you do then?'

'I went to see the manager and squared it with him.'

'Did they let you off?'

'They charged us for the cup but agreed not to press charges.'

'That was lucky.' Eric smiled indulgently; he could not be expected to know, since Christopher had not told him, what a hideous betrayal Marie-Louise's act had seemed of everything that the enchanted space had to offer, of all faith and trust and beauty. 'Yes, that's Mom for you,' he said. 'She can never quite see why she can't just have what she wants.'

'I suppose we none of us can. But we don't always grab, regardless of consequences.'

'Don't we?' Eric laughed. 'Speak for yourself, old man!'

'Oh, I'll take it upon myself to speak for you,' Christopher said, as they got up and left the beautiful room.

It occurred to him as he re-entered his little room and opened the windows to let in the night air, that he had, in a manner, spoken for Eric in his email to Daniel; and that in all probability the father's response to his speaking was now waiting for him. He was tempted to leave it to the morning; he had no inclination to spoil the evening's impressions with what would undoubtedly seem like a violation of grace and good humour. But nor did he want that potential violation to lurk like an evil genie in his little electronic lamp. He powered up the computer and called up his inbox. There it was, the reply, from De Villiers, D:

Christopher,

Your letter was not as much of a surprise to me as you may have thought. I've been prepared for something like this by your silence, though I didn't imagine to what extent you'd actually gone against the spirit and the letter of our agreement. I didn't ask you to go to Paris to tell me that my son had received, at the hands of unnamed 'associates', the education that I had failed to give him. If I understand you correctly, Paris has miraculously civilised him, rescued him from barbarism.

Well, that's good to know. But, as you say, it's not a discovery I can be expected to sponsor, so I must ask you to return to South Africa immediately. It seems to me that you have been working against my interests rather than promoting them. Since you provide so little detail, I have no way of knowing who or what these 'associates' are that have transformed my son. It's clear that they have managed to persuade you, at any rate, of their superiority to your friends at home, and I hope they will console you for what you have sacrificed. I am flabbergasted that a man of your maturity can, in just a fortnight, find reason to discard a long-standing friendship so lightly.

Daniel

The tone of Daniel's letter was, he supposed, to have been expected. Daniel was not a man who took kindly to being crossed, and he had got into the habit of regarding Christopher as appointed to his convenience, as not having an independent mind and will. That, no doubt, had been Christopher's own fault, for making himself smaller than he was, as Beatrice said, for consenting dumbly to the role apportioned to him. He now felt as if the survival of the friendship had been more a question of his tenacity than of any reciprocity on Daniel's part. At most, Daniel had consented to being loved, not displeased at being admired, not averse to having an undemanding friend as company during those periods when the depletion of his personal life left him rather blankly surveying his domain, like a king without subjects.

There was, to Christopher's sense, a kind of poignancy in the fact that, after so many years, the friendship should be terminated by his embroilment with Daniel's son; but perhaps the friendship had run its course long ago, and it had taken this return to Paris to bring home that fact. It was in Paris, after all, where Christopher had, for a brief period, most enjoyed Daniel's friendship, and it was in Paris that he had felt most betrayed. To see again the scenes of his youthful exhilaration and devastation – and he felt, now, that those terms were not too extravagant – was in some measure to relive them, their intensity wadded, no doubt, by the complacencies and compromises of middle age, yet still disconcertingly undiminished.

For it had been a process, he now realised, the gradual recovery of that time; but realising that, it occurred to him to wonder whether, potent as the Parisian medium was, it could have achieved just that effect without the presence of Eric de Villiers. For all the differences between father and son – and they were manifold – what the young man's energy and undaunted assault upon life most resembled was his father's unquenchable enthusiasm and indomitable conviction that, for all his faults, he could and would be loved. It was a conviction so entrenched as to impress itself upon anyone within its sphere of influence, as Christopher himself had experienced – to his detriment, Martha would surely say, and who was to say Martha was wrong? It had the quality, this conviction of Daniel's, of making everybody else seem ordinary by comparison; or, more positively, to Christopher's beguiled vision, to irradiate the ordinary with its own lustre and its own glamour.

All this Christopher now turned over in his mind as he stared bleakly at the small screen transmitting in 12 pt Calibri his old friend's indignation. He knew Daniel well enough to appreciate the restraint marking this peremptory missive. It would have been far truer to his temperament to rage and rant: it was a measure of the depth of his disgust that he should have recourse to a mode so alien to his nature as irony. Well, Daniel's disgust was now Daniel's portion; he, Christopher, need no longer make it the rule of his existence to please Daniel de Villiers.

He could see no call to reply to Daniel immediately – or, indeed, ever. Yet, Christopher conceded, he might in due course come up with something suitably abject or even uncharacteristically defiant.

CHAPTER 18

Sunday morning brought neither compliance nor defiance: Christopher decided to put Daniel on hold, and pretend that he was simply a tourist intent on seeing the sights. One sight he had been wanting to see, in fact, was the Picasso Museum, which had opened a few years after his last visit. He had never been sure whether he really *liked* Picasso; his own bent was altogether towards the muted warmth of Degas, with his tired ballerinas, resigned laundresses and wistful absinthe drinkers.

But on this visit, the vivid Mediterranean flare of Picasso's canvasses, all the more strident for their setting in the restrained sandstone rooms of the museum, affected him unexpectedly. They were grotesque, they were distorted, these paintings, but they were alive in their very rapaciousness and yet, at times, serene in their repose. They had little to say about Degas's world of working and enduring; they were perversely pagan in their celebration of brute energy and exuberant sensuality.

Christopher paused in front of a painting of two creatures on a beach, apparently female and male, in the process of either devouring each other or making love, in a clumsy consort of confused limbs not so much entwining as colliding. It was unhelpfully entitled 'Figures at the Seashore'. He stood staring blankly at the painting. It had power, certainly, but an irreverent mind could also have found scope for comedy in the ecstatic contortions of the two figures, apparently intent upon spearing one another with their pointed tongues, each at some risk from the other's serrated jaws.

He stepped back to gain perspective on the strange composition, and brushed against someone standing to the left of him. As he apologised, he glanced at her face; she returned his look, seeming to recognise him. He was nonplussed for a moment, and then her face found its slot in his memory: she was the woman in black whom he had seen at Beatrice's apartment. Now, in the generous light of the museum, her features stood starkly revealed. Her face he could only describe as desiccated, in the parchment-like brittleness of her complexion, emphasised by her hair, which was the colour and texture of straw. Against the pallor of her skin her eyes shone deep blue, the sole aspect of her face betraying any vitality.

'Oh, hello,' he said. 'I didn't recognise you for a moment.'

She inclined her head and smiled. For a moment he wondered if she could speak English, then remembered that she had done so before.

'Do you like Picasso?' he asked, for want of anything else to say, as she still looked at him as if anticipating some communication.

But if he was expecting the conventional enthusiasm, he was surprised. 'Like?' she replied. 'No. No, I do not like Picasso.' Her face assumed a startling sinewy energy under the pressure of her emotion. 'I hate him. But he fascinates me, he makes me understand something about men and women.' Her English was careful but fluent; her accent was not French, but he could not place it more positively than that.

'May I ask what it is about men and women that he makes you understand?'

'Ah, I do not know how to say it, he says it through his pictures. You see that picture?' she said, pointing at the painting in front of them.

'Yes, I was just contemplating it when you arrived.'

'So, you have contemplated it, you should know what I mean. It shows the man needing to destroy the woman in order to make love to the woman.'

Christopher said nothing as he peered at the painting, trying to make it fit her interpretation. She continued, as if eager to convince him, 'You know the painting in the Louvre, by Gericault, of a lion attacking a horse?'

'Yes, I have seen it.'

245

'Well, that is what this is, a wild animal destroying another animal.'

'But isn't the woman also destroying the man?'

'No, if you look closely, you see he is all power, she is all submission.'

Christopher looked closely, but still failed to see. 'But doesn't she *want* to submit?'

'Yes, yes, that is the worst, that she wants to submit, that she wants her own destruction from the man. It is, I think, a very terrible painting. Beautiful, but terrible. It is always terrible, for the woman.'

It would have been open to him to protest that, in Picasso's rendering, male and female were so intertwined that it was difficult to see who, if anybody, was subjugating whom; it was at least open to speculation that the woman might be the aggressor. But he guessed that his interlocutor was not open to a more playful interpretation of the situation: she was glowering at the picture as if contemplating an attack with a nail file.

But her aggression subsided into a more resigned mode. She shook her head. 'It's always terrible, for the woman,' she said again – which, Christopher decided, was a termination of the conversation rather than an invitation to further discussion. There was a moment when she seemed to be on the point of saying something more, but she bethought herself, and relapsed into silence. So they vaguely drifted apart, as strangers in a museum do, drawn in different directions by their different interests, driven by the fear of having to make conversation with a stranger about room after room of paintings.

Christopher spent another two hours amidst the exquisite excesses of Picasso's imagination. There was power, certainly, in the writhing lines and the ferocious colours; but was the woman a victim or a partner? Did she suffer it or perpetrate it? As he mused, Zelda's warning – was it only a week ago? – flashed into his mind: Beatrice was … *lethal*, her word had been. He'd failed to see the slightest sign of this, but then, wasn't that precisely the mark of the most lethal predators? Christopher shook his head and smiled to himself – no, far more likely that Zelda had been motivated by the aggrieved spite that seemed to be her mode of interaction with the world.

He caught another glimpse, once or twice, of the woman in black, immersed, he supposed, in horrified contemplation of the affront of Picasso's genius; but he did not approach her, and she seemed oblivious to his presence.

Strolling through the Sunday-afternoon lethargy of the Marais, Christopher contemplated the prospect of his return, now that his mission had been officially terminated. But he was too curious to leave; he felt that he had seen but half the drama and would never know the ending if he left now. And it was not, he reminded himself, for Daniel de Villiers to prescribe to him when to return; he could stay on, for a while at least, at his own expense. His seat was booked for his return in a few days' time, but it was an open ticket that could be changed; and he had been assured by Monsieur Marcel that he could keep his room as long as he wished, with only a twenty-four hours' notice of intention to leave.

He had hardly reached his room, when his phone rang. 'Christopher? Zeevee.'

'Zeevee!' He was absurdly pleased to hear the American's leisurely vowels.

'I'm phoning with an invitation. Are you free on Tuesday evening?'

'Yes. Yes, I am.'

'Good. Gloriani has asked me to invite you to a little reception at his apartment.'

'Gloriani? I didn't imagine he'd even remember meeting me.'

'You're underestimating both yourself and Gloriani. You are eminently memorable, and he has an excellent memory. So you can make it? Eric will be there too.'

'That's good'

'That's excellent. I'll send round an official invitation to your hotel, with the details.'

'Will it tell me what to wear?'

'No, Gloriani would never dictate to his guests on that front. But don't wear a Gloriani, that would seem obsequious.'

'I don't actually own a Gloriani. But what *do* I wear?'

'Anything you feel good in. There will be people dressed to the teeth and there will be people in almost nothing at all; but they will all try to look as beautiful as they can.'

'Looking beautiful is more than I can undertake, but I shall do my best to look at least decent.'

'I'm sure your decent will be beautiful.'

'Is the decent ever beautiful?'

'Or the beautiful ever decent? It's a good question – but yes, as you do it, I'm sure you'll make the decent look beautiful.'

Christopher smiled at the familiar honking laugh at the end of the line. 'I'll try to be worthy of your faith in me. And at what time do I turn up?'

'The invitation will say at eight, but make it a bit later. You don't want to be the first to arrive. Not after nine, though. There will be food, so don't eat before you come.'

Un-dined, then, at a quarter past eight on Tuesday evening, Christopher set off, once again, for the Marais. Gloriani, it appeared from the card that had been duly delivered, lived on the Place des Vosges. In the charmed world where Christopher had latterly found himself, it seemed only appropriate that Gloriani should live at that address – and yet, of all addresses ...! If Eric had in his early days felt his exclusion from the gracious places of Paris, he must be more than satisfied now.

The walk to the Marais, across the river, across the two little islands, was now acquiring the ease of familiarity, without sacrificing any of the charm of its variety, the succession of vistas and panoramas, the broad spread of the river, the buttressed bulk of the cathedral, the prim rectitude of the little park, the inconsequential pomposity of the miniature bridges, the tortuous succession of narrow streets, to issue at last in the sublime redbrick rectangle of the Place des Vosges, now, in the evening light, softening into shade and lamplight, the trees absurdly clipped into a kind of suspended hedge, obsessive in its symmetry and yet whimsically eccentric; the houses fringing the square, peering over their gracefully arched arcades, also partaking of this play of the formal and the fanciful.

Gloriani's apartment was on the south side of the square. Entering through one of the inconspicuous doors leading off the colonnaded arcade, and mounting a severe stone staircase to the first floor, Christopher found an ornate double door standing open to the landing, leading to a high-roofed room of generous proportions. The room had been kept, Christopher imagined, close to its original design, a simple oblong space opening, through a series of French doors, onto a balcony. Heavy curtains were swept away from the doors, affording a partial view onto the lamp-lit square beyond. A massive chandelier suspended from the ceiling dimly illuminated a tapestry covering an entire wall; a quick glance revealed a hunting scene, bounding dogs in pursuit of terrified deer, armed men following.

The size, proportions and relative bareness of the room suggested a stage set, awaiting the entry of the cast – unless, indeed, the performance had already commenced, for in the far corner a group of people stood clustered – or *arranged*, for there was something in the symmetry of the grouping that seemed not merely random, but suggested a single centre of interest around which a tableau was composed. The illusion of formality was enhanced by the dress of those in the group: the men were in dinner jackets, the women in evening gowns that blended with the sumptuous, though faded tones of the room. There was a low murmur of conversation; from a far room came the sound of a chamber group playing a Schubert trio. The whole picture, dim, subdued, with its mellow colours and its muted sounds, had about it a ripeness that spoke of sociability and amenity and unostentatious power.

Christopher did not recognise anyone in the group; indeed, most of its members had their backs towards him, engrossed as they were in conversation. At that moment the composition shifted, relented, and revealed Gloriani himself, who now stepped forward to greet Christopher, the group turning to watch him, like courtiers in an opera following the movements of the Duke. The theatrical air of the occasion was intensified by the music from the further room, which had now modulated into the lovely Andante from the E-flat major Trio.

'Ah, Mr Turner,' Gloriani said, in his perfectly modulated voice, 'I am so glad you were able to come.'

'I am too,' said Christopher. 'Thank you for the invitation.'

'The privilege is mine entirely. I had feared you may have returned to your native country, but Zeevee reassured me that you were still with us. Would you like something to drink? You'll find the drinks in the next room.' He gestured towards the double doors behind him. 'We must talk, you and I,' Gloriani said, 'before the end of the evening.' He put a fine-boned hand on Christopher's sleeve for a brief moment, then turned back to his coterie, which parted to receive him and then closed around him jealously.

The next room was less muted – here, guests were standing in twos and threes, their voices raised above the musicians plying their instruments as earnestly and intently as if on a concert stage. The lighting was brighter, too, and the decoration more lavish: sofas and easy chairs and precious rugs, and a large oil painting that could only be a Renoir, a boating party on a summer's day, with fair, plumply smiling women and gallant straw-hatted men in easy, sunlit concourse. Here, in this wondrous room, was also what Gloriani had called 'the drinks' – a fully equipped bar staffed by two young men in tuxedos. Christopher speculated, unkindly, that they were probably *claqueurs* moonlighting as waiters; yet they were so expert at dealing with the complicated requests of the guests that they could, he concluded, be nothing but professional barmen. He himself asked simply for a glass of champagne and withdrew from the press of people into yet another room, even more lavishly furnished than the previous one, where food was being set out on a long table. Here, he was relieved at last to find a familiar face, all the more welcome for being the amiable, ugly face of Zeevee, who was standing on his own, apparently engrossed in studying a painting on the wall, a gloomy generic still life of slaughtered pheasants surrounded by freshly picked pomegranates and parsnips.

The American's lugubrious features relaxed into a lopsided

250

smile as he recognised Christopher. He extended a huge hand; Christopher shifted his glass to his left hand to shake the proffered paw. 'Quite something, isn't it?' Zeevee asked, gesturing around him at the brocaded walls and the gleaming parquet floor. 'It's the real thing.'

'The real thing?'

'Yes, the original furnishings and finishes. Well,' he relented, 'there may have been a tactful touching-up here, a copy substituted for an original there, but not so you could tell.'

'Certainly not so *I* could tell,' Christopher confessed.

'When the imitation is made by an expert, it defies detection.'

Around them the room was filling, as several large platters were uncovered. The press of hungry people in search of food, the surge towards the more exotic delicacies on offer, gluttony precariously kept in check by decorum: Christopher was amused to see the stately occasion relapsing so readily into honest voracity.

'Are you hungry?' Zeevee asked. 'Do you want to pile in?'

'I don't think I'm hungry enough to do battle for it,' Christopher replied.

'No, I'd also rather stand here and talk to you.' Zeevee said, which struck Christopher as so exactly the right thing to say that he couldn't think of a reply that wouldn't spoil the moment; but Zeevee seemed to understand that, too, and they stood for a moment in companionable silence. From where they were positioned, there was a clear vista through the interleading rooms to the entrance, and to their left, to further rooms Christopher had not explored. The two men stood and watched as guests arrived in the vestibule, where Gloriani was still tirelessly greeting new arrivals.

'I don't think I've ever seen such a consummate social creature,' Christopher remarked, half to himself.

'Yes, isn't he amazing?' Zeevee said. 'He's as smooth as silk and yet not the least little bit insipid. It comes with having complete control of his environment. And *that* comes with being absolutely expert at what he does.'

'But what is it that he does? Apart from designing clothes, I mean.'

Zeevee looked at Christopher. 'I think Gloriani would not understand that question. He'd say what *is* there, apart from designing clothes?'

'Then his environment is quite a small part of human endeavour?'

'Yes, if you count human endeavour in terms of its contribution to the gross national product. But if you consider that what almost every man, woman and child on earth has in common is the need to clothe themselves, then, well, that's quite important.'

'But it's not as if every man, woman and child on earth can afford to be clothed by Gloriani, is it?'

'No, indeed,' Zeevee said, moving into his ironic discursive mode. 'But don't you see, by setting the highest standards within his admittedly narrow niche, he creates, indirectly, a yardstick? And however remote its form, it's a yardstick that affects the production of clothing in general.'

'No, I'm not sure that I do see that. But I gladly accept that Gloriani is a highly accomplished person.'

'Oh, he's a genius,' Zeevee said, as if that disposed of the question, and they stood for a moment again in silence. Their communion was invaded by a woman with a plate in her hand, on which two lobster tails lay in unadorned isolation. Peering at Christopher closely, she said, 'Well, hi! You're the gentleman from South Africa, aren't you?'

'He is, indeed,' Zeevee intervened. 'You remember Zelda, Christopher?'

Christopher remembered Zelda, but he would not have recognised her in her present manifestation: her hair was now a vivid red, and where before it had been drawn back severely from her face, it now surrounded her features in an abundance of ringlets. The eyes, formerly so prominent, now all but disappeared in a vast abyss of dark make-up. Her voluminous wine-red dress was draped around her spare frame as if to obscure it from view. The total effect would have been sinister had there not been something innocent about its very excess, something of a young girl playing at dressing up like an adult.

'Don't you just hate a boo-fay?' Zelda asked Christopher,

lowering her voice as if inviting him into a subversive conspiracy. 'People clambering all over each other like puppies trying to get the best nipple.'

'There's nothing puppy-like about them,' Zeevee said. 'More like crocodiles competing for wildebeest on National Geographic.'

'You know I hate that channel?' she said. 'Are they really called wildebeest – as in wild beasts?'

'As in, yes,' said Christopher. 'I think you would call them gnu.'

'I wouldn't call them anything. Not that I've got anything against them, I just don't like watching animals being torn apart by each other.'

'You haven't done too badly, my dear,' Zeevee said, pointing at the two lobster tails on her plate.

'You're kidding, right? Two measly tails was all I got for getting my Manolos trampled on.' She giggled. 'They're crocodile skin, so I guess you could say the gnus have had their revenge.'

She wandered off, looking waif-like and lost with her plate held before her like a begging-bowl.

'I wouldn't have recognised her,' Christopher said. 'Nothing about her is the same, not even her voice.'

'Oh, Zelda reinvents herself every month or so. She's had about twenty different incarnations since I've known her. She is really one of my best friends.'

'But how do you sustain a friendship with someone who's never the same from one month to another?'

'Oh, there is a stable core of innocence under the trappings. Zelda is only a slightly more pronounced form of the general rule of social interaction here, which is not to repeat oneself if one can help it. Which is really also a law of nature, if you think about it.'

Christopher shook his head. 'You mean like the butterfly and the chrysalis? Or the tadpole and the frog? I'd find it confusing if my friends kept metamorphosing. Surely you rely on a certain amount of repetition in your friends? You can hardly be expected to get to know them afresh every time you meet them.'

'Quite. That's where the stable core is useful.'

'I'll drink to the stable core,' Christopher said, lifting his glass.

253

'And I'll drink to the metamorphosis.'

'To each his own. But you seem to me not to be the butterfly type.'

Zeevee laughed. 'Yes, I know, I'm a perpetual grub. But a man can hope, can't he?'

'You're the least grub-like person I've ever met,' said Christopher, suddenly feeling the need to be serious with this ugly, ironic, melancholy man. 'What I meant was that you don't strike me as flighty and changeable. You'll stick to what you've chosen.'

'I'm not sure that that's a virtue,' Zeevee said. 'Shouldn't one adapt to one's environment?'

'That depends on the environment, I suppose. Now *this* environment ...'

'Not the kind you think one should adapt to?'

'I don't know. It's a very beautiful environment. But I seem to feel ... well, that the price of adaptation may be very high.'

Zeevee laughed. 'For me to adapt to a beautiful environment, the price will be high indeed!'

'That's not what I meant,' Christopher said, 'as you well know.'

'Whether you meant it or not, my dear sir, it's true.' He said this comfortably, inviting neither assent nor dissent, looking about him with his alert, interested gaze. Then he observed, 'Now *there's* somebody who is beautifully adapted to his environment.'

Christopher followed Zeevee's glance and saw, in the far room, Eric de Villiers. The young man had evidently just arrived, being greeted by his host with the double kiss on the cheek. 'Eric? Ah yes, beautifully is the word.'

Under the mild glow of the chandelier, Eric shone gold; and on his face, as he emerged from Gloriani's greeting, was a smile of such candour and joy as to constitute a motion of confidence in his host, in the gathering as a whole, in the evening: whoever else is here, it seemed to say, will be delightful, and my mere presence will make them more delightful still. Adapted to his environment, yes, but at the same time so constituted as to form a defining part of that environment.

Zeevee inclined his head towards Christopher and said,

254

'Beautifully indeed.' But he said this with an expression of such forlorn admiration that Christopher felt moved to say, 'I think I know something of what you feel. I once felt something like it for his father.'

The American turned on him a gaze so mournful that it would have been comical had it not been so heartbreaking. But all he said was, 'You once felt? So you no longer do?'

'No. No, I think I have seen through my feelings.'

'Seen them for what they are, you mean?'

'Well, seen them, at any rate, for being futile, a waste of time.'

'And how long did it take you to realise that?'

'Thirty years, more or less. It has taken the son to make me see the father for what he is.'

'Because the son is like the father?'

It was extraordinarily as if Zeevee's candour released some corresponding spring in Christopher, leading him to say things he hadn't been aware of thinking. 'No,' he said, 'because the son is what the father could have been, if he'd followed the generous impulses of his nature rather than the promptings of his caution. In Eric I can see what I loved in Daniel, as I once knew him.' It was not often that Christopher used the word 'love', to himself or others, in relation to his feelings for Daniel de Villiers. It was surprising how natural it seemed; that, too, was an effect of Zeevee's simplifying directness.

It was in keeping with this directness that Zeevee turned to face Christopher and asked, 'So that now you love Eric?'

'Only in a hypothetical sort of way. At fifty – well, one doesn't love as one loved at twenty. And fortunately, there is a kind of inhibition against falling in love with somebody twenty-five years one's junior.'

'I don't know,' Zeevee demurred. 'History is littered with the corpses of those who fell in love with people twenty-five years and more their junior.

'No doubt. Perhaps the inhibition is less developed in some people than in others. I, at any rate … no, I'm not in love with Eric de Villiers. Fortunately.'

'It would have been a complication, certainly.'

'Certainly. Whereas you …'

'I?' Zeevee seemed discomfited.

'You don't have the wisdom of age – or call it, then, the grim acceptance of the inevitable – to protect you.'

'Is that a warning?'

Zeevee asked this lightly, but Christopher was still under a spell of seriousness. 'No,' he said. 'No, I don't think I would want to warn you against your own emotions. They are what they are and you are who you are. They may not bring you happiness, but they are part of being young, part of the life force in you, part of the passion that you can't deny.'

Zeevee gave this proposition his attention, as seriously as it had been offered. 'And yet, what did your passion bring you,' he asked, 'if I may be so impertinent?'

'In a sense, nothing. There are those, Martha among them, who will maintain that I have wasted my life on a useless passion. And as I have just said, I can now see how futile it has been.'

He was formulating his ideas as he spoke, making them out for himself as he explained them to Zeevee. 'And yet,' he continued, 'I wouldn't *not* have had it, this passion. Such as it was, with its stern demands and its meagre rewards,' he smiled self-consciously, 'it has been my life. And it has sustained me. No doubt it couldn't have been otherwise. I could say I was fated to love Daniel de Villiers; I was not, at any rate, aware of having a choice. Until…' – he was still figuring it out for himself – 'until, perhaps … well, till this last week. I have abdicated my self-appointed role as guardian of Daniel de Villiers's interests. I am a free agent.'

Christopher was conscious of a certain swagger in this declaration, and Zeevee's smile seemed to indicate that he, too, was not entirely persuaded by its force. 'Are you really free?' he asked. 'Or have you just changed sides?'

'Ah, that I don't know. I don't even know if there are sides. But I do think that Eric … well, is a better prospect than Daniel ever was.'

'Prospect for what?'

'Well, in your case, for friendship, if that's all that is on offer.'

Zeevee looked away, seeming to contemplate Christopher's statement. Then he slowly asked, 'What, then, is your advice to me?'

'I wouldn't presume to advise you. I'm too poor an example to serve as a model for anyone. And yet I wouldn't want to advise you to a contrary route either. All I can say is that you seem to me to be very fortunate, to have this, at any rate, to have your youth and your opportunity here, now, in this place and at this time; and to have such a friend as that. Even if you cannot have him on your terms, you can have him on the terms of Paris, which seem to me to be more generous than any terms that were ever offered to me.'

'The terms of Paris? What do you take them to be?'

Christopher could feel himself flushing under Zeevee's ironical regard. 'I must strike you as very presumptuous, pronouncing on the terms of Paris after a fortnight. But yes, with whatever allowance for my over-hasty judgement, I would say that Paris is still an enchanted place to be young in, because unlike – shall we say? – Houston, Texas, she softens the brashness of youth, lends it something of her own age-old accommodation to history and to legend. To be in love in Paris is to be part of that history and that legend. To be young in Houston is *only* to be young; to be young in Paris is to be young in the light of all the ages. Am I talking the sheerest nonsense?'

Zeevee was looking at him soberly. 'No, I don't think you are,' he said. 'I'm listening with the greatest interest. But it does sound to me as if you think, even though you're too tactful to urge it upon me, that I should indulge my infatuation – I mean, continue to do so.'

'I don't think it's an infatuation and I don't think it's an indulgence. But yes, to permit yourself the luxury of being in love, as long as you don't count upon its ever being returned in just the same form. To settle for half a loaf.'

'You call half a loaf a luxury?'

'Compared with no bread, it is a luxury. But then,' he continued, the champagne suddenly letting him down, 'the truth is I am not in a position to advise anybody; I'm too much at sea myself. For a moment, there, I thought I'd achieved some kind of clarity, but listening to myself, I seem to have arrived only at contradiction upon contradiction.'

'What is clear, at least, is the beauty of your intentions.'

Christopher looked at Zeevee to ascertain whether this last statement was ironically meant: beautiful intentions were so manifestly futile in the circumstances. But irony was not now Zeevee's mode, and he looked at Christopher with only his usual guileless gaze – which suddenly, to Christopher, had an extraordinary beauty of its own. They stood for a moment, not saying anything, looking at each other in a kind of community of desolation. For they had both lost what they had never so much as had.

Christopher put his hand on Zeevee's shoulder. 'My dear young man,' he said, 'the beauty you see in the intentions of others is the beauty of your own nature. May you never lose it.'

It sounded, he knew, paternal, even patronising; but he trusted Zeevee to ignore what was awkward about it, and see only the truth of the feeling. Zeevee, indeed, looked at him as if not quite knowing how to deal with the unexpected tribute, but before he could reply, his attention was claimed by the mewling of Zelda, who had returned in search of more lobster tails. Zeevee offered to brave the crush of humanity on her behalf, and Christopher excused himself, his mind too full of matter to make space for Zelda's chatter.

He wandered down the series of rooms, one opening from the other, most of them with a balcony onto the square. They were sparsely furnished, with at most a few easy chairs and low tables, all severely under-utilised, Christopher speculated. The rooms seemed to serve no function other than to form the harmonious but empty vista he had admired from the main room – unless their function was merely to be looked out from, for which indeed they were admirably equipped, with their large windows and generous balconies. But if they had been intended to relieve the crush of people in the main room, they had failed: the rooms were entirely empty, except, in the furthest of them, for a solitary woman. Since she had chosen that room, she must be assumed to be avoiding company, and yet Christopher felt an uncharacteristic impulse to intrude upon her solitude. He couldn't have said what it was in her attitude that touched him; perhaps he projected upon her state his wistful alienation from the glittering gathering inside. *She* was not glittering; her black dress, though of manifestly superior cut and cloth, was designed to deflect attention rather than to attract it.

She was standing at a window – this was one of the rooms that did not open onto a balcony – looking out over the quiet lamplit square. As he approached, she turned to face him, and only then did he recognise her as the woman in black. From her smile, re-served as it was, he gathered that she had recognised him too.

'Hello,' he said. 'We meet again. I didn't recognise you immediately. I suppose I didn't expect to find you here.'

'No,' she said, 'I am not often in this kind of place nowadays. But I used to be a part of it.'

'You were part of the fashion industry?'

'Yes, I worked for Gloriani too.'

'Ah, Gloriani …! He seems to be, I don't know …' he groped to express the realisation that was just dawning on him.

'You mean,' she said, 'that he is the power controlling us all. Yes, you could say that. But I was never a very important part of his domain. I was a stylist. And then when I met Beatrice, she asked me to become her personal stylist, so I worked for her until she retired and then I became … well, what you have seen. A kind of housekeeper and secretary.' If she resented a position denot-ing possible servitude, there was nothing in her manner to sug-gest this. But then, her manner at that moment was too neutral to suggest anything as definite as resentment. It left Christopher stranded, conversationally speaking, in that it did not invite any particular response.

'So you have known Beatrice for a long time,' was the best he could produce.

At this, her features opened into a smile. 'Oh, for ever,' she said. 'She couldn't do without me.'

This left Christopher wondering what advantage there was for her in this arrangement, though he guessed that the dependence was mutual.

'I don't think we've actually been introduced,' he said. 'I'm Christopher Turner.'

'I know that, of course,' she said. 'My name is Olga Tomanová.'

'You are Russian?'

'No, Czech. But I left Prague many years ago, as a young girl, in 1968, when travel became possible for a short while.'

'Ah yes, the Prague Spring.'

She smiled. 'Yes, the spring that never had a summer. But for me ... well, I was young and I was happy to be in Paris. But of course, I discovered that even in Paris, if you have no money and no friends ...'

It was extraordinarily as if she had some need to tell him her story, to involve him in the life she had led. 'I almost died of hunger and cold, that winter of 1968,' she said. 'I begged outside the stations, for the few centimes people had left over when they travelled on to other countries. I slept on the station platforms until I was chased away by the police, then I moved to the bridges of the Seine. I was always cold, always hungry, always scared.'

Her face was set in a kind of trance of memory; then it acquired a fiercer energy, a contraction of bitterness. 'People talk about the Seine,' she said, 'about its bridges, how beautiful, how romantic, but for me ... for me they will always smell of piss and shit and unwashed clothes and unwashed people, dirty people.'

She paused again, and Christopher waited for her to resume, as she was clearly intent on doing. 'By the time I realised that I was worse off than I would be in Prague,' she continued, now more calmly again, 'I didn't have the strength, even if I'd had the money, to go back.'

Unsure how to respond, Christopher said quietly, 'Then how ...?'

'How did I become a stylist? I wish I could say I was spotted by a talent scout and asked to come for a try-out. That fairy tale ... well, it is a fairy tale. I *was* spotted, by a kind of scout, you could say. A woman came to me and asked me if I wanted a job, a well-paid job. I said yes, of course; I'd have said yes if she'd offered me a hot meal. It turned out that she was recruiting, if that's the word for it, for a brothel in Pigalle.'

She was quiet, staring out of the window, and Christopher could only wait again for her to continue; a statement like that did not invite or permit a response.

'It was horrible at first, of course. I was eighteen and I had never been with a man. But the other girls were kind, in a rough sort of way, and the conditions were … well, the place was warm, and we had enough to eat.' She looked at him. 'Are you shocked?'

'No, no. I'm not shocked, just … well, surprised.'

'Surprised that an ex-prostitute should seem so respectable? Of course, not all of my … colleagues ended up so well. I was lucky – every whore's dream, the lucky break: one of my clients turned out to be a fashion scout – this was at the beginning of the fashion for very thin models – Twiggy had been the face of the year a couple of years earlier – and it was not necessary for me to go on diet to look as if I was starving. So I went for a try-out, and I started modelling. I was so-so successful, but after a few years I got very tired of walking up and down a piece of plank, showing off clothes. It is not a very interesting occupation, no?' She looked at him as if anticipating a reply.

'I don't know,' he said, 'I imagine not. But a lot of people seem to want to do it.'

'Yes, I wanted to do it, too. At first it seems better than prostitution, because you do not get paid to sleep with the men, so you can think you are doing it because you want to. But of course, after a while you realise you have no choice, you are sleeping with these men because you *have* to, because if you don't, they don't photograph you any more – the photographers, they were the gods, they could make you, and they all said that to make good pictures the photographer must sleep with the model, so that the picture has the feeling of sex. So it is just indirect prostitution.'

She looked at him; there was something unnerving about her blue eyes in her pale face with its papery skin. 'I know you are wondering how I could ever have been a model, as ugly as I am now. But I was once beautiful, like everyone else in my world. And

261

then, one night, I was coming home with a photographer after a shoot and of course a party, and he was drunk and drove into a concrete pillar. My face was – it was destroyed. What you see is what plastic surgery did for me. So that was the end of my modelling career. But I was not sorry. My beauty had been a curse for me. And in any case I was more interested in styling, it is more creative, at least you are asked for an opinion. A model is never asked for her opinion; you don't ask a horse for its opinion on the kind of saddle you put on it. So I asked Gloriani if I could become a stylist and he said okay. I think he could see I had an eye. But he is a good man, too, in his way, so perhaps he was sorry for me.'

'Is that where you met Beatrice?' Christopher asked; it was becoming clear to him that Olga's story complemented the one he had heard so recently from her employer.

'Yes,' Olga replied. 'She came to us, she was very young, very scared, very inexperienced. I was sorry for her. I wanted to help her not to make the mistakes I made.'

'And did you?' Christopher asked – disingenuously, he knew, but not feeling at liberty to let on that Beatrice had confided in him.

'Did I what?'

'Did you help her not to make mistakes?'

'Ah, you want to know whether Beatrice made mistakes. Listen, you know, everyone makes mistakes, even with someone to help them. So yes, of course she made mistakes. But I looked after her, I helped her through her mistakes. And I am still helping her, when she allows me.' She did not volunteer any more information, and Christopher had no desire to delve any deeper. It would be an affront to the dignity of Beatrice du Plessis to pry into her past or, even more, her present. She was what she appeared and what she had told him she was; that was, for the time being, his only article of belief.

But Olga, having opened her reserves of confidence, seemed oddly intent upon sharing them with him. 'Sometimes,' she said, 'the mistakes of our past follow us into the present and force us to make more mistakes.'

This was cryptic, but Christopher forbore from pursuing

her implication. It seemed likely that she would do so herself unprompted.

In this he was proved right. 'I am speaking to you, Monsieur Turner, like this, because I do not know what else to do,' Olga said. 'I am desperate with worry about Beatrice and about Jeanne.'

'Is it to do with Charlie Winthrop?' he risked.

'Charlie Winthrop?' She looked at him in mild surprise. 'Ah, you know about Charlie Winthrop. No, not Charlie Winthrop. He is, how do you say, *vieux jeu.*'

'And yet Beatrice was very concerned.'

'She was concerned, yes, but it is possible that her concern was also a little over-done.'

'Why on earth would that be?'

Her tone had abruptly hardened. 'I think that she may see Jeanne's situation as a way of interesting Eric de Villiers.'

'I'm not sure I follow you. Isn't Beatrice interesting enough in herself?'

'So you think, and so I think, but Monsieur de Villiers is young and restless, and he needs excitement. And he likes to think of himself as the protector of helpless women.'

Taken aback at her candid appraisal, Christopher replied, 'That is, as far as it goes, surely quite an admirable aspiration?'

'Admirable, yes, and I am not saying that Beatrice is not truly concerned about Jeanne.'

She was silent for a moment, her attention apparently drawn to a solitary pedestrian walking his dog in the street outside. Then she took a deep breath. 'But unfortunately her plan, if it was a plan, may have been too successful.'

'*Too* successful? I'm afraid I do not follow you.'

'I mean in perhaps making Monsieur de Villiers too interested in Jeanne.'

'Too interested?' Christopher asked mechanically, though he had no wish to encourage her, wished only he could stop her relentless revelations.

'Well, I mean that *she*, Jeanne, may have fallen in love with him. Can you blame her, when a young man as attractive as that comes all the way to Firenze to collect her – and who knows what arguments he used to bring her back?' She looked at him searchingly. 'Do you perhaps know?'

'No, I don't know.' It struck him that he knew very little about anything. 'But let us say that Jeanne has indeed fallen for Eric. I can see that that is cause for concern. But cause for despair?'

'Despair, yes, Mr Turner,' she said almost gloatingly, as if claiming a triumph. 'You see, Monsieur de Villiers – well, Jeanne says that he has told her that he loves her too.'

She said this in a voice so low that Christopher had to lean forward to catch her words. There was a horrible fascination in the stream of words coming from the woman; he felt compelled by the sheer energy of her malevolence to give her his attention.

'He told her this?'

'So she says. She confided in me when she came back from Italy; I have always been her confidante, ever since she was a little girl. He talked to her in Italy, he talked to her on the plane. She was very excited, but also scared. She doesn't want to hurt her mother, of course. And yet, of course, she wants the man as well.'

'Of course,' Christopher repeated, too dismayed to question her certainties. 'How do you think Beatrice will take it?'

'Take it? Oh, you mean, how will she feel? She will be destroyed.'

He allowed the full impact of the word, pronounced so matter-of-factly, to sink in. 'Is that how much Beatrice cares for Eric?'

'After her daughter, Monsieur de Villiers is the most precious thing in her life.' Was there a touch of bitterness in Olga's voice as she said this?

'But why?'

'You are asking me why he is precious?' She asked with a kind of fierce humour.

'No, that I think I can understand. But why would Eric leave Beatrice for Jeanne? Next to her mother she is like – like a cover photo next to an old master.'

She smiled her wan smile. 'Some people prefer cover photos to old masters. And youth is always overestimated, especially by the young.' She paused, weighing her words. 'Also, I think he is tired of being a *claqueur*.'

'What does that have to do with Beatrice?'

'I mean that being around her, being with her, he remains the *claqueur* applauding the beauty of others.'

'And with Jeanne?'

'With Jeanne he can be the impresario, the designer, the agent, the owner. He will take charge of her career and build his own career on hers, he will build an agency on her.'

'But he could do that as Beatrice's companion too.'

'He could have done that if Jeanne had not fallen in love with him. Now she will consent to his terms only on her terms. She is young, but she is old enough to know her own market value.'

'But how can you know all this?' Christopher asked.

'I have listened to her. He has talked to her of starting his own agency, with her as his main asset.'

'And she has consented to this?'

'So far, they have only talked. But that is what will happen. Unless …'

'Unless what?'

'Unless Monsieur de Villiers can be persuaded to leave Paris.' She looked at him with glittering eyes. 'To go back to South Africa, for instance.'

'You think I can make him do that?'

'I think you can try. I think you can try harder than you have so far, to put before him the advantages of leaving.'

'How do you know how hard I've tried?'

'I have listened to Beatrice. She, too, has made me her confidante.'

'Then you will know that she very much wants Eric to stay. And you will betray her like this?'

'Pardon me, but I am not betraying her. I am doing what is best for her, sparing her the unhappiness of being cast aside for her daughter. And I will be sparing Jeanne the unhappiness of being married to a worthless man who will exploit her and then cast her aside.'

'You are very hard on Eric.'

'I am hard because he is hard. I have known enough men like

265

him: good-looking men, charming men, men who make you feel you are the most special person on earth, and then, when someone else or something else comes along, they step over you and leave you lying in the gutter.'

'You may well have known such men,' he said, 'but consider where you met them. Why should Eric be like them? I can't believe that he would deliberately mislead Beatrice or Jeanne. There must be some misunderstanding.'

She shook her head. 'There is no misunderstanding. You know only the part of Eric de Villiers he wants you to see. You do not see the ambition, the hunger for fame and recognition. I know the signs, I have seen it often, how a person can become dissatisfied with his own achievements because he sees around him the achievements of others. And I have seen the signs in him; he will not rest until he has made his name and his fortune.'

Her conviction was unshakeable, he could see: there was no point in arguing with her. 'But what is there I can do about it?' he asked, conscious of how this made him seem to be deferring to her view of things.

'You can take him home, as I have said.'

'I can't, as I have said,' he countered obstinately. 'Nobody can force Eric to do something he doesn't want to do. Especially not if, as you say, he has his mind set on succeeding here in Paris.'

'But you can try. You have influence with him. I know he likes you.'

Olga's insistence had yielded to something more insidious; she was looking at him for all the world as if expecting some hope or succour. It was almost comical, he felt, that he should be looked to for light, when he was so much in need of enlightenment himself; but his strongest sense was a desire to divest himself of the responsibility she had inflicted on him. . He shook his head. 'Look,' he said, 'what you have told me has come as a shock. I need to get my head around it. I really can't give you any undertaking when I don't even know what I think or feel.'

'I see,' she said, lapsing again into bleak indifference. 'You are on his side. The men always side with each other.'

'It's not a matter of sides, can't you see? It's a matter of what's right and what's wrong.'

'That *is* a matter of sides. What is right for one side is wrong for the other.'

'Look, I'm sorry, there are just too many questions that I have to answer for myself before I can give you an answer.' Then he said, and it was the only thing he could say with any certainty, 'I must get out of here.'

'You can get out of here, but you can't get out of the situation.' All in black, in the dim room, she was sphinx-like in her gravity.

'You must forgive me if I leave it there for the time being,' he said, with what he hoped was convincing finality. He turned his back on her and made his way through the rooms beyond, most of them now thronged with people. He felt unable to speak sensibly to anybody; he needed to get out and collect his thoughts.

He registered, in passing, Alessandra Giovanelli in animated conversation with Simon Cleaver, she all gesticulation, nostrils and teeth, he all cool concentration, his amazing eyes fixed on her neck as if with an intention to rip out her jugular with his amazing teeth, Rimbaud gazing up, his head at an angle, as if considering his own options, were jugulars to be ripped.

Zeevee was standing on his own, apparently pondering a mysterious object on a plinth, a jawbone of some huge animal, conceivably a hippo. In a more detached moment, Christopher might have found something poignant in the young man's solemn absorption in the grotesque object; but as it was, he felt mainly relief that he did not have to explain his own flight to him. Because flight was what he was intent on; he could not, after such knowledge as Olga had imparted, have lingered on exchanging pleasantries, even with Zeevee.

His escape was not to prove a simple matter, however. There was a light touch on his shoulder; he turned round to find himself confronted with the smiling regard of Gloriani.

'Mr Turner?' he said. 'You seem to be in a hurry, but may I beg for a moment of your time?' His manner was all courtesy, but there was not the slightest implication of tentativeness; he was not a man who would ever beg for something he didn't know he could have without begging.

'Of course,' Christopher said. 'I was just ... but never mind, I am quite at your disposal.' He could do no less, given that his host was making a point of engaging him in conversation.

'Thank you. I shall not detain you for long. It is, as you may have guessed, about our young friend Eric de Villiers?'

'Eric?' Christopher felt for the moment that he never wanted to hear the name mentioned again.

'Yes, you will forgive me taking this liberty after such a regrettably short acquaintance.'

Christopher muttered his assent; his forgiveness was clearly not his to withhold.

'You see,' Gloriani said, as if imparting an important secret or a personal confidence, 'Eric has, I think, at last found his feet.'

'I am pleased to hear that, of course, but ...'

Gloriani held up his hand. 'Please. Allow me to elaborate. I shall be frank with you, there were times when I would have given him up for lost, when he seemed, how do you say, all at sea. But now – well, as I say, I think he has found his feet.'

He moved fractionally closer to Christopher. 'You may wonder why I am telling you this. I shall tell you: it is because Eric has asked me to. He is, I think, afraid that you do not have faith in his abilities. And also, I think he hopes that you will tell his father, explain to him why it would be a bad time for him to return to your country now.'

'Then what ...?'

'What is it that he has done? To be frank with you, he has done nothing as yet, but I think he is on the verge of doing something great. I shall not spoil it for him and for you by giving you the details, because I am sure he would like to tell you himself; but he wanted me to let you know that he has my blessing, and will have my support.'

Gloriani stood there under his chandelier, shining with goodwill and generosity and self-satisfaction amidst his accumulations, animate and inanimate, and for the first time since Christopher had laid eyes on him, the man struck him as vulgar – vulgar in his self-assurance, in his perfectly turned-out clothes and his perfectly composed manner, his perfectly styled hair, his perfectly preserved complexion and his perfectly-toothed smile. He was beautiful, beautiful, beautiful; but he was hollow. He was a simulacrum, a trademark, a label.

Christopher extended his hand. 'Thank you for your confidence,' he said, 'and for the invitation to this wonderful gathering. I unfortunately have another engagement which I've not been able to cancel.'

Gloriani clasped his hand in his own smooth palm. 'But of course, I am sure you are much in demand. I am all the more grateful to you for honouring us with your presence.'

Christopher felt that enough professions of gratitude had been exchanged, and withdrew from Gloriani's benign countenance, feeling that he'd somehow failed a test – though of what, he couldn't quite say.

But in turning his back on Gloriani he had, he found, turned to face Eric, who was now bearing down upon him with his shining visage.

'Ah, there you are at last! I've caught sight of you a couple of times, but I keep losing you.'

'Yes,' said Christopher, 'I seem to have been wandering through about twenty different rooms.'

He was hardly conscious of what he was saying, but Eric gave his words his earnest attention. 'Yes,' he said, 'isn't it amazing? Gloriani has such taste.' Then, without waiting for a reply to this proposition, he continued, 'Beatrice sends her regards – and her regrets.'

'She's not coming tonight?' Christopher asked, his mind still refusing to engage in the conversation with any energy.

'No, it's a bit awkward, with tomorrow being a school day. Jeanne is writing an exam, and Beatrice thought she'd stay home for moral support.'

At this, Christopher at last felt a slight check, the torsion of his own will asserting itself. 'Jeanne is fortunate,' he said, 'to have the support of such a mother – and then of you as well.'

269

Eric's smile was just a trifle too bright, as he replied, 'Oh, fortunate indeed, and of course I help where I can.'

Christopher could see that if he wanted things named, he'd have to name them. 'So I believe,' he said. 'I am told that you have interested yourself in Jeanne's career.'

His dry manner checked the other's enthusiasm for only a moment. 'Oh, who told you? Was that the good Olga I saw you chatting to? She shouldn't really be jumping the gun, things are at a very early stage of development.' But then he continued, as if imparting news of the happiest import. 'But yes, to an old and discreet friend like you ... yes, I am hoping to launch Jeanne in the new season. That's partly what I tried to get her to see in Florence, you know, not to spoil her lustre now, not to feature as just another face in the tired line-up of Charlie Winthrop models.'

And then, as Christopher could only gape in silence at this extraordinary effusion, the young man continued: 'Jeanne is the face of the future, the style of the future, you know. All those expressionless masks, the empty eyes and the the slack jaws, the seen-it-all attitudes, the Kate Moss clones – all those are passé,' he gestured dismissively. 'Jeanne will restore the idea of fun and high spirits to fashion, she'll remind us that clothes aren't meant to be draped over impassive forms, they're supposed to be worn as part of an active life, as an expression of animal vitality.'

He fixed Christopher with his bright regard as if expecting delighted assent; then, as the older man still just stared, he continued: 'Those old coke queens represented exclusivity, untouchability, the whole stultifying ethos of haute couture, or at least its boutique version. But Jeanne, she'll embody a new spirit of liveability, of *life*. The world is tired of paying homage to gorgeous zombies; people want their beauty fresh, thrilling, unspoilt.'

'You seem very sure of what the world wants,' Christopher said. 'Isn't it a matter rather of what you want?'

Eric flushed slightly, and hesitated; then he seemed to make an effort to refrain from plumbing Christopher's implication. 'Yes, I suppose it's true enough,' he said, with his genial smile, 'that I'm relying on my instinct – but what else does a man have? My instinct and a certain amount of market research. But of course Beatrice has been useful, she's helped me make important contacts, people like fashion journalists, and Gloriani's making a bit of a comeback, launching an absolutely new look and a new line at Paris Fashion Week, and he's agreed to make Jeanne the face of the new look. He hasn't been … well, very productive in the last few years, but has suddenly, he says, been inspired to create … well, it's all very hush-hush, but I have seen some of the designs, and they're stunning. He really is taking off in a new direction.'

'And you will be taking off with him?'

'Well, naturally I hope that this'll be an opportunity to launch myself as an agent and – again in strictest confidence – a kind of adviser to Gloriani.'

'Your experience as a *claqueur* qualifies you for that?'

If Eric was hurt by the evident scepticism of this enquiry, he concealed it under his easy laugh. 'Well, yes, apparently so. I'm told I have a good eye.'

'Oh, I'm sure you have an excellent eye.'

'Gloriani seems to think so. He trusts me to help him reach a younger, more adventurous market, naturally without sacrificing the classic principles that have made him a revered designer.'

'Naturally. He has in fact just delivered the testimonial you asked him to provide.'

Eric kept his countenance. 'That's excellent. Then you know.'

'Yes, I know.' Christopher paused. 'And Beatrice?'

'What about Beatrice?'

'What will her part be in your new career?'

'Oh, I'm hoping, of course, that she'll be part of the enterprise. She has so much to teach Jeanne – and, I daresay, even me.'

'Even …?' Christopher fairly gaped at him.

He smiled his easy smile. 'I suppose that sounds conceited. Of course she had a lot to teach me, she's already taught me so much.'

'I think she has done more for you,' Christopher said deliberately, 'than I have ever seen done by one human being for another.'

If Eric thought this was an extravagant claim, he accepted it as he accepted, it seemed, all of life, with his bright bland readiness.

'Oh, don't think I don't realise that, and I'm only too pleased that you've noticed it for yourself. All I meant was that compared with Jeanne, I may be a bit more wise to the tricks of the trade.'

'I have no doubt that you are wise to the tricks of the trade, or will be soon enough.'

'That's what I'm hoping for. So you see,' and he urged his point with shining candour, 'it would be the worst possible moment for me to leave Paris.'

'Oh, I can see that.'

'And do you think you'll be able to get Dad to see it, too?'

At this, Christopher laughed. 'Do you think I've ever been able to get your father to see anything he didn't want to see?'

'I don't know. I've assumed that you have influence with him, otherwise why –'

'Otherwise why would you have bothered with me?'

This, at last, tested Eric's good humour. 'I don't mean that at all, you know that. What I mean is why would Dad have sent you here, unless he trusted your judgement?'

'I think he trusted me to act according to *his* judgement. So that now he no longer trusts me. But what is it to you, what your father thinks, given that you are now all set for a career in Paris?'

The smooth features just perceptibly registered a qualm. 'Well, that's just it, can't you see? A career in Paris could be a pretty precarious affair, even with Gloriani's backing.'

'Whereas a farm in Africa will always be a farm in Africa?'

If Eric saw the sarcasm in Christopher's question, he evaded it. 'Well, yes,' he said, 'and I wouldn't want to burn my boats altogether now, if it can be avoided with a bit of tact.'

'Then I'm afraid you'll have to exercise your own tact, of which I'm sure you have quite sufficient. I've done with tact, at least as far as your father is concerned.'

Eric looked at him as if seeing him for the first time. 'Hey, you really are worked up about something, aren't you?'

'Yes, I'm sorry. I'm not feeling too well. I've just made my excuses to Gloriani.'

'You're not leaving?' the young man asked. His solicitude, which until recently had seemed to Christopher such a fine product of his emotional education, now sounded hollow, the pretended concern of an insurance salesman for the health of a prospective client.

'Yes, I am.' Christopher said. 'Yes. I find … I find I'm rather worn out by …' he gestured ineffectually at the rich interior surrounding them, at the voluble assembly in the muted lamplight, at the two of them standing in the middle of the splendid parquet floor, 'by all this.'

'All of this? All of Paris?'

'I don't know.' Christopher knew that he must seem very flat to the young man, after the liveliness of their previous conversations – which, he now realised afresh, he had delighted in. But liveliness seemed out of place, seemed fraudulent in the glare of what he had just been told.

Eric was indeed looking at him quizzically. 'You're not feeling quite yourself?' he asked. If there was an edge of impatience to the question, it was expertly dissimulated the next moment by the concerned hand he placed on Christopher's shoulder.

He shrugged, which had the effect of displacing Eric's hand. He had no desire to explain, let alone justify, his state of mind to Eric. He was finding it difficult to look into his face, into his earnestly enquiring visage, fearing what he might see there. 'I don't know,' he said again. 'Perhaps I'm feeling myself for the first time since I've arrived.'

He wasn't quite sure what he meant by this, and from the slight frown on Eric's face he could see that he, too, was puzzled; but the young man had the advantage, always, in his easy social manner. 'You mean you've been misleading us all this time with a false persona?' he asked, so lightly that it did not seem to require a reply.

And yet Christopher gave the question the consideration it had not asked for, and produced a reply. 'Perhaps,' he said. 'Perhaps I have been under a kind of charm.'

'And what has broken the spell?'

Christopher looked, then, at the face in front of him, the charming, half-smiling, *plausible* face, and now for the first time really saw it, saw in the glint of the teeth and the lustre of the eyes, the

273

truth of its origins and its upbringing; saw the father looking through the eyes of the son, the brutality beneath the beauty, the final indifference of youth and strength to all but its own supreme claim to life.

'I do believe *you* did,' he said, and turned his back on the young man in the beautiful room.

CHAPTER 19

He went downstairs without looking back, and started walking without plan or direction. The streets were now full of evening diners and flâneurs, the never-ending parade of people to whom the streets were home, and his progress was slow, all the slower for being purposeless. So that when he found himself next to L'Étoile Manquante, and saw, miraculously, a vacant table in the front row, he sat down without reflecting. He had been walking and standing for a couple of hours now, and sitting down was, suddenly, a welcome relief. He felt tired, though he couldn't tell whether this was a physical or a mental state.

He ordered a glass of wine and sat back in his little chair, less observant of the passing scene than turning over in his mind the events of the evening and his part in them. In particular he reverted to his exchange with Eric. His act of cruelty – because that was what his parting comment to the young man now seemed to him – haunted him; for even if it had been deserved, it had yet been cruelty, with the brutal intention of inflicting hurt. He hadn't been able to help it, seeing the young man in the arrogance of his strength and beauty, disposing of Beatrice as if she were a cold dinner. And yet, wasn't that the prerogative of youth, to live at the expense of others?

He lingered over his glass of wine, not in a hurry to return to his hotel room, where he would have to face the blank stare of his laptop, awaiting some kind of response to Daniel's missive. The evening was mild, and the street was congested with pedestrian traffic. He was gazing at nothing in particular, marvelling as often before at the random forces – economic, aesthetic, expedient – that had produced just this conglomeration of humanity in just this setting.

He mulled over the events of the evening. Uppermost in his mind was Olga's plea: please take Eric away before he causes more harm. It was not in his power to take Eric away, any more than it was in his power to make him stay; and yet the alternatives presented themselves to him as a quandary, as a choice he had to make, if not for a practical purpose then for the orientation of his own moral compass. Was Eric's continued presence in Paris in Beatrice's interest, as she believed, or her ultimate ruin, as Olga maintained? And if it was odd that Beatrice's welfare should have become the decisive factor in his decision, that, no doubt, was but part of the oddness of his situation all round. From the moment he had ceased being Daniel's envoy, he had lost any clear notion of his function. It was not even clear that he *had* a function; would it make any difference to any living creature what he did or didn't do?

Engrossed in this probably wine-induced speculation, he failed to take note of the person taking the empty chair next to him, even though he and the man were now technically sharing a table. So it came as a surprise, almost a shock, when he found himself addressed: 'Excuse me, but are you not the gentleman from South Africa?'

Looking up, he found himself subjected to the sardonic regard of Fabrice. For a moment he was at a loss for words, then said, 'Yes, indeed, I'm Christopher Turner.'

'And I am Fabrice, the friend of Simon Cleaver.'

'Of course. I remember.'

'And also the friend of your good friend, Eric de Villiers.'

'Yes, I remember.'

'How is he, our friend, Eric?'

'I believe he is very well. I left him, in fact, about half an hour ago, at a reception.'

'At Gloriani's, yes, I know he was going there.'

'You know Gloriani?'

'Of course. Everybody knows Gloriani. But we are no longer on visiting terms. Gloriani, I think, does not approve of me.'

This did not surprise Christopher, but he couldn't say so. He merely nodded and took a sip of his wine – his glass was, however, empty.

'Ah, allow me –' and before Christopher could object, he had raised a peremptory finger for and ordered another glass of wine.

'Thank you,' Christopher said, 'but I really have to be going.'

'Of course. But first we will have a glass of wine together. I need to practise my English, and I am sure we will find many topics of common interest.'

'Your English is very good,' said Christopher, taking refuge in the impersonality of lukewarm courtesy.

'Thank you very much,' said Fabrice, as if he had been paid a heartfelt compliment. 'My mother was English, and sent me to school in England. I have always been very grateful to her. It has made me so much more socially pliable than most Parisians.' He gestured at the passing throng. 'It is getting better of late, but at heart they still think that because they live in Paris they don't need to know any language but French. They don't know that Paris no longer belongs to them.'

Christopher did not really want to get involved in the man's conversation, but instinct suggested that blandness would better pass the time than open rudeness; so he replied, 'To whom does it belong, then?'

'To the rats,' Fabrice said, with startling vehemence. 'Where do the rats go when they abandon a sinking ship? To Paris, to Amsterdam, to the tolerant northern democracies. And the rats will take over those democracies and turn them into the same kind of hell that they fled from.'

Christopher was not surprised to find that Fabrice was a run-of-the-mill xenophobe. But he seemed to expect some response, so Christopher said, 'But who are these rats? I don't see any of them around.'

'Don't you? That is because you don't have eyes to see. Me, I have an eye.' He looked around him, as if for something on which to demonstrate the power of his eye. Then he said, 'You see that *mec*, coming out of the Bar Central?'

Christopher looked where Fabrice pointed. A young man had

indeed just emerged from the bar across the way; he hesitated at the door, lit a cigarette. In the yellow light spilling from the bar he seemed very pale. He was lean as a greyhound and casually dressed – low-slung jeans showing the top of Calvin Klein underpants, a Lacoste shirt, citified sneakers. Something about the awkward fit of the clothes on his bony frame suggested that the conspicuous logos were fake. The hair, carefully gelled into disarray, had gold highlights that glinted in the light from the bar. The effect was garish and slightly pathetic.

'Yes, I see him,' said Christopher, as Fabrice seemed to be waiting for a prompt. 'What's special about him?'

'Nothing. He's one of a hundred, a thousand, as common as the pigeons that shit on the statues or the rats that scurry in the sewers. But keep watching.'

The young man stood smoking at the entrance to the bar. There were several other men out there smoking, now that smoking was banned in public places. But the one pointed out by Fabrice was not simply having a leisurely cigarette; whereas the others stood talking to each other or staring vacantly at the passing parade, he kept glancing back into the bar, as if expecting to be followed. After a few minutes another man, older and considerably more fleshy, emerged from the bar and came up to the young man; he asked him something – evidently for a light, because the young man produced a Bic and flicked on the older man's cigarette. They stood for a moment, smoking; there was a brief exchange, and the two men walked off down the Rue Vieille du Temple, in the direction of the river. As they walked past the café, Christopher registered their expressions: the older man nervous, licking his lips; the young man dully uninterested in his companion, even resentful, morosely staring ahead of him. His sneakers, Christopher noticed as they walked past, were dirty and scuffed.

'A successful negotiation,' commented Fabrice, his grimace a mixture of amusement and contempt. 'The young man will get about fifty euros for an hour of his time, or perhaps more, depending on how much of his person is involved. It's not much, but for him, it's a fortune, compared with what he was earning in Romania.'

'Do you know him?'

'No, but I know the type. I have an eye. He is not from Paris, he doesn't inhabit his clothes as if he belongs in them, he doesn't walk the street as if he's at home in it. And most of the foreign boys are Romanian. Romania is very homophobic, so they can't ply their trade there. And Romanians tend to be very good-looking, before they lose their teeth. But of course, this young man could be from anywhere.' He paused, glanced at Christopher, then said very deliberately: 'After all, your *petit gars* was from South Africa.'

'My – ?'

'Yes. Your Eric. I take it that you do know that I met him there, at the Bar Central?'

Christopher had a sense, triumphant as far as it went, of being prepared for information that he suspected was intended to take him by surprise. So he said, as casually as he could, 'Oh yes, he told me that he met you in a gay bar. I just didn't know that it was this gay bar.'

'And he told you that he went home with me?'

This, too, Christopher was prepared for. 'Yes, and he told me that nothing happened.'

'That depends on how you define happening. But yes, we didn't fuck. It's not my, how do you say, cup of tea?' There was another one of Fabrice's timed pauses. Then he said: 'But it was Eric's cup of tea, or perhaps just his daily bread.' He chuckled, pleased with his own wordplay.

Christopher tried for a moment to pass this, too, off as stale information, but there was, after all, a limit to his *sang-froid*. 'You mean, I take it, that Eric was ...' he couldn't bring himself to utter the word that hung in the air between them.

'Yes,' Fabrice said, 'I mean that Eric was hustling when I met him, a taxi-boy, as we call them. He didn't tell you that? Ah, he must have forgotten that detail. Yes, that is how I met him. He asked me for a light for his cigarette – just like the little encounter you've just witnessed, just the other way round – and in those days you could still smoke inside the bar.'

'But Eric doesn't even smoke,' said Christopher, his protest sounding irrelevant even to himself.

'That is as it may be. A cigarette has many uses, apart from being smoked, as you will know if you are a fan of old movies. It's a very useful negotiating tool.'

'But if you weren't … if it isn't, as you say, your cup of tea, what were you doing in the Bar Central?'

'Call me a public benefactor. I rescue deserving young men from walking the streets.'

'And in this public service you are motivated purely by a spirit of benevolence?'

Fabrice smiled, a smile like moonlight on ice. 'Perhaps not *purely* – we must not expect purity in this old whore of a city. But I did rescue your young man from ending his days giving blow jobs in the Bois de Boulogne for ten euros a shot to feed a crack habit.'

'You are telling me …?'

'No, no, rest assured, Eric has no crack habit, not yet, and not as far as I know. But he would have developed one if he had carried on in his chosen field of work, as sure as …' – he looked around for inspiration and found it in the street in front of them – 'as sure as dogshit sticks to your shoe. Your young friend is very beautiful, but potentially he's just another rat. And he was, when I met him, not too far from that.'

'Excuse me if I ask what was in it for you? Since you're not the Salvation Army, what *are* you?'

'I am a facilitator. I provide services to people who need them. And one of my services is providing hand-selected escorts to discerning gentlemen.'

'You mean you're a pimp?'

The man spread his hands in mock horror. 'Please, we no longer use that word outside Pigalle. I am a modelling agent, with a business on the side as a social coordinator catering to a niche market. It's really a very tasteful business. I think you saw me here the other evening with Simon Cleaver?'

'You know I did.'

'Yes. Well, Simon occasionally works for me, when he needs a bit of extra money. When he has money to spare, he sometimes makes use of my services. It's really a very reciprocal relationship, and as I say, quite civilised. The thing is, dear Simon actually enjoys the job, and when he doesn't – well, he is an actor, after all, and can act any part very convincingly. Which is all that the market requires. I am told the majority of clients prefer what is called the GFE, the Girl-Friend Experience, which is really quite innocuous, a kiss and a cuddle. It seems people are starved for a bit of affection, or its pretence.'

'And they're prepared to pay your rates, which I take to be high, for that?'

'Tell me, my dear sir, wouldn't *you* be prepared to pay, let us say five hundred euros, to be allowed to believe for a night, and with hard evidence, that your young friend Eric loved you?'

Christopher had thought that by now he could deal with anything Fabrice lobbed at him, but this question winded him for a moment. Then he said, 'I don't think I have to answer that.'

'No, you're right, you don't. I have eyes, I can see for myself. I saw you the other evening at La Coupole, with Eric. Ah yes, you didn't see me, because La Coupole is big and I didn't want to be seen. But me, I could see; and I could see from the way you spoke to Eric, from the way you carried yourself, so different to the way you're carrying yourself now, that you love him. And I know, too, that it would be worth five hundred euros to you to believe for a night that he loved you in return.'

His shallow blue eyes rested for a moment on Christopher's face, but the older man was determined not to betray anything, not to be goaded into a reply. 'Ah,' said Fabrice, with his mirthless smile, 'perhaps he gives it to you for free? That would be uncharacteristically generous, though strictly speaking a violation of his undertaking with me.'

'He still has an undertaking with you?' Christopher asked, seizing at the diversion.

'Theoretically, yes, although he seems inclined to forget it, and I am not so ungentlemanly as to remind him of a gentleman's agreement. You see, in a sense he is where he is because of me.'

'That's all very well – but where exactly is he?'

'That is a good question, an excellent question. He has moved on and moved about so much … yes, it is difficult to tell exactly where he is. I shall have to discuss it with him quite soon. But in the meantime, what I do know, as I say, is that I took him off the streets of Paris and placed him in its drawing rooms and salons.'

'You? Not Zeevee?'

'Why Zeevee? Who do you think introduced him to Zeevee?'

'I thought Gloriani did,' Christopher said, reluctant to admit ignorance or error to this shiningly smug man.

'No. Not so. I introduced Eric to Zeevee and Zeevee introduced him to Gloriani. You see, or perhaps you don't, since you seem to see so little, Zeevee was one of my most regular and valued clients.' He paused to test the effect of his revelation, but Christopher refused to give him the satisfaction of a reaction, and he continued, 'Yes, I supplied him with boys. When you look – how shall we say? – well, the way Zeevee looks, and you have as much money as he has, it is easier to buy company than to, how shall we say, barter it.'

'And Eric ….?'

'Yes, Eric. I sent Eric to Zeevee as I had sent any number of other young men to him. The complication, really quite an inconvenient one, came about because Zeevee fell in love with Eric.'

'And Eric with him?'

'Who can tell? Eric is not the romantic type, I think. But he told me that he wanted to move out to live with Zeevee, where I have no doubt the accommodation was superior to my poor little apartment, and where of course the pocket money and fringe benefits would have been considerable. Also, Zeevee could introduce him to people – like, for instance, your friend Gloriani, who lost no time in recruiting him as a *claqueur*. And to give Eric his due, he played his advantage like a master, in no time knew everybody and went everywhere, and poor Zeevee had to stand by and watch Beatrice du Plessis fall in love with Eric.'

'And Eric with Beatrice?' It was absurdly as if Eric would somehow be redeemed in Christopher's eyes if he could be imagined to have been driven by love rather than calculation.

'As I say, who's to tell? Let us say that he found Beatrice more expedient, in terms of his public image – it always has more cachet to be the lover of a beautiful woman than to be the plaything of a rich man. And Beatrice, after all, was not poor.'

Christopher looked with revulsion at the man facing him. There was nothing to say to him; but Fabrice did not need encouragement.

'Not that Eric has severed all relations with me. We are neither, Eric or I, such a fool as to let personal differences interfere with business. He remains a valuable contact for me in the fashion business, and a link with your estimable embassy through the kind favour of one Xolani, whom you may have met...?'

'I have seen him, yes.'

'Yes, then you will know he is very beautiful. He was also in my stable, as it were, for a while, until he struck out on his own, into the world of fashion and the world of ... well, of all those wonderful substances that your national airline and your embassy, or certain functionaries within it, so generously distribute to the rest of the world. Unofficially, of course. But the point is that Eric has retained his links with Xolani and with me, much to the chagrin of Zeevee, who thought he was extricating Eric from our clutches. But Eric, sensibly not wanting to be wholly dependent on Zeevee or for that matter on Beatrice, has kept up the French connection, as I believe it used to be called.' He smiled unpleasantly. 'The fashion people, fortunately for me and for him, need to nuke their few brain cells into oblivion to tolerate one another, and they can afford to pay for the means.'

'And Zeevee is trying to sever the connection?' Christopher asked. It was monstrous to have to discuss such enormities as if they were making small talk; but he was compelled to take his tone from his interlocutor.

'Yes, poor man,' Fabrice continued, not without relish. 'He really still is in love with Eric, even though Eric abandoned him for Beatrice. Zeevee thinks he can reclaim him, from us if not from Beatrice. But all he has to offer Eric is his money. And Eric has discovered that he can fend for himself.'

Christopher felt sick and empty. He loathed the man he was talking to, who sat there with his self-satisfied grimace like a well-fed dog. He would have liked to get up and leave, but there was something hypnotic about the man, about his chemical-blue eyes fixed, now, on Christopher, as if waiting with interest for his response.

'Why are you telling me all this?' Christopher asked, in what he hoped was a tone of neutral enquiry. 'What do you have to gain by it?'

'Ah, you are too cynical. You must not assume I am always motivated by personal gain. Perhaps I am just sorry for you, deluded as you have been by your excellent young man.'

'Thank you, but you needn't waste your compassion on me. I don't need it.'

'You mean you don't want it. I can understand that. But to answer your question truthfully, then, I am telling you this because I have been told you are here to recall your young man to his native land, and it is my calculation that if you know all there is to know about him, you will be less eager to do so.' He leant forward, in his intensity spraying little drops of spittle. 'I want to help you to see, in short, that he is damaged goods, a toxic asset, not a young man that you would want to present to his father. The story of the prodigal son is very beautiful, but alas, very few fathers would act as the prodigal son's father did.' He leaned back in his chair again, all urbane irony once more; but this did not prevent him from, at last, calling things by their name. 'Perhaps the prodigal son was not a hustler and a drug dealer.'

Christopher resisted a sudden impulse to spit in the man's complacent face, and asked instead, 'But what is it to you whether Eric stays or leaves?'

'It is in fact a matter of some import. To me he is not a toxic asset; indeed, I look on Eric as an investment that is about to start yielding a handsome return, as he digs himself deeper into the *beau monde*. I think I deserve some gratitude, after all I've done for him.'

'You mean you gave him board and lodging in return for his services as a drug runner and a prostitute?'

'Ah, you are blinding yourself with externals. I did not simply use him as one uses some dumb animal; I trained him for his function as a companion to gentlemen of taste. You have noted, perhaps, an improvement in the manners, in the – *tenue* of your compatriot?'

'Yes, but I ascribe that to the influence of Beatrice du Plessis.'

'Ah, she is a true lady, or has become one in her middle years, and she may well have contributed, as no doubt did our friend Zeevee, but I, I, Monsieur Turner, I am the one who laid the foundation and made the rest possible.' He noted, without rancour, Christopher's sceptical expression. 'You don't believe me? I know very well, I don't come across as a paragon of the social virtues. But I can teach what I don't practise; I know the tastes of people who pride themselves on their taste, and I know how to satisfy those tastes. And I can recognise potential in unpromising material. I cannot, how do you say, make a silk purse out of a sow's ear, but I can make a very good Moroccan leather wallet, which is after all more serviceable than a silk purse. You must not judge me by appearances; I have had the upbringing of a gentleman, and I have the ability to impart my *savoir-faire* to others, as I did to Eric de Villiers. You yourself, I think, will have noticed that he has a particularly happy knack of dealing with older men. I flatter myself that I helped him in that respect, as in others, that I taught him to be properly … what is the word?'

'Solicitous?' The word came unbidden to Christopher's lips.

'Yes, that is an excellent word. I taught him to be solicitous. Which is why I think I have a legitimate claim to his services.'

'Might it not have been preferable to use him as a model? I mean, as opposed to a prostitute?'

'Yes, modelling was my original idea, and I did try him once or twice. But it didn't work. He is really too *nice* to be a model. The modern model has to exude an air of, how shall we say, of *fuck you*, of bad-tempered rejection of the gaze that he or she courts. Now, your friend is too eager to please, too puppyish – it comes across as naive. When last did you see a model smile? And even when he didn't smile, Eric, his manner was too accommodating, too compliant to the desires of the spectator. It's obvious that he has grown up trying to please. But the true model does not try to please; the true model has a kind of hauteur and a blankness of expression, often the result of a vacancy of mind, whether inborn or drug-induced. The great model is a highly specialised creature: her sole function on earth is to be looked at, and she does not allow anything, least of all a sense of other people, to distract her from that calling. In a way, it's very pure. Models refer to the rest of the world as *civilians*; they think of themselves as some kind of über class. Escorts, on the other hand, have to be aware of other people, and respond to them. A good model is an object creating a need; a good escort is a human being fulfilling a human need.'

Christopher was too sickened by the man's claims to have a ready reply. But the small penetrating eyes were fixed on him mockingly; Fabrice was not going to let go without some rejoinder from Christopher.

'Either way, it sounds pretty appalling,' Christopher said at last. 'But if Eric, then, to his credit, is too human to be used as a model … are you not assuming too easily that he will be happy to be used by you indefinitely?'

Fabrice laughed. 'My dear Christopher – you don't mind if I call you Christopher, do you? – Eric's happiness is more than I ask for or need. All I need is his cooperation, which he will continue to give me because it is in his own interest to do so. The arrangement runs quite smoothly, and you will forgive me if I say we don't need outsiders to interfere with it. You may also just drop a hint about this to your friend Zeevee.'

'I'm sure you are more than capable of dropping your own hints.'

'Thank you, I value your little compliments. But it would per-haps be more pleasant for Zeevee to receive the hint from you than from me or one of my … assistants.'

He looked at his watch, something slim and streamlined and expensive-looking. 'But I am afraid I must interrupt this pleasant tête-à-tête. Late as it is, I have business to attend to. My hours, alas, are irregular.'

He got up, and bowed. 'I am pleased to have had the opportu-nity for an open-hearted talk. I think it is good that we understand each other. In short, Monsieur Turner, let us have Eric de Villiers. We can put him to better use than you. And please … allow me.'

And he placed a note in the little saucer containing the bill.

Christopher felt as if he had been picked up bodily and flung into some heap of garbage. Whatever he touched would be garbage, and would only pollute him further. And yet, to remain still was to be choked by ordure. He got up – his table was immediately claimed by an impatiently waiting couple of young men – and started walking in the direction of the hotel slowly, irritably aware of the human crush in the narrow streets of the Marais. It seemed impossible to avoid the contamination of touch, the clammy breath of the crowd. The evening, so clear and shining at its outset, had turned hideous; it seemed to him that all beauty had been mired by the touch of Fabrice, all virtue made suspect by the dark confidences of the woman in black. The streets were just extensions of catwalks, the shops just purveyors of enhancements to the display of human flesh, the cafés just seating for phalanxes of *claqueurs*.

He left the oppression of the Marais with relief, crossed again to the Île St Louis. On an impulse, he turned off to the Rue de Bretonvilliers. Zeevee's great entranceway, of course, was closed; but he still had in his wallet the slip of paper where he'd noted the code. He keyed it in; the door, indifferent to his motives, accepted the code and clicked open.

The courtyard was, after the hubbub of the streets, almost eerily quiet. The fountain was trickling gently, and somewhere, upstairs, someone was playing a violin. There was light downstairs, in Zeevee's apartment, and the entrance doors stood open to the summer night. Christopher approached over the gravel, his footsteps sounding preternaturally loud in the hushed courtyard. He stopped by the door and stood waiting. Perhaps he should have announced himself on the intercom at the gate; but having come this far, he continued, still without any clear notion of what he was doing and what he had in mind.

At the open front door he paused, his hand poised to knock. The room inside was dimly lit; its preposterous interior mutely shone forth into the darkness. Voices floated from the room leading off the entrance.

'So why did you tell me you were going to marry Beatrice?' Zeevee was saying.

'What difference does it make to you,' came Eric's comfortable baritone, 'who I'm going to marry, as long as I'm not going to marry you?'

'But with Beatrice, there would have been room for me in your life, you know that.'

'Yeah, right – as a trusted family friend, as a confidant, listening to Beatrice bewail my infidelities and imperfections? As a kind of best friend to the wronged wife?'

'I don't know why you assume that you'd have been unfaithful.'

'That's just it, don't you see?' Eric's tone was reasonable, plausible as always. 'I could never have been faithful to Beatrice. I need a stronger stimulus, a greater challenge. If I'd wanted peace and security I could have gone home to Franschhoek and married my neighbour's daughter and reminisced about Paris with poor old Christopher.'

'And this impulse and challenge – you expect Jeanne to provide that? A seventeen-year-old girl?'

'She won't be seventeen forever. And she's already showing signs of knowing her own mind. She'll give me a run for my money, and in the end she'll defeat me. Because she's younger and stronger than me.'

'That's perverse, surely, wanting to be defeated.'

'I don't *want* to be defeated, nobody wants to be defeated. But nor do I want to be driven by time and circumstance to abandon Beatrice when she needs me most. Far rather abandon her now, while she still has resources and resilience.'

'Let me get this clear. You're abandoning Beatrice now in order not to abandon her later?'

'You're deliberately making me sound more calculated than I am.' There was at last a scratch of impatience in Eric's voice, but it yielded immediately, as if instinctively, to his normal equanimity. 'I'm drawn to Jeanne for obvious reasons, her youth, her beauty, and the sheer excitement of being with her. That's surely understandable.'

'You forgot to mention her potential as a model.'

'Okay, that *is* part of the excitement. She's at the start of her career and her life. And I'd like to be part of that.'

'And to blight her life just as Beatrice's life was blighted.'

'No, Zeevee.' Eric's quiet patience would have been admirable, Christopher thought, if it had not been so provoking, such a demonstration of final indifference. 'I want to look after her and protect her. But yes, I also want an active role in her career. I'm sick of just sitting there, applauding the achievements of others. If I don't want to go home and stand in my father's shadow, why should I stay here as Beatrice's toyboy?'

There was a moment's silence, the scraping of a chair, and then Eric continued. 'Look, I know this is a shock for you, and I know how close you are to Beatrice. But there'll always be a place for you in whatever business I set up – and for her, too.'

'Do you really imagine that she'll consent to some part in an enterprise you set up with her daughter?'

'I can't see why not. What has been, has been. We can all move on.'

'Perhaps we can't all move on with the same ease as you – from who-knows-who to Fabrice, and from Fabrice to me, and from me to Beatrice, and now from Beatrice to Jeanne.'

'I never contracted for permanence with anybody; it's not my fault if other people's expectations exceeded my commitment. I've provided excellent value, and I never pretended to be anything I was not.' Then Eric's tone softened. 'Look, I'm sorry if you're disappointed. ….'

'I'm not disap*point*ed. I'm disgusted.'

'Whatever. What I'm saying is that I'm sorry that we don't see eye to eye on this.'

'Sure. See it your way, is what you're saying.'

'No, I accept that to you what I'm doing seems … well, irregular.'

'Irregular! That's rich. Fucking reprehensible, I'd say.'

But Eric's good humour, which had, after all, always been his strongest quality, was proof against even this. 'As you wish,' he said accommodatingly. 'You choose the adjective. But bottom line is we're going to be working together, and I'd rather work together as friends than as enemies.'

'You'd rather, would you? Why must what *you'd* rather do be the rule of my existence?'

'It needn't be. I'm just saying it'd be more pleasant.' There was a silence, during which Christopher imagined poor Zeevee trying to catch hold of something, get some purchase on the slippery surface of his friend's appeal. But before he could do so, Eric continued: 'Look, I'm really grateful for what you've done for me. You've been more than a friend to me, and I don't want to lose you.'

At this, Zeevee seemed pacified, or acquiescent, or defeated, because he didn't reply. Christopher turned to leave; then, just as he was about to do so, his eye fell on the portrait that had so intrigued him on his previous visit, the painting of the nude woman with the white socks. In the dimly lit room she had escaped his notice; but looking at her closely now, he saw with a shock that the subject was a young Beatrice du Plessis, only it was a Beatrice that seemed infinitely more experienced, more cynical, than the serene woman he had got to know. The portrait leered at him, mocking his assumptions with its worldly-wise assurance; look at me, it seemed to say: I am what it's about, why things are as they are, the half-truth, the mixed motive, the hidden agenda, the possible other case.

Christopher turned his back on the knowing grimace and on the ugly room, and made his escape as noiselessly as possible. He turned over in his mind the conversation he had just overheard. He had advised Zeevee to persist in his infatuation, and no doubt Zeevee would do just that – not because of his advice, but because that was what one did with an infatuation. And even Beatrice, superseded by her own daughter, relegated to being useful – even Beatrice would no doubt accede to her new role, because that was the only one available. In the end, he thought wryly, we are all *claqueurs* to Eric's act.

So Zeevee had lied to him about the nature of his relationship with Eric. Well, no doubt he had wanted to be lied to, had not wanted to face the truth of Eric's charmed existence. And Zeevee had discerned this, had lied in all charity and compassion – not to mention his famed discretion, and his forlorn loyalty to his friend and occasional lover. No, Zeevee could not be arraigned for duplicity, or at any rate for bad faith. But Martha? As a friend of Zeevee's, she must have known more about Eric than she'd let on; what was remarkable, as he thought back, was how little she had told him. But there, too, what claim did he have on her loyalty? He could imagine her smiling grimly at being asked to help Christopher to help Daniel de Villiers to find his son – Daniel de Villiers, who had ruined her summer and, conceivably, her life. Why should she feel obliged to give Christopher access to the existence she had constructed in his despite? The simple fact of the matter was that he had arrived in Paris as an outsider, and had too soon assumed, on slender evidence, that he was being treated as an insider. The young girl at the Gare de Lyon had simply been more direct about disabusing him of this illusion.

He traversed the little island and crossed to the left bank of the river. Generously, as always, the Seine opened up the view to its series of bridges, its clustered banks. The sky on this perfect evening, the first warm breath of summer, was a deep, deep blue, luminous over the brash glare of streetlights and the headlights of the endless cars plying the banks of the river. It was as it had always been, a great human experiment in living, imposing a civilisation on a marsh and a river and two small islands, giving shape and form to the needs and desires of its people, evolving, somehow, a city uniquely beautiful, and establishing its stringent aesthetic standards as a law and a morality. Thou shalt be beautiful; thou shalt not grow old or tired, thou shalt pay my price in blood, sweat and tears. And, of course, it was beautiful, Christopher knew this. But he knew, too, that underneath the tranquil river and the glittering squares slithered the humid corridors of Châtelet, endless ramifications and intersections of human purpose blindly pursuing its ends. Piss and shit, Olga had said, piss and shit.

He was not ready to return to his garret, to spend the night with the bitter dregs of the evening. Instead, he allowed the flow of the river to direct his steps, on his right the great bulk of the timeless cathedral, brilliantly lit against the dark-blue sky: another beautiful empty shell. He carried on walking, and soon, perhaps by unconscious design, he reached the Pont des Arts. He mounted its steps and made his way past the usual charivari of lovers, musicians, street artists, vagrants and beggars, until he found a spot at the railing overlooking the Île de la Cité. He stood gazing out over the great river. Here, thirty years ago, he had contemplated the loss of Daniel de Villiers; and here, now, he was contemplating the loss of Daniel's son. It was in neither case a recordable or quantifiable or even legitimate loss, because in neither case had there been a substantial possession; and yet it was a loss, if nothing else, of a possibility, a loss of what beauty seems to promise, a loss of the illusion that beauty can be possessed on terms other than its own. For whatever concessions one thought oneself prepared to make to the claims of beauty, they were never enough: beauty does not negotiate compromises; it does not have to. It is ruthless, because it knows that when its time comes, it will be ruthlessly cast aside.

He became aware, above the hubbub of performers, passersby and onlookers, of a single strand of sound, simple and sustained and serene. He looked behind him and noticed, for the first time, the young woman standing across from him, against the opposite railing. She was dressed in a simple white frock, a blue scarf draped loosely around her neck. Her black hair was tied back from her pale face, in which her dark eyes seemed startlingly large. She was singing – one of Mahler's Rückert lieder.

Liebst du um Schönheit, o nicht mich liebe, she was singing, without visible emotion or effort, a simple neutral request, If you love for beauty's sake, oh do not love me, followed by the sardonic proposal, Love the sun, for it has golden hair. *Liebe die Sonne, sie trägt ein goldnes Haar!*, she sang, her warm mezzo gaining urgency as she immersed herself in the song's hypnotic repetitions: *Liebst du um Jugend, o nicht mich liebe; Liebe den Frühling, der jung ist jeder Jahr*, If you love for youth's sake, oh do not love me.

In her hand she held a small tape recorder, to provide the lush orchestral accompaniment, over which her voice flowed limpidly, negotiating the unadorned rise and fall of strophe and antistrophe

292

in a kind of controlled rapture. She sang as if she were alone on the bridge, alone on earth, with only her little music box and her voice and her song, and an absent lover. She gazed ahead, without seeing the passersby, the onlookers, the whole glowing evening. She was entirely contained within herself and yet pouring out, measuring out, the lovely strains: *Liebst du um Schätze, o nicht mich liebe! Liebe die Meerfrau, sie hat viel Perlen klar!*

There were not many people listening to her; but standing next to Christopher, he now noticed, were two young men. One was leaning back against the bridge railing, the other leaning into his friend, their heads touching, lost in the song and each other's closeness, believing with the blessed solipsism of young love that the song was theirs and theirs alone. As, on the song's sublime change of heart, the singer ecstatically proclaimed, *Liebst du um Liebe, o ja mich liebe!*, they tightened their embrace, their eyes closed: *Liebe mich immer, dich lieb ich immerdar!*

Mahler's glorious orchestral muttering reached a kind of equanimity in resolution, but the voice was as if left suspended in the fragile promise of eternal love; the singer stood quite still, not asking for applause, not soliciting contributions, though an open purse on the ground in front of her suggested that they would be not unwelcome. The two lovers stood lost in the moment in each other's arms. *They* would not love for beauty, for youth, for riches, their attitude said: *they* would love for love's sake alone, oh yes, and love for ever, as they were loved. Christopher turned his back on the singer: to applaud would have been to appropriate the song to himself, to reduce it to just another performance. His eyes were misted over; to clear his vision he focused on the little island glimmering in the dark water. Behind him, the singer was venturing into the dark waters of *Ich bin der Welt abhanden gekommen*, I have done with the world.

On the island, on the narrow strip of land lining its prow, next to the water, a straggling of young people were sitting and standing, smoking, drinking wine. One of their number, shirtless, shaggy-haired, was preparing, with glistening self-awareness, to perform some feat on his rollerblades. There had been several such displays in front of the cathedral, but this seemed to be a private performance for the small group gathered on the quay. The performer had constructed a ramp, and he was with some bravado preparing himself and his audience for his act; there was some strutting to and fro, some testing of the ramp, some flexing of muscles and cracking of knuckles. Then, ungainly for the moment on his blades, he retreated down the bank and turned round for the approach. The onlookers grew quiet; he rubbed his hands together like a trapeze artist, paused a moment, smoothed back his hair, and gave one, two tentative steps forward as if testing the surface; then, rapidly picking up speed, he fell into a powerful striding rhythm, his body swaying in perfect counterweight to each thrust and glide. Faster and faster he went, the uneven paving under his feet seeming to sustain him as air sustains a bird; as he reached the ramp, he was flung forward and upward by his momentum, escaping gravity and taking off into air, his torso gleaming in the brilliant light on the bank, his energy contained in the leap. At the extreme point of his trajectory, he flipped over in a somersault so controlled that it seemed to take place in slow motion. For a second there was silence as he hovered in the air, his companions raptly intent on his flight. If he miscalculated, he would come to grief, he would smash into a wall or rush headlong into the Seine. But he wouldn't miscalculate, couldn't miscalculate, didn't miscalculate: his movement was a thing perfect and complete in itself, not subject to vacillation or deviation, a thing of brute beauty and valour and act, Christopher found himself reciting, oh, air, pride ... and he landed, to the cheers of his friends, a few metres from the low parapet by the water's edge. He twirled around and acknowledged the applause with an ironic bow and a radiant smile. He shimmered in triumph. He was young, he was in Paris, he was beautiful and strong and would forever remember flying through the air on an evening in June to the enchanted acclaim of his friends.

Christopher found he had tears in his eyes: whether for the grace and flair and energy and power he had witnessed, or for its inevitable corruption and decay, he could not have said. Perhaps they were just different parts of the same process, the flight and the fall.

He felt old, and lonely, and betrayed; but, somewhere, he felt consoled, by the consolation that beauty brings, however tainted its sources and vile its ends. Angels are bright still, though the brightest fell, he quoted to himself.

Ich bin gestorben dem Weltgetümmel, the young woman was singing, I have died to the world's hurly-burly, with an almost voluptuous savouring of the song's extravagant asceticism, *Und ruh in einem stillen Gebiet*, and have found rest in a quiet realm. Christopher took out a twenty-euro note and placed it in her purse, as poor tribute to the power of her gift. *Weltgetümmel*, he thought, what a wonderful concept. He turned his back on the island and the bridge and the singer and the lovers and made his way to the Hotel du Carrefour.

ACKNOWLEDGEMENTS

I am grateful to my first readers for their patient scrutiny and helpful suggestions: Christine Roe, to whom this book is dedicated; Lou-Marie Kruger, André Crous, Arnold van Zyl and my agent, Isobel Dixon. Their comments have helped to make this book much better than it would otherwise have been; no doubt it would have been even better had I accepted all of their suggestions. As usual, I am indebted to my editor, Lynda Gilfillan, for her sharp eye, sense of style and indefatigable labour. She has trimmed the novel of many of its excesses, but she is not to be held responsible for those I have persisted in.

My thanks, too, to my publisher and his production team: Jonathan Ball, Jeremy Boraine, Francine Blum, Valda Strauss and Kevin Shenton, with Michiel Botha once again producing an exemplary cover design. This is the sixth novel of mine that they have seen into press, with their customary patience, efficiency and good humour. I very much appreciate their unstinting support over the years.

Readers of Henry James will recognise in my novel the plot outline and some of the characters of *The Ambassadors*, as well as some of the thematic concerns. I believe, though, that my appropriation substantially recasts and reinterprets the Jamesian given.

I have consulted the following books: *A Model Summer* by Paulina Porizkova; *Model: The Ugly Business of Beautiful Women* by Michael Gross; and *Fashion Babylon* by Imogen Edwards-Jones.